CW01665416

MAUREEN [illegible]

A novel by Peter F Doyle

© Peter F Doyle 2020

All rights reserved. No part of this publication may be reproduced, stored in a retrieval system, or transmitted in any form or by any means without the written permission of the publisher, nor be otherwise circulated in any form of binding or cover other than which it is published and without a similar condition being imposed on any subsequent purchaser.

All rights reserved.

ISBN: 978-1-8381836-0-8

MAUREEN KELLEHER

Beret Press

For Catherine, my mother,
and Dominic, my son.

PART ONE

CHAPTER ONE

Mrs Shaughnessy didn't seem an unfriendly woman, that first evening, when she said that she liked things to be clear, liked things to be understood. A bit stern, possibly, but not actually unfriendly.

'I like things to be clear Maureen, so we all know where we are. You've come up from the country, Maureen, and things will be different here in Bray, I would say. Oh, and while you're here with us, obviously, you'll find it'll be better if you eat in the kitchen, easier for all of us.'

So Maureen Kelleher ate in the kitchen. She could hear the family, easily, from there. Eating and talking a bit, not much. Mrs S, the two children, and Mr Shaughnessy, usually, as well. He, a bit loud, laughing, when he'd been in the pub too long, with his pals, after work. When he'd drink taken. If the truth be told she was glad not to be in there with them, although it did, sometimes, feel lonely here on her own, sitting at the kitchen table. Not like back home in Dungarvan, with her family. There, it was always noisy, laughing. Or that's what it seemed like now, anyway.

It was Mama and Dada who'd said she had to leave the school, especially as there was a job available in the railway boarding house, where the drivers and the firemen stayed when they finished late, or had just done a night shift. She'd only been thirteen. It was strange to go to work, but Mrs Kennedy, who ran the place, had been very nice, very kind to her. They tidied up, and they washed the bedding, and they cleaned the floors. The men cooked their own food. It would have been impractical to do that for them. 'Coming in at all hours, like they do, and

Dublin jackeens most of them, too. Take care not to encourage them, now, Maureen, ye hear?', Mrs Kennedy had said. Maureen was never exactly sure what being a Dublin jackeen actually meant, but she agreed nevertheless. The work was not that different from what Mama did at home, more of it though, but not hard work, not really. And the men, when she met them, were generally pleasant enough. Most of them knew Paddy, who was a signalman and Conny, who was a porter at the station. And some knew Dada as well.

When Maureen was fifteen she went to work for an English family who lived in one of the larger houses in town. He was the manager in one of the bigger local businesses. When he saw her he always said, 'How are ye today, Miss Kelleher, how are ye?' in a kind of silly Irish accent. He went off in his car every morning at a quarter to eight, always exactly at a quarter to eight. Mrs Graham stayed at home. She was very nice, very friendly, but she did nothing, absolutely nothing, in the house. It was different from the boarding house though. It was the Graham's home. And it was very different from her own.

The railway cottage where she'd been brought up had been comfortable enough, but very crowded when they were all there, Paddy and Conny, and Theresa, and Danny and Dympna as well. The older ones had gone. Michael had got married and Tommy joined the navy in England, the merchant navy he called it, and Nan and Angela had gone to work in London. Mama said she'd heard that they were going to work as nurses if they could.

Mama cooked on the open fire. The bread as well, a big loaf every day. They got vegetables from the haggart next to the cottage, Dada planted potatoes there, and onions and cabbage and carrots as well, and the boys gave a hand, now and then anyway. Sometimes Maureen had to cycle up to Maggie Connolly's for stuff, on the big bike. It was difficult going up the hill to Maggie's, but great fun on the way down, although you had to be careful not to crash into the dyke and lose the whole lot. Paddy had once broken six large eggs on his way back, and Mama, after scolding him, had used them immediately, from the bag, because it would be a terrible sin to waste them, she said, picking the shell from the yolks.

But it wasn't like that at the Graham's. They had their groceries, their bread, all delivered, and there was a kitchen with a large stove. Mrs Delaney came in to do the breakfast and then in for the evening meal as well. Maureen helped her if it was necessary, but mainly did the washing up and then cleaned the house and made the beds and, sometimes, did shopping. She still lived at home. It was easy to get home on the late bus from the centre of town, which she did after she'd helped serve the evening meal and then washed up. Mrs Graham paid the fare.

When Maureen was seventeen Mama and Dada had agreed it would be better if she got a job in Dublin or thereabouts. Theresa was in Dublin, now, anyway. She worked in an office and she said it would be a great thing altogether if Maureen could come up as well. She said it was fun at the dances and there was loads to see, and boys to meet as well.

Theresa looked in the Dublin papers for a job for Maureen. When she came home for a weekend she had some newspaper clippings, clippings from the adverts. And Maureen saw two jobs that she thought she could do. One was in the city itself and one was in Bray. Theresa told her that Bray was a little outside the city but it was easy enough to get to on the train. Both of the jobs were housemaids' jobs really, cleaning and shopping and looking after the children. Babysitting in the evening as well, when required.

She sent a letter to each, Theresa helped her write them. She'd asked Mrs Graham if she would give her a reference and was surprised at how upset Mrs Graham was that Maureen wanted to leave, not angry though, just upset. Mrs Graham said how much she and Mr Graham would miss her if she did go, but, of course, she would give her a reference. A jolly good one, Maureen, she said.

The job in the city had already been taken but Mrs Shaughnessy, in Bray, telephoned Mrs Graham and asked her questions about Maureen's suitability for the job, and whether she was punctual, and whether she'd taken time off. Mrs Graham told Maureen about the phone call and said she'd given her a perfect reference. And then Mrs S. offered Maureen the job, on a month's trial, initially.

Maureen talked it over with Mama and Dada. They said she should take it. Dada said he had been to Bray and it was a lovely sea-side town, maybe a bit like Youghal, really. He said it might be better than the city itself, 'And, if it doesn't suit, ye can be back here, home, before nightfall.'

Maureen was excited about leaving Dungarvan, but scared too. She was relieved that Theresa would be there, in Dublin anyway. And Theresa had agreed to meet her at the station and go out with her to Bray, as well.

She had been to Dublin before on the train, once with Mama and Dada to see one of her aunts, Mama's sister Helen, and twice with her sister Theresa and Theresa's friend Grace, to spend a weekend in the city with another cousin. Those journeys had been different. With Mama and Dada she had only been ten, or eleven, was it? It had been fun. She'd never been to a big city before. It was near Christmas as well so there was lots going on. And with Theresa and Grace she had been just following them really, a little sister kind of thing. Fun as well, but in a different sort of way. She remembered sitting there, on the train, opposite the other two, watching them smoking their cigarettes, and laughing, and having a joke with the guard when he walked on through.

But this journey was different. Mama and Dada came with her to the station, Dada carrying her suitcase. She hadn't dressed up for the journey but she had made sure that everything was clean, and pressed, and smart. Jimmy and Mick at the station knew she was going, and wished her luck.

'Be careful now, up there, won't you Maureen? And watch out for them Dublin boys whatever you do!'

They'd all laughed together. And then it was just the three of them standing on the platform waiting for the train. All of a sudden with nothing to say.

She saw the train arriving. She could see it puffing slowly into the station past the signal box, the driver leaning slightly from the cab, and the thought came upon her, definitely, that she was leaving home, leaving Mama and Dada.

The train stopped and she kissed them both quickly, hugged them too, and lugged her case onto the train and then poked her head out of the window. They were looking up at her now and, in that instant, she saw them differently. Differently from ever before. A man and a woman together, he in his suit, she in a dress. They were like two adults who she knew very well but, in a funny way, were different from her Mama and Dada. Different from the woman who had looked after her, and told her off, and cuddled her, and laughed with her; different from the man who had sung and played his accordion to her, and walked with her in the garden, and shown her how to water the plants and pick the cabbages, and held her tight when she'd fallen and cried.

The guard held up his green flag, at the same time shouting something to the porter, who laughed and shouted something in return, and she heard the steam and the whistle, and the oh so slow movement as they started to move along the platform away from her mother and father. Both smiling and waving as she went, waving her away from them. And she kept looking until they were almost out of sight, already walking together along the platform towards the exit, only Mama now still waving though.

Her carriage was empty apart from two men at one end and an old woman at the other so she sat in the middle, away from either. She sat on the left-hand side but, with no other passengers near, she could easily see through windows left and right, and knew she could move across when the fancy took her.

This part of the journey was to Waterford where she'd change to the main line. She done this trip a few times but, once again, this seemed different. For what seemed like the first time she saw everything in a more concentrated way. Looking out over the narrow causeway she saw the beginnings of the sea; they crossed that water and then she saw the wide, real, sea to her right, beyond the fields that seemed to go to its very edge. She could remember walking across the causeway and walking down to that exact bit of sea, she could recall laughing and playing and running on the beach near there, not once but a number of times. The two viaducts at Ballyvoyle and Durrow, flying high over the trees and the valley. And the tunnel too. Five hundred yards Dada had told her. And then the road with a lorry flying along, faster than the train. The driver waving. She waved back but she didn't imagine he could see her.

And at every level crossing she waited to see someone or something that she recognised, and, at last, she saw a girl waving at the train as they trundled slowly past, a girl smiling up at Maureen, shyly almost. Doing what she had done herself so many times back at home. Back at home.

She sat back, almost exhausted. Exhilarated by being on her own, but so scared of what was coming. Sitting there she felt the start of a tear, but stopped it. The train moved on until the bigger river appeared on her left. The Suir. She could see the city of Waterford ahead where she had to change. The train was slowing now as it moved on to the steel river bridge, making its way to the other side and then moving along the other bank, slower and slower and then, as slow as could possibly be, sliding into the platform and stopping.

As she stepped down from the train, with her suitcase, Maureen knew she was really starting her journey now. The ride from Dungarvan had been a kind of stepping-stone for her, a stepping stone into another kind of life.

The Dublin train was crowded. There was a match on later that day, the All-Ireland Final between Cork and Kilkenny. Dada had said the trains would be very crowded to Dublin, but they had no option because she'd agreed with Mrs Shaughnessy that she would arrive that very evening. And she'd got the impression, from Mrs Graham, that Mrs Shaughnessy was a bit of a stickler for things.

Maureen had felt confident on the platform in Waterford, well, more confident shall we say. She had started to feel optimistic about the job, and, anyway, she'd soon be seeing Theresa as well. And Theresa was always a great old laugh. Theresa seemed to take nothing very seriously but she was always encouraging to Maureen and, for all her laughing and joking, she had found herself a great job with some solicitors in Dublin, as a secretary of all things. Maureen could never imagine having a job like that, a secretary in a solicitor's office sounded really important. But she'd bet that Theresa would still be laughing, important or not.

Thinking about Theresa helped her but, on this crowded, noisy train, she felt small again, sitting on her suitcase in the corridor, men and woman laughing, drinking, shouting, pushing past her. All friendly enough, but she wasn't really part of it. And she had other things to worry about. All these red-faced people, shouters and smokers and drinkers, all they were worried about was whether Cork or Kilkenny would win the hurling.

She sat and watched them. Occasionally a man or a woman would catch her eye and give her a wink or raise their glass to her, but then they'd turn away and continue their conversation or their argument or their joke. Maureen half-hoped that someone would talk to her but she'd not the slightest idea what she would say if they did.

She sat on the case, everyone else above her, boxing her in. She couldn't even see the windows, couldn't see outside, and she realised, looking at everyone else, that she was just a poor mite really. Her clothes were not smart, or new, and her case was just an old cardboard thing, worn and scruffy. And she was just seventeen. Just a girl. It felt like everyone else knew what they were doing. Back on the platform at Waterford, just for a moment, she'd felt confident that she knew what she was about, but when she saw all these people, some of whom wore very smart, probably expensive clothes, she felt like a country girl, a plain country mouse.

'What'll you have to drink, young lady?'

She heard a big voice above her. She looked up.

A large man, in a big jacket, with a big face and a wide moustache, was looking down at her. Smiling. Kind. She knew he had been part of the group sitting right near her.

'No, thank you, I'm fine.'

She heard her voice come out, almost squeaky, and she felt silly.

He laughed.

'No. come on now. Have something soft. You can't go all the way to Dublin without a drink. A Club orange? Go on now!'

The others in the group, two women and a man were looking at her, smiling. One of the women in particular was nodding her head and encouraging her to say yes.

'OK, A Club orange would be nice. Thank you, sir.'

'Great!'

And he pushed his way through the crowd towards the bar. The others smiled at her for a second and then looked away and continued their chatting.

She felt better. Sort of. It took him about ten minutes to come back, the drinks held precariously in his hands. And there was a bottle of Club orange with a straw.

'There you go. Take it out of me hand wouldya? Before I drop the lot.'

He laughed, and his friends laughed. Maureen stood and took the small bottle of fizzy orange from his hand, sitting down quickly again on the case, careful now because it had started to bend a little under her weight. The encouraging woman stood as well, and she helped the man put down the other drinks. Relieved of his burden he smiled and winked at Maureen, taking a Penguin biscuit from his pocket and giving it to her.

'Here, that'll cheer you up, now.'

And he left her to it.

She ate the biscuit first and then sucked on the straw, tasting the tangy drink in her mouth. They were both lovely, absolutely delicious, the biscuit and the drink. She still felt silly, but happier now. Occasionally she caught the eye of the friendly woman, who gave her a smile or a little blink of an eye, not a wink but a little movement which said hello, I can see you there. And Maureen was grateful to her for that, because it made her feel part of what was going on. Even if she was on the outside, she could still be a part of it all. Even if she didn't really care who won the Final. Maybe that women didn't care either, maybe she just enjoyed being happy with her husband and her friends, enjoying a grand day out.

She knew when they were approaching Kingsbridge Station. Everyone had started to get themselves ready. Finishing their drinks. Some standing from their seats, others getting their coats and their hats together. She felt a change in the atmosphere, everyone had been noisy but sort of relaxed for most of the journey, but now they were excited, looking forward to the game, laughing in a different kind of way almost.

She stood as well. Close next to the group who had been kind to her.

'Where are you off to then? You're definitely not going to the match are you? With your case an'all?'

It was the friendly woman. She was taller than Maureen, and close enough so that Maureen could smell the scent of a perfume.

'No, I'm starting a job today. In Bray. My sister's meeting me here at the station.'

'And what will you be doing, if I may ask?'

'I'm working as a maid in a house. With a family. Mrs Shaughnessy.'

'Oh, Bray's a lovely place altogether. I'm sure it'll be great. Have you met the family?'

'No.'

'Well, I'm sure it'll be fine. But don't let them take advantage now, you hear?'

Maureen wasn't altogether sure what that might be about, but she knew the woman meant well.

'No, of course, I'll be sure not to. Thank you.'

The train stopped with a little lurch which made everyone lean forward slightly off-balance, almost falling, all in time, like dancers, and then they were straight again. And the doors slammed open as the more enthusiastic fans set off at a pace, laughing still, and shouting.

'Ah well, we're away now. Look after yourself. Take care now.'

She smiled and touched Maureen for a second on the shoulder and then turned to follow her husband, if that's what he was, towards the doors. The man himself turned towards the wife, checking she was there, he caught sight of Maureen as he did so and gave her a wink and a smile before they disappeared down on to the platform.

The carriage was all of a sudden almost empty.

She picked up her case and followed everyone else down on to the platform. They had been nice people. A bit like the Graham's in a way, but Irish not English, so more like her.

'Maureen!'

She looked along the platform and there was Theresa, waving, at the very end. It was a relief to see her. If she could have ran, she would have, but the case made it awkward, so she walked as fast as she could.

'How are ye? Was the journey OK? God, I forgot about the match, it must have been packed on that train. You look great. Smart and tidy, that's good. How were Mama and Dada? Did you get anything to eat?'

As always Theresa was full of energy and questions. She looked very smart, a lovely dress and a cardigan. She looked sophisticated. That's what Maureen thought, she looked sophisticated. She loved that word. She remembered Dada had used it once when they were talking about Theresa. Theresa had become a bit different to them, in a way, a bit of a mystery to them all, with her success, and her job in a solicitor's office. Maureen remembered Dada, in front of the fire, thinking for an awful long moment and then saying, slowly, that he thought Theresa was now a sophisticated young woman. And they'd all agreed.

They were walking along the platform. And Theresa said, first thing, they had to go and get a cup of tea and a sandwich, because she was starving herself and she was sure that Maureen had eaten nothing. There was no space to tell her about the Penguin and the Club soda because she just kept talking, but Maureen didn't mind because being with Theresa gave her confidence. This was her big sister.

They went into the cafeteria and each had a cup of tea and Maureen had a cheese and tomato sandwich but Theresa decided she wasn't hungry after all and just had a cigarette. And Maureen told her about the journey and the people on the train and about Mama and Dada seeing her off.

Theresa listened and smiled. And she said that the woman was right about not letting Mrs Shaughnessy take advantage of her, which actually Maureen thought was a bit unfair on Mrs Shaughnessy because she hadn't even had a chance to take advantage yet, had she?

Theresa told her a little bit about where she worked and how she hoped that Maureen would have the time to come into Dublin, and how they'd have a great time. And maybe she would come out to Bray now and then, when she could manage it.

When they had finished their tea, Theresa said they'd better get going because they shouldn't be late for getting to Bray. They took the bus to Connolly Station and waited for the train to Bray.

Maureen realised now that pretty soon she'd be starting her new job in a place she didn't know, and, despite being with her sister, she felt a bit sick in her stomach with the worry of the job, and the worry of Mrs Shaughnessy as well.

Because they weren't exactly sure where to go they asked at Bray station. The ticket collector said they should walk along towards the Killarney Road, follow that, and it would take them fifteen minutes or so.

The case wasn't heavy but Maureen was tired and nervous, and the walk turned out to be longer than she expected She had gone to an early Mass with Mama that morning and had been travelling ever since and now she was close to something, which, if the truth be told, was a bit of a mystery to her. Not the work especially, she was used to that. No. It was living in someone else's house. Not having her own family to talk to at the end of the day. Getting used to other people's ways.

They passed a load of shops, all shut of course. And she could smell the sea that they had travelled beside for the journey out from Dublin. Theresa had been friendly but, in a way, seemed a bit distant now. For some reason Maureen had expected her to be more happy to see her, not that she hadn't been welcoming, of course she had. But Maureen got the impression that she wanted to get back to the city as soon as possible. Maybe she had things to do, or had a date, or needed to get ready for work tomorrow. And, when they found out where to go, they walked along not saying a great deal.

Maureen had also realised, seeing Theresa again, but away from home this time, how much of an age gap there was between them. For all her laughter and her joking, Theresa wasn't a girl like Maureen, she was six, almost seven years, older then her. Theresa had said about going to dances and the like but Maureen wasn't sure, now, that there would be a lot of that. For a start, Maureen would only be able to go out in the times that Mrs Shaughnessy had said she could have off, she'd mentioned Thursday afternoon and Sunday. If that didn't fit in with Theresa, which it might not do at all, there wouldn't be a lot she could do, and she couldn't go gallivanting off to Dublin on a Friday or a Saturday night could she?

Still it was a comfort to know that Theresa was less than an hour away on the train and would be sure, sometimes at least, to come out to Bray to see her. It was nice place to come to, so why wouldn't she?

'OK, Maureen we're almost there, it's just this next one I think.'

They'd checked again with a passer-by that they were going in the right direction.

They turned into the street. The houses were not quite as big as she expected, for some reason she had been expecting something grander. They weren't that much different from the place that the Graham's had lived in, back in Dungarvan, and in a way not even as nice as that.

They slowed slightly walking down the street.

'I'll come with ye to the door anyway, Maureen.'

They had reached the house. A garden at the front. Lights in the windows, two storeys with a small window above.

There was a knocker on the door. Theresa lifted it and let it fall. She turned to Maureen as it clanged against the door, and they giggled. And then they turned immediately, with serious expressions on both their faces, to wait for the door to be answered. After a few seconds a light came on in the hall and they could see the shadow of someone walking towards the front door.

Maureen breathed in deeply.

The door opened and a woman stood there. A tall woman, taller than Maureen or Theresa, and thin as well. At first Maureen couldn't quite make out her face because the light was coming from behind her, from the hall.

'Hello, Mrs Shaughnessy, I'm Maureen Kelleher.'

'Well hello, Maureen. I was expecting you a little bit earlier, but that's fine, you've come a fair way today, I'd say.'

Maureen thought she was more or less exactly on time.

'And you are?'

She was talking to Theresa.

'Hello Mrs Shaughnessy, I'm Theresa Kelleher, Maureen's sister. I work in Dublin so I thought it'd be best if I came along with Maureen today.'

She put out her hand to shake Mrs Shaughnessy's, who was not expecting this, obviously. They shook.

Maureen was so proud of Theresa, so glad she had come along with her.

'Well, come in, come in. I'll show you your room. Your sister will probably be wanting to see where you're sleeping, where you're working too. Isn't that right?'

And Mrs Shaughnessy showed them. The bedroom and the house. Just a brief introduction to Mr S, who was smiling and charming, especially to Theresa, and a hello to the two children, Maria and Stephen.

And then they went to the kitchen where Mrs S made a cup of tea and explained to them both what Maureen's duties would be, that she would eat in the kitchen, and how she could have Thursday afternoon off and Sunday afternoon off, and she could go out after dinner was done in the evenings, as long as she was back by nine, except by special arrangement, and she told her the times of Mass and how far away the church was. And she said that she, Mrs S would show Maureen her duties, even help for the next couple of days but, by Wednesday, she would expect Maureen to know, for the most part, what to do. And if she had any questions she must ask.

'Is that all clear Maureen? I like things to be clear.'

Maureen nodded. Mrs S sounded like she was a strict woman but not unfair. Maureen thought, as well, that she had a long, rather sad face.

'Miss Kelleher, do you have any questions?'

This to Theresa.

'No, I think that's perfectly clear, don't you Maureen?........Occasionally it would be nice to see Maureen on a Saturday night in Dublin, maybe even stay over with me, once on a while. Would that be a problem?'

Maureen looked at Mrs S's face. She wasn't altogether pleased by the idea, that was obvious, but she was not unreasonable.

'After a while I'm sure we can come to some kind of arrangement. Initially I'd say it would be better for Maureen to get used to her work without too many disruptions, but after that, as I say, I'm sure it might be possible. Occasionally.'

'Fine.'

'Well, I'll leave you to say your goodbyes, and then, Maureen, there's a sandwich and a piece of cake under that plate there for you. After that you might get some sleep after your long day.'

She stood up and shook Theresa's hand, with a shadow of a smile, and left them to it.

They walked outside and gave each other a hug.

'She seems alright, underneath it all. Anyway, you'll be fine. I'll see you in the next week or two OK?'

They hugged again and Theresa set off, quite quickly, for the station, waving like Mama had done, as she went out of sight,

It was strange. The first week or so. Mrs S showed her exactly what she had to do for those first couple of days. Help Mrs S with the breakfast and then, on her own, wash up and tidy away. And then do the bedrooms, the children's first, and then Mr and Mrs S's, when she gave permission to go in there. She was told on what days she had to wash what. Obviously, Mondays mainly with the bed linen and the towels. She was surprised that Mrs S helped her on that first day, did most of it herself, in fact, with Maureen helping. And the ironing of course. And the children's clothes and the shirts and the underwear. And cleaning the house as well, sweeping and dusting and mopping. It was more than she was used to but there was nothing unusual about any of it. Mrs S was a stern woman, most of the time, but she was always helpful. She didn't smile much, or at all, and she never joked. Mrs Kennedy, in the railway dormitory, has always been ready for a laugh, especially when they sat down for a cup of tea and a cigarette, Maureen didn't smoke though. But she remembered the two of them laughing about the men in the place, or something that had happened at the shops, or even at Mass. Like when Bridie O'Connor marched young Sean up the aisle for communion after she found him mitching off from Mass, but she'd brought him too late, and Father O'Brian just ignored them. She gave up eventually and marched him back down the aisle, a barely hidden grin on Sean's face, the little imp.

Maureen slept in a small room at the top of the house, almost a part of the attic you might say. There was a bed and a chair and, not a chest of drawers exactly, but a small cabinet with three drawers she could put her underwear and her socks and some of her tops in. She had some hangers for her frock and her work clothes. There was a mirror on the wall and a small piece of carpet on the floor, and you could see out of the window right down the street. The same window she had seen at the top of the house when she'd arrived, late that Sunday afternoon, with Theresa.

Maureen had never had a room of her own. She'd always shared with someone, sometimes there'd even been three of them, and the bed itself was often shared as well, although with more of them leaving home there was greater space these days. And even more now that she, herself, had gone as well.

When she'd closed the door behind her on the Sunday evening she'd felt lonely for a second or two but then, standing with her back to the closed door, she realised what she'd been given. She'd got her own little place. She walked across to the window, just three big steps, and then from wall to wall, three steps as well although the last step was cramped a bit by the wall. And she sat on the bed. A single bed, with sheets and blankets and an eiderdown. They'd seen better days but they were fine. She lay on the bed and bounced once and it creaked quite loudly so she didn't do it again.

She discovered that if she lay on the bed the wrong way round she could see out of the window and, on that first night, she did exactly that. Back home the sky was full of stars, you only had to go out the door to see them all spread out above, and Dada had showed her the plough and the bear with the north star. She couldn't see a whole sky from her bed but, with the light off, she could still see the stars twinkling and she spotted the plough as well. It was great to see the sky like that, a connection with home almost.

That first night she was nervous obviously, but it wasn't as bad as she had expected, although she wasn't quite clear what exactly it was that she had expected to be bad.

Mrs S had given her an alarm clock and told her she must set it for six-fifteen every weekday and six forty-five on Saturday and Sunday. She was to be in the kitchen at six thirty to get everything ready. To get the fire going and to make sure everything was out and ready for breakfast. Mrs S would come along at seven and, for the moment, at any rate, would supervise the cooking. When she and Mr S and the children had eaten their breakfast she was to clear the dining-room table and then she could have her own breakfast before doing the washing-up. Mrs S said she wanted all that done by eight-fifteen, and eight forty-five on Saturday and Sunday. They would go to ten o'clock Mass on Sunday and Mrs S would like it if Maureen would accompany them, although she might prefer to sit by herself for the Mass itself so she could say prayers for her family back home.

The first Monday morning was scary of course. She came downstairs, in a quiet house, not exactly sure what to do. She was wearing the black dress that Mrs S had given her. It fitted more or less, and she looked like a maid. At the Graham's she had just worn her ordinary clothes but here Mrs S preferred her to look like a maid. And in a way so did Maureen.

She entered the kitchen, timidly, and there was Mrs S waiting. And she gave out instructions so that Maureen knew what she had to do. She said she would come early one more time, tomorrow, but after that she would expect Maureen to get on with things on her own. And she did. In fact, Maureen liked that first half hour. On her own, thinking what she wanted, getting everything ready for the day. That and being back to her room, in the evening, were the best bits of every day.

And, of course, she got to know the family better over the first week and the weeks after, as she became a sort of part of the household. The children were not that much younger than she was in fact. The boy, Stephen, was almost fifteen, and

Maureen felt kind of sorry for him. He didn't say much and he didn't have much about him you might say, and he had spots as well. He said hello to Maureen, usually with his head bowed, but he wasn't actually unfriendly at all, more shy really. The girl, Maria, was more confident, she bullied poor Stephen, or derided him. She talked to Maureen as if she was a bit below her, which, Maureen thought, she was in a way, as a servant, if you like. Maria, of course, was her father's favourite, of the two of the children. Mr Shaughnessy was irritated by Stephen because, although he was a clever boy at the school, he wasn't what you might call a real boy, didn't play sport and have rough and tough friends who liked a laugh and would like a drink in later life. Maureen thought he might be a bit disappointed in Stephen, but he made up for it with Maria, who could do no wrong as far as he was concerned, and played up to it as well.

Mr Shaughnessy, himself, was, when you met him, a friendly enough fellow, even a bit charming. But there was something about him that Maureen didn't quite like. She remembered the way he looked at Theresa on that first night. He looked over her body, Maureen had seen that even though it was just a few seconds, it seemed like he was pricing her up, like a farmer might a cow. But, she supposed, he was friendly enough, and he wasn't in the house that much anyway, she hardly saw him from one week's end to the other.

The truth be told, she didn't think Mrs S liked Mr Shaughnessy that much either. Obviously nothing was ever said, but Maureen couldn't think of a time when she'd seem them together, talking or having a joke, or even discussing something seriously. Mrs S ran the house and he came in and ate, and slept, in the same room as her admittedly, and went out again to work or to meet his friends. Maureen couldn't help but compare them to Mama and Dada. They always had to work hard, Dada often working nights as well, but when they were together, they were close to each other, even when they weren't actually speaking. She missed them when she thought about them.

Maureen discovered, quite quickly, that she'd come to like Mrs S. She started to call her Mrs S, in her own mind that is, not out loud of course, during that first week. And it was in an affectionate sort of way. Mrs S was almost always quite serious. And she wasn't a beauty. That had to be admitted. Her face had a longness to it, and she was long in the body as well, tall, and not shapely. In truth, she was not an attractive woman. If you compared her with Theresa, in her bright fashionable clothes, you would see the difference immediately. Theresa was younger obviously, and single as well, but Mrs S didn't try in that same way; she surely had the money to buy nice clothes and have her hair done and make herself look as nice as possible, but she didn't.

Despite all that Maureen realised that she was a good woman. She treated Maureen with respect. Of course, she told her what to do, and she did get a little annoyed when Maureen, to her own horror, had dropped a dish and broken it during that first week. But Mama would have been annoyed about that too, it was only natural wasn't it?

But you did see the occasional little smile, almost not even a smile, the shadow of a smile, just the tiniest hint when she was pleased; when Stephen had told her he had come first in Latin that week, the first time he'd managed it; when she had trusted Maureen to make the steak and kidney pie and Maureen had taken it out of the oven and they had both looked at it, proudly; and that time, in the kitchen, when she heard Maria play a whole tune, a tune that Maureen didn't recognise, on the piano in the other room. Then there was that tiny flicker, and Maureen liked her for it.

When they went to Mass that first Sunday, Maureen was not quite sure where to go until Mrs S touched her lightly on the shoulder and pointed her into the pew with the family after all, and Maureen sat at the far end, near the column, just a smidgeon separate from the others. Mrs S was a kind woman.

And in that way Maureen understood why Mrs S had told her about eating in the kitchen. She didn't want there to be any misunderstanding, she wanted to be clear, exactly like she had said, and she knew, straight away, that Maureen would not have been comfortable there. And Maureen liked her for that as well. She hadn't really expected to eat with the family anyway, and she wouldn't have wanted to, even less so after she knew them a little bit. Not because she didn't like them, but it would have been a strain for her, and, listening from the kitchen, it didn't sound like much fun for them either. No great laughing conversations there, apart from Mr Shaughnessy rattling on, about not much at all, when he'd had a little too much to drink.

CHAPTER TWO

Once she got into the swing of it, got into the timetable, so to speak, everything was relatively easy. Mrs S was always around but she didn't interfere or even check up on Maureen, not obviously anyway. And she treated her like someone who worked in her house, but wasn't a servant, treated her like another adult in fact.

'Do we need more soap powder, Maureen?', she might say, or

'Will that lamb last another day or will I order some sausages from Flattery's?', or

'Pop into the Post Office for me would you, when you're out, and get me a dozen stamps?'

It was as much the way she spoke as what she said. Friendly, or friendly in Mrs S's sort of distant way.

Mrs Graham, back in Dungarvan, had sat around all day doing virtually nothing, Maureen thought she drank a little in the afternoon, but Mrs S was always busy, or occupied, in some way or another. Sewing, and mending, she liked to do all of that, which Maureen was grateful for, because she was hopeless at that kind of thing. And reading sometimes, the newspaper or a book. And she went out to things. She was involved in the church and a charity as well, something to do with the nuns.

And once in a while, every few weeks though, she had a group of women around for tea in the afternoon. They were the wives of her husband's friends and women from the church, people who knew in each other in the town.

Mrs S got a bit nervous before these teas. It wasn't that obvious, but Maureen could see it in her, dashing around a bit, and checking up on things. So Maureen did her best, made sure that they had ordered everything and she made scones as well, Mama had taught her how to, and put everything out on the table ready. The sandwiches and the bits of cake and the scones and the tea things. And when she knew the women were about to arrive she made sure that the kettle was boiled for the tea. And, of course, they used the nicest tea service and the best, matching, teapots and milk jugs, and linen. And she served everything in the nicest possible way. She always made sure she looked smart for these little do's, ironed her black dress and made sure her hair was tidy.

Some of the women smiled at her and said hello, and others ignored her while they took a sandwich or held their cup out for tea. She didn't mind. She just made sure that there was sufficient of everything, which of course there always was because most of them, not all, most of them, ate very little.

And Mrs S might catch her eye as she walked round, just catch it nothing more. And when it was over she would come out into the kitchen to help Maureen tidy everything up and away.

'That was grand Maureen, thank you. And Mrs Doyle loved your scones.'

For Maureen that was enough.

After two weeks she got a little note from Theresa, which she was glad about, because she'd heard nothing at all from her since that Sunday when she'd started.

Dear Maureen

Sorry I haven't been in touch. I can come to Bray next Sunday. We can go for a walk and have some tea. Meet me at the station at three o'clock if you can. I'll expect you unless I hear from you.

Love

Theresa

Maureen had sent a letter home to Mama and Dada at the end of the first week saying that all was going well, and they had sent a short letter back saying they were glad that everything was fine. Apart from that, Maureen had had no contact with anyone else, which was one of the reasons she was glad that Theresa had got in touch. It would be someone who she could talk to; Mrs S was very nice in her particular way, and the rest of the family were pleasant enough, but they weren't people she could chat to, and talk to about this and that, not yet anyway. She was also just a bit worried that Theresa had not been her normal bouncy self when she'd met Maureen at the station in Dublin, she'd been friendly and interested, but Maureen couldn't help feeling that she hadn't been as jokey as she sometimes was, although maybe it was just that day. No-one can be happy all the time, she thought.

They went to Mass on Sunday as usual. She sat at the end of the family row, next to the pillar, and she went to communion behind Mrs S and the two children. Mr S stayed in his seat, reading the missal, not looking up. After Mass the family stood around outside the church talking to their friends but Maureen said to Mrs S that she would go back and check up on the dinner. As much as anything she wanted to make sure there were no hitches today so that she could get away on time.

All went well. She got the dinner out, and ate her own meal in the kitchen. She cleared the dining-room table when they'd finished, washed up and put everything away. It wasn't difficult because the Shaughnessys didn't hang about at the table chatting and drinking, laughing and talking. No, they ate their meal and spoke a little about this and that, but they didn't linger. It was almost like they all wanted to get it over with and be away. Which suited Maureen, especially today.

She tidied herself up. A quick wash and a brush of the hair and she set off to walk into town. Normally she'd be walking to the shops to buy something or other, with the shopping basket on her arm, but today she was free of that, just her small handbag to carry.

It felt like she'd been there ages, in Bray. It had only been a couple of weeks, obviously, but she felt as if she knew the place quite well already. She saw the same people around, said hello to the same people, and went to the same shops; the butchers, and the grocers, and the greengrocers, so it was all becoming very familiar. And even going to Mass, just the couple of times, she'd got an idea of the people who lived around or near the Shaughnessy's.

As she walked along into town she realised she was happy here. Obviously she missed Mama and Dada, and she did feel lonely sometimes. At home she would always see her friends, Annie and Ann, and Greta as well, she might see them, or one or two of them, almost every day. She would call round, or they would call round, or they'd stand outside just chatting and laughing. She did miss that, but not as much as she would have expected. She was discovering that she quite liked being on her own and being sort of responsible for herself; and she liked the fact that Mrs S seemed to trust her.

It was a bright afternoon, sunny, a blue sky, warm enough, but not hot by any means. In the town, and as she approached the station, she saw couples and families walking out, mainly down towards the Strand Road and the Promenade. She was early, it was a little before a quarter to three when she passed the town hall clock, and before ten-to when she arrived at the station.

She didn't mind, it was great to be out and about on her own, and, better still, she was meeting Theresa, and she hoped they might have a couple of hours to walk and chat, and get a cup of tea as well. Mrs S had said that she was welcome to bring Theresa back to the house, they could use the kitchen for themselves, she'd said. But Maureen didn't want to do that unless she had to, if it was raining or something, really she wanted to be away from there for a while, free of it all for an hour or two, if you like.

She walked up to the station. It was busy, people still coming out from Dublin in early Autumn, especially with the weather being so fine. And there was Theresa! Looking in the other direction. Maureen ran across to her and as Theresa turned, hearing her steps, they hugged and looked at each other, smiling.

'You look great Maureen! How are ye?'

'I'm grand, really good. How are you, are you well?'

'I'm fine, better than fine. It's great to see you, Maureen...Now look, shall we walk along the Promenade before we get a tea or something?

Theresa did not really look that great at all. In fact, she looked rather tired and pale, rather worn out.

They walked together, linking as they went out of the station, walking towards the sea.

Once they were across the Strand Road Theresa asked her how things had been for the last couple of weeks.

'Now tell me, how is it with Mrs S, is it all OK there?'

And Maureen told her. About Mrs S, about her room, about the Shaughnessys, all of them, about going to Mass and going to the shops, and baking the scones, and dropping the dish, and the first of the tea parties for Ms S's friends. About how it was all fine and really how she liked Mrs S, although she might have seemed a bit, how would you say, standoffish at the beginning.

And Theresa was pleased that she was happy and wasn't really homesick, and seemed to be enjoying her job, and was sorry that she hadn't been in touch earlier.

And they walked along the Promenade, right along to the end, and turned and walked back, all the time linking, and chatting, looking at the people, laughing at children playing, and laughing at some of the adults as well, for different reasons altogether.

Maureen was glad that Theresa had come. She hadn't properly realised how much she missed having a friend to talk to and having the comfort of them walking along together, their arms intertwined, almost cosy in the slightly cold sea breeze, laughing together, chatting together, close as close can be.

Yet at the same time, almost at the back of her mind, while she enjoyed the walk, and the talk, and the laughter, Maureen was aware that there was something different about Theresa. She had noticed it before, those two long weeks ago, and in a way, whatever it was, it was more pronounced now.

They found a café and went in and ordered a pot of tea and two small cakes. The waitress brought their order over, Maureen stirred the tea and then poured it out. Theresa's first, because Maureen knew that she liked her tea weaker, with more milk, than Maureen did. Theresa watched her and smiled, and took a sip of the tea when Maureen had finished and had poured her own stronger tea. Maureen took a bite of her cake but Theresa ignored hers, lighting a cigarette instead, blowing away the smoke through the side of her mouth.

There was a silence, just for a second or so. A silence that Maureen could hear even within the noise of the crowded café.

'I've got some news Maureen, which I'm really sorry about, especially after persuading you to come to Dublin, or Bray anyway. I've decided I'm leaving Dublin, to go and live in London. On Tuesday, I'm leaving on Tuesday.'

Maureen didn't know what to say. And Theresa wasn't saying anything more. She was just looking at Maureen with a sort of regretful, sad, smile on her face. Older now.

'Why are you going? Because Nan and Angela are there, is that it?'

'No, not really, or not just that. I'm fed up with my job at Joyce's for a start. I mean it's interesting sometimes but a lot of it is just plain old office work, filing and the like. And I'd like to spend a bit o' time in London you know, before I have to settle down. It'll be great. And, who knows, maybe I'll be back in six months.'

The truth was that Mama had been wondering about Theresa for a while, wondering if she was ever going to settle down, find someone, get married. She was older than Nan and Angela, and both of them were already engaged, in London of course, but engaged nonetheless. Both to Irish boys.

Maureen wasn't convinced either, by what Theresa had said. Oh, sure, it was a perfectly good reason to go to London. That's why everyone went wasn't it? For a well-paying job and to see something different. And just the idea of London was exciting as well. But, no, she wasn't convinced. Theresa had a good job, better than any of them, in fact, and, sure, she might have married a solicitor or something if she'd wanted to, here at home. Up to recently Theresa had always said how great the job was, and the people, and the social life. Maureen even remembered her saying once that going to London was a waste of time, you could get all the life, all the fun you needed, in Dublin. She remembered her saying it, laughing.

There at the table, opposite Theresa, Maureen realised that she didn't really know her sister that well at all. She was a lot older, wasn't she? Maureen had only been ten or so when Theresa had left home, and she'd never really been close to her, the gap was too wide for them to have played together, or had little secrets, or got into trouble together.

She would have liked to say, 'Come on now, there must be something else that's making you go,' but she couldn't, she almost didn't feel it was her place to say anything like that. And she was disappointed. She couldn't help it. Disappointed that she wouldn't see Theresa in Dublin and maybe go to a dance or two with her. But she was also disappointed that Theresa, maybe, wasn't telling her the whole story.

'So you're going from Dún Laoghaire?'

'I am. And getting the Irish Mail to London for Wednesday morning.'

She thought Theresa was glad they were on to the practicalities.

'And I've been before of course, three or four times. To see the girls and such.'

'So are you staying with one of them? For a couple of days anyway?'

'No, they live way out, in Watford for God's sake! I prefer it nearer the centre. A friend of mine has a couple of rooms in Willesden Green and they said I could stay there while I sort myself out.'

'OK.'

Theresa looked at her with concern on her face, at the same time taking out, and lighting, another cigarette.

'I'm sorry Maureen. That I've let you down a bit really. But I have to go. I could have told you, but that would have got in the way of you coming here, and I wouldn't have wanted to do that. There's not enough in Dungarvan for you, for any of us really.'

They both looked at each other for a second, saying nothing again. And Theresa glanced at her watch.

'Begod is that the time! I've got to fly, Maureen. I've things to sort out this evening. There's a train in five minutes or so. I'll just pay and we'll be off. Do you want my little cake there? I'll get a bag for ye.'

And within a minute or so they were out of the café, hurrying down towards the station. Theresa linking arms with Maureen again, but this time it felt like it was to drag her on quickly towards the station.

When they got there they hugged briefly before Theresa ran through the ticket barrier, turning to wave quickly before she got on the train. Maureen wondered if she would look out of the window and wave again. But she didn't.

Maureen walked back through the town. The time now, she saw, was only four twenty-five. Theresa hadn't stayed very long at all.

She ambled slowly back along the road to the Shaughnessy's. It was still light and bright, with people walking about, strolling here and there. She thought about Theresa and what she was going to do, and she was surprised at herself, because she realised that it didn't really matter if Theresa wasn't in Dublin. She probably wouldn't have seen her that much anyway, although it would have been nice to have her older sister close by, of course.

But she was happy with her job, happy with being in Bray, she was content enough.

When she got back to the house she went up to her room. Everywhere in the house was quiet. She sat on the bed and took the small paper bag out of her handbag, and ate the little cake that Theresa had left on the plate. It was a fondant fancy, with icing on it, very sweet, and a little bit sticky. Afterwards she wasn't sure that maybe she should have left it till later, or even till tomorrow.

After ten minutes or so she got changed and went downstairs to start preparing the Sunday tea, setting the table, getting the kettle on, making sure that everything was ready for the family. And then she heard the front door open and heard the four of them come in, heard the voices of Mr and Mrs S, and the two children as well. Mrs S popped her head round the kitchen door.

'Oh, you're back already, that's great, everything go alright with your sister?'

'Yes, fine thanks, ma'am. Everything's fine.'

'Good. Can we eat in a quarter of an hour or so? I see it's almost all ready.'

'It's all done bar the tea itself. I'll have it ready for you when you sit down.'

'Fine, Maureen, you're a good girl, you know, I'm so glad you're here.'

CHAPTER THREE

Theresa sent her a letter the following week saying she had arrived safely and was staying with friends, if anyone needed to contact her they could write to that address. Maureen wasn't sure if she was the only one Theresa had written to, so she wrote to Mama and Dada and mentioned, just in passing, that Theresa seemed OK in London. Mama wrote back and said that Theresa had been in touch with them as well.

Maureen forgot about Theresa then, not totally, of course, but put her to the back of her mind while she got on with her life in Bray. Theresa was old enough to look after herself anyway, wasn't she?

Maureen was enjoying life now. She had got into a kind of rhythm with everything, in the house anyway. It wasn't very hard work and Mrs S and the others were not that demanding and everyone was friendly enough. And friendly enough was fine with Maureen. She didn't want to become pals with the children, whom she regarded as both being a little odd in their own separate ways. And she was discovering that she didn't really like Mr S, he seemed pleasant enough, almost cheery, but there was something about him that she didn't entirely trust. Very occasionally he might come into the kitchen, usually when she was preparing dinner, or clearing up after, to get a glass maybe, and she didn't like him being close to her. And he did come close to her on those occasions, by accident, really, she supposed, but she could always smell the drink on him. And, to be fair, it was never anything more than that, just a slight uncomfortable feeling with him near.

Mrs S was a different matter altogether. She was still almost stern but Maureen had got to know her better over the weeks and could tell when she was pleased, with a meal, or the ladies' teas, or with something that had happened at the shops, or with the children. And Mrs S asked Maureen about her life back home, and about Mama and Dada, and the family, about Dungarvan, and where she'd worked before.

Almost every day they would sit down together for a cup of tea and a rest, sometimes mid-morning, sometimes late afternoon, depending on things like shopping and the meetings Mrs S had to go to.

She would come into the kitchen and sit down at the kitchen table and ask Maureen to make the tea. She was still the mistress, of course. But they would talk. About house things first, if necessary, but then she might tell Maureen about Maria's progress at school, or the trouble she had got into, which she did regularly, with the nuns, just silly things really, homework and being late to lesson. And Stephen as well. Mrs S would almost laugh about Maria, but with Stephen she was always a little worried for him. And Maureen knew why, because he was not a confident boy and might find it hard there at the Christian Brothers.

And Mrs S would always ask about her own news, had she got letters from home and the like. She was always interested and Maureen told her about whatever was going on, like when she got a letter from Tommy posted in New York, with a picture postcard of the city tucked inside, or when Angela got her qualification as a nurse in England, or when Michael and his wife had their first baby, a girl, and Maureen became an aunt.

It was never more than fifteen or twenty minutes but Maureen looked forward to it. Looked forward to hearing Mrs S walk down the hall and come into the kitchen.

'Will you make us both a cup of tea, Maureen? And then take the weight off your feet for a few minutes while we have a biscuit and a chat.'

About four weeks after starting in Bray, when, to be honest, Maureen was only just getting used to sitting down with the mistress for tea and a chat, Mrs S mentioned that Mrs Doyle, who she knew from the teas, had a new girl start only at the beginning of that week and had asked if Maureen could show her around, take her down the town, show her where everything was. The girl, apparently, was a bit meek and a bit homesick as well. Mrs S said, if they got on, it might be nice for her to have a friend to walk out with. Maureen felt quite flattered really, because she, herself, had only been there a few weeks. Maureen said that would be grand and Mrs S telephoned Mrs D to say that Maureen would come over at three the following afternoon.

That day she had some ironing to do after lunchtime, but when she'd finished she made herself look respectable, tidied herself up and, after telling Mrs S that she was going out to Mrs Doyle's as agreed, and would be back definitely before five, she set off. Mrs S almost smiled and said she hoped she had a good time.

Mrs D lived just two and half streets away. Maureen knew where it was because they passed her house on the way to Mass every Sunday and Mrs S had pointed it out to her one week. The same kind of house as the Shaughnessy's although, maybe, just a touch bigger and smarter. Mrs Doyle's husband was a little more important than Mr S, he was a long-established councillor who might be mayor of the town at some point, it was said.

Maureen walked round there quick enough. She was a bit nervous though, or not nervous really, more wary she supposed. Supposing she didn't like this girl? Julia was her name, Mrs S had told her. But she didn't have to like her, did she? All she had to do was take her down the town and show her around, tell her which shops she used, maybe take a look at the Promenade, perhaps have a cup of tea as well. They didn't need to become pals or anything although, of course, it would be good to have a friend to go out with sometimes. She'd met a couple of girls at Mass, after Mass, outside the church. But they were already friends and, although they were nice enough, Maureen hadn't felt they were particularly interested in her. They hadn't said they would meet her next Sunday or suggested going out together on their afternoon off.

She started down Mrs Doyle's road and, when she came to the house, walked up the path and pulled the bell. It did feel strange, almost like being a real visitor; she wondered what it would be like to come to a place like this and have the door opened by the maid, and her coat taken, and be welcomed by Mrs Doyle, taken into the lounge and offered tea, and maybe something to eat. She had watched others doing just that, and she had taken other people's coats, herself, and had shown them in to the lounge.

The door opened wide.

'Maureen! Great! You're exactly on time, what a fine girl you are!'

Mrs Doyle was always ebullient, always friendly, down to earth as well, even though she was quite an important person here in Bray. She didn't stand on ceremony and she spoke to anyone and everyone in much the same way. Usually with a laugh.

Mrs Doyle wasn't fat, not fat at all in fact, and not especially tall either, but she did seem take up rather a lot of space. Maureen had noticed that at Mrs S's, you always knew when Mrs Doyle was there, laughing, talking, moving about, taking up more of the room than anyone else. Mrs S liked her, Maureen knew, but she had watched some of the other women looking at her in an irritated way occasionally.

Maureen smiled hello, and then noticed the other person, a person hidden to some extent by Mrs Doyle, Maureen could only see the edge of her really.

Mrs Doyle moved to the side and then Maureen saw fully who was behind. A girl. A girl who looked young. If she had seen her in the street Maureen might have thought she was fourteen, or thirteen even. She was not tall and she was thin, her legs were definitely skinny. And she was dressed to go out in a dark blue coat that was too big for her with a kind of beret on her head. Her face was pale and she looked almost scared. Not completely scared, but only almost, because there was the try of a smile on her face.

'Now, Maureen, this is Julia. Julia this is Maureen, who works for my good friend, Mrs Shaughnessy. Julia has come from Kerry and is just getting used to the ways of Bray and the like. It'd be grand if you could show her around, Maureen. And look, I've given Julia a couple of bob for some tea or something. Not that I'll make a habit of it, you can be sure of that.'

She winked at Maureen when she said this and then pushed Julia out the door, not roughly, but definitely.

'Enjoy yourselves. Back by five Julia, to get started on the supper, mind!'

She smiled again and shut the door leaving the two girls alone, outside, on the top step.

They looked at each other.

'Let's go then eh?'

Maureen led the way and Julia followed, they turned onto the road and aimed themselves towards the town. They had two hours, but they had to get there and they had to get back, and they had to have a look around, and get a cuppa as well.

They walked along in silence for a while, Maureen leading the way.

‘So you’re up from Kerry eh?’

‘Yes.’

‘So when did you get here?’

‘Sunday I suppose, Monday really. Work I mean.’

Silence as they walked.

‘So, is Mrs Doyle alright to work for, then?’

Silence. They walked.

And then Julia spoke, in a strong, fast, Kerry accent

‘She’ll be OK I suppose, nice really, except she never stops, she never stops talking, laughing, telling her husband what to do, telling her children what to do, telling me what to do. Never still for a moment. And, by the way, whenever I’m doing the tea she goes on and on about your scones, so you’d better give me that feckin recipe today, so at least I can shut her up about that.’

Maureen was taken aback, not shocked at all, but taken aback, and she hadn’t expected the ‘feckin’ that’s for sure. It seemed so odd coming out like that from this slip of a girl, right there in the street. Looking at her you wouldn’t have expected her to say boo to a goose.

She stopped and so did Julia They looked at each other for a second and then they burst out laughing. Maureen pulled Julia’s arm under hers and they moved off towards the town without saying another word, but giggling together now.

When they sat down in the café Julia told her about home. They lived on a smallholding, her Da worked that, and worked for a nearby farmer as well, but it was a difficult life and there was no work at all for her or her sisters, so each of them left as they got to fourteen or fifteen. Julia was seventeen and she'd actually worked in Cork for the last eighteen months before coming to Bray. She seemed happy talking about home, said she hadn't enjoyed Cork much, but Mrs Doyle, for all her busy-ness, seemed OK so far.

And Maureen told Julia about Dungarvan. Different but the same in many ways. Family, happiness, very little money, a hardship of sorts. And everyone moved away, everyone always moved away. It was the same for both of them.

Maureen liked Julia. She was an odd girl that was for sure. Waif-like, almost poor-looking, pale skin and a thin face. You almost wouldn't have been surprised to see her begging on the street. And there she sat in the café smoking a cigarette in a very brazen kind of way as well. Maureen realised that she, herself, looked different from this. Sturdier, more rounded, older certainly. And prettier, she thought, as well.

They chatted about this and that. Julia was definitely more scurrilous than Maureen, talking about Mr and Mrs Doyle and what they got up to, for instance. And a dreadful story about the woman of the house in Cork. It almost made Maureen blush to hear her, but she was funny alright, they laughed out loud, looking around as they did so, aware of the noise they were making in the small café. And Julia was pleased to make Maureen laugh.

And so they became friends. They walked back that afternoon and agreed to meet on the Sunday, they'd see each other at Mass anyway, but they could go out for a few hours in the afternoon as well.

When Maureen got home that first afternoon Mrs S asked how things had gone and she said fine, they'd gone fine. And as she started to get the tea together she felt happy. Because she had missed her friends back home, and it would be nice to have a friend here for a chat and a gossip and a laugh. And someone to go out with as well. She'd enjoyed being on her own for a few weeks but it would be great to have a pal again.

Everything fell into a kind of routine now. As the winter evenings closed in Maureen did her work, and did the shopping, and chatted to Mrs S most days and saw Julia a couple of times a week and wrote to Mama and Dada, and went to Mass. She was comfortable with it all.

CHAPTER FOUR

Initially, of course, Maureen and Julia just met for a chat and a walk. Or sometimes, as it got colder, they would sit together in the kitchen of either house, when all was quiet, and talk about this and that. Sometimes it would be serious stuff, about home or their families. In November Julia's mum was ill for a week, maybe pneumonia or something similar, and Julia was worried sick, herself, about what might happen because, it seemed, her Ma was not a strong person, generally that is. And Maureen told Julia about Theresa, about how strange that she should disappear off to London like that. Julia said there was nothing strange about that at all, who wouldn't want to go to London, especially a girl like Theresa who was capable of getting a good job as a secretary or the like in a solicitor's office. Julia said she, herself, would be off like a shot if she thought she could get an important, well-paid, job like that. It would be miles better than skivvying like she was now.

Maureen didn't agree with Julia on this. Maureen liked her job. Oh, it would be a fine thing if she could get an important job, wearing fancy clothes and the like, but that wasn't possible, at the moment anyway. And she liked working for Mrs S. She didn't feel she was skivvying as Julia put it, didn't feel she was actually a servant, if you like, even if she knew she was, in a way. Maureen felt part of what was going on in the house, and she had her own room, and she had a little bit of money, and she had her chats with Mrs S. And she had Julia as a friend.

Back home Maureen, before coming to Bray, had started going to the odd dance with her friends, Ann, and Annie and Greta. They had been to the céilís which took place in one of the places in town, in the function room and they'd been to a dance hall as well. Really, they'd only just started going out together because they were still a bit young but it had been great fun, the atmosphere, and the laughs and the dancing itself, whether doing the Irish dances, which could be wild, or the more modern stuff as well. It had all been great.

Here in Bray she hadn't known anyone and while she wasn't exactly a shy person she was sure she wouldn't be going to the dances on her own. It wasn't long, however, before Julia and she started talking about doing something more exciting than just going up to the town, and having a walk and, maybe, a cup of tea and a cake together. And, of course, Julia was desperate to go dancing. And Maureen thought she should like it too, although she was, for some reason, nervous about the prospect as well. In the first place she was worried about what Mrs S might think. She wasn't sure if she would disapprove. And she didn't want that, she liked Mrs S and she liked that they talked together, she liked it that Mrs S treated her, if not exactly as an equal, but with respect anyway. She was worried that if she started going to dances, and the like, Mrs S might look at her in a different way, not as friendly, become more distant in some way.

And maybe the same thing with Julia as well. At the moment they were just two friends together, if they went out dancing they were bound to meet more people and Julia could also become more distant in some way, pick up friendships with other girls maybe. But when Maureen thought about it a bit more she knew she was just worrying too much.

And, anyway, there was the thing about boys. She had known boys back in Dungarvan obviously. Danced with them, and she'd even kissed one. Bridie O'Connor's other boy, Michael. They were at a dance and had gone outside, for a break, for a rest. And he had kissed her, and she hadn't minded at all, but it had only been a short kiss and then it was like they both forgot about it, as if it had never happened. She'd known Michael at school, and he lived down the road, he was a year older, but she'd known him all her life really. And that's what it was, that was the problem, the kiss had been nice but she knew him too well.

So when Theresa had mentioned dances, and boys as well, she had liked the idea, of seeing other people, seeing other things, and meeting other boys. Boys she didn't know every single thing about already.

It would be wrong to say she hadn't met boys here in Bray either. There were the delivery boys coming to the house, she might have a chat with them, especially if they brought stuff right into the kitchen. And the butcher's boy, Jimmy. For some reason he always seemed to be riding his big old delivery bike back into town when she was going for shopping or something, At first he had just kind of wheeled along slowly next to her, with his howarya's and the like, and then he'd stopped occasionally and pushed the bike along for a couple of hundred yards or so, walking with her, before leaping on again and belting off back to the shop because, he said, Reilly, the butcher, could get awful fierce if he took too long with the deliveries. She liked him, he was funny and friendly, and he'd said about the dances and things, but he wasn't for her, she thought, not in that kind of way. Not that she wouldn't have a dance with him if he'd asked, she would.

Julia had said they should go to the dance this Saturday night. So when she sat down with Mrs S on the Tuesday, for their cup of tea together, she said she and Julia were thinking of going to the dance on Saturday. She'd decided she'd just say it, not ask if she could go, but just say it as if it were the most natural thing in the world. Which of course it was. And she had every right to go if she wanted, Mrs S couldn't keep her locked up in the house, could she?

Mrs S didn't blink an eyelid at the idea. She said that would be fine and she hoped she would enjoy herself but that she should not be back too late. And they left it that. Except Mrs S also said that she should keep an eye on Julia because she thought that maybe Julia could be a bit on the wild side, if you know what I mean, she said.

And Maureen thought she did know what Mrs S meant. The two of them had been in a sweetshop just the week before, Maureen wanted to buy a small bar of chocolate for herself, the Five Boys one that she liked, a little treat. And when they'd come out and walked along the street a bit, Julia showed her two packets of mints she had stolen from the shop. Laughing about it, and popping a mint into her mouth, she offered a packet to Maureen. Who refused immediately. For some unknown reason Maureen was not surprised at Julia acting like this, doing this kind of thing. They got on fine together but she knew Julia was very different from her. Maureen told her that if she ever did that again she would not go into any shop with her ever again, she might not even go out in public with her. But Julia just laughed and gave her a friendly shove before stuffing another couple of mints into her mouth.

On the Saturday night, after tea and everything had been dealt with, Maureen spent a while getting ready. She'd put curlers in to get a bit of a wave to the hair and she ironed the one frock she had that would do for a dance. She was worried that she didn't really have a good dress to go out in. The one she had would have been fine enough at home but she thought it might be a bit plain for here in Bray. Because it was different here, there was no doubt about that. There was more money for a start, more people, and, of course, people came here on holiday as well, and for the weekend, and for days out. They splashed out a bit you might say. But, anyway, there wasn't anything she could do about that at the moment. And then she giggled to herself wondering what Julia would do, looking as young and skinny as she did.

So she got herself ready and put on her lipstick and all the rest and looked in the mirror and checked her stockings were straight. Julia would call for her at eight thirty. She went downstairs and sat in the hall. Mrs S heard her and came out, she said she looked fine, and the two youngsters peeked around the door at her. Both smiled, but Maureen wondered whether Maria wasn't actually looking down at her a bit, smirking rather than smiling. The front door bell rang and Mrs S said to be sure she had a great time, and to remember what she'd said about Julia.

'Not too late now, you hear!'

Exactly like Mama might have said.

Julia, standing there in the door way, looked both strange and attractive at the same time. She was still the same skinny waif and in that way she looked absurd, but all dressed up, and made up, she did look attractive as well. Dressed up, and made up, exactly like Maureen really. Best frock, stockings, hair done, lipstick and make up. They were both the exact same person as they were before, the girls going to the butchers or to the greengrocers but they were also totally different. They were dressed as women now, or as women might be, or as they might be as women.

When they saw each other at the door, they both laughed. Not loud. Just laughed in a kind of complicit way. Both knowing what the other one was covering up with all this palaver, all this sheen, all this gloss. But they were happy with it.

Maureen pulled the door to.

'Bye Mrs Shaughnessy!'

'Yeah. Bye, Mrs Shaughnessy!'

Maureen meant it but Julia was being almost sarcastic, or silly at the very least. But anyway, no matter, thought Maureen.

They set off down the road arm in arm. Julia smoking already.

The Arcadia Ballroom was in the centre of town near the station. Maureen was a little nervous about going there because it was a place like nothing she had ever been to before, much, much, bigger anyway, and she knew you got a great crowd there, including Dubliners who'd come out on the train. Julia, of course, showed no sign of nerves at all and when they got there she was straight in, pulling Maureen along, chatting to whoever they were behind or in front of.

And inside it was wild as well. The music and the chat and the dancing. A lot of boys, some not quite so happy with the dancing, lined up on the opposite side to the girls. Well, that was the same as Dungarvan anyway, thought Maureen.

Maureen danced with Julia, and they met some of the girls who worked in the other houses, girls she'd seen at Mass, and a couple of the girls who worked in the shops she went to as well. It was like when you saw them all in here, in the ballroom, you had something in common with them and it was easy to chat, and laugh, and dance, and discuss the boys on the other side of the hall.

And she danced with three of those boys, or was it four, as the evening went on. Just boys, nothing special. One of them asked her again, asked her if she'd like a drink, a mineral, but she didn't want to dance with him, or have him buy her a drink. Julia, of course, was all over the place, mad as they come, somehow louder and more extravagant than everyone else. Maureen thought she might be drinking, or have drunk something before she came, and as the evening went on she became even more visible. Screaming with laughter, encouraging the boys, and even, once, falling over on the ballroom floor. Maureen somehow knew that Julia would be like that, it would have surprised her if she wasn't.

At half eleven Maureen thought she should be getting home. She wasn't really sure what Mrs S had meant when she said don't be too late. She certainly didn't mean she should stay out till two or three o' clock, Maureen felt pretty sure of that.

Julia couldn't believe it. She said it was far too early to be going home, she should stay, she had to stay. But Maureen said she was going anyway, and Julia just shook her head in disappointment, gave Maureen a kiss and said she'd see her tomorrow at Mass.

Maureen got her coat and made her way through the crowd and out of the main doors on to the street.

She wasn't really sure whether she should have left Julia there, but it would have been impossible to persuade her to come home, she would have refused point blank. And Maureen, herself, really wanted to go home. She had enjoyed the dancing and the craic with the other girls, and she'd enjoyed being with Julia as well, but she'd had enough now.

She walked back through the town and then hurried along the road back to the house. She thought about the dancing and the laughter and the boys, and knew she had enjoyed it all, but she also knew she didn't want to spend hours and hours at dances, or to go dancing every night of the week, which she knew some of the girls loved to do. But she would go again, she would go again, for sure, for definite.

The house looked quiet, why wouldn't it be at that time of night? Maureen had never heard the Shaughnessys stay up very late, as far as she knew they all seemed to be in bed by eleven or earlier even, although it was true Mr S did come in late once or twice a week. Once she had heard him knock the telephone off the hall table and swear quite loudly. Maureen opened the front door as quietly as she could and went into the hall. There was some light coming from the kitchen. She wasn't sure if she should go straight upstairs or say hello to whoever it was in there. If it was Mr Shaughnessy she didn't want to, she didn't want to talk to him alone, especially this late at night when he would definitely have had a drink. There wasn't a night went by that he didn't drink something, she knew that. And he never had just a glass, she knew that as well.

But she also knew it would be very bad manners to ignore whoever it was. And it might just be that the light had been left on, in which case she should turn it off, anyway, before going up to her bed.

She took her coat off, put it over her arm and walked across the hall and down to the kitchen door. The door was a quarter open and there was light from inside. She pushed the door wider and peeked around it, as if just to say, it's me I'm home from the dance, just a couple of polite words before disappearing up the stairs to bed.

The light was coming from the bulb which was by the back door of the kitchen, in the little alcove there, the only light that was separate from the switch here at the door. You might use it if you were taking stuff out the back in the evening for instance. The overhead light was off, so the kitchen itself was quite dark. Maureen could see the figure of Mrs S sitting at the kitchen table in this semi-darkness, almost eerily shadowed there. From where she was, at the door, Maureen could see, just feet away, the other woman's back, sitting up straight in the wooden kitchen chair, hands folded in front of her, placed on the kitchen table. Almost like praying but not quite.

Maureen realised that she had never been in the kitchen at this time of night, probably past midnight now. It was possible, she thought, that Mrs S had a habit of sitting in the kitchen on her own when it was late, with a cup of tea maybe, after the children were asleep and all the day's work had been done. Mama sometimes did that at home.

'Hello, I'm back.'

She said this in almost a whisper, unwilling to speak too loudly in the quiet of the night.

There was no response for a second or two. Mrs S didn't turn around to her even then.

'Right you are, Maureen, I'll see you tomorrow.'

Her voice was flat. Not welcoming, or even efficient as it sometimes was. Just flat. Not Like Mrs S at all.

Maureen hesitated. Part of her just wanted to leave and go upstairs to bed. It was late anyway and she still had to get up early in the morning. At the same time she had a feeling that something was not right, but she wasn't sure if it was any of her business.

'Could I make a quick cup of tea, ma'am? I'm parched after the dancing.'

She had no idea where this came from; she was astounded, in a way, at her own cheek. She stood, still at the door, still with her coat over her arm. She'd only been in the house a minute or two even now, although it seemed longer.

Mrs S didn't reply immediately, but then Maureen heard her breathe in before speaking.

'Quickly then. You can leave me a cup too, before you go up.'

Less flat now, her voice, but not chatty, not chatty at all.

Maureen came in and went over to fill the kettle and put it on. And she got the teapot and the cups out. Quietly, quietly, not letting them rattle, putting everything down softly on the side. She didn't look towards Mrs S although, obviously, she could feel her there, see her, even, through the corner of her eyes. She felt that her own moves were being followed as well. The kettle took a while to boil and Maureen just stood there in front of the milk, the teapot, the sugar bowl, the cups, the saucers, all on the side, all of them, her included, waiting for the kettle. Not turning to look at, or to say anything, to Mrs S. She felt awkward, almost trapped there, and part of her, a big part of her, wished she had kept her mouth shut and gone upstairs.

And she made the tea. Now, of course she had to wait for it to brew.

'Sit down at the table, Maureen, have your tea here if you wish.'

The voice sounded softer now, not as flat or harsh, closer now to the voice that Mrs S would normally use, perhaps not over-friendly, but yes, normal, let's say.

Maureen stirred the tea in the pot and then transferred the pot to the table, and the cups and saucers and the milk and the sugar. A thing she had done a load of times, because it was exactly like this that they would sit, when they had their chats with their tea and biscuits, most days of the week. But not the weekend usually.

She sat down at the table concentrating on the tea, and the pouring, aware that Mrs S was watching her every move.

'So how was the dance Maureen, did you enjoy yourself?'

'I did. It was great.'

Maureen smiled and looked up from the cups, ready to talk. Mrs S's face was shadowed because there was still just the light from the back-door bulb. Sufficient to do the tea, as the stove was near to the back-door alcove, but not really shedding any proper light into the room.

Her face was shadowed but immediately Maureen could see

something different about it. In fact she knew, immediately, that Mrs S had something wrong about her face, but for a second or two she didn't quite register it as that, because she didn't want to. She didn't want to see, or know, that Mrs S had been hurt, been hit maybe.

The right eye was swollen quite badly till it was virtually closed, and there was a slight darkness, or bruising, on the upper part of her cheek.

There was a shock between them now. Maureen was shocked by what she saw, but had no idea what to say next, no idea at all. And Maureen knew that Mrs S had decided to let Maureen see the damage, after all, she could have told her to go straight upstairs, but she hadn't. She'd let her stay. She showed her what had happened. And there was a shock between them now, inside them too, inside them both.

Maureen gulped as if to start to say something, but as she did so she caught Mrs S's eyes, and they were saying NO. I have shown you but please don't ask. And Maureen understood.

Ask me no questions and I'll tell you no lies.

'The dance was great Mrs S, it was just great.......'

She couldn't say anything more. She knew it would be best to go up.

'Would it be alright if I leave you to it now, ma'am? Otherwise I'll never be up for the breakfast?'

'No, you go ahead, Maureen. Get some sleep. You sleep well now, you hear.'
Maureen got up to go, leaving her tea to go cold, and as she passed Mrs S she touched her arm, just touched her arm lightly, to tell her that she understood.

CHAPTER FIVE

She was ready for sleep as she climbed those stairs, away from the kitchen and its shadowed light. If she hadn't gone in there she would have been going up to bed in a different mood altogether, she would have been pleased that she had enjoyed the dance, pleased that she'd left when she wanted to, laughed a little at Julia's antics, glad that she'd met some of the other girls, looked forward to going again next week. She still felt those things but they seemed unimportant now, for the moment anyway.

Even in those few short weeks she had grown to like Mrs S, the woman who had said, in that funny way she had, that Maureen should eat in the kitchen, and, at the beginning, had been kind of stand-offish if you like. Maureen knew, now, that she was a good and kind person, if you got past her rather stiff ways.

And what she had seen in the kitchen had shocked her. God, she knew these things went on alright, the Murphy family down the road in Dungarvan was a good example of that, Billy Murphy hitting Breda was just a fact of life in that house. Especially after a few drinks, and sometimes without even that excuse, if that's what it was. But she was shocked because she would never have expected to see that here. Not in a well-off house like this one, and not with someone like Mrs S who seemed to be in charge of things.

When she had seen her face across the kitchen table she had seen the bruising first, but she'd seen, in a moment, something else as well, she'd seen that Mrs S was sad and worn down, seen, maybe, that her way of talking, her efficiency, her briskness, covered up something else. Covered up herself.

Maureen got undressed, hanging up the frock but leaving the other stuff on the floor to get washed. She put on her nightdress, shivering now, it was cold up here away from the bit of warmth downstairs, and she climbed into bed. She wondered where Julia was now, and she slept.

She woke on time and went down to prepare everything for the Sunday breakfast. She wasn't sure what would happen with Mrs S, she would have to wait and see.

Normally Mrs S would appear at seven fifteen or so, sometimes a bit later, sometimes a bit earlier. Maureen wondered if she might have a word with her about last night, say something about it. But what that word would be, she didn't know. Mrs S did not appear.

At about half seven she heard Mr Shaughnessy coming down the stairs, noisy and heavy.

He came into the kitchen.

'Good morning Maureen.'

'Morning, sir.'

'I've some bad news for you I'm afraid. Mrs Shaughnessy has been taken ill, she's got an awful cold, flu even, maybe, pretty bad it looks like. We've decided that she'll have to stay in bed for a few days.'

'OK, sir. I can take her some tea and a bit of breakfast upstairs.'

'No. No, that's not necessary. We don't want you catching the flu as well. She'll just have some tea and a slice of toast. If you do that when breakfast is ready I'll take it up. No need for you to go in the room at all. I'll take her meals up for the next day or two. I've been in contact with her so I've already got the flu if I'm going to get it.'

'Yes, sir.'

'Oh, and I'll not be going to Mass this morning. I'll go later, I mean. You go along with Maria and Stephen.'

'Yes, sir.'

He stood there for a moment. In his trousers, braces, and his shirt. No collar, no tie.

'Right, then, breakfast at eight as usual.'

And he left. She heard him climb the stairs again and then hurry the children up.

She made the breakfast and made sure it was all on the table for the three of them. And she made a tray for Mrs S as well. A pot of tea and two slices of toast, and butter and marmalade. He took that straight up before sitting down for his own breakfast.

And once they were eating she had her own fried breakfast, sitting by herself at the kitchen table.

The house was quieter than normal without Mrs S chivvying the children, and the husband, to get ready for Mass, making sure they looked presentable, making sure their shoes were shined. When Maureen had taken the cooked breakfast in the three of them were sitting there. Not talking. Quieter than it would usually be, the two children looking subdued, glancing at Maureen and saying a brief hello but nothing more. She left them to it.

And when they walked along to Mass the children barely said a word to each other, or to Maureen. They knew, or they knew something was up, anyway. If Mrs S just had a cold they might have made some kind of comment, but, apart from that, they would have been as chatty, and argumentative as they were normally, Maria would have been anyway. But they said little.

And, at the church, the three of them stood, and kneeled, and prayed in the pew. Not looking at each other, not communicating at all.

They left Mass together, following each other in the queue down the aisle and then out into the sunshine, a bright but cold day.

The children, and of course they were teenagers not exactly children, drifted off to chat with their friends and Maureen looked around for Julia. She hadn't seen her in church but wondered if she'd been at the back. The girls she knew, the shopgirls and the like, were all together, laughing and looking around, on the other side of the road. There was no Julia there. Maureen waved across to them but decided she had to get back to the house to get started on the dinner because there'd be no Mrs S keeping an eye on things, and helping where necessary, today. She quickly told Stephen she was going back and left them to it. They knew they had to be back within half an hour or so otherwise there'd be trouble with the father.

She wasn't worried about Julia. She could have gone to an earlier Mass although that was unlikely considering the state of her the night before. Or she might have decided to go to the evening Mass instead. Maureen'd know soon enough.

Back at the house it was very quiet. All the quieter really because she knew that someone was there in the house, Mrs S was upstairs, in her bed presumably. Although Maureen knew, at the same time, that there was no real reason for her to actually be in bed. What was she doing then? Sitting in her room. Looking out the window? Reading?

Mr S wasn't in the lounge, maybe he was upstairs as well.

She got on with the dinner. She'd got the potatoes and the other veg ready before going to Mass and put the meat in on low, so it was just a matter of getting it all going. And she was used to this, she'd been doing it almost all on her own for the last few weeks, Mrs S trusted her to do it, and she'd more or less done the same thing back at home for years. Helping Mama anyway.

The children were back on time and Mr S appeared from nowhere, had he been in the garden maybe. Who knows? It wasn't like normal. At the best of times there wasn't a huge amount of laughter and conversation but today there was even less. There was a mood on the house, a quiet thing where nothing was said, nothing was mentioned, no idle chatter took place, no joking was heard, no teasing of Stephen by Maria. Maureen just kept going, hearing, all the time, that difference.

She served the dinner. And made a tray for Mrs S which he took upstairs before sitting down to his own. They ate the meal, the pudding as well, apple pie and custard today. She had hers at the kitchen table. And then she cleaned up. Mr S brought down the tray, the food had been picked at not eaten.

It was just an awkward day.

At half two or so Mrs Doyle turned up. This was very unusual, for her to just turn up without some kind of arrangement or even a phone call. She'd come to ask after Mrs S, having been told by the children, after Mass, that their mother was unwell.

Maureen answered the door and saw, immediately, that Mrs Doyle intended to just go straight upstairs. Maureen said that she was sure that Mr Shaughnessy would like to chat to her first and would she like a cup of tea? A scone maybe? Mrs Doyle was a very pleasant woman but she did like to get her own way, she was irritated that she had to talk to him. And, no, she didn't want tea and scones, so soon after dinner. But she said that pleasantly to Maureen, with a smile.

Mr S took her into the lounge. Maureen could hear the buzz

of them talking. She had been pleased to see Mr Shaughnessy looking very uncomfortable when he'd come into the hall to greet Mrs Doyle.

They talked for just five minutes or less. Maureen hung around in the hall, waiting to see what the outcome would be. And Mrs Doyle came out looking very annoyed, underneath a kind of smile and some politeness. He had managed to divert her and she was leaving.
She saw Maureen. She seemed to consider if she was going to say something, and then she did.

'Maureen, my dear, I'm afraid Julia has let us all down and I'm going to have to let her go. She came home in a disgraceful state last night, and couldn't be woken at all this morning. And that's not the first time I've had problems with her. Other things which, truth be told, I cannot mention at all. Lord have mercy on, her that's all I can say! She'll be gone by the end of the week anyway. I wish we'd had the good fortune to take you on, Maureen, before Mrs Shaughnessy found you. You'll look after Mrs Shaughnessy, won't you? Make sure she's warm, and has enough to eat and drink?'

'I will ma'am, I'll make sure of that.'

'Good girl.'

And she went with hardly a word to him. A murmured good-bye maybe. She wasn't pleased with him, or with Julia, either, obviously.

Mr Shaughnessy stood by the front door for a second or two then turned, and seeing Maureen still standing there, asked if she was going out. She said she was. And he went into the lounge with not another word.

CHAPTER SIX

Maureen walked around to Mrs Doyle's that afternoon when she left the house, hoping to have a word with Julia. It was still a bright and cool day, as it had been when she'd walked to Mass earlier, although she could feel that the evenings were starting to draw in now. She wasn't sure what reception she would get at Mrs Doyle's. Mrs D would probably be pleasant enough to her, she always was, but she wasn't sure she would like the fact that she had come to see Julia. If Julia was there anyway, she might well have taken her afternoon off, never mind the fact that she had got up late and all the rest of it. Or told Mrs D to stick her job and left immediately.

Julia answered the door, looking very subdued, wearing her working dress. Mrs Doyle was in the hall behind her. It was clear that Julia wasn't quite sure what to do and she glanced backwards towards Mrs D.

'Come in now for ten minutes Maureen. Go in the kitchen with her. But no more than ten minutes, mind. Julia has a load of work to catch up on.'

They went into the kitchen. It was tidy enough and Maureen could see that Julia had started on the tea.

They sat down.

'She told me you got in awful late?'

And Julia told her all about how she'd been dancing and how things had gone on, even after they left the dance hall, she wasn't too explicit about that. And, yes, she'd had a few drinks but nothing major, like. And she hadn't got home till half past four and she'd knocked something over in the hall which woke up Mr and Mrs Doyle, who came downstairs. Knocking over something in the hall reminded Maureen of Mr Shaughnessy, who she didn't want to think about at all. And then Julia had slept in, even though Mrs D had tried to wake her.

And Maureen asked her about the other things that Mrs D mentioned but not specified. And Julia wouldn't say, apart from the fact that it was, 'nothing at all, nothing at all.' And what was Julia going to do now? She thought there might be a job in one of the hotels where one of the other girls worked, she'd look tomorrow.

And she said she'd better get on with the work because she'd need some kind of reference from 'that feckin eejit'. She said this in a whisper. And Maureen got up to go, saying she'd see her during the week.

Julia followed her out to the hall. Mrs Doyle was waiting for her to go, she smiled, nicely enough at Maureen and glared at Julia, who said bye and went back to the kitchen.

Maureen was glad to get out of there. She walked up the street towards the town. Not for any purpose but just to have a walk on her own. To relax herself a bit before going back and sorting the tea out.

It was a strange week that followed.

Mr S obviously went to work as normal and the children went to school. This left, on Monday morning, Maureen in the house with Mrs S upstairs. She hadn't seen her on the Sunday although she thought she'd heard her have a bath. Mr S said very little to her. He made sure, though, that he took the breakfast up to his wife before leaving for his work that morning.

'Be sure not to bother Mrs Shaughnessy will you Maureen? She needs her rest and I don't want you going down with the flu as well. Then we'd be in a right pickle altogether!'

He said this with a smile. As if they were friends or something. Maybe he didn't even suspect that she knew anything.

She got on with her work. Cleaning up after breakfast and then doing the beds, sorting out the washing and getting on with it. In an odd way it was quite pleasurable knowing that she knew exactly what she had to do, and being in control of her day. Knowing when she would go to the shops and deciding what the meal would be tonight. Being Monday it was little more than using up stuff that was left over from yesterday, but there were still a few things that were needed to be bought.

Mr S had said he would come back at one and Maureen should get a sandwich or some soup ready for him to take up to his wife. He turned up at twelve forty-five and took the tray up and left immediately to go back to work.

Maureen thought she would go up to the town at half twoish.

At just after two, directly just after the clock in the hall had chimed, she heard footsteps coming down the stairs. And Mrs S appeared at the kitchen door.

'Hello Maureen.'

She was dressed, the same stuff as normal, a blouse and a skirt, the type of thing she wore round the house. Comfortable. She was carrying the tray. She had eaten half the sandwich that Maureen had made.

Maureen looked at her.

The bruising on her face was blue and yellow now. If anything, it was more noticeable even though it was probably healing at the same time.

Mrs S smiled at her, a wan, sad smile. She sat down at the table.

'Let's have a cup of tea, shall we? And a biscuit?'

So Maureen made the tea and put a few biscuits on a plate and sat down. She said nothing. For one thing she wasn't sure what she should say, and for another it really didn't seem necessary to talk at that moment. They were relaxed together in the kitchen. There was no particular tension between them even though there were obviously things still unsaid, and other questions that could reasonably be asked. But weren't.

Nothing was mentioned to Mr S, of course, or to the children, about Mrs Shaughnessy coming downstairs during the day. They didn't have a spoken agreement not to say anything, it was understood. For the next two days Mrs S came down after lunch and had a cup of tea and a biscuit, they talked about house matters, the shopping, and the children, about Julia's escapades as well, but nothing pertaining to the incident or the Saturday night in the house. There was no need to discuss it. Maureen knew what had happened, she might not have known the reason for it, if, indeed, there was any definable reason, but she knew what had happened. Mr S had hit his wife, probably after drinking too much and getting angry with her, exasperated with her, about something or other. Maureen didn't really know what that might be, but she expected it was about him being master in his own house. He had used the expression 'not even master in my own house' from time to time before, sometimes as a sort of joke about Mrs S, when he hadn't got his own way about what time they were going out, or where they were going to, some matter of little real importance. Sometimes he said the same thing, sometimes about the same type of trivial incident, but with an angry edge, with a touch of fury; walking away and slamming a door the last time it had happened.

Maureen wondered what Mrs S felt about him, about her husband. Sometimes, lying in bed at night thinking about this and that, she thought about those two. At first she'd imagined they'd got on well, in their own kind of way, they had their children, they had their house, they led a comfortable life. Mrs S seemed contented in a quiet kind of way. But seeing her sitting at the kitchen table, that Saturday night, she thought that there was a dreadful unhappiness there as well.

Talking with Mrs S at the table on those afternoons, during that week, Maureen felt close to her. They had a sort of secret between them, a trust. And this was something that Maureen had never really experienced before. She had been close to her family, close to Mama of course, but never close to another person in this kind of way. And of course, she couldn't help but feel flattered that a woman like Mrs S who, after all, came from a different level of society was able to trust her and confide in her, even if only in a limited way.

She was close to Julia, as well, of course. But that was totally different. The two of them were just two youngsters, from similar backgrounds, enjoying life, sharing gossip, and supporting each other as they could, looking after each other, if they were able. But with Mrs S she felt, in a way, more like a grown-up, more like a woman on an equal footing, and she liked that, she liked that very much.

Maureen met Julia in town on Wednesday. Julia had a good idea when Maureen would be out shopping and made sure to find her. They had a cup of tea in the café they usually went to.

Julia was not really any more forthcoming about the stuff that had been left unsaid at the weekend, by both Mrs Doyle and by Julia. Maureen dreaded to think what she might have got up to and, in one sense, was glad not to know the gory details. At the same time, of course, she would have loved to know what had gone on. She had run into a couple of the other girls on Tuesday and they were full of Julia's bad behaviour, which they thought was absolutely hilarious, and they were both shocked, and sort of delighted, by the fact that Julia had got the sack from Mrs Doyle's. They knew who Mrs Doyle was, of course, and had been somewhat mystified by how Julia had got a job there in the first place. In the past Mrs Doyle had tended to have meeker, mousy, girls or sometimes older, more settled, types. That'd teach her they said. Stick to the quiet ones in future. They roared with laughter.

Julia said she had looked for the job in that hotel but it had turned out there wasn't a vacancy after all. She thought of going to look for work in Dublin itself but, she said, then she'd seen a postcard advertising a maid's job in one of the smaller Bray hotels and she'd gone for that. It wasn't as nice as the other place at all, but it would do. They had spoken to Mrs Doyle who had not given her a great reference but, apparently, hadn't damned her totally, and the hotel said they would take her on a fortnight's trial. So she started there at the end of the week.

Maureen was glad that Julia would be staying in Bray. They got on well and she was good company, usually anyway.

On Thursday evening Mr S came into the kitchen and said that Mrs S was better now and would be down for breakfast on Friday. Everything would be back to normal, he was pleased to say. A bit of bad luck though, he said, it never rains but it pours; Mrs S had slipped when she was in the bathroom the other day and had bashed herself on the face, and there was still a bit of bruising he said, but they hoped it'd all be out of the way by Sunday Mass. It'd better be, by the beginning of next week anyway, he said with a laugh, because there's one of those afternoon teas coming up with all the ladies, including Mrs Doyle and the rest. She'll want to look her best for that.

CHAPTER SEVEN

It was the actions of others that had changed things, she knew that. From that week where she had sat, almost secretly, with Mrs S, the week where Julia changed her job as well, from that week she'd felt more at home. Or more established, more part of things, more settled. And it was not because she herself had done anything in particular, except be there, maybe. Mrs S was not really any more demonstrative on a day to day basis, it wasn't really in her character, but, despite that, there was something between them now, a shared secret, almost a friendship. And Maureen liked that idea, she liked the idea that she was a friend of Mrs S's, it flattered her to be so.

And, oddly, Julia treated her differently as well, from that time. Julia was happy to be working in the hotel, it was more suited to her character; busy, changing, interesting, and with those little intrigues and dramas that always take place in pubs and hotels and the like. And Julia decided to treat Maureen, now, a bit like an older sister, laughing at her because she was sensible and because she liked working in that stuffy old house but, at the same time respecting her for exactly the same things, asking her advice and seeking her opinion. Except about dancing and boys, never about them.

So things settled down.

She worked every day, and had her time off, and met Julia, and some of the other girls as well, and went for walks. And she went dancing, once a week usually, sometimes twice. And as it led towards Christmas there was loads more to do, in the house and outside the house as well.

She enjoyed this time, because it was busy there was more to do, Mrs S had more of her teas and she was planning a drinks party in the week before Christmas. Maureen met one boy, Christie was his name, at the dance, who she liked well enough, and saw a couple of times, walking along the promenade and the like, but it didn't quite work, she didn't know why, except she was relieved that he seemed to think the same thing, so that now they said hello in a friendly way when passing, but that was about it.

Mama and Dada had got in touch to say that they were coming up to Dublin to stay just a night with Maureen's Auntie Helen and would it be possible to meet? Maureen arranged a long afternoon off with Mrs S on that day so she could at least meet them and have tea before they got the bus to Helen's.

She was excited. It was actually the first time she had gone into Dublin from when she'd arrived in Bray those few months ago. She sat on the train, and that felt like the first day as well, steaming out of Dungarvan station on the way to something new.

She was slightly early at the station so she just stood and watched the crowds going past, seeing at least three girls of a similar age to herself arriving in off trains with a suitcase, like she had, herself, not that long ago. Nervous, looking around, hoping to be met, hoping to be looked after.

Mama and Dada's train arrived more or less on time and Maureen waited at the end of the platform, watching for them. They were slower than most of the other passengers, not hurrying at all but, eventually, Maureen saw them clearly, on their own, walking towards her.

And she was shocked. She was shocked by two things. By what she saw, and what she felt.

She hadn't seen Mama and Dada for three months and what

she saw now were two old people walking towards her, older than she had expected, or had wanted, smaller than she had expected. Walking slowly and carefully as two older people might do. As they came nearer she saw that Mama looked like an old woman now, thinner, face lined, hair grey and straggled. And Dada too, a small, slightly overweight, bald man, who walked in an awkward sort of a way, smiling, and waving with his free hand as he saw her, and saying to Mama that he had seen her, indicating with his head as he leaned over to speak to her. They were dressed as they had been when she left, in their smart clothes. Not so smart here, however, on a Dublin city station.

And for a second, not much more, she felt ashamed of them, she felt ashamed to be meeting them, to be seen with them. With their shabby country clothes, and their obvious country ways, and their slowness, and their poorness as well, so obvious to anyone with half an eye. Yes, she felt that for a second, and then she felt her own shame for allowing any such thought to even enter her head.

They came through the barrier and she embraced her mother first and then her father. And she could feel their warmth for her as she did so, feel how glad they were to see her.

And they stood back to look at each other.

'You look great Maureen, they must be feeding you well anyway, wouldn't you say so Dada!'

He laughed, just enjoying being there, enjoying standing next to his daughter.

'You look grand too, the pair of you, with your smart city clothes on. Was the journey OK?'

'It was fine, just delayed for a few minutes here and there, but it was nothing. And we met James Murphy on the train as well, so we had a good old chat with him which passed the time.'

James Murphy was a cousin of sorts, a gossip and a chatterbox, so that would certainly have passed the time without any shadow of a doubt.

'I was thinking before you have to get the bus to Helen's we could go to Bewley's for tea, and we can have a grand chat as well. How would that suit you?'

They agreed. And then they discussed whether they would walk or get a bus. As they didn't see Dublin that often Mama said they'd be happy to walk, and so they did. Maureen carried their small bag and they went slowly along by the river, looking at this and that, talking about this and that. They told Maureen about all the gossip at home, which wasn't much at all, in fact. One of the Gaffney boys getting into trouble with the Garda, Father O'Brian getting angry at Sunday Mass because, he said, not everyone was contributing enough to the collections, Mama said he was turning into a very bitter old man after having been so mild as a young priest, Philly Duggan disappearing overnight, her mam saying she'd gone to stay with an aunt, there was thought there that she might be pregnant. The usual stuff, really, thought Maureen. It wouldn't surprise her about Philly though, she was always wild, not unlike Julia in a way.

And Mama said they'd had a letter recently from Theresa, which Maureen hadn't, telling them she had moved into a better place, somewhere in North London. Theresa said she was working but she didn't say exactly what she was doing. Mama said she was a bit worried because Theresa had been the type of person that would always tell you everything, and now she didn't say much at all, in her letters, anyway.

When Maureen had said to Mrs S that she was meeting her mother and father Mrs S had said it would be a great idea to take them to Bewley's. It was a little bit different she said, and a bit of a treat as well. She'd asked Maureen if she was alright for money, to pay for tea and everything, but of course Maureen had no problem with money at all, because she spent very little of her wages. She was saving up. She had no idea what she was saving up for, she had no specific aim, she was not saving for an expensive coat or anything like that. She was, in fact, saving for her future, she knew that, she was saving for her future, whatever that might be.

And so they arrived in Grafton St, the walk had been slightly longer than they had expected but it was no problem. As they approached Bewley's Maureen felt nervous. She had never been in there before and wasn't quite sure what you had to do. And she realised also that, all of a sudden, it seemed to be her looking after Mama and Dada, rather than the other way round. It would only have been a year or two before, even less than that maybe, when she would have expected to be following them and expecting them to organise everything. Now, in Dublin, it was her.

They went in and it was great. Noisy and crowded, but they got a table and the uniformed waitress took their order for some tea and some scones. She was friendly and helpful to them all, especially Mama who had a bit of trouble making up her mind. And once they'd ordered they could relax and look around a bit. All the different kinds of people, some of them obviously quite well off, some of them not so.

Maureen was relieved. She had done the right thing. This was a treat for Mama and Dada that they wouldn't forget, and when they got home they'd be able to say how Maureen had taken them to Bewley's in Grafton Street and treated to them to tea and cakes, which were all very nice, and they'd be able to say how well Maureen was doing in Bray, and how, now, she knew her way round Dublin almost like a native, so to speak.

They sat there for almost an hour, talking about nothing in particular, watching what was going on about them, Mama pointing out someone's dress or coat or shoes, watching people going, and people coming in, and people staying, and the noise and sometimes the laughter, and waitresses nipping in and out, efficient and fast. And they themselves, drinking tea and eating cake and scones, which Maureen and Mama admitted were almost as good as their own.

And then they had to leave.

They walked slowly back to the quay where Mama and Dada would get the bus to Helen's. It was only fifteen minutes, or twenty at the most, from the centre of Dublin to her house. They waited ten minutes and the bus arrived, on they got, not forgetting their bag which Maureen was still carrying, and not forgetting a hug before they went.

Maureen watched the bus go and then turned to get back to the station. Mrs S had told her not to worry about tea but she wanted to get back to Bray now anyway. The train was crowded with people finishing work and on their way home. In a way, it was a bit like Bewley's on the train, crowded and noisy, with a bit of laughter, a bit of joking here and there, and the smoke as well of course. Maureen didn't smoke and didn't really like the taste or smell of it, sometimes it reminded her of Mr S, which was not pleasant at all. But sometimes, also, it reminded her of her Da smoking his pipe which she did like, which she was comforted by, and for some reason the smoke on the train, that late winter afternoon, took her to that memory rather than any other.

She got off at Bray and walked out of the station, along with all the others rushing to get home, this time knowing exactly where she was going, knowing exactly which direction to take. And fifteen minutes or so later she arrived at the house, taking her coat off as she entered and going to the kitchen to help Mrs S finish making the tea.

And then it was Christmas.

Christmas was a very busy time for Maureen, doing loads of shopping and cooking, often with Mrs S, which was actually fun at times, but a bit stressful as well when the little parties were coming up. There were great laughs at a few dances, a bit of loneliness on Christmas Day, although the family were very nice to her and bought her small presents, gloves and the like. And there was a rush home to Dungarvan for a couple of days, between Christmas and New Year, when Mrs S gave her time off to see her family. Mama had not been well, just a cold, or a touch of flu, and Mrs S knew that Maureen was worried and would feel better for having gone to see her. And when she got home Mama was already better, so they had a great couple of days, and Maureen popped out, as well, to see Ann and Annie and Greta and told them about Bray, and Julia, and most of the other things she'd seen and done in the last few months.

Mr S celebrated a lot over the Christmas, over most of December in fact. Drank a lot. The worst time of the whole festivities was when Maureen and Mrs S had to carry him upstairs and put him to bed, because he had come home and just collapsed in the hall, unconscious. Maureen thought he should be just left there really, but at the same time it wouldn't do for the children to come downstairs in the morning and find their father spread-eagled on the hall tiles, fully clothed. They dragged him up the stairs and put him in the spare bedroom. He slept there now, although it was never admitted that this was the case. Maureen was surprised the children didn't hear all the noise, they probably did, of course, but chose not to come out and see what was going on. Carrying him up there might have been quite funny in different circumstances. If he'd been a man who got drunk once a year, if he'd been a nice man, a friendly man that they liked. But he wasn't. Maureen could see contempt on the face of Mrs S as they manoeuvred him up the stairs and dragged him into the bedroom, laying him on the bed in his clothes and leaving him there, Mrs S pausing just a second, after a minute hesitation, to remove his collar and tie so he didn't strangle himself, somehow, during the night.

CHAPTER EIGHT

It was during January that Maureen met Michael. After Christmas things were generally a bit quiet, it was cold anyway, although everyone was hoping that the winter would not be as dreadful as the year before, with its snow and its ice. Anyway, Maureen and Julia went to a Saturday dance, it was in the middle of the month. The seventeenth of January. Maureen remembered that.

He asked her to dance. In many ways he was no different to look at than any other boy that had ever asked her to dance. He wasn't like Gene Kelly or Cary Grant either, not film star handsome. But he smiled at her and asked her to dance and she felt comfortable with him, and she said yes when he offered to buy her a soft drink. She rarely did that, agreed to have a drink. And when she looked around she saw Julia looking at her, winking at her, and laughing, in a silly way. They went outside for a little while, not for long because of the cold, but he said he'd like a cigarette if she didn't mind, and she'd said no that was fine. And he told her a bit about himself, that he worked on the railway, that he came from Greystones just down the way, and he was surprised he hadn't noticed her before, because he came here to the dance in Bray pretty often. And she told him where she came from, and how they had the railway in common, because Dada, and two of her brothers, worked for them as well. And she felt comfortable with him.

They went back in and danced another dance and then Maureen said she had to get home. He looked disappointed but he asked her if he could walk her. She said it was fifteen or twenty minutes each way, and he said that was no problem. So they walked together. He didn't try any of the things that boys did, he didn't try and put his arm around her or try to kiss her or even really flirt with her. They walked along comfortable in each other's company. He described his family, his mother and father and his three brothers, and told her which one was sensible and which one was wild. The wild one, James, lived in London. Making loads of money so he said. The sensible one was a schoolteacher, here in Bray in fact. And the other, middle, one was the quiet boy who worked in a small factory somewhere. And Maureen told him about her family, but there was too many of them to describe in that short walk. And then they got to the house.

They stood for a few seconds. She was relieved again that he didn't try to kiss her, but after a little hesitation he asked her out the next day, just for a walk in the afternoon, said he could call for her, so at least she could finish telling him about the rest of her family, he said. She laughed and said yes. And then she said goodnight and went up to the house and let herself in. Without looking back. She dearly wanted to take a little peek before she closed the door. But she didn't.

CHAPTER NINE

He turned up exactly at the agreed time. Maureen would have expected nothing else, of course, she would have expected nothing else whoever the boy was. To turn up late was not the right thing to do, to turn up early was almost as bad because it put everyone in a bit of a spin, but to turn up late suggested you didn't care sufficiently or were arrogant in some way.

She had told Mrs S at breakfast time that she would be going out with a boy that afternoon, taking her Sunday afternoon off and going out with someone. Mrs S smiled at her and asked her if he was a nice boy, and Maureen said he seemed to be, but she would see.

Maureen got ready after Sunday dinner. Just tidy and smart, some make up but not too much, hair brushed and bounced a bit. She looked at herself in the mirror and thought she looked alright, alright for a Sunday afternoon walk anyway. She could see that the frock was starting to look a bit old and her shoes, as well, could do with being mended. But, anyway, all she was doing was going out for a walk with a boy. Part of her felt he'd just have to put up with it, like it or not, and part of her felt she would dearly like to have some nice clothes, some smart shoes, look a bit like a lady. And, while she herself was still looking in the mirror, she thought about Mrs S, Mrs S had the money didn't she? She wasn't rich but she had money to buy clothes and she didn't seem to bother did she?

Maureen twirled around and thought she looked fine. She went downstairs. Mrs S was round and about, and the children were there as well. Not standing in the hall or anything, but nearby. Interested.

Oddly enough Maria had become friendlier over the last week or two. After the Christmas break she had walked home with Maureen a couple of times after school, running into Maureen with her shopping, Maria carrying her schoolbooks. They hadn't talked about much at all, Maria had told her a bit about the school and the nuns, and a bit about the trouble she got into. It was pleasant to walk along with her, a change to before. Not friends but friendly if you like.

At three o'clock the doorbell rang, chiming with the hall clock which was striking three. She opened the door and there he was. He was smaller than she had expected. In her mind he was taller. A shortish broad man in his twenties, brown hair with a bit of a curl in it. A nervous smile, a pleasant face. Certainly not handsome, but pleasant to look at. In a way she was disappointed. She would have liked it if he had been handsome, and taller and smarter. He was wearing a brown suit and, obviously, a collar and a tie. Shoes shined as well. He looked fine. The disappointment was just an emotion on the way to reality. He was fine.

He stood there on the step. He'd said hello but he wasn't sure what to do next. She stood there looking at him as well, both paralysed for a second. She felt someone behind her.

'Will you introduce me, Maureen?'

She turned slightly, feeling awkward, almost embarrassed.

"Oh, yes, of course, Michael this is Mrs Shaughnessy, who I work for. I told you?'

Michael smiled, just about, and extended his hand.

'Pleased to meet you Mrs Shaughnessy.'

'Pleased to meet you Michael. Well, Maureen we'll see you later.'

And Maureen found herself through the door and outside, not pushed, she had gone of her own accord. She turned to see Mrs S just closing the door behind her.

They walked down the path and then turned towards the town. Luckily it was not a very cold afternoon, especially for that time of year, although Maureen wondered why Michael had not worn a coat as well. Perhaps he didn't have one? No, that couldn't be true. Perhaps he though he looked better just in his suit? She hoped he wouldn't be cold. She had put on her blue overcoat and a pair of gloves, and her beret, while she had been waiting for him. In fact Mrs S had said that it definitely would not be warm, especially if they went down to the Promenade, which of course they would.

'She's a strange looking one. That Mrs Shaughnessy I mean.'

"What do you mean strange?'

'She's a thin old thing, isn't she? And a bit horsey looking as well, wouldn't you say?'

Maureen was upset by this.

'She is not so! Mrs Shaughnessy is a very nice woman indeed.'

'I didn't say she wasn't nice. I just though she looked a bit odd, that's all.'

Maureen did not want to talk about Mrs S. Not in such a way certainly. She found that, inside, she was bitterly disappointed in him, in the whole situation. They had hardly reached the end of the road and already she was regretting agreeing to see Michael. At that second she would have happily gone back to the house. Gone back into the warmth of the house and forgotten she had ever met Michael. Had a rest and then gone down to start to make the tea.

There was silence as they walked along. She could feel that he knew he had done something wrong, or done something, said something, which had annoyed her.

'I'm sure she's fine. She was friendly enough anyway.'

He was trying to make amends.

And then he asked her about Dungarvan and her sisters and brothers and she relented and told him about home, told him a bit more than she had the evening before, and he told her a bit more about his family. And he told her more about his job and where he went on the railway. And he asked her what she wanted to do, did she want to stay here doing this type of work forever? And she said she had no idea, no idea at all. And he said he would probably go to England because there were more opportunities there.

They walked down to the Promenade and strolled along it like everyone does, like she had done with Theresa and with Julia as well. It was friendly enough, the tension had eased a bit. She already knew, in a way, that he was not a bad person, but she felt he had let her down. Poor man, he had just not lived up to expectations.

When he relaxed he was good enough company, though. Telling funny stories about his brothers and the people he worked with on the railway. Of course she'd heard these stories, or stories very like them, before, they were the usual stuff, but at least they could laugh together.

They went for a cup of tea as well. He bought them tea and cakes. And then she said she'd better be getting back. His face gave him away immediately. He had hoped for more, he hadn't wanted her to say she was going home. He had wanted them to enjoy so much being together that it would be a wrench for them to part. And, the truth be told, that was what she would have wanted as well, what she had, in a way, expected. But now she wanted to go home. She had spent almost two hours with him, and apart from the beginning, she had enjoyed his company, but she wanted to go home now. If he wanted she would consider seeing him again, but all this had not been what she wanted, not at all.

They walked slowly back, she wasn't going to deliberately rush him, not deliberately rub in the fact that it hadn't gone great. And she felt a bit sorry for him as well, he was nice man, she knew that, and he was almost blue with the cold as well; as the afternoon drew on the temperature had dropped, she was cold in her coat and gloves, and beret as well, God knows how he must have felt.

They stopped at the gate. And he said would they see each other next week maybe? And she said she wasn't sure, maybe she'd see him at the dance. And he understood.

They said goodbye and she walked off down the path towards the front door, hearing the clicks of the metal tips on his shoes as he also walked off, slowly, in the other direction.

When she got in she immediately felt the warmth of the house envelop her. She could hear the other people in the house, hear noise in the kitchen, and hear the children talking in the sitting room.

She went straight upstairs. They would have heard her come in.

She undressed down to her slip and lay on the bed for a minute or two. Just thinking. Wondering what it was she wanted. He had asked that question hadn't he? Was she going to be a housemaid for ever?

Well she wasn't. She knew that. But she wasn't sure what she wanted to be. Wasn't sure, at all, what she wanted to do.

In the end he had not been good enough. Poor man. Saying the wrong thing, wearing the wrong clothes. She had thought when she met him, at the dance, in the dark, that he had been more than he had turned out to be, she had actually been full of hope. It had taught her a bit of a lesson really.

She got dressed and went downstairs.

Mrs S was making soda bread. Once or twice a week she made it, plain usually but sometimes with mixed fruit in it. She looked across as Maureen entered the kitchen.

'You're back early. Earlier than I expected anyway. He seemed nice enough. Michael. Although he'd have froze out there without a coat, wouldn't he?'

'Yes, he was fine.'

'You don't seem too sure.'

'He was fine, but maybe not what I expected.'

'Will you see him again?'

'Probably not.'

'OK. Will you help with tea?'

'Sure.'

And the two of them prepared the Sunday tea.

CHAPTER TEN

On Tuesday of that week Maureen and Mrs S sat down together in the afternoon. There had been no time on Monday because Maureen had an enormous amount of washing and housework to do and Mrs S had to go to a meeting of some kind with her women friends in the afternoon.

They sat down at about three thirty. The children would not be home for an hour or so. It was a good time for a bit of peace and quiet before the evening rush started. Mrs S told Maureen about her meeting, a charity thing it turned out. Telling her Mrs Doyle had upset a few of them, with her bossy organising ways.

And she asked Maureen about her afternoon with Michael. Obviously Maureen didn't tell Mrs S what Michael had said about her, about her physical appearance. The truth was he hadn't said anything that was actually untrue, but it was unkind and unnecessary. No, Maureen just said that she hadn't found him to be as mature as she had expected. And this was true. She had expected something more from him than those silly comments about Mrs S. What a thing to say to someone when you don't even know them properly, when you would have no real idea about what they were thinking themselves. He had assumed she would agree with him, that she would laugh and agree with him. Reflecting on it she thought that she did know one person who would have laughed out loud at what he'd said, Julia. She would have loved those comments, and would have laughed out loud. But she wasn't Julia and, even though she liked her, she had no intention of being anything like her.

Mrs S said she was young and there would be plenty of time to find a boy that suited her, and that she must always be sure when she made her decision, sure that the man she was going to marry was the right one for her. And Maureen was embarrassed because Mrs S had obviously made the wrong decision. She had married a man who hit her, and, even if you ignored that, he wasn't a particularly likeable man either. Maureen shuddered inside thinking about having to live with a man like Mr Shaughnessy.

Nevertheless Mrs S had her children, who, Maureen, knew, she loved dearly. And they were the product of him and her. And, just for a second, she had an image of those two making the children and she thought how absurd it all was. It was like a grotesque nightmare thinking of that drunken man and that woman, skinny and plain as she was, in a way, having sex and producing those children. How many times had they done it? Just those two times? No, it would be more than that, and maybe that was what drove him to violence. Did she refuse him? Or make it plain that she didn't want to do it?

Maureen had drifted in her thoughts, Mrs S was talking about something else now. It was an early Easter this year, Ash Wednesday was the following week, not that far off the beginning of February, and, by the way, don't forget there's the general election tomorrow. Mr Shaughnessy had been going on about the election over the last few weeks because he liked to think he was closely involved with the local councillors and the political party bigwigs. Maureen couldn't vote so any interest she had in it was only because it was happening, little more than that. And Mrs S hadn't really mentioned it, although she'd had a tea the previous week and the women had been going on about it. It was an event after all.

Anyway, said Mrs S, I'm going into Dublin on Thursday, a bit of a treat before we have to think about Lent and the like, and you'll come with me. We won't tell anyone.

Maureen was pleased and excited and a bit nervous. She worried over the next day or so. It was all very well the two of them having their chats in the kitchen, almost every day now. That seemed easy to do, there was no-one else around and they could chat in a personal kind of way without having to be the mistress and the maid, if you like. But going into town was something else altogether. For a start they'd spend most of the day in each other's company, which was a lot longer than twenty minutes around the kitchen table. But, maybe, she thought, she was worrying over nothing.

On the Thursday morning they walked down to the station. A little after nine, when the children had gone to school and he was at his work. It was the oddest experience for Maureen because she realised she had never been out like this with Mrs S. In the first week or so Mrs S had taken her to the shops, so she knew which ones to go to, and which ones not to go to, but this was different.

Of course, in Bray, Mrs S knew loads of people so she was saying hello to this person and that person, avoiding stopping, if she could, by saying she had to catch a train. Which was true. Maureen noticed that she said that she had to catch a train not that they had to catch a train, not making it obvious she was taking Maureen with her. Whenever they had to stop briefly to talk to someone Maureen hung back slightly, taking the right kind of place. And then they got to the station and Mrs S bought the tickets and they waited for the train, and got on, and Mrs S sat down and patted the seat for Maureen to sit down next to her. Which she did.

There was something intimate about sitting next each other in the carriage. Of course it was still winter and they both had their coats on, both larger than they normally would be so they were sort of pressed together, and it was comfortable.

If it had been Mr S. sitting there, God forbid, Maureen knew she would have made every effort not to be touching him, but with Mrs S, they were comfortable together, warm together, on the rocking, half-crowded, train.

Mrs S pointed out a few things here and there, but they didn't really speak, didn't converse at any rate. And then they reached the city.

They spent a lot of time in the shops near Grafton Street which Maureen recognised from her trip to Bewley's with Mam and Dada. Mrs S seemed to be looking for a new dress and a coat of some kind. She tried things on and asked Maureen's opinion. Mrs S was definitely not Theresa, that was for sure. Theresa would have been having a go at all kinds of things and laughing, trying on things she could never afford, trying on flamboyant things which she could never use. But Mrs S was trying on things which were practical rather than glamorous. Maureen tried to encourage her to try something a bit brighter, one dress in particular which might have suited her, but she shook her head, almost shy, almost embarrassed, even at the thought.

It was an interesting time for Maureen because she saw another side to Mrs S. This woman whom she liked very much was, in some ways not confident in herself at all. When she spoke to the shop-girls she was treated with respect and she didn't show any weakness there, but there was a way about her that suggested she didn't have a certain kind of strength, even when she tried on the dresses there was an uncertainty when she looked at Maureen for an opinion, an uncertainty not a hope.

There was something about her not feeling fully herself as a woman, maybe he had removed some of that from her with his violence, and his arrogance too.

After a while Maureen found herself manoeuvring Mrs S towards making a purchase of a particular dress and coat because she felt that, if she didn't, they would go home empty-handed, which would have been a great disappointment. She could see that Mrs S would not get anything very noticeable but she could get something with a bit of style. There was a blue dress that looked good enough and flattered Mrs S's rather meagre figure so Maureen encouraged her to buy it. It was dear, lots more than Maureen would ever dream of spending, but it did look smart on her. After humming and hawing and checking with Maureen, and with one the girls from the shop as well, she decided to buy it. And she bought a smart coat as well, an easier purchase but still expensive.

'We'll go to Bewley's Maureen. And by the way call me Margaret, for God's sake, when we're out of the house at any rate. I'm sick of you saying Mrs Shaughnessy this, and Mrs Shaughnessy that, all the time.'

And so they did, and so she did.

Apart from saying her name for the very first time when it took just the slightest effort, just the slightest bit of nerve, it came very easy to call her Margaret, very easy indeed.

They had a great time at Bewley's laughing about Margaret's faffing around with the dresses, always choosing the most conservative colours and cuts, but she said she couldn't do anything else, that was just how she was, how she was made. But she thanked Maureen for at least making her buy something because there was a definite danger she'd go home with absolutely nothing, that had happened before, she said, more than once.

They finished in Bewley's and strolled around, looking in a few of the bigger shops and then they went to Hodges bookshop to get a little something for the children. Maureen had never seen a bookshop like it, in fact she had hardly ever been in a real bookshop before in her life so she was bemused and fascinated by everything in there. She had read a few books at school, and she glanced at the newspapers in the house, but she had never really read a book for enjoyment.

Margaret bought a science book for Stephen and a novel for Maria. Not that she'll ever read it, she said, with a laugh.

And then they had to get back.

Margaret had smoked after they had left the dress shop. Maureen was surprised in a way, although she'd had a suspicion she might have smoked because she smelt it on her sometimes, but of course he did as well, so it was always a possibility that the smell of the smoke had transferred itself from him to her in some way. But while they were out she smoked. And it looked like she enjoyed it, in fact it reminded her of both Theresa and Julia, puffing away. It was strange how she looked like a different person with a cigarette in her hand, or when taking a puff and blowing the smoke away, making a little, but definite, performance of it.

Once they got on the train the atmosphere between them changed, or they became quiet at any rate, not talking just travelling. It was as if they were each preparing themselves to go back into another kind of existence. For Maureen it was not an unpleasant existence she was returning to, just a different one, a more formal one where she had work to do, work to get on with. She wondered whether she would just say ma'am to Margaret in future, in the house. She would avoid the Shaughnessy word except when talking to him, of course, and she would keep Margaret to when they spoke alone, or for when maybe they might have another excursion together. And she wouldn't tell anyone else about it. Especially not Julia. Julia would be quite likely to start calling her Margaret whenever she came round, just because she couldn't resist anything that would rock the boat, she was totally incapable of resisting being a troublesome rapscallion. No, she definitely would not tell her.

From the station they walked quickly back to the house. Maureen carried one of the bags, the one with the dress in it, Margaret carried the heavier one with the coat. They didn't talk, although at the station Margaret had said she hadn't realised it was so late and that the children would be back soon. Maureen wondered whether they would run into Maria but she was nowhere to be seen.

At the house they went in quickly, taking their coats off as they walked into the hall. Stephen appeared and said he had got home early that day, for some reason or other, but Maria wasn't around.

Margaret put her coat up on the hook and then pulled out the bag with Stephen's book in it. She gave it to him. He looked at it, opened it, flicked thought it. He looked really pleased. And so Margaret was pleased as well, that he seemed to like the book so much, that she had bought him something that would give him pleasure

'Thanks Mam, that's great, just what I needed.'

Maureen waited till they had finished dealing with the book, and then she hung her coat up as well.

'I'll get on with the tea then, ma'am.'

'Right you are Maureen. I'll be there in a minute if you need any help. Oh, and thank you Maureen, you've been a great help today.'

'It was a pleasure ma'am, I really enjoyed it.'

CHAPTER ELEVEN

Lent was just around the corner now. Margaret discussed with Maureen what they would be giving up, a discussion in the kitchen, not over serious but focussed. Margaret said she would give up cigarettes, but no-one would know about that so she would also give up sweets and sugar in her tea and coffee, and Maureen said she would give up chocolate. She bought a bar most days and would miss it. And Margaret said to make sure there was flour and milk and sugar and lemon for the pancakes on the Tuesday.

Recently Maria had started to come into the kitchen when she got home from school, not every day but often. She would sit and watch Maureen start on the evening meal and talk to her about this and that, other girls at the school, what she had seen in the street, and sometimes she would ask Maureen about her life before she came to Bray. She seemed interested, and Maureen was happy to tell her about Mama and Dada and her brothers and sisters and what it was like in Dungarvan, what was the same as Bray and what might be different. Sometimes Maria would say little at all but, instead, would get on with her homework on the kitchen table. Her Mam was not altogether pleased with this because it got in Maureen's way and there was the danger of getting the books spoilt with something spilt or knocked over. At the same time, however, she was glad to see Maria doing her work.

Stephen did his homework in his room. He took his schoolwork seriously but he also came into the kitchen when he got home, for a cup of tea or a piece of bread and jam.

So it could be that there might be the four of them in the kitchen at four-thirty or five of an afternoon. Maureen enjoyed those moments and so did Margaret, she believed.

On Shrove Tuesday they were all there as Maureen was preparing the pancake mixture before getting on with the meal. They hadn't had pancakes before, while Maureen had been there anyway. Why would they? In the main it was the type of thing you would eat once a year, all the better for only happening on pancake day.

They were there relaxed and laughing, only Maureen working really, the others sitting at the kitchen table when they heard the front door open. Obviously this could only be Mr Shaughnessy. And the atmosphere changed in an instant. Maureen could see the two children and Margaret stiffen, see them become anxious. They were not scared exactly, that would have been too strong, but, it seemed to Maureen, that they did not want to be caught here in the kitchen enjoying themselves together. And, of course, there was nothing they could do. It was not a huge house. It would take him but a few seconds to walk from the front door to the kitchen, and it would be obvious that there was no-one in the sitting-room or the dining-room, and the light from the kitchen could be seen from the hall.

Maureen carried on with what she was going to do next, peeling some potatoes. The other three sat, and Margaret started to say something which would have been, 'Isn't it time that you two got upstairs with your homework and got out of Maureen's way, the poor girl has enough to do without you two cluttering up the place?' She would have said something like that, eventually she would have said it anyway, even if he had not turned up. She wanted to say it at that moment as if it was the most natural thing in the world.

But he appeared at the door before she could put the words together. The family turned to look at him and Maureen just carried on with the potatoes.

'What's going on here then?'

He had a smile on his face, he was being friendly. And he was wavering slightly from side to side, hardly noticeable, but there nevertheless.

It was Stephen who replied, as he stood up and gathered his books.

'We were just checking that Maureen had got the stuff for the pancakes Da.'

'Well I'm sure she has. Isn't that so Maureen?'

He was still friendly.

'Of course, sir, I wouldn't forget, sir.'

There was a bit of a silence. Stephen still standing, Maria kind of pushing her books together, Margaret sitting, looking at him almost over her shoulder.

'I'm not keen on you bothering Maureen here. She's plenty to do without you crowding out the place. Off you go you two, get your work finished before tea. Margaret, there's a thing I need to discuss with you.'

'Sure.'

The children went first, squeezing past their father, he touched them both, almost affectionately as they passed him. And Margaret rose and went out too, in the same manner. He was waiting for all three of them to leave the kitchen before he left too.

'I'll look forward to your pancakes Maureen, make enough now, won't ye? We've got a big old fast ahead of us after all.'

He smiled at her and left, fully closing the kitchen door as he did so. Separating her off from the rest of the house. She liked to keep the door open normally, often because it helped to keep the heat down in the kitchen, but more, really, because it made her feel part of what was going on, so she could hear the voices, the radio sometimes, hear whatever life there was.

But as he had closed the door she didn't dare open it, not for the moment anyway, that would have seemed impertinent.

She continued with her work. Listening all the time. The closed door made it difficult to be absolutely sure, but it seemed like there was very little noise in the house. Stephen and Maria had gone upstairs first, she had heard them going, almost scampering to get up to their rooms, relieved to be out of the kitchen or, more accurately, relieved to be away from their father's annoyance. That was it she thought. It was annoyance rather than anger, she thought he didn't like to see them all together, without him. Enjoying themselves. And maybe Margaret and he had gone upstairs as well.

She could do little other than continue with the tea. Listening still, at first, but then just concentrating on what she had to do.

After about fifteen minutes she had time to go and make sure the table was set. She knew it was ready, but it was a reasonable excuse for her to leave the kitchen and see what was going on, if anything. The ground floor of the house was empty. There was no-one in the sitting room or the dining-room. He had hung his coat up in the hall, she could see that.

She listened again. Stood in the hall for maybe half a minute, absolutely still, trying to direct her hearing upstairs. She heard nothing, or no voices anyway. Once or twice a creak of floorboards which could have been anything at all.

For a second, standing there, she felt almost lucky. Lucky that she wasn't one of those two children, and luckier still that she wasn't Margaret, subject to his whims and his anger, and worse. He had always been pleasant enough to Maureen, at most he had ignored her occasionally, but he wasn't really interested in her, she knew that.

She went in and looked at the table, everything was there as she knew it would be.

They all came down at six. She heard the children first so she went out of the kitchen as if to see if they were all ready. Both children half-smiled but said nothing, nothing to Maureen, nothing to each other, as they took their places at the table.

And then she heard the two grown-ups. No voices, just steps. They reached the bottom of the stairs and entered the dining room. He was looking pleased with himself, slightly jollier than before, she looked sad. Margaret gave Maureen a quick look, almost a smile maybe, as she sat down and Maureen saw that she might have been crying as well.

'Whenever you're ready Maureen.'

She brought the food in and left them to it as they said grace and got on with their meal. She could hear him talking, heard his lower voice, and the short responses from Stephen and Maria. She sorted out the pancakes and got ready with the lemons and the sugar. Made the pan ready on a lower heat, and warmed the plates.

After about ten minutes she went back. They had finished. As usual it had not taken them long. They handed over their plates and Maureen said she would do the pancakes now so it would just be a few minutes.

'That's fine Maureen, that's fine.'

It was only him doing any talking it seemed.

She went back and started on the pancakes. Slightly nervous because she wanted to get it right. She regretted the others weren't there to see it all being done, to have a go at it themselves. At home with Ma and Da they would have had a great laugh tossing the pancakes, at least one of them falling on the floor and having to be thrown away. For her, pancake day wasn't just eating the pancakes it was seeing them being made, enjoying the whole thing. Enjoying it all before the rather gloomy days of abstinence started on the following day.

She made a batch of ten and took them in.

'I'll make a few more now.'

She went straight back and did another eight. Keeping a couple for herself she took the rest in.

They were all quiet, the children eating, squeezing lemon juice, sprinkling sugar. Him as well. It looked like Margaret had maybe eaten one, and not all of that. She was saying nothing but she smiled at Maureen in a sad, destroyed kind of way. And Maureen thought how happy they had been less than an hour ago.

'They were great Maureen, well done, but that'll do us. Get yourself sorted out now.'

Him again.

She went back to the kitchen and tidied up. She had put a plate aside, for herself, of meat and potatoes so she sat down and picked at that, not particularly hungry, and then she ate her two pancakes. Nice enough, having been kept warm on the oven. But it wasn't the same.

She heard movement. They had finished. Sitting at the kitchen table she heard him in the hall saying something, to Margaret presumably, and then she heard the front door open and close. He had gone out, for the rest of the evening probably.

Margaret brought the pancake plates into the kitchen and Maureen went to clear the table. They said nothing to each other. The children went straight upstairs without another word.

Once Maureen had cleared everything she organised the washing up. Margaret sat at the kitchen table still not speaking, not helping Maureen either, she usually helped in some way or other but today she sat at the kitchen table saying nothing.

Maureen was happy doing the washing up, there was a little bit of satisfaction in cleaning the plates, removing the stains, making them gleam white again. She just got on with it, knowing that Margaret was sitting there behind her. There was no need to say anything really.

When she had finished, and put everything away, she filled the kettle to make some tea.

Margaret saw what she was doing but said she would go up now and would see her tomorrow. She got up and left the kitchen and Maureen heard her steps slowly going up the stairs, across the landing, and into her room. The door shutting quietly behind her.

CHAPTER TWELVE

The next day was Ash Wednesday. When Margaret came down she said little. But that was sometimes the way, probably two days a week they would just get on with things, making sure the breakfast was ready for him and for the children, Margaret concentrating on the youngsters really, making sure they were up, making sure they ate something, making sure they had their books ready. Maureen concentrated on the food although that would be slightly different in Lent. But it was still important to make sure that the children had some breakfast before they went out.

Some days the two of them talked about this and that and even had a laugh occasionally but today nothing much was said. Maureen didn't want to talk about the last evening and wouldn't really have known what to say anyway. It was none of her business what Shaughnessy had said to his wife when they left the kitchen, none of her business what had happened upstairs. And Margaret wouldn't have said anything, she never actually said anything about him at all, there was no need. Maureen had seen what he could do and had watched him with his bullying ways, which were sometimes little more than what had happened yesterday, an insistence that everyone did what he wanted. Said in his friendly fashion, with his smile and his expectation that there would be no objection from anyone.

Margaret said she would be going to mass later on in the morning for the ashes and they could go together. Maureen had been expecting to go to mass. There would not have been a time in her life, a time that she could remember anyway, when she would not have got that little cross of ashes on her forehead.

Julia was very dismissive about religion and the priests and the mass. A couple of times Maureen had been sitting at Mass with Julia, one time, at least, she remembered when Margaret's family were staying and it would have been a bit of a push to have them all in the pew. And Julia did a kind of scurrilous running commentary to the Mass, maybe not so much about the religion itself, about the communion, but more about the people, about the priest and the pomposity of it all. Who had the loudest voice in the prayers, who was standing first and kneeling first and genuflecting lowest so that everyone could see how saintly they all were. And when the priest was in the pulpit with his readings and his sermon she had something to say about him as well.

Maureen's Da was not a great fan of the religion either. He didn't say much about it but he would have as little involvement as possible, and would virtually ignore the priest if he called at the house. Mama, of course, couldn't get enough of it all, which amused Dada sometimes and annoyed him at others.

Although Maureen didn't think about it a great deal, it would be true to say that she regarded it all as something that had to be done, little more than that. And the truth of the matter was that if she said she wasn't going to attend Mass or made a fuss about religion she would have found it very hard to get a job like the one she had. There wouldn't be a respectable household that would put up with that from the housemaid, it would have been unheard of.

Shaughnessy went to Mass as well, of course, good Christian that he was. It was one of the places that people like him made his contacts, it was necessary to be seen there, to chat with your cronies, maybe to nod a greeting to people who might be useful to you, people who you would like to know. And he knew the parish priest as well, Father O'Sullivan. He came around to the house now and then, said hello to Margaret and the children and spent time with Shaughnessy shut in the sitting room. Laughing, and drinking as well. Maureen knew they were drinking because she had to tidy up afterwards. He nodded at her, O'Sullivan did, when she opened the door to him and she took his coat, but he didn't actually talk to her. The curate, Father Pledger, was young though, and the couple of times that she had spoken to him outside the church he had seemed pleasant enough.

It was probably no different in Dungarvan, though, to what it was here in Bray, probably the same everywhere when you thought about it. Julia had told Maureen some terrible stories about her priest back in Kerry but, of course, you never knew if she was just making it all up, or exaggerating at the very least.

They were to go to the 10.30 Mass so Maureen made sure that she'd sorted most of her morning work out by then, finishing the breakfast stuff and doing the bedrooms as quickly as she could. In Margaret's bedroom she noticed that there were more of his things there than had been for a while. So he was probably sleeping back there. It made her shiver with a feeling of disgust, she couldn't help it. The idea of getting into bed with that man every night was not something she wanted to think about.

She put on clothes for Mass and met Margaret downstairs.

They said little as they walked to the church, and when they got there they went straight to the pew and waited for Mass to start and queued up during the service for the ashes to be placed on their foreheads. Maureen could feel it there as she walked back to the seat. They went to communion as well.

After the Mass Margaret had a brief word with some of her friends and acquaintances but Maureen could see that she wanted to get away, and it was only a minute or two before she rejoined Maureen and they started on their way back.

'Will we go down to the town, Maureen? Take a quick turn along the Promenade?'

Maureen was surprised. She hadn't expected that. It was a bit like going to Dublin the week before. The two of them together, and work not really being a part of it. Of course she had things she had to get on with at home but that could wait. And she couldn't say no, anyway, could she?

They walked along, comfortable, Maureen thought, with each other, no need to talk unless there was something to say. It was a chilly day, but not unpleasant, and they both had their coats on and their hats. And they both still had the ashes on their foreheads, she could see Margaret's and feel her own.

They didn't stop until they reached the sea, a bit blowy there; they walked and then Margaret sat down on one of the benches along the Prom. Maureen followed suit. They said nothing for a minute or two. Just looked out across the Irish Sea.

'What do you think about it all, Maureen?'

'About it all?'

'You're young Maureen, seventeen. Eighteen soon I expect. What do you think about things?'

'I'll be eighteen in April....Margaret, I'm not quite sure what you mean.'

For the first time she felt awkward calling Margaret by her first name. She wasn't sure why. Up to that point, except maybe that very first time, it had felt natural enough. Perfectly normal. But now it felt odd.

'I mean, here we are in Lent now, atoning for our sins and all that, fasting, do you think it makes any difference?'

Maureen thought about it for a second or two.

'To be honest, I have no idea if it makes a difference. It's just something we do. Although I know not everyone believes in it. My Da for a start. He doesn't like the priests, doesn't like our Parish Priest anyway.'

'So, does he go to Mass?'

'He goes most times although if he has any excuse, not feeling well, or if he's been working overnight, he'll use that to avoid Mass and the like. He thinks the priests are parasites, that's what he says, although Mama tells him he shouldn't speak like that.'

'Maybe he has a point.'

Silence between them.

'What do you think of my husband, Maureen?'

'I'm not sure what you mean.'

'Do you like him?'

'Well he can be a bit fierce can't he? He likes his own way. Like most men I suppose.'

She tried to say this as a kind of a joke, but it wasn't funny. And beneath all this was her knowledge of what Shaughnessy had done to his wife, she knew he had beaten here at least the once. They both knew that, it was never anything that was discussed, or mentioned by them, but they both knew.

'Well, yes, he certainly can be a bit fierce, you're right there.'

They sat in silence and then Margaret suggested they walk to the end before getting on home, before getting back to get on with the rest of the day.

They stood and started to walk.

'Link with me, Maureen, would you?'

So she did and they walked together against the sea breeze towards Bray Head, Maureen's arm through Margaret's. Not talking. Maureen glanced over once and thought she saw that Margaret was crying, but it may have only been the wind. It was probably only the wind.

CHAPTER THIRTEEN

To Maureen's surprise, and shock, Margaret disappeared from the house the next day.

Shaughnessy had said at breakfast time that Mrs Shaughnessy had not been feeling too great and was not to be disturbed; he said Doctor Glancey would come during the morning. Shaughnessy didn't go to work. Maureen went into town to do some shopping and, when she returned, Shaughnessy told her that Margaret had gone to stay with relations because she needed a bit of a rest. Doctor's orders, he said.

He said that he would be relying on her, Maureen, for a little while although maybe his sister might be able to come and help if Mrs Shaughnessy's illness continued for any length of time.

'Will ye be OK with that Maureen? Looking after things for a little while? While we sort things out I mean. Mrs Shaughnessy says you're a good girl and more than capable, and the children think you're great.'

He was being his friendly, charming self. Which Maureen did not like. But she knew, as well, that she wanted to look after the children, wanted to look after the house if Margaret was away, because she knew that Margaret was relying on her. She was one hundred percent sure about that.

'Of course, sir, everything'll be fine with me. Will the children be visiting their Ma at all, they'll be awful worried?'

'Probably not, it's a little distance away, and they've got their schooling to get on with. Maybe when Mrs Shaughnessy's improved a bit we'll manage something. Don't you worry about that for the moment. Just try and keep things ticking over OK?'

He didn't want to discuss Mrs Shaughnessy at all really, he just wanted to make sure that Maureen would manage things for the moment at least.

'Will you tell the children yourself, sir? Or...."

'Yes, don't you worry, I'll see them today, when they get home. It'll be a shock alright but, if they know you're here to look after them, they'll feel better about that, at any rate. Now, as I say, don't you worry, just get on with things as normal, do ye hear?'

He was almost sharp at the end. Telling her to get on with it. Smiling still though. He gave her a little wink and left her to it in the kitchen. A few seconds later she heard the front door shut as he went out.

He was back by three. He briefly said hello to Maureen, putting his head around the kitchen door, and then disappeared into the sitting room. Shutting the door. He had a desk in the alcove in there and used the place as kind of office or study now and then. She peeked out into the hall after he'd shut the door, for no real reason, and she could smell the tobacco and the drink. But he had been courteous enough when he'd said hello.

Stephen was home first, as he usually was, Maria being more inclined to dawdle and gossip. He came straight into the kitchen and Maureen felt awkward, embarrassed, not entirely sure what to say. Shaughnessy had to have heard the boy come in, Stephen was never noisy but the house was virtually silent, so anyone coming through the front door would have been noticed.

She said hello, smiled at Stephen. She was sitting at the kitchen table at that moment, just finishing a quick cup of tea.

She thought she should say something to him; it would be ridiculous to chat away as if nothing had happened, but she didn't want to break the news about Margaret. Shaughnessy had said he would do it, and he might be angry if she said anything first and, anyway, it was his job to do that, as the father.

And then she heard the sitting room door open. She heard his steps and, once more, he put his head around the kitchen door.

'Stephen, I need a word.'

Shaughnessy disappeared immediately going back to the sitting room, expecting the boy to follow him.

Stephen looked at Maureen, unsure of what this was all about, worried maybe that he was in trouble for some reason unknown to him. Stephen rarely, if ever, did anything that would merit being in trouble, but he knew his father could be unpredictable at times. Maureen smiled and nodded him to follow his father. He put his bag down and went out into the hall. She heard the sitting room door open, and then click shut.

And two minutes later Maria arrived. Noisier of course. Straight into the kitchen.

'Maureen, is there anything to eat? I'm starving, the dinner was today uneatable, like stuff even the cows would refuse. Just because it's Lent.'

'I'll get you something. But go and see your Da in the sitting room first, he needs to speak to Stephen and you. Stephen's in there already.'

'Jesus! Am I in trouble again? Have the sisters been on to him?'

'No. Nothing like that. Just go and see him.'

She went.

They were not in there very long. Five minutes at the outside. The three of them came back into the kitchen.

'Maureen, I've told Stephen and Maria the situation. That their Ma'll be away for a short while, and for the time being at least you'll carry on as usual. We'll see how things go. I'm away out now, things to catch up on at work. Make sure you get your homework done, both of you. I'll check up on it later.'

And he left.

The two children sat down at the kitchen table. They both looked blank, not upset, just blank. Yesterday Margaret had been quiet, it was true, but she could often be like that. In fact, sometimes it was a source of amusement to the children how quiet and taciturn their mother could appear to be, without actually being so. Both of them could laugh her out of it, Maria in particular taking the mick out of her, for her apparent solemnity, and making her mother first smile and then laugh. So yesterday she had been no different to how she could be at any time.

Shaughnessy had insisted the children didn't disturb their mother that morning, so the last time they had seen her was the last evening. After he had kicked up a fuss about them all being in the kitchen, after they had pancakes together, almost silently, at the evening dinner table.

'Did you see Ma this morning, Maureen?'

'No I didn't. And the Doctor came while I was out at the shops. She went away soon after that, before I got back I mean.'

Stephen looked unhappy.

'So how did she go? Da said she's gone to Limerick to relations. She couldn't have gone on her own could she, if she was ill I mean?'

'I've no idea, but no, I wouldn't say so. Your Da just said she'd gone, she needed a rest. I'm sure she'll be back soon. It'll be good for her to have a little break maybe. Don't worry too much about her, she'll be in touch.'

'I didn't know we had relations in Limerick, did you Stephen?'

'No, not really, one of Da's cousins lives that way, I think he said that once.'

Maureen looked at the two children. They were close to their mother, both of them a lot closer to her than to the father. In their school uniforms they looked young, but as Maureen often had to remind herself Stephen was no more than a couple of years younger than her, less than that, and Maria not far behind him either.

Maureen didn't believe any of it. Margaret wasn't ill, not physically ill, although she'd obviously been worn down by him and had been ill-treated by him. When they walked along the Promenade yesterday Maureen had seen Margaret's tears, she'd pretended it was the wind, but it wasn't, they were real tears. And Margaret had given Maureen an opportunity to support her. When she'd asked the question about her husband. 'What do you think of my husband, Maureen?' Maureen had avoided the question, hadn't she? She could have said the he was a brute, she could have said that he was despicable. But, of course, she didn't. How could she have said something like that?

But Margaret'd be back. Maureen was pretty sure about that. She had an idea that people went into those places, big houses in the country usually, run by religious, and stayed a while and then came home, she'd heard about such things. People having a rest because they were exhausted, or sometimes because of the drink, but that wasn't the case with Margaret. A week, a month maybe. She'd be home before Easter. That's what you had to believe.

'We'll have dinner at six, as normal, you two. Go and get your homework down and we'll have dinner at six. Your Mam would want things to be the same. OK? Get on with you then!'

It was like she had to pretend to be their mother, like acting the part, she thought.

The children sat for a second and then picked up their bags and left the kitchen. She heard them both go upstairs and go into their rooms. She wondered for a second if they would stay together, talk together about what had happened. Comfort each other. But they didn't. Perhaps later.

At six they came down. They went to the dining room and then came into the kitchen.

'We'll eat in here. It'll be easier. I'll serve your father's meal in the dining room when he gets home.'

And so the three of them sat down at the kitchen table to eat the soup and bread that Maureen had made for them.

The kitchen was warm and although the meal was a simple Lenten thing there was a comfortable feeling between the three of them, or at least as comfortable as it could be with Margaret not being there.

CHAPTER FOURTEEN

As the days went past Maureen realised a surprising thing. That, almost no matter what happens, people get on with their lives.

The children now had their breakfast and their supper with Maureen in the kitchen, a bit rushed in the morning but more relaxed in the evening. Stephen and Maria appeared to enjoy this, and Shaughnessy seemed to accept it. He was often not at home till late evening, but once or twice he had appeared at supper time. The first time he was surprised to see the three of them sitting in the kitchen, but after a second's thought he'd just left it, left them to it. He rarely ate at home anyway, Maureen had no idea where he got to, and wasn't particularly interested. When he was eating at home, he told Maureen beforehand, and then she served him something in the dining-room, usually later than the children ate.

Although Maureen still had much the same work to do, and the responsibility to organise it herself, she now had the advantage that she could, more or less, do things when it suited her. She didn't have to wait to see what Margaret wanted doing, and Shaughnessy himself showed no interest at all in what was going on in the house.

There were two people who did show an interest, however. One was Julia and the other was Mrs Doyle.

From the second day of Margaret's absence Mrs Doyle made a point of calling in. Either first thing in the morning, around nine let's say, or towards the end of the afternoon. And Maureen was surprised to realise that she looked forward, usually, to these visits. Mrs Doyle made no secret of the fact that she despised Shaughnessy, although she didn't actually use the word 'despise' of course. And she was the one that put a name to what had happened to Margaret.

'She'll have had a nervous collapse, a breakdown you might say, Maureen. And no wonder with what she's had to put up with.'

Maureen was careful not to actually say anything detrimental about Shaughnessy herself but Mrs Doyle was less discreet.

'I'd say you have to be careful with him Maureen, especially if he's been out with his friends.'

But she was helpful and she inquired after the children, and she made sure that he knew she was calling round.

'Tell him I'm coming around every day would you Maureen? And I'll get Mr Doyle to let him know as well. So there'll be no doubt in his mind, no doubt at all.'

It was Mrs Doyle who told Maureen where Margaret was. Mrs Doyle had an unerring way of finding out things. She said Margaret was in a kind of nursing home run by nuns, as Maureen had thought in fact, and it was only about twenty miles away. Mrs Doyle said she should keep it to herself for the moment at least, she was sure Margaret would be in touch soon enough.

'It'll be a relief for her to be away from him at any rate, even though she'll miss the children terribly. But she'll know you'll do a good job looking after them, Maureen, she'll know that at any rate.'

Julia, in a strange way, was not a lot different from Mrs Doyle.

'You don't want to trust that feckin' Shaughnessy, Maureen. It's his fault she's cracked up, the way he treated her. It's no secret in the town by the way, no secret at all.'

Maureen didn't like being in the house with him, without Margaret there she felt vulnerable. There was a lock on her bedroom door, with no key. But in a drawer in the scullery there was a red Oxo tin with all kinds of bits and pieces in it, including an old brown envelope with keys inside. She took the envelope upstairs and tried the keys. One worked, although it creaked. There was a little oil can under the kitchen sink as well, she oiled the lock so it worked almost silently. And every night she locked her door.

The Saturday after Margaret had disappeared Shaughnessy came home very late. After she had gone to bed. It was a clear night, cold outside, and she could see those stars through her bedroom window. She heard him come up the stairs and stop outside his bedroom downstairs, and then his door opening and closing. She lay awake for a while. Listening to the house. Not that long after she heard again the creak of a door downstairs, followed by almost silent steps coming up the last flight to the landing outside her little room. She heard light, uncertain, movement, she could almost hear breathing. And then there was silence. For what seemed like years. And then she heard quiet, careful, steps go downstairs again, followed by the muffled closing of a bedroom door, below.

CHAPTER FIFTEEN

Lent, in its own way, made things easy. There was not a great deal going on outside for the children, or for Maureen either, the meals were simple enough, shopping was straightforward. Maureen just did what had to be done.

In the second week after Ash Wednesday, on the Tuesday, Mrs Doyle turned up in the late afternoon. She didn't usually stay that long, having a quick look round and a quick word with Maureen. Maureen felt there was an element of checking up on herself by Mrs Doyle, she trusted Maureen certainly, but she liked to just make sure that everything was going right.

On her way out she stopped for a second in the hall.

'Are you busy tomorrow, Maureen?'

'No more than usual, Mrs Doyle.'

'Would you be able to take a few hours out?'

'I could, I suppose, that wouldn't be a problem.'

'Right then, be outside, at the gate, at nine-thirty sharp. There's no need for Shaughnessy to know.'

'Yes, Mrs Doyle. OK.'

'Nine-thirty then. On the dot.'

And she left, leaving Maureen a bit mystified. Mrs Doyle was not a woman whom you questioned or turned down. Never unpleasant, not to Maureen anyway, but strong-willed. Maybe she had another girl starting who needed help, or she wanted some work done in the house.

Maureen got everyone sorted the next morning. Just her luck that Shaughnessy took longer than normal to get off to work, but in the end he was gone by half-eight. That would have been a relief anyway, but was a particular relief today. Even though she'd said she wasn't particularly busy on that day she still wanted to get the bedrooms done, and the breakfast things sorted before she went out. She didn't want to come back to a mess. She had thought for a second, with him delaying, that he might say he was coming home at lunchtime. But he didn't. And if he did, she could say, afterwards, if she wasn't back, that she had just gone shopping, not expecting him to turn up.

After the beds and the washing-up she had a quick wash and put on clothes to go out in. Nothing special. And she was ready, coat and hat on, by nine twenty-five. She waited two minutes, standing there in the hall, and then she went out to the street, standing by the garden gate.

And a car pulled up. A small car, with Mrs Doyle driving.

'Get in Maureen.'

And so she did. And away they went.

Maureen had been in a car before, obviously. Mr Graham, back in Dungarvan, had given her a lift home a couple of times, and her Uncle Jimmy, in Cork, had a car which she'd been in. And her teachers, a married couple, had a car that they shared although, thinking back, Maureen couldn't remember Mrs O'Gorman actually driving it.

The truth was that she was amazed to see Mrs Doyle in the driving seat, she'd never seen her in a car before, not driving. For a start she always walked round to the Shaughnessy's. She'd seen her as a passenger of course, Mr Doyle sometimes drove them both to Mass, in a bigger car than this though.

It was a real novelty to be sitting in the front seat next to Mrs Doyle, it was fun.

'I didn't know you could drive a car, Mrs Doyle?'

'Well I can. This is my little car. Which is especially nice to have in the summer months for a trip out, or a picnic, or to visit my daughters.'

'Can I ask where we're going?'

'You'll see soon enough.'

It was just a few minutes that they were out in the country. A beautiful day, still cold though. Maureen was glad she had put on her beret and gloves, and her scarf at the last minute.

'Tell me about yourself Maureen. Where are you from, now.'

And so Maureen told her about Dungarvan and the family, and where she'd worked with the Graham's and in the railway dormitory, and why she'd come to Bray. Mrs Doyle said she had grown up in Cahir herself which was not a great distance from Dungarvan, and she'd come to Dublin where she'd worked in one of the big shops before she met Mr Doyle. On a trip out to Bray, one summer Sunday, she said.

And then she asked her about Shaughnessy. Were things alright there? Maureen didn't want to tell Mrs Doyle about him on the stairs, on the landing. It had happened twice, that first time and then on the Wednesday, a week ago in fact. But nothing had really happened, had it? And the door was locked anyway.

'Everything's fine Mrs Doyle. Really. To be honest I don't see a great deal of him. I get the breakfast which he eats and then he tells me if he's coming home to dinner and I prepare something. The children eat with me in the kitchen, and they seem happy with that.'

'He's got a bad reputation. I shouldn't say this but he has. He used to be a nice man, respected, but now he's got a problem with the drink. Makes him a bit of a bully as well, not well liked at his work. And, of course, he treats Margaret badly, he's hit her hasn't he? Recently I mean?'

'Well, I'm not sure I should say.'

'You're a loyal thing, Maureen, but it's no secret, no secret at all. Anyway, it's great out here isn't it? The Wicklow mountains are beautiful aren't they?'

It was definitely beautiful and there was something exciting about driving along the winding roads, being in a car, going quite fast it seemed to Maureen. She turned to look at Mrs Doyle. Wrapped up she looked as if she took up even more space than usual. And, as always, she looked confident and in charge. And looked, as well, as if she was enjoying her drive, bibbing some sheep out of the way with the car horn, laughing as she did so, and waving to the odd person that they saw on their way.

'Have you known Margaret, sorry Mrs Shaughnessy I mean, long?'

'Since they moved in, since they married, before the children of course. Nineteen hundred and thirty, I'd say it would be. Mr Doyle knew Shaughnessy himself before that, they're both from Bray, Shaughnessy worked for my husband for a while. A good worker then, by the way.'

'I was born in nineteen thirty. They've been there all that time!'

'God, you're only a slip of a thing Maureen! And are you eighteen yet?'

'April the fourth'

'That's better than April the first anyways. Yes, Margaret wasn't much older than you are now when she moved in, when she married him. Maybe just a year or so, nineteen maybe? God, she looked awful young. They met through their families, they're not exactly related I'd say, but their families are close, and it was kind of arranged.'

Maureen hadn't really thought of Margaret as a young woman before. But, of course, she had been once, and then she'd had Stephen when she was twenty or so. Maureen couldn't think what she would have looked like then. And she'd moved into that big house as well, when she was just a girl really. And Maureen couldn't really imagine, either, what it would be like to have a child at her age. But that wasn't unusual at all, two of her sisters had children young, one at seventeen and one at eighteen. It was just that she, herself, couldn't imagine what it would be like, couldn't imagine it happening to her, at this age.

'Was she happy? Then I mean.'

Even as she said it she knew what a stupid question that was.

They'd reached some crossroads and Mrs Doyle was concentrating on checking where she was going, looking at the signpost and turning the car right, onto a slightly bigger road; they'd come down from the hills now.

'I can't say I knew her well then, but yes, she seemed, happy enough. She had her house and her child. And he was attentive enough I suppose. He was a kinder man then and he can put on the charm when he wants, which can fool you for a while, nowadays anyway. As I'm sure you're aware, Maureen. And then, not long after, there was the second child. That wild thing, Maria! God, I bet she was a shock after Stephen. Stephen was quiet and as good as gold, just like he is now. But Maria was something different altogether.'

They drove on for a couple of minutes.

'We're going to see Margaret, Maureen.'

Maureen had thought this was probably the case, but there had been no way of knowing for certain.

'Have you spoken to her then?'

'No I haven't, but I know the Mother Superior, and two of the sisters as well. Let's just say I've made sure I've kept in touch. It's easy enough to get information out of Doctor Glancey, and he won't tell the husband that I've shown an interest. He knows which side his bread's buttered. By the way, it's important you don't tell anyone about our little trip, Maureen, do you understand that? The sisters won't say anything to him either, about us I mean, so we can keep it just between ourselves.'

'I understand Mrs Doyle.'

'Good girl, I knew you would.'

Maureen had heard stories about some of the places that the nuns ran. Where girls with babies got sent. Maybe even Philly, from back home, had ended up in one. She hoped not. She wasn't sure about this kind of place though, the place they were going to. Maybe they were less severe with people just having problems, who probably paid them as well. To be honest Maureen hadn't really liked many of the nuns she had met, they had a way with them that was not friendly, and even Mama was not awfully keen on the sisters who sometimes turned up at the house. Maureen was a bit nervous about meeting the nuns today as well, although Mrs Doyle seemed pretty relaxed about it.

They were going through a small village, hardly even a village, and Mrs Doyle was not driving fast now, she was checking where she was going. Keeping an eye out for something.

'There'll be a turning here on the left somewhere, keep a look-out now Maureen, so we don't miss it.'

They kept going for another quarter of a mile or so.

'Here it is, here it is!'

Mrs D steered the car into the driveway and motored up towards the house at the end. It wasn't a house, it was a convent. It looked more enclosed, more forbidding than a house. Fewer windows and more walls. As if everything was kept inside, secured inside.

She stopped the car and they sat for a short while not moving. The engine ticking in the silence as it cooled down.

'It'll only be a short meeting Maureen, we'll have to start back fairly soon. And remember you're not to say anything, not to the children either. You promise me?'

'I promise, Mrs Doyle.'

'Let's go then.'

Maureen followed Mrs Doyle towards the main entrance. She discovered that she was worried now. She was worried about Margaret, worried what state she might be in. Would she be in some kind of cell, like a jail or something, locked in? Had she gone totally mad? Would she be restrained, tied up, in some way? Surely Mrs D would have told her already if it was as bad as that.

Mrs Doyle rang the bell and within a few seconds a little panel in the door opened to check who was there and, just seconds after that, the door opened.

It was a nun who opened the door. She seemed to be expecting them, a brief smile and waving them in. And she indicated that they should wait there in the hall. Not a word was said. Maureen looked at Mrs Doyle, who seemed comfortable enough, noticing Maureen she smiled and then looked away again.

After a couple of minutes another two nuns appeared. One seeming more important than the other.

'Mary.'

'Julia'

The two women embraced for a second. They obviously knew each other well.

She's not at all like my Julia, thought Maureen.

'Say hello to the Reverend Mother, Maureen.'

'Reverend Mother.'

'Maureen. It's nice to meet you, young lady. Margaret Shaughnessy is looking forward to seeing you, I know. Mary, Mrs Doyle that is, says you're a sensible, intelligent young woman, and I hope you are. You can spend a bit of time on your own with Mrs Shaughnessy, talk to her, don't upset her, bring her good news from home if you can. And, as I'm sure Mary has told you, this visit is in the nature being confidential, it's not necessary for everyone, or indeed anyone, to know it took place. Do you understand?'

'I do Reverend Mother.'

The nun had a way about her, she was serious, scary almost, but seemed to be kind as well.

'Good, good. Sister Patricia here will take you to see Margaret. Let's say about twenty minutes shall we?'

And the other nun indicated that Maureen should follow her leaving Mrs Doyle with the Reverend Mother.

They went through a door and down a short corridor, rooms along one side. Sister Patricia stopped by one of these doors and opened it. Maureen had been half expecting that she would unlock it with a huge key attached to her habit but she just turned the handle, opened it and ushered Maureen in, then disappeared quietly after closing the door again behind her.

And there was Margaret. Sitting at a small table looking towards her. Smiling, sort of. The room was small and basic but it was more than a cell, or more than what Maureen would have expected in a cell. Not that she'd ever been in a nun's cell, she hadn't. There was a bed, a table with a chair, a small easy chair in a corner and a small chest of drawers. The window, normal sized, looked out on a garden. Crucifix above the bed. Three books on the desk and some writing paper. A glass and a jug of water. A blue rug on the wooden floor.

Margaret got up from her chair.

'Maureen, it's good to see you.'

She looked smaller and thinner, older, almost curved, misshapen, in her body. She was wearing clothes that Maureen recognised, normal day to day skirt and blouse and cardigan and her brown walking shoes.

She came to Maureen and gave her a brief hug.

'Sit down now.'

She looked around.

'Sit there in the comfy chair.'

And Maureen sat, and Margaret sat back on her chair, at the table, moving around so that she faced Maureen.

'Tell me first, how are the children, are they OK. Are they missing me?'

Her voice was the same voice, it was definitely her voice but it lacked something, it was weaker, quieter, not confident any more.

'They are both fine, Margaret. Absolutely fine, although they're missing you of course and, to be honest, a bit mystified by everything. Mr Shaughnessy told them you weren't too well and were spending time with relations, near Limerick I think he said.'

'Right.'

'And I'm trying to sort them out for school and everything, and I think their father checks their homework, usually anyway. I hope you don't mind but they spend a fair amount of time in the kitchen now, me and the children eat there, it seemed easier.'

'That's fine, Maureen, that's perfect. I'm sure you're doing a great job, and that's what Mary Doyle says as well.'

'Has she been to see you before? Mrs Doyle?'

'No, but she left a message with the Reverend Mother last week, or a few days ago anyway, I'm not even sure when last week was, to be honest, you lose track of time a bit in here.'

'But, look, are you OK, Margaret? I mean, what happened? Sorry, Margaret, it's none of my business really is it?'

Maureen didn't know what she could ask Margaret and what she couldn't.

'You'll know what happened Maureen, maybe not the details, but you won't want to know the details I can assure you. But you know what it was like. And, look, I couldn't take any more, that's the truth of it. I just fell apart that night. He was angry about that, of course, really angry. Christ, it was like a nightmare that I couldn't get out of. Jesus!'

Margaret had stopped talking and seemed to tense up immediately, seemed to almost go rigid sitting there in that upright chair by the table. She went paler, whiter, tauter, than she'd been already. And using words that she'd never used in that way before, not in Maureen's hearing.

Maureen was scared, now, because just asking that question had made Margaret change almost instantly. A second or two ago she had seemed tired, stressed maybe, she had looked ill, but she could easily have been anyone with a physical illness. Now it was different. Maureen wondered whether she should go and find the sister before things got worse.

And then she relaxed. Not completely by any means, but the tautened tension, the memory, the fear, seemed to go out of her body.

'Sorry Maureen. Sometimes I just have to think about being there, in that house I mean, and I fall apart again, I don't know what's happening to me. And, at the same time, I want to be there for my lovely Stephen and Maria, I want to be there for them so much.'

And now, not taut anymore, she was crying bitterly, head sunk towards her thin concave chest. Like an old, crying, haggard, woman.

Maureen got up and did the only thing she could. She put her arms around Margaret and she held her, and the woman buried herself into Maureen's body and sobbed. She held her for a long while, as long as was necessary. And when she heard the crying subside, and felt the body in her arms relax, she loosened her arms slowly and went to sit on the bed, closer to Margaret than if on the other chair.

'I didn't want to marry him, Maureen. Not because he was a bad man, not really, he wasn't, then I mean. He drank, of course, but so did most of the boys. I just didn't want to marry him. I felt nothing for him, there, that's the truth of it, I felt nothing for him. I never have and I never will. And he knows that, and he hates it. He hates it, he hates it!'

And now her teeth were clenched again, her body tightening up, her own anger, against him, making her tense to a point that Maureen didn't even know how she could breathe, how she could live even.

'And my lovely children are the victims of all this, my lovely children. Lovely Stephen and that wild one, Maria.'

She spoke through gritted teeth and then, almost inexplicably, laughed through her tears when she mentioned Maria, probably remembering her vivacity, her life, her impudence and cheek that she showed so often.

But not so much now, with her mother away, with little or no explanation.

She stopped for a second and then looked at Maureen.

'They won't be like him will they Maureen, they won't turn out like him, will they?'

Maureen got up again and held her tight. Margaret didn't cry this time but she wound her arms around Maureen's body, almost clinging on in desperation, terrified of sinking into an abyss that was too appalling to contemplate.

'No, Margaret, they won't be like him. They will never be like him.'

But, she thought, despite herself, what do I know? I have no idea if they will turn out like him. No idea at all.

Releasing herself she sat back on the bed again, looking at Margaret, trying to force her to look back at her.

'Margaret you must try and get better. You must try and calm yourself so that you can come home and see the children. They miss you and they need you, you know that. The sisters here will help you, and the Reverend Mother seems very nice. Nicer than any nun I've ever met I'd say. They can help you. I'm sure they can.'

Margaret looked at her.

'I'm desperate to see my lovely children but if I go home he'll be there, won't he? He'll be there as well, don't you understand? If I go home to my children I will see him again. He will see me again. He will do what does. Don't you understand Maureen? Don't you understand?'

'Just try and get better, Margaret. Let the nuns help you.'

'What do the fucking nuns know Maureen! Living here in this place. What do they know about anything. Tell me that, if you can!'

'They'll help you Margaret, they will help you.'

Maureen realised that Margaret had tried hard. At the beginning. To be sitting there, composed, in that seat at the table when Maureen had come through the door. She had tried hard to show that she was fine, that she'd been ill but she was improving, that she was getting better, that she could manage. But she couldn't. She couldn't hold herself together for more than a few seconds at a time.

There was a knock on the door. Sister Patricia put her head around the door.

'You'll be needing to finish off now, I'm afraid. Just another minute or so.'

She had a soft face and she'd smiled this time. A pleasant open smile.

'Yes, sister.'

The nun closed the door again but Maureen could see her outside waiting, just keeping an eye as well.

'I have to be going Margaret.'

'I know you do, I know. Thank you so much for coming. I'm sorry if I was emotional, but I am getting better, I am, Maureen. I'm getting much better. Every day I'm better, I really am. Will you tell the children that, tell them that you've seen me and I'm getting better and I'll be home for them soon? Will you tell them that, Maureen?'

Maureen knew that she would not tell the children anything at all about her visit to their mother. Or him either, but that was another thing altogether.

'Of course I'll tell them and they'll be pleased to hear it. They're looking forward to you coming home, I know they are. Maybe by Easter eh? You can open your eggs together.'

'That would be great, Maureen. That would be great. To be there on Easter Sunday, we could all go to Mass together; me, and the children and you as well. And then we could have a big Easter meal, couldn't we? All together. That would be great.'

'Here now, give me hug.'

She pulled Margaret to her and held her tight as she could, feeling her thinness, her boniness, her meagreness. It was almost like she was disappearing.

The sister opened the door.

'Are you ready now?'

'We are. I'll see you soon Margaret, make sure to get yourself better now, won't you?'

'I will. And come and see me again, Maureen. Please come and see me again.'

'I will.'

She edged through the door that the sister was holding open, giving a little wave. And seeing Margaret instantly return to her seat by the table, seeing her face already losing its animation, losing any happiness, just falling back into a state of vacant despair, staring blankly at the white painted wall in front of her.

The sister led the Maureen back along the corridor and through the bigger door back into the entrance hall where she had arrived.

The nun left her there. Suggesting she sit on one the two chairs before she went. Which she did. Maureen felt cold in the building, only now realising that there was a spartan feel to the place. Not unwelcoming in any way, but not unnecessarily comfortable either.

She heard voices and another door opened. Maureen stood up. The Reverend Mother came through followed by Mrs Doyle.

She thought this door must lead into the convent itself, Margaret's room was probably in an area separate from that, an area for guests or whatever. She wondered if Margaret could walk in the garden she could see from her window. It would be a sort of punishment, in itself, if she could only look at it through the glass, so to speak.

Mrs Doyle smiled and the nun did also.

'Everything alright, Maureen?'

'Yes, fine thanks.'

'Well, let's get on our way. Julia, Reverend Mother, thank you for letting Maureen see Margaret, and thanks also for your discretion, I appreciate it.

'God works in mysterious ways, Mary, we all know that. It was nice to meet you Maureen, and if necessary, you'll come to see Margaret again?'

'Of course, Reverend Mother. Thank you for allowing me to

see her.'

She smiled. She was waiting for them to go, not impatient but expectant.

'We'll be off then.'

'God be with you, safe journey now. Be careful in that machine of yours, Mary.'

'I will.'

Sister Patricia appeared, out of nowhere it seemed, and opened the front door, closing it again immediately when they were both outside.

It was raining now, not heavy, a soft drizzle. A calming rain.

They got into the car and Mrs Doyle started it up, and started the windscreen wipers to clear the rain away.

They didn't speak until they really got going, until they had gone again through that little village and turned left then on the road back towards Bray.

'So. What was it like? How was she?'

Maureen thought about what she could say, thought about how she could explain.

'I was thinking, at first, that she was fine. She was sitting there in her ordinary clothes, she could have been back home in Bray, sitting at the kitchen table or something. We could have had a chat and everything would have been fine, that's sort of what I thought. But as soon as she started to talk about anything back there, the children, or him, or whatever happened she just seemed to fall apart. I mean really fall apart, like a different person altogether.'

'The Reverend Mother said things were not going well.'

'Well they're not, not from what I saw. And Margaret asked me to tell the children she was getting better and I said I would. So I lied to her really as well, which I feel bad about, I really do.'

'You can't tell anyone Maureen, you do understand that, don't you?'

'I know I can't. But I felt it would comfort her if she thought the children thought she was improving.'

'You did the right thing, Maureen. And I'll tell you, it's an awful responsibility you have. Was she crying or what?'

'Crying, holding on to me, and language as well. Nothing terrible really, but she doesn't ever talk like that at home.'

'God save us! And the Reverend Mother thinks it'll be months rather than weeks before she's ready to go home.'

'Well she doesn't want to go back to him that's for sure. She wants so much to see the children, but she doesn't want to be in the same house as him, that's a definite.'

'If she wants to go back to the children she'll have to go back to him. That's the way it is, Maureen.'

They were driving back through the mountains. Misty rain made it difficult to see any great distance and Mrs Doyle was driving quite slowly now. In the sun on the outward journey it felt like they had sped along, it had been fun and fast, but now the roads were wet and slippy, and the rain was falling, the journey felt risky, almost dangerous.

Maureen said nothing for a while, and Mrs D concentrated on her driving. They had a slight shock at one stage almost running into the back of donkey and cart which was making its way along with a farmer, or whatever, driving it. You couldn't see his face because he'd put his big coat right over his head to keep the rain off. His hand appeared in a wave as they edged past him, but that was all they saw of him.

'You know the Reverend Mother?'

'I do. Julia. She's my cousin. We went to school together. She's a very bright woman. I didn't expect her to become a nun that's for sure.'

'She said about going there again. Do you think we should do that? Do you want to do that?'

'Let's see how things go. It's possible that she'll just get better, of course. It happens sometimes, even if it doesn't seem likely at the moment. He goes to see her by the way, he's been a couple of times and according to the Reverend Mother she's as good as gold when he's there, almost as if nothing's wrong. But as soon as he goes she's screaming that she's not going back to him, whatever happens she's not going back to him. It takes her twenty-four hours to calm down after he's been apparently.'

They were coming back to the coast now and would be in Bray in a few minutes. It was only just after half-twelve, they'd only been gone three hours and a lot had happened.

'Can you walk back from my house Maureen? It might be better if I don't stop outside the Shaughnessy's, he could be home for dinner I suppose?'

'Of course. He might be there. It's unlikely but not impossible.'

'If anyone says to him that they saw me pick you up you'll just have to say I was passing by chance, and I gave you a lift into the town. Is that alright. We don't want him getting suspicious if at all possible.'

'Fine.'

And so they went the last few minutes in silence. And when Mrs D stopped the car outside her house Maureen just said goodbye and got out and walked back down the street towards the Shaughnessy's house.

CHAPTER SIXTEEN

She'd arranged to meet Julia the next day when she went into town. Julia said the afternoon was a better time for her because there was a load of things that had to be done in the hotel in the morning, but things eased off a bit in the afternoon.

Maureen sorted the house out in the morning and had a bit of lunch, a sandwich and a cup of tea and then walked into the town. There was a small amount of shopping to do and she got that out of the way before meeting Julia at the café that they liked.

And, of course, Julia was late. There had never been one meeting, apart from the very first, when Julia had been on time. She always had an excuse of course, usually because her boss had been unreasonable, whatever the excuse, it was always someone else's fault.

Maureen sat at a table by the window and ordered a tea, she would have liked a cake but it was Lent. She watched the people walking by and realised she knew a lot of the faces now, recognised the faces even if she didn't know who they were. As she would have in Dungarvan of course, although she would probably have known exactly who many of those people were, might have known their children, or someone in their families, even if she didn't know them directly.

And she saw him as well. She did see him occasionally in the town, it was unusual but not unknown. She hadn't seen him at home yesterday after her visit to Margaret, she hadn't want to see him either, and he had come in very late. She had heard him but not seen him.

Now she saw him in the street. He was talking to two men, familiar faces. They were laughing, standing there laughing. He was bigger than both of them, broader as well. It was interesting to watch him because, if you looked at him, you'd think he'd not a care in the world. It didn't seem like his friends, if that's what they were, were asking him how his sick wife was. No, they were having a laugh and a joke, as if all was well with the world. And then he left them, laughing with them as he did so, roaring with laughter at something one of the other two had said. And laughing to himself as he walked up the street and turned the corner back to where his offices were. Maureen knew where he was probably going.

She was surprised. Not because he laughed with the men, with his friends. No, not because of that. She was surprised that he continued to laugh as he walked away. For some reason she wanted his face to change after he had done his social duty and laughed at his cronies' jokes, when he turned away she wanted it to change to the face of someone who was worried about his wife and children, change to the face of someone who cared.

But it didn't.

'How are ye? Have you ordered me a tea and one of those fancy cakes that you like?'

She hadn't seen, or heard, Julia coming in. Hadn't been expecting the slap on her shoulder.

'No, I haven't. If you were ever on time I'd have ordered it. But you never are and I'm not wasting money on tea that's just going to go cold on me. And no cakes in Lent.'

'God, you're a tight old thing, Maureen, that's for sure. A cup of tea over here would'ya! And a fondant fancy too!'

She sat down. Smiling. And her smile made Maureen smile.

Cheered her up.

'How are ya?'

And they chatted about nothing at all. Or Julia chatted about nothing at all. What was going on at the hotel, who she'd seen out in the town, who was going out with whom, who had split up.
And she offered Maureen half her cake as well, but Maureen refused to be tempted.

'So, and what about Margaret? What news there? Is she on her way back or what?'

'I don't know. There's no news at all.'

'God there must be something. She can't have just disappeared. Didn't you say she was in Limerick or something.'

'That's what I heard.'

She looked about her and then leant towards Maureen, and started to speak quietly.

'Well, I've heard different.'

'She's in some convent or other, over the mountains there. Not that far away. A place people go when they crack up, when they go mad, or because of the drink sometimes as well. Not cheap they say.'

'Well, I don't know. I heard she was with relations in Limerick.'

'No, she's in this convent. Definitely. He told one of his pals, so it's no secret now, even if it ever was. That stuff about the relations was rubbish, just to cover things up. But he couldn't keep his mouth shut, could he? I'm surprised he hasn't told you, I mean you've sort of got a right to know, haven't you? Looking after the kids an' all?'

'What else did he say?'

'Nothing as far as I know. Eddie Clancy told me, but that was it. She was in this convent, that was it. Oh, and they say he's been seeing another woman as well. I forgot that.'

'What do you mean another woman?'

'Oh, I don't know if that's true at all, someone saw him in the street with a woman. To be honest he's such a bad reputation people will think anything about him.'

Maureen could well believe he was seeing someone else. He was that type of person, wasn't he? He'd come up to her landing a third time. It scared her so much when she heard his steps. He'd tried the door but it was locked. He didn't make a fuss or rattle the door or anything, she just saw, heard, the doorknob turn, felt him push lightly against the door, and when it stayed shut she heard him go down again. That had been a week ago and since then there had been nothing. And she hoped that was the end of it. And when she'd seen him at breakfast, and a few times in the evening since then, he'd been pleasant enough, asking after the children, were they behaving themselves and the like, and asking if she was doing ok, and how grateful he was for her work. And telling her also that he would increase her wages because of the extra work she was doing.

Maureen would have liked to tell Julia about her trip to the convent. It seemed almost silly not to say anything about it, because, in actual fact, Julia already knew almost everything anyway. But she didn't let on. She had told Mrs Doyle and the Reverend Mother that she wouldn't and she wanted to keep that promise, and, almost more importantly, she felt it would be betraying Margaret as well. She didn't want to tell anyone about the state that Margaret was in, it would definitely be a betrayal of their friendship.

And she realised that Margaret and she were friends now. In a certain kind of way she probably knew more about Margaret than she knew about almost anyone else. It was a queer feeling to realise what that friendship was. Margaret was twenty years older than her, something like that. God, she might almost be closer to Mama's age than her own. And she was different to her as well. She'd had money, a lot more than Maureen anyway. And mistress of that house from when she was a girl, from when she was nineteen or twenty or whatever it was. And she'd finished school properly and passed exams which Maureen never had.

She couldn't tell Julia anything at all, she couldn't even hint that she knew about the convent because Julia would know that she knew more, and then she wouldn't stop till she had found out everything.

'God, I'll be glad when Lent is over. There is nothing to do, nothing. And there's still three weeks, or is it four? I'm not sure. At least there'll be Paddy's Day soon, won't there? That'll be a break at least. God, Maureen, is that the time? I've got to get back. I'll love and leave ya.'

And she was away. The good thing about Julia was she could rabbit on about anything and sometimes it didn't really matter if you listened or not, because she'd keep going regardless.

CHAPTER SEVENTEEN

'My cousin is coming to stay, Maureen. She'll be arriving this afternoon.'

He was eating his breakfast after the children had left. She had brought some more tea in for him and was about to return to the kitchen.

Maureen was not sure what to say.

'She wanted to come and just check that everything is going alright with the children and everything. Miss Driscoll is her name. She never married unfortunately. You'll get on fine with her, I'm sure.'

'Will she be staying long, sir?'

'In the first instance, it'll just be three or four days I'd say. If Mrs Shaughnessy is still away for a while she might come and stay for a longer period. Possibly.'

'And Mrs Shaughnessy is she doing OK sir? We're all anxious about her to be honest.'

'She's not too bad at all, not too bad at all. Improving all the time. I hope she'll be home in a week or two with a bit of luck. But don't say that to the children, we don't want to set their hopes up until we're definite.'

'Right, sir.'

'So can you make the sure the spare room is ready for Miss Driscoll, Maureen.'

'I'll do it right after I've cleaned the breakfast things. What time will she be here?'

'She said she'd aim to get to the house at three. I can't be here, so you'll let her in and show her everything?'

'I will, sir. Will Miss Driscoll have come from Limerick, sir?'

'Why do you ask that, Maureen?'

He looked puzzled for a second.

'I thought that Mrs Shaughnessy was with family in Limerick, I'm not sure where I got that idea from.'

'No, no, no. Miss Driscoll, Auntie Deirdre to the children, she lives near Meath, not too far away. Yes, Mrs Shaughnessy is in the country with, she's with one of my other cousins.'

'I'll get the room sorted anyway.'

'Good, good girl. Oh, and by the way, I was looking to see if the locks on all the doors are working, is there a key in the door to your little place up there?'

'There is sir. It works fine.'

'Good. And also, while Miss Driscoll is here at least, we'll all be eating in the dining-room, can you sort that out, Maureen, for tonight?'

'I will, sir.'

She left him to it and after breakfast she went and checked the spare room, aired the sheets, and dusted, made sure there was no cause for complaint.

She realised that things were going to change, even if it was just while this cousin was staying. She decided, also, that she better give the house a good going over, dusting anyway, before the woman arrived. She'd be bound to be looking for something to criticise.

She arrived at just after three. The bell rang and Maureen opened the door. A woman of about thirty, for some reason Maureen had expected someone a lot older, because of the way he'd said about her not marrying. She looked like anyone really, nicely dressed, with a small suitcase. Smiling in a friendly way.

'Hello, I'm Deirdre Driscoll, and you must be Maureen. You are expecting me, aren't you?'

'Yes Miss. Of course, come in.'

She came in and put her case down, took her coat off and hung it up herself on the coat stand.

'Can I show you your room, Miss.'

'That'd be grand, Maureen.'

And she followed Maureen upstairs. Maureen showed her the room and where the bathroom was. And pointed out the children's rooms and the staircase that led up to her own room.

'It's a great house isn't it, Maureen? Very spacious. Lovely. Now, look, what about a cup of tea. You and me, eh? You can show me the kitchen and we can have a chat about things.'

Miss Driscoll left her case unopened on the bed and they both went down to the kitchen.

When they got there Maureen put the kettle on and got things ready for tea. Miss Driscoll sat at the kitchen table and, for a minute or two, said nothing.

'So, how long have you been here Maureen. A few months now is it?'

'About six months now, Miss.'

'And you came up from the country?'

‘Dungarvan, Miss.’

‘Lovely….Now, how are the children?’

‘They’re fine, although they miss their Ma, as they would. But they’re doing fine, doing their school work and everything.’

‘Of course, of course. And I suppose you’ve been working extra hard with their mother being gone?’

‘Not really. Well maybe a little bit, but it’s no hardship. Excuse me, I’ll just do the tea.’

Maureen made the tea and put it on the table, with cups and saucers and milk.

‘Will you want sugar, Miss?’

‘No sugar for me, Maureen! That’s what I gave up, sugar and cakes and the like. What about you. Did you give up the drink or what?’

Maureen wasn’t sure if she should take this as a joke.

‘I don’t drink Miss, anyway, Lent or not. No, I gave up the sugar and the sweets and things.’

‘I was joking about the drink Maureen, you don’t look like a drinker to me. Too young anyway. What age are you now?’

‘Seventeen, Miss, eighteen in April.’

‘So how do you like your tea Maureen. Strong or weak?’

‘Strongish really, Miss.’

‘Great, me too.’

And the woman stirred the tea and then put milk in the two cups and poured out the tea herself.

‘Tell me about the children Maureen. Stephen and Marie. How

are they doing?'

'Maria it is. She'll get awful annoyed if you call her Marie.'

'Of course, sorry. I have another niece called Marie, I'm always confusing them. So how are they doing?'

'Good, Stephen's great. He's very quiet and he does all his school work, and he's always very pleasant. And Maria, she's a bit wilder sometimes, but she's calmed down a touch recently, she misses her Ma. Well they both do, obviously.'

'Of course, any child would miss their mother, wouldn't they? Now look, I've had a little bit of a journey today so I'm going to have a sleep before tea. Mr Shaughnessy said he'd be home for dinner at around six, is that right?'

'Six is when they eat, yes. You'll all eat together in the dining room.'

'Great, and I can meet the children then. I haven't seen them since they were tiny, so they probably won't remember me.'

'OK. Do you want me to give you a shout at half-five or something, in case you're still asleep?'

'No, no, I'll be fine. Thanks for the tea Maureen and the little chat. I'll see you a bit later.'

She got up and left the kitchen, Maureen heard her go up the stairs and into the spare room, heard the door shut behind her.

The woman seemed very pleasant to Maureen, not really what she was expecting. For some reason she thought it would definitely be an older woman, someone who marched straight in and checked the dust on the skirting board before she even said hello. But this woman seemed pleasant enough, even easy-going in a way. She hadn't even looked around the kitchen or asked what they were having for tea or anything like that. The children might even like her.

Half an hour later Stephen arrived followed by Maria a couple of minutes after. Maureen told them that their Auntie Deirdre had arrived. Which mystified them. It was obvious that Shaughnessy had not told them anything about the visit. Neither of them were even sure who she actually was. When Maureen said that she had come from somewhere near Meath, Stephen seemed to recognise a kind of family connection with the place. Maria said she wasn't sure where Meath exactly was.

Maureen asked them about their grandparents and family and Stephen said that they didn't really have anyone left really. He remembered meeting both grandparents when he was very small but they had all died over the next couple of years and, although cousins and aunts were mentioned sometimes, they never seemed to meet them. Maria said most of her friends had loads of family and that they were really the odd ones out with that kind of thing. Even at Christmas there was usually just the four of them, although their father's brother, Martin, used to turn up now and then, but he'd gone abroad to work in America.

Maureen asked about Margaret's family. Stephen said she'd been an only child and now her parents had died there wasn't really anyone, as far as he knew anyway.

Maureen then shooed them out of the kitchen saying she had to get the dinner ready, and that tonight, and for the next few nights at least, they would be eating in the dining room.

It was a very basic meal of course. Colcannon of sorts and soda bread. Maureen wondered if she should have tried to make it something more, with the new woman there. Not try and impress her exactly but show what she could do, but as it was Lent there wasn't much alternative was there?

He was home a bit earlier than usual and seemed pleased that the cousin had arrived, and the lot of them sat down at six.

Maureen brought the food in and saw that the aunt was sitting in Margaret's place. Of course, there was no reason why she shouldn't. Normally the parents sat at either end and the two children at either side. She could have sat on the side with one of the children, next to Maria maybe, but that might have seemed a bit odd as well. Nevertheless, it wasn't nice to see someone sitting in Margaret's chair, it felt like she was kind of trying to take over, even if you knew it wasn't true.

The atmosphere was fine. The children were talking to her, and she seemed to be pushing the conversation along, asking them something or other about their school.

'Thanks Maureen. That's fine.'

She left them to eat their tea and went back into the kitchen where she ladled out a meal for herself and sat down at the kitchen table to eat.

She felt lonely all of a sudden. For the last few weeks, and that's all it was, the children had eaten in here with her and it had been fun. Even though they were all aware that Margaret wasn't in the house, and that they missed her, it was comforting to chat with the children and eat with them as well. In some ways she had felt more part of the household, part of the family almost, when they ate together in the kitchen.

But she guessed that Shaughnessy would be happier with this new arrangement. He'd never liked the children to have too much to do with her but he'd given in, because he had to really. There was no alternative. But now he could move things back to the way they were. For a few days anyway, the aunt was only meant to be here for a few days, he'd said.

She heard them all laughing about something, something the woman had said, she heard her voice, a high tone, and then the laughter. And now Maureen felt a little jealous as well. For the first time in ages she thought about home and wanted to be back there again.

They spent longer at the table than normal, even sitting there for a few minutes after Maureen had cleared away the plates. The children left the table and Shaughnessy asked Maureen to bring some tea into the sitting room for himself and the cousin.

The children followed Maureen back into the kitchen.

'She's real nice Maureen, she's a laugh actually, I like her. What do you think?'

'She seemed very nice, you're right. Very pleasant, we had a cup of tea together earlier and she seemed OK. Do you like her Stephen?'

'She's OK yeah.'

He smiled.

'Anyway, get on with your homework now.'

'Can I do mine in here, Maureen?'

'Better not, I think your Da would prefer it if you didn't spend too much time in here.'

Maria made a face but followed Stephen out of the kitchen and up the stairs.

Maureen made the tea and took it into them. They stopped talking while she put the things out and when she left he got up to shut the door behind her. Doing the washing-up she could hear them talking and laughing. Not something she could remember hearing before in this house, certainly not between him and Margaret anyway.

He went out about half an hour later and she went upstairs to her room. Although she did poke her head in the kitchen on the way, and thanked Maureen for the lovely tea.

Maureen put on her coat when she'd finished clearing up and went out for a walk. Just down to the town and back. She didn't tell anyone she was going. She didn't really have to but, normally, she would have let the children know, or Margaret, that she'd be out for an hour or so. She just wandered around the town, said hello to a couple of girls she knew and started back. It was cold, she had thought she might take a quick look at the sea, spend a few minutes on the Promenade, but it was too cold. She'd just needed to get out.

She knew she was being stupid, but she was upset. The aunt, who seemed very nice, had upset things really. Her coming had sort of pushed Maureen out of the way, pushed her back down a peg if you like, pushed her back to being a servant. She had enjoyed managing things and helping the children, she had enjoyed being left to do what she wanted but that had probably changed now.

And it was almost like Margaret didn't exist anymore as well. The aunt hadn't really mentioned her. Maybe she didn't know her? Maybe she'd never met her.

The house was quiet when she returned. His coat was back on the coat stand, so he'd returned. A lot earlier than he would have normally, or usually anyway. The lights were off in the dining room and the sitting room. Maureen went into the kitchen and quickly sorted out the breakfast stuff for morning and thought about having a cup of tea. Ideally, she would have wanted to sit down with Margaret and have one of their chats, chats about nothing really, just comforting. But she wasn't here. So, Maureen decided to go to bed.

At least with the aunt in the house there was very little likelihood of him trying her door. She went upstairs, washed, went to bed, and fell asleep.

CHAPTER EIGHTEEN

Things were normal the next morning. The children had their breakfast and went to school and he had his breakfast and went to work. He said nothing, which is about as much as he would say on any day. Apart from goodbye.

The aunt didn't appear for breakfast, Maureen had expected her and had laid a place at the dining room table. Breakfast had gone back in there from the kitchen as well, she thought that was what he wanted.

Maureen cleared up and wasn't quite sure what to do, wasn't quite sure whether she should wait for the aunt before deciding on the shopping, on the meals.

At just after nine the doorbell rang and she knew who that would be. Mrs D.

'Hello, Maureen, how are you, how's things?'

She was in the house before you knew it, and after putting her coat on the stand, she was straight to the kitchen.

'Let's have a cup of tea Maureen, I had a very early breakfast this morning because Mr D was off on some trip or other, just for the day but he had to set off early. I got up as well, I've no idea why, I should have just stayed in bed and had a rest. But I didn't. Anyway, a cup of tea would be great.'

Maureen put the kettle on.

'Mr Shaughnessy's gone to work I assume?'

'He has, Mrs Doyle, but his cousin is staying now. She hasn't come down yet.'

'His cousin? Who's his cousin then?'

'She's called Driscoll. Deirdre, I believe. She comes from somewhere around Meath. I'm not sure where.'

'So when did she turn up?'

'Yesterday. Mr Shaughnessy just told me in the morning that she was coming, and she arrived in the afternoon. She seems very nice. She might be down in a minute, you can talk to her.'

'I'd like that. Maybe, if she's not down before I'm ready to go, you could pop up to see whether she's available to say hello?'

'If you like I can do that.'

Mrs D got up from the kitchen table and shut the kitchen door.

'Leave the tea for the moment, Maureen. Sit ye down.'

She did.

'The Reverend Mother got in touch with me yesterday. She said that your visit had helped Margaret a bit. I mean she's still more or less the same, but she was talking a bit more about getting back home which is encouraging. So the Reverend Mother thought another trip next week sometime might be useful. What do you think? Will you able to get away? Will this cousin be a problem?'

'She's only meant to be here for a few days, three or four I think he said. But maybe she might come back for longer, I'm not sure.'

'Well it would be possible for me to go on Wednesday so let's try that shall we? I'll let them know we'll come Wednesday if at all possible'

'Fine.'

Maureen got up to finish making the tea and, as she did so, she was aware of the kitchen door opening. The aunt.

‘Good morning, Maureen. Oh, and hello.’

Mrs D hadn’t realised for a second that the aunt had come in but stood up as she heard the voice.

‘Oh, Mrs Doyle this is Miss Driscoll, Mr Shaughnessy’s cousin who’s staying for a few days.’

‘It’s very nice to meet you Miss Driscoll, Maureen here was telling me all about you.’

‘And it’s very nice to meet you too, Mrs Doyle.’

Maureen wasn’t sure whether she should try and tell the aunt that Mrs Doyle was quite an important person. And she wasn’t sure how to either.

‘Would you like to take your tea in the sitting room?’

And, now, she wasn’t even sure which one she was asking.

‘That’d be nice, thank you Maureen.’

Miss Driscoll was the one that answered and stood aside to let Mrs Doyle out into the hall.

It took Maureen a few minutes to get the tea stuff ready and when she took it in they were sitting down, smiling at each other, talking. Mrs D telling her about the people she knew in Meath and whether they had acquaintances in common. As far as she could tell Miss Driscoll was saying she knew the names but didn’t actually know the people. Which was a pity, says Mrs D, because they’re an awfully nice family, beautiful house, beautiful gardens as well.

She left them to it.

She would have quite liked to have stood outside and listened, but that was not the type of thing she did.

After about twenty minutes or so she heard their voices change in that way that they do when people are getting ready to leave, and heard them getting louder when the door to the sitting room was opened again.

Maureen went out into the hall. The two women were standing there still chatting. Maureen took Mrs D's coat off the hook and helped her to put it on. She waited till it seemed right and then opened the door for Mrs D. to leave when she was ready.

'Anyway, I'll see you at Mass on Sunday, if you're still here that is. Give my regards to Mr Shaughnessy won't you? Thank you for the tea, Maureen.'

And she was off. Maureen looked out but there was no car today, walking all the way. She turned at the gate and waved before she disappeared down the road.

Maureen shut the door. Miss Driscoll was standing waiting, watching

'Well, you get on very well with Mrs Doyle, don't you?'

'She's a very nice woman, very helpful, always interested. Especially now with Mrs Shaughnessy away. Always offering to help.'

'I'm sure she is, I'm sure she is, Maureen.'

CHAPTER NINETEEN

As luck would have it, in the first instance, Deirdre Driscoll only stayed till the following Tuesday. And in that time Maureen got to know her a bit better.

She was a friendly woman or, to be more accurate, she was a woman who liked to be around, liked to chat, liked to have a cup of tea and a cigarette, and have a joke about this and that. She would come into the kitchen, like she had on the day that Mrs D arrived, later, after the others had gotten up and gone. She didn't get up to see the children off to school or anything like that which, to be honest, both Maureen and the children found a bit odd. It didn't bother them, the children weren't disappointed or upset, they were just a bit mystified. If an aunt came to stay, with Mama not there, they sort of expected she would bustle around sorting things out and seeing them off. But she didn't. She never appeared until about nine. This meant that on two days the children had their breakfast in the kitchen because Shaughnessy had left the house early as well. And the three of them enjoyed those breakfasts, without actually admitting it, without saying anything about it to each other.

The problem with the aunt getting up late was that it upset the rhythm of Maureen's morning. Normally, not always, but normally, everyone would be gone by about eight-fifteen and Maureen would have all the breakfast stuff sorted by half-eight. She might have a cup of tea then, or not, as she fancied, and she'd get on with the bedrooms. But now that was impossible because the aunt hadn't got up yet, and she felt she had to wait and get her some breakfast when she turned up. Which she did about nine.

And she took her time as well. She might only have a bit of toast to eat but she'd have three or four cups of tea and she would smoke as well. One cigarette or two. Maureen didn't like the smoking in the kitchen because you could never get rid of the smell. About the only good thing about Shaughnessy was that he didn't smoke, not at home at any rate. And then she would insist that Maureen sit down with her and she would talk about this and that. Mainly asking questions about the house and the children and Bray and a bit about Dungarvan. And about Margaret. She wasn't obviously nosey, she didn't seem to ask direct, personal, questions about Margaret, about her illness or anything like that. She might ask where Margaret got her clothes, or who were closest friends round and about, stuff like that. But Maureen knew what she was doing. She was finding out as much as she could, and she was finding out because she didn't know anything about her. She admitted as much. She said that the two of them had never met, she actually said 'I'm pretty sure we never met, pretty sure about that', and she explained this by the fact that she had spent some time in England, working over there, and then she had gone to America as well. But, anyway, now she was back home, she was glad she could be of help to Mr Shaughnessy.

Maureen didn't tell her anything much. She certainly didn't tell her that she and Margaret were friends and that she had gone to visit her at the convent. She did wonder, though, if the woman had heard anything before she came into the kitchen on the day when Mrs D was there, but she didn't see how she could have done. And she realised, as well, talking to the aunt, that she, Maureen, didn't really know a lot about Margaret herself. Didn't know a lot of details about her life, hardly anything in fact.

On the Saturday and Sunday the aunt still got up a bit later than the others but she did manage to get to the breakfast table while Shaughnessy was still there, so she had her cup of tea and her toast and her cigarettes with him. Chatting and laughing. She was a great one for the laughing.

Maureen was told to leave her bedroom, not to bother cleaning it. She'd sort it out herself, she said.

'I make a terrible mess, Maureen. Clothes all over the place. I wouldn't want you to have to plough through all that. I'll do it myself. Don't you worry yourself about it.'

Maureen was happy enough, in one sense, to leave it to her, although she was surprised that, at the same time, she felt it was really her job to get things done, to keep the whole house tidy. She didn't like the idea of one room descending into chaos and her not being able to do anything about it. But, anyway, the woman was only here for a few days, Maureen would sort it out when she left. On the Friday, the aunt went into town to do some shopping and Maureen thought she might take advantage and have a quick look at all this mess.

She went upstairs and, even though she knew that there was absolutely no-one in the house, she almost went on tiptoe. She went to the spare room and turned the handle. It was locked. She was surprised, but realised that Shaughnessy had spoken about the locks, hadn't he? He must have given her a key.

Maureen went downstairs again, a bit quicker than going up, and went to the Oxo tin. She took the brown envelope out, there were four keys still in there. Perhaps he didn't know about the Oxo tin? He'd have a set of keys of his own anyway, wouldn't he? She took the keys upstairs and tried each one in turn, the third opened the spare room.

When she heard the key turn she was pleased, it a was bit like discovering a secret. But immediately she had her doubts as well. The woman had locked the door because she didn't want anyone to go in there, and it was her right to do that. If it was Julia in her place there would have been no hesitation at all, she'd be in there like a shot. If Maureen went in there, though, she might have to say something when she went to confession. Would she be obliged to say she had broken into someone's room without their knowing? Was it like some kind of burglary, or breaking and entering or something?

She stood on the landing, unsure whether she should go into the bedroom. Why did she want to go in there anyway? She definitely wasn't going to steal anything. The truth was she just wanted to have a look. She wanted to get some idea about Deirdre Driscoll. And if the door had opened straight away, without the key, she knew she would have just gone straight in. She would have just gone in there. She would have opened the door carefully and gone in, and had a quick look round, and left again. She was just being nosey, that's all, and that wasn't a sin in itself, was it?

And why would she lock the door anyway? There shouldn't be anything to hide. Shaughnessy didn't lock his room, he didn't seem to care that she went in there every day, went in there whenever she needed to.

She turned the handle and pushed the door open. Slowly, as if she was scared the aunt might be in there waiting for her. Waiting till she got in and then jumping out from behind the door and saying 'Gotcha!' But she wasn't there of course.

Being the spare room it wasn't that big, although there was still enough space for a double bed and a wardrobe and a dressing table. The curtains were drawn and the window had been opened slightly to let in some air. Despite this there was still the tang of perfume and powders in the room, and the smell of cigarettes as well.

There were clothes over the back of the dressing table chair, what looked like a frock underneath and a nightdress on top, and a pair of stockings hanging down as well, the feet of them visible below the end of the nightdress. On the dressing table itself, there was nothing out of the ordinary; hairbrush, small face mirror, face cream and powder, and a small bottle of Chanel No 5 which Maureen knew was quite an expensive perfume. And hair grips and little bits and pieces in a dish that had always been there in front of the big mirror. On the floor, next to the chair, there was a woman's magazine, Vogue, an old thumbed copy, lying as if it had been thrown there after reading. Maureen was tempted to pick it up and have a look, but left it where it was.

The bed was unmade but had been tidied. There was nothing much on the bedside table, an ashtray with cigarette ends still in it. On the other side of the bed, away from the door, was her suitcase. It was open. There were still some clothes, underwear, folded in the bottom of it. And a washbag sitting on the open lid.

The room was untidy but nothing particularly out of the ordinary, Maria's room could be easily twice as bad as this on any day of the week. Perhaps she just didn't like the idea of people in her room.

Maureen went back to the bedside table and opened the top drawer. A packet of cigarettes, a box of matches and a packet of sweets, a tube of mints. She opened the second drawer. What looked like a diary with a letter folded inside its pages, the envelope of a letter.

Maureen had never kept a diary, she wasn't sure she knew anyone who had ever kept a diary. She knew that people did, they wrote about their lives, what happened to them and everything. Mrs O'Gorman, her teacher, had told them about diaries. She'd told them about an Englishman who wrote a famous diary, Samuel Pepys, and Maureen remembered that name because Pepys sounded like peeps, she'd thought of him peeping round a corner and then writing down what he saw. Stupid, really. And Mrs O'Gorman had made them keep a diary in their workbooks, every day for a week.

She looked at the diary sitting there in the bottom of the drawer. Part of her wanted to pick it up and read it. Part of her wanted to look at the letter. She wondered what Deirdre Driscoll would write in a diary. She wondered what secrets were in there. Wondered what she would find out if she just leaned over and picked up that little book, with the letter peeking out from it.

She knew it would be wrong to look. And she didn't, but, in her head, she could hear Julia shouting at her.

'Take a look you eejit, no-one's going to know are they? Have a look, why don't ya?'

But she didn't. She closed the drawer, reluctantly, and turned to go. There was nothing much else to see.

On the back of the door, there were two dresses hanging. Pretty dresses, one mainly blue, the other a kind of pink. She liked nice things, the aunt.

She went out of the door onto the landing. And, as she did so, she heard the front door opening. She felt her heart instantly pounding, she felt almost sick.

'Maureen, are you there? I'm back. It's too dreary to stay out there any length of time. There's not a great deal to be seen in Bray anyway is there? Maureen, are you upstairs?'

Maureen quickly locked the door, fumbling, almost dropping the key before she managed to turn it. But she did manage to turn it, quietly, quietly. She put the key with the others in her pinafore pocket and went downstairs, breathing in deeply as she did so. Thanking God that she hadn't stayed to look in the diary, thanking the Lord she hadn't stayed in there any longer.

As she came down the stairs she saw Miss Driscoll, standing in the hall waiting for her, smiling up at her in a friendly way.

'Oh, there you are. Can we have a cup of tea Maureen, I'm parched? God, I'm always parched aren't I? Are you OK, you look a bit pale you know, did you eat breakfast? You've got to eat something you know, Lent or not, remember that, Maureen, you have to keep your strength up, you know.'

And Deirdre Driscoll followed Maureen into the kitchen for her tea.

CHAPTER TWENTY

The aunt left on the Tuesday morning. Shaughnessy had already told Maureen that she would be back by the end of the week and would stay as long as necessary. She took her suitcase and, that morning, Maureen went to clean her room along with the others. It wasn't locked, the door was open slightly. She saw that Deirdre, that was how she thought of her now, although she called her Miss, she saw that Deirdre had tidied up and had made the bed, not perfectly but in a polite way. There were some papers in the waste basket and Maureen looked at them, but there was nothing on them, a few scribbles, but nothing recognisable, there was a handkerchief as well, thrown away for some reason, and a lipstick and a small powder puff. Both of those were still just about usable, but Maureen thought she'd probably had a bit of a clear out before she left, when she was packing. She felt a bit grubby looking in the waste paper basket but, she thought, she would have taken all the stuff out of there anyway, to be thrown away. And she did. And at the bottom, scrunched up, was an envelope. When she unravelled it she saw that it looked like the envelope she'd seen in the diary.

It was addressed to Mrs D. Maguire, with an address in Dublin. There was no sender's name on it but the stamp was English, the postmark London. Maureen looked inside but there was nothing. She was disappointed, although she knew that Deirdre would be extremely unlikely to throw away a personal letter, very unlikely to put it in the waste paper basket where anyone who saw it could read it. And she thought it wasn't just Deidre who wouldn't do that either, no-one with any sense would just leave a personal letter lying around would they? They'd take it with them or destroy it, tear it into tiny pieces.

She looked in the bedside table. The mints were still there but nothing else. She looked in the drawer of the dressing table, a few hairpins and a slide, nothing else. She looked under the bed. Nothing there either. Deidre had removed everything. She could have left some things behind if she'd wanted, because she knew she was coming back, but she hadn't. Then Maureen, looking round, saw the blue dress on the back of the door. She had left something after all.

In those last few days Maureen had kept an eye on Deidre. She was interested in what was going on, but, to be honest, there hadn't seemed to be anything particularly odd about her being there. Deidre seemed quite straightforward, she supposed, although she did spend time in the evening with Shaughnessy in the living room, and there was a fair amount of laughter. And she knew they were drinking as well. Which, in a way, Maureen disapproved of. For a start, it was Lent and secondly it just seemed not right to be enjoying yourself in that way when Margaret was away in the convent.

She had wondered a bit more on the Saturday night though. She was lying awake in bed. She was thinking about writing to Mama and Dada which she hadn't done for at least two weeks now, and she was thinking about Julia as well. She had said about Deidre to Julia. And Julia had just asked what she was like, was a she a nice woman, she hadn't made any connection with that 'other woman' thing that she'd mentioned in the café. And Julia was usually very quick on things like that.

Maureen was lying there, everyone had gone to bed, him included. She felt safe now, of course, there was no way that Shaughnessy would come up to her room, with the other woman in the house. But then, lying there, she heard someone walking about downstairs. Not walking loudly, she could just hear the creak of the floorboards, not even the steps themselves. And a door shutting, very quietly. From where she was, above them all, it was almost impossible to work out who it was and where they were going. She listened and listened, for as long as she could. But she heard nothing more.

And then, of course, it was Sunday.

They all went to Mass together, Shaughnessy introducing Deidre to a few people afterwards. Saying hello to Mr and Mrs Doyle. Maureen was a little way away and, from that slight distance, she could see some of the men looking at Deidre in that way that men have, and then passing a few words between each other, with a laugh as well, and dig of the elbow from one of them to another, and another, bigger, laugh. Shaughnessy heard them and looked across, with that potentially angry look that he had. The men stopped laughing but smiled, smirked almost, to each other, nevertheless.

Before Maureen set off back to the house Mrs Doyle sought her out for a second and said for her to come to the Doyle's house on Wednesday at 9.30.

'Easier that way, I think.'

So Deidre went on Tuesday. As she had come, with her small suitcase, and she left at just after nine.

'Thanks Maureen for looking after me, and making all that tea, I hope you didn't mind all my questions. Anyway, I'll be back on Friday when I've sorted out all my business at home. I'll see you then.'

'What time do you think you'll arrive, on Friday I mean? Just so I know.'

'It'll be about three I'd say. About three.'

It was a relief to see her go. First of all because it made it easier for her trip with Mrs Doyle the next day, there'd be no need to make excuses, or worse, cancel. Secondly, Deidre seemed to take up Maureen's time, wanting to sit down and have tea, or even just coming in to the kitchen for a chat. If it had been Margaret she wouldn't have minded at all, she would have welcomed it, but with Deidre it was a bit of a chore, not that unpleasant really, but a chore nevertheless.

She found she was looking forward to Wednesday now. There was some trepidation of course, she wasn't sure how Margaret's health would be, but at the same time it was quite exciting to go on a trip. And, in an odd way, it made her feel more important again. During the last week she felt she had been relegated, back to being just a maid, being at everyone's beck and call. Even the children had changed slightly because she wasn't sitting down chatting with them so much, and she was serving them meals again in the dining room, they almost looked a bit embarrassed now when she put their meals down in front of them.

CHAPTER TWENTY-ONE

As with the previous time Maureen did her best to get as much work done as possible before going out on the Wednesday morning. Shaughnessy had said he would be late home that evening, not before eight he said, so that would make it easier for her getting the tea for the children, they could eat in the kitchen and it would all need less preparation. She did the beds quickly and left the house at nine twenty-five.

It was bright day. Maureen had noticed, although Lent was not over, that the weather had been mild and the spring was starting. It was nice to see, with the evenings getting a bit lighter as well. When she got round there the car was out in the road but Mrs Doyle was nowhere to be seen, so Maureen went up to the house and knocked on the door.

The door was opened by Mr Doyle. She knew he was an important man and he kind of looked it. He was not a big man, but he had a way about him that made you take notice. Like Mrs Doyle herself, in fact. He was wearing his suit. He always wore a dark suit, with a watch chain across his waistcoat.

'Maureen, come in, come in.'

He was friendly. For some reason she was surprised that he called her by her Christian name. There was no reason that he would not know her name, but it was strange to hear him say it.

'Sit down for a second, the boss'll be along shortly.'

Winking at her, with a bit of a smile, he pointed her towards one of the upright chairs in the hall. She sat down, and found herself looking up at him, a bit like being at school.

'So, how is everything at the Shaughnessy's? With Mrs Shaughnessy not being there I mean.'

'It's fine sir. Well, obviously, it's a terrible shame that Mrs S, Mrs Shaughnessy I mean, is ill, and the children are missing her. But everyone's managing, I'd say, sir.'

'And you're doing a grand job yourself according to reports, young lady, a grand job.'

Maureen felt herself blush.

'And there's an aunt there as well I believe?'

'Miss Driscoll, sir, yes. Although she's gone home, I think for a few days, she'll be back on Friday.'

'And she'll be a help as well, of course?'

'Of course, sir.'

As she said this she realised that it wasn't true. Deidre was no help at all, she was just one more person to look after. Anyway. She heard steps coming from upstairs and Mrs Doyle appeared, on her way down. 'Everything all right, Francis? Is he looking after you, Maureen?'

'He is ma'am.'

'Well, we'll be on our way.'

'Safe journey now. Give my regards to the Reverend Mother, won't you?'

'We will, Francis, we will.'

And they left the house. He watching them for a few moments before shutting the door.

They both got in the car and set off.

‘How are things Maureen?”

‘They’re fine ma’am.’

‘Tell me about this Deidre then. The aunt.’

‘Oh, she’s pleasant enough I would say. Friendly anyway, she likes a chat and a cup of tea.’

‘Well, we all like that, don’t we? And she gets on with him, with Shaughnessy, does she?’

‘They get on fine. I mean they all eat together, the children as well I mean, and then she and Mr S sit in the lounge and talk a bit and have a drink.’

‘Are the children there?’

‘No, they’ll have gone upstairs, or maybe come into the kitchen for a chat maybe.’

‘So, him and her, what do they talk about?’

‘I’ve no idea. Although they seem to laugh a lot. But they shut the door, he shuts the door, so it’s difficult to get any idea of what they might be discussing. Not that I’d be listening anyway.’

‘You might not be listening, Maureen, but with the door open you’d probably get an idea anyway, wouldn’t you?’

‘I’d say I would, yes.’

‘And she’s from Meath you said?’

‘She is, she says she is. Although she’s lived in England and in America for a time. She told me that. And she doesn’t know Margaret, I mean she says she’s never actually met her.’

‘Well, that’s a strange thing.’

They drove along the same route as previously. Another

lovely day, a bit warmer if anything. Mrs Doyle didn't talk for a while, just drove, and Maureen didn't see what else she could say. And then Mrs D slowed the car down and pulled into the side of the road. There was a little dent where it would be possible to park without getting in anyone's way, not that there was any traffic to get in the way of, there wasn't.

Once she had put the brake on and everything she half-turned towards Maureen.

'Do you think you should say anything to Margaret? About the aunt, I mean.'

'I don't know.'

And she didn't.

'It's possible she knows of course. It's possible that Shaughnessy has told her. I know he's been to see her.'

'He never said about going to see her.'

'Well, he's been there a few times. And he might have discussed Miss Driscoll with her, or told her.'

'Well, to be honest, I don't think there's any need to tell her because if she already knows she'll probably say something, and if she doesn't know it might be best not to say anything. Because if I do she'll know that Mr S has been keeping things from her. If you get what I mean?'

'Yes, yes. You're right of course, you're a bright girl, Maureen.'

And they set off again. Not talking at all this time until they reached the convent.

When they got there Sister Patricia immediately took Maureen through the door and down the corridor to Margaret's room. She had smiled at Maureen but had said nothing, just led the way.

She opened the door and Maureen went in, the door shut quickly, it seemed, behind her.

She was sitting in the same place, at the desk

Maureen immediately saw that Margaret was in worse shape than before, or maybe she just wasn't pretending any more. She looked even more haggard, the same clothes almost hanging off her now. And her face as well. It was always a thin face but now it seemed so drawn, it was almost like Maureen could see the cheekbones through her skin.

When she saw Maureen come in she smiled briefly and stood up. It was an effort for her to get to her feet.

'Maureen.'

She came across with her arms out. Thin arms out. And she embraced Maureen. Except it was hardly an embrace because there was so little strength in it. Maureen held her tight, feeling though, that she had to be careful not to break the woman in two, she felt so fragile.

Holding her so close she could smell her as well. A clean smell of soap, but an old decaying smell underneath it, almost as if she was dying. No fragrance, no sweetness any more. Like an old, old woman.

After a few seconds holding her, Maureen led Margaret the foot or two to her chair and held her arm as she sat down again.

'Can I sit on the bed?"

'Of course, you can, Maureen, of course you can.'

Her voice, the last time, had lost some of its strength but now it was little more than a whisper. But she was looking at Maureen almost affectionately, a pathetic small smile on her face now.

'How are you Maureen?'

It was pitiful, the slowness of the voice, the quietness of it.

'I'm fine Margaret. I'm fine.'

'And the children? How are they?'

'They're missing you Margaret, but they're all right.'

'I so much want to see them. But I can't, can I? He says it wouldn't be right for them to see me while I'm so ill.'

'He? Mr Shaughnessy? He came to see you?'

'Yes, didn't you know? He came on Friday I think, or Monday. I'm not sure.'

She looked confused for a moment.

'I told him you'd come to see me. How grateful I was that you'd come to see me.'

Maureen was shocked. She'd never thought that Margaret would tell Shaughnessy that she'd come to visit. Although why wouldn't she? The state she was in. She hadn't a clue what was going on really. And she'd never even asked Maureen how she'd got here, to the convent, either. Perhaps she thought there was a bus or something, she might not even know exactly where she was. Maybe she thought they were just outside Bray, in Greystones or somewhere near like that. These thoughts went quickly through her mind, and she realised that she hadn't really understood how ill Margaret was.

Maureen smiled a big smile.

'And what did he say to that?'

'He said you were doing a grand job, and he said he was going to put up your wages as well.'

'Yes, he's done that. What else did he tell you about home?'

'He just told me about the children, that they were doing fine, and you were doing fine, and I was not to worry. But he said, as well, that I wouldn't be going home till I was properly better and that the children shouldn't visit because it would be too distressing for them. Too distressing.'

She started to cry.

'Margaret, have you had any other visitors? Is there any of your family you'd like to see? I could write them a letter or something if you'd like?'

'No just you. And him. He pretends to be nice to me. Especially in front of the sisters. He pretends he cares. But he doesn't. He'll keep me in here for ever if he can. That's what he'd like best, I think. To keep me in here for ever. For eternity.'

'But have you any family I can contact for you?'

'No family. No family. I haven't even got my own family, my own children. If Mama was alive she'd look after me, but she went a long time ago. And Dada too. There's no-one else to look after me. Just you and the sisters.'

Maureen looked up towards the window.

'Do you go out in the garden, Margaret?'

This thought seemed to change her face slightly, stopped her crying, made her smile a bit again.

'Every day Sister Patricia and I go out in the garden. As long as it's not raining, even then if it's not too hard. We walk around and around. Just slowly. Sometimes you can see the water from the rain on the leaves, they're beautiful, the drops lying there, still as anything, on the green leaves. And the flowers are starting as well. Crocuses and daffodils. It's lovely. And we talk too. She's so kind.'

'What do you talk about?'

'I tell her about the children. When they were small. All the little things they did, all the things I remember. Their drawings and Maria helping me make cakes, and Stephen showing me his drawings. Oh, and Christmas as well. Opening their presents. I used to love it when they were small and they opened their little presents. And I told her about Mama and Dada who I loved so much as well. I was an only child and I loved them so much. I just don't know why they agreed to him, why they wanted me to marry him. I don't understand that at all. Maybe they didn't know. Do you think that was it, Maureen? That they didn't know?'

'I'm sure that was it. There was no reason for them to know was there? Maybe nobody knew.'

She wasn't listening.

'And Sister Patricia says I can help with the garden as it gets warmer. But she has to make sure that Sister Judith agrees because she's in charge of the garden. But I'm sure she will. She will agree, won't she?'

'I'm sure she will, Margaret.'

Out of the corner of her eye Maureen could see that Sister Patricia was outside the door. It had only been a few minutes it seemed. There was light knock and the door opened.

'It's time to go I'm afraid.'

As before Sister Patricia waited outside while Maureen and Margaret embraced and said goodbye.

They walked quickly back to the entrance hall. Not speaking.

The Reverend Mother and Mrs Doyle were waiting for her. It looked like they were just finishing their conversation and Mrs D was ready to go.

'Thank you for coming Maureen. We'll see you again I hope.'

The Reverend Mother smiled briefly as she said this and then left through the other door, not saying anything more. Sister Patricia let them out and they walked over to the car and set off back home.

'How was she?'

'A lot worse I think. I'm sure she was better than that last week. It's like she's falling apart, I'm not even sure she knows what day it is. Is it doing her any good being there at all? I'm not sure it is.'

'Well if she went somewhere else it'd probably be a lot more unpleasant I would think, like a hospital or something. At least the sisters are kind enough, and the convent itself is pleasant, isn't it?'

'It is. She likes the garden she says. But, look, she's told him that I visited.'

'And he hasn't said anything to you has he?'

'No. Nothing. He's been no different at all.'

'And so do you think he's told the aunt?'

'I have no idea. It wouldn't surprise me. And thinking about it, I said to her how helpful you were, and her reply was a bit odd in a way.'

'How so?'

'She just said something like she was sure you were a great help, or something like that, but it was the way she said it, I'm not sure if it wasn't a bit sarcastic. I could be imagining it though.'

'Well, I'm not sure about her at all. I talked to an old friend of mine in Meath and she didn't know her and she said she'd ask around, check her out if you like. And no-one knew her. That could be nothing of course but usually there's a trace, usually someone will know someone won't they? It's not that big a place for mercy's sake.'

'Well she did say she'd been away, didn't she?'

'So you said.'

She stopped speaking while they overtook a donkey and cart, it could well have been the same one from the week before, she bibbed, he waved.

'Maureen, I'm sorry, I've put you in a very difficult position. I shouldn't have done that.'

'What do you mean?'

'Taking you over there without telling Shaughnessy. I didn't think that Margaret would tell him, and I knew the sisters wouldn't. But I didn't realise how ill she was. She doesn't know what she's doing, does she?'

'Mrs D, look, I was wondering why didn't you talk to her yourself, why haven't you gone in to see her?'

'Maybe I should have. I thought about it. But, God forgive me, I thought she might find it a bit shaming for someone like me to see her in that state. I thought it might make her worse in some way. Feel humiliated by him and then by seeing me as well. And I knew that you and she had become friends, so I thought that would be the better thing. For you to see her, and not me.'

'Well I'm glad I have seen her, but I'm not sure it does her any good.'

'Who knows what does her any good, Maureen? We can only do what we think is right.'

'Do you think I should tell him that I've been to see her?'

'If we'd told him after the first visit it wouldn't be too bad I suppose, but he knows, now, that we've kept it from him. But, look, I'll go and see him. I'll say I made you go. He knows what kind of person I am, always wanting to get my own way, a busybody. I know what people think Maureen, oh, I know what they think!'

She laughed as she said this last bit and Maureen did as well, almost giggled actually. But then Mrs D was serious again.

'You can apologise for not telling him, say I made you promise to keep it secret, something like that. But don't talk to him until after I've spoken to him. Don't worry, though, he won't want to upset me, and he definitely won't want to upset Mr D, that's for sure. Will he be in tonight?'

'He said after eight.'

'I'll come at eight fifteen then. Better dealt with sooner rather than later.'

They drove, leaving the subject behind, chatting about the countryside, and meals for Lent, and St Patrick's Day. And it wasn't long till they were back in Bray. Maureen left Mrs D at her house and walked home. She realised, as she walked back on her own, that she was frightened now. She could almost imagine him being there now, waiting for her, already knowing that she'd been to see Margaret. And being furious with her from the moment she entered the house, and Mrs Doyle not being there to protect her.

But, of course, he was not there. The house was empty and quiet when she opened the front door and, after changing, she got on with preparing the children's tea.

The children came home, and they all ate together at around six. They chatted normally of course, but Maureen found herself preoccupied. Even if Shaughnessy was wary of the Doyles, which he was of course, that didn't mean he couldn't make life difficult for her. He could easily make her uncomfortable without doing anything that the Doyles could actually complain about. He did that already didn't he? And if the aunt came back, and was on his side, it could all get very unpleasant. In different circumstances, she knew that she would just look for another job, it'd be easy enough to find one, Mrs Doyle would make sure she got something in Bray if she wanted it, or she could go elsewhere, even go to London. But she felt for the children and for Margaret, as well. She didn't want to just desert them, although she had no idea if she was really helping them in any way at all.

Shaughnessy came home exactly at eight. The hall clock chimed as he came through the door.

She came out into the hall.

'Evening, Maureen. Is everything Ok?'

'It is, sir.'

'Right, I'll just wash up and I'll eat. Is it ready to serve?'

'It is sir.'

'Five minutes then.'

He went upstairs. She heard him say hello to the children and then go into the bathroom. She went into the kitchen and got his meal ready to take into the dining room. And a couple of minutes later she heard his steps again on the stairs, coming down for his meal.

She looked at the clock as she passed it with his food on the tray. It was about eight twelve. He had time to start before the Mrs Doyle said she'd come.

At eight sixteen there was a ring at the front door.

'Oh hello, Maureen. Is Mr Shaughnessy in? Would you mind

asking him if he's got a few minutes for me?'

'Of course, Mrs Doyle. Right away. Mr Shaughnessy's having his dinner at the moment, though.'

'Well, ask him, anyway, would you?'

All this loud enough for him to hear. Mrs Doyle looked serious, but gave just the slightest wink and a touch of the hand as she passed her coming into the house.

Maureen went into the dining-room.

'Mrs Doyle is here, sir.'

He didn't look pleased, but got up from the table.

'I'll see her in the sitting-room.'

He went through the door connecting the rooms and Maureen went back to the hall and showed Mrs Doyle into the sitting-room. She left them to it. Shaughnessy shut the door, and Maureen went back to the kitchen and sat down to wait.

She heard the murmur of their voices, she was expecting anger or raised voices at some point, but there was none of that.

They were in there for fifteen minutes, sixteen minutes to be exact, on the kitchen clock.

She heard the sitting room door open. And his steps coming towards the kitchen.

'Maureen, come into the sitting-room would you.'

He had just looked around the kitchen door and then disappeared again.

She took a deep breath and went after him.

Mrs Doyle was sitting down, looking relaxed enough, giving nothing away.

He sat down as well, leaving Maureen standing there trying to look at the both of them.

It was Mrs Doyle that spoke.

'Maureen, I've told Mr Shaughnessy about our two visits to see Mrs Shaughnessy. I said to him that the Reverend Mother, a cousin of mine as you know, had specifically asked for you to go to the convent because Mrs Shaughnessy, herself, had asked to see you. And, for whatever reason, Margaret had requested that no-one be told about it, had asked that it be kept confidential. That was the word she used. Confidential. So we, myself and the Reverend Mother I mean, decided to respect her wishes. In hindsight though, and as you said to me yourself Maureen earlier today, we should have told Mr Shaughnessy. And I apologise for that. It was done with the best of intentions I can assure you, Mr Shaughnessy. And Maureen is absolutely blameless.'

He was just watching. His face gave little away, and then he spoke.

'Maureen, Mrs Doyle has explained everything to me and, although, I have to say, I'm disappointed that you didn't tell me, I do understand why. You're only a slip of a thing after all, and you'd find Mrs Doyle and the Reverend Mother a formidable pair. Anyone would I'd say.'

He smiled at them both as he said this.

'Anyway. All I would say is please don't tell the children anything about your seeing their mother. And any visits in the future, by Maureen I mean, not you Mrs Doyle, of course, should be agreed with me in advance. Is that reasonable?'

He was being charming.

'It is, sir.'

'Good. Are we OK then Mrs Doyle?'

'We are.'

'Grand. Would you like a drink of something before you go?'

'No, no, Francis is expecting me back, he'll be wanting to know how things went.'

'Well then, give him my regards, would you?'

'I will, of course. Will you show me out Maureen?'

Maureen looked across to him, and he nodded.

'I will, ma'am, of course.'

CHAPTER TWENTY-TWO

She lay awake that night, longer than usual. And woke earlier the next morning as well. Things had changed and she wanted to make some kind of sense out of it.

During her visits to Margaret, her secret visits, there had been a kind of hope. It had seemed somehow worthwhile, even though, admittedly, Margaret had seemed worse that second time. But Maureen had still felt that it was all a temporary thing that would be solved after a few weeks rest and quiet with the nuns, after some gardening with Sister Judith, after some quite kindness from Sister Patricia.

She blamed Shaughnessy for her being there, she had no doubt that he was to blame, with his aggression and his violence, and his coldness. But at the same time there was something else as well. Although Maureen had recognised that Margaret was ill she had, up to last night, blamed it all on him. But now, and she didn't know exactly why, now she understood that the illness was more than that, more than the result of his attitudes and actions. He had made it worse but there was something wrong inside Margaret herself. She was sad. She was lost. She was alone. And it seemed to Maureen that Margaret had probably always been lost, and lonely, and sad.

There was a slight lightness of dawn visible through her attic window and she knew she had to get up soon. Had to get the day started.

And she wondered about Margaret, also waking up, maybe, at that very moment. What was she thinking? At that very moment? Maureen had never thought that before. Never thought of Margaret waking up in that small, sparsely furnished room. Every day, waking up and realising that she was alone again. Did she have a waking moment when she was not aware that she would not see her children that day, when she was not aware that she was unhappy. Did she have a moment when she looked forward to the day? And then the truth fell on her, again, each day, the truth toppled on to her, crushing her yet again.

Margaret was ill. She was very ill. He had made it worse, she knew that. Without him Margaret might have stayed at home. She would still have been sad and alone, but she would have seen her children, she would have had some kind of hope.

Maureen heard movement in the house. Even though she was always first up she often heard the start of people waking and moving, mattresses creaking, feet on floorboards.

Did the children think about their mother when they woke up? Did he think about Margaret when he woke up? Did he think he loved her, did he think he cared for her? Maureen had no idea.

She got up, and washed and dressed, and went downstairs to start the breakfast.

On the Friday Deidre turned up as she said she would. Maureen was surprised that she was almost glad to see Deidre when she opened the front door and saw her smile. She had two big suitcases with her, and there was a car pulling away, so Maureen thought she must have taken a cab from the station. It would have been difficult, almost impossible, to carry them all that way on her own.

The children were glad to see Deidre as well. They didn't jump up and kiss her, or embrace her, or anything like that, but Maureen could see that they were glad she was back. She lightened the atmosphere in the house, so everyone felt better, including him it seemed.

And Lent was coming to its close.

St Patrick's Day was in the week before Palm Sunday. Maureen made a good meal for everyone on that day, breaking the fast, and she heard the four of them, the two children and Deidre and Mr S enjoying the meal and laughing as she ate her own meal in the kitchen. The children and Deidre came into the kitchen after they had eaten, thanking Maureen, and doing a bit of the table clearing themselves, to help her.

Julia had suggested that she got out with her that evening, but she didn't want to. Instead saying that, straight after Easter, she would definitely be out dancing with Julia.

During Easter week she went again to see Margaret, with Mrs D. And this time Mrs D came into the room with her as well. Margaret was surprised to see Mrs D, but after a moment's hesitation, she seemed pleased to see her. She said all the usual things, about the children, about him, and she said she had been doing some gardening with Sister Judith. Then she just seemed to drift away from them, as if she had forgotten they were there.

They drove back. Not talking about Margaret, there seemed little to say.

And Easter Sunday came at last. After Mass they had a good dinner back at the house, relieved that Lent was over.

To Maureen's total surprise Shaughnessy took the children to see their mother that very afternoon, after they had eaten. It was the first time they had gone. Deidre went as well.

'We're going to the convent Maureen, we'll be back for tea as usual.'

She opened the door to them at about five. The two children came in first, Stephen and Maria looking sad and unhappy. The two adults behind them looking serious.

Maureen went back to the kitchen, and after a few minutes Stephen came in followed by Maria.

'Why didn't you say, Maureen? Dada says you've seen Mama, and you didn't say anything?'

Maureen felt guilty.

'Your Ma didn't want anything said. Not just yet, not at the time anyway.'

She knew this wasn't the real truth but she couldn't think of anything else.

'Was she pleased to see you? Did you all go in at the same time?'

'Deidre stayed in the car. Dada and Maria and I went in.'

'It was awful, Maureen. She looked so ill, and so sad. When will she be better do you think?'

Maria was almost in tears.

'Come here, darling, let me give you a hug.'

And she held Maria tight.

'Hopefully she'll be better soon. God willing she'll be home before you know it.'

She saw Stephen's face over Maria's shoulder. He didn't believe a word of it.

CHAPTER TWENTY-THREE

It was only a week after Easter that Maureen became eighteen. With all the stuff that had been going on she had virtually forgotten about her birthday, but at the end of that Easter Sunday after the children had gone to bed, when she was sitting in the kitchen alone, she remembered the date.

Mama wrote to her regularly, not a long letter or anything, just a short note in her rather scrabby handwriting, and a couple of weeks ago she had mentioned the birthday and said it would be nice to see her then, if it was possible. Maureen hadn't really thought about it, she had put it to the back of her mind. But now she thought it would be great to see her parents. To go home for her birthday.

On the Monday morning she spoke to Mr Shaughnessy as he was eating his breakfast. He was on his own at the table.

'I was wondering if it would be possible to take next Sunday off, sir? It's my birthday and my Mama has asked if I could go home and see them.'

'And how old would you be, Maureen?'

'Eighteen, sir.'

'Eighteen eh? And it's the Sunday that's your birthday is it?'

'It is.'

'Well I would say, Maureen, that you deserve the whole weekend off. You could go home on the Saturday morning and come back Sunday evening. It would give you a bit more time at home, wouldn't it? Or come back Monday morning. I'm sure we can manage.'

He was looking at her smiling, in that friendly way he sometimes had.

'That's very kind of you sir. I could get back Sunday, that wouldn't be a problem.'

'Fine. Well, let's say after breakfast on Saturday then. Would that be OK?'

'That'd be great, sir.'

And it was. She'd have a bit of time to get home, and maybe she could go out on the Saturday with Ann and Annie and Greta, and she could have most of the Sunday with Mama and Dada. He had been kind.

She wrote home and said she would be home on Saturday afternoon and she would have to go back again on the Sunday afternoon.

She told Julia, of course, that it was her birthday on the Sunday, and Julia absolutely insisted that they would go out on the Friday night.

Needless to say, on that Friday, Julia told everyone that it was Maureen's eighteenth birthday and it took a great deal of resolve for her to avoid the excesses that Julia was prone to. Julia, herself, did not avoid the excesses, but they all had a great time, a dance, and a laugh together. And they sang Happy Birthday to Maureen. And she went home, not too early and not too late.
On the Saturday she dealt with the breakfast quickly and then, as she was clearing away the crockery in the kitchen, the two children and Deidre and Mr S came into the kitchen.

It was Maria that spoke.

'Maureen we'd like to wish you a very happy eighteenth birthday because you've been so kind to us, and we love having you here.'

And she handed Maureen a little parcel and an envelope.

Maureen didn't know what to do.

'Open it, go on open it.'

So she opened the little parcel and inside was a brooch with a beautiful green stone in it, and she opened the card and it was signed by them all. She wanted to cry, all of a sudden, she wanted to cry.

'Thank you so much. Thank you, thank you.'

And then Shaughnessy spoke.

'We won't hold you up now, but we hope you have a great birthday, and we'll see you back tomorrow evening.'

Maria and Deidre each gave her a little quick kiss before they trooped out. Shaughnessy was last and, as he left, he put something down on the table.

'Just a little something for the journey.'

A ten-shilling note. He'd disappeared before she could thank him.

She had everything ready to go, of course, so as soon as the kitchen was tidy she went upstairs, put her coat on, and left for the station, shouting a 'bye' as she shut the door.

It was a bright morning, and she was warm after hurrying with the breakfast and everything.

Walking up to the town, to the station, she felt free. It was good to leave the house behind even if only for a couple of days. Getting into Dublin was easy and, then, it felt great to be on the train down to Waterford, not particularly crowded on that Saturday morning.

As the train moved out of Dublin her mind wandered. Thinking about the crowds on the train she had gone to Dublin on, the woman giving her a little encouraging smile. She remembered that woman now, almost with gratitude, because of her kindness, because she had taken the trouble to speak to her. She must have known that Maureen was anxious. It was probably absolutely obvious. She must have looked like a meek little frightened mouse on that crowded, noisy, train. Obvious to her husband too, buying her that drink and that Penguin biscuit as well, and smiling, to cheer her up

And Theresa meeting her. Theresa had been preoccupied hadn't she? She was thinking about something else. Maureen realised that now, but she hadn't then, not really. Because Theresa was a grown woman, to her, a grown-up. Theresa had written a couple of times, in the last three months, just to say that all was well in London and they were not to worry about her. And the fact that she said that made Maureen worry, a little bit anyway.

The business with Mrs S, with Margaret, had changed Maureen, she knew that. She wasn't so naïve that she didn't think that adults never had problems, but actually seeing it in reality had made her realise what could happen to people when things go wrong. And made her realise, also, that Theresa had been really troubled about something or other. But they weren't close enough for her to ask. Maybe it was just a boyfriend, maybe she'd had a crush on someone and it hadn't worked out. Maybe it was just as simple as that.

As they travelled she could see the mountains in the distance and that made her think more about Margaret as well. She was over there somewhere. In her little room. Or maybe in the garden. It looked like a fine day to be in the garden. And she wondered how that dreadful change in Margaret could have taken place. From the seemingly confident woman who had opened the door to Theresa and herself, to that frail, breakable, meagre-looking soul she had seen just a week or so ago. But the woman who opened the door, on that September, had not been strong either, she knew that now. She had seemed assured, seemed in charge, but she hadn't been. She couldn't have been could she? She was already tormented in some way or other. And then she thought of the bruising in that darkened kitchen. She had shown it to her deliberately. She could have hidden away, that would have been quite possible, it would have been what he wanted. But she didn't. She waited in the kitchen knowing that Maureen would come home, knowing that she would come into the kitchen. She wanted to show her, she wanted to share her pain with someone, and she had chosen Maureen.

Yes, she had chosen Maureen. Was that because there was no-one else? She had no family. She could have told Mrs Doyle. But at the same time that would have been impossible too. Poor Margaret could never tell one of her women friends, they didn't do that, they didn't tell about such things, they couldn't do that. Even if they already knew. Mrs Doyle had known, she may not have known exactly what was happening, but she knew that he was unpleasant and she knew that Margaret was suffering. She definitely knew that. But there was nothing that could be done.

What did the children know? Was it a bit like Mrs Doyle? That they knew things weren't right, but didn't know exactly what that meant, in reality? They must have known that their mother was unhappy. But how would they know that? Margaret had never given much away, she kept things inside her. Did Stephen have an idea, or Maria? Maureen felt it was more likely that the boy understood that things were not right. He was quiet, he listened, he saw things, he was her firstborn, he was close to his mother. He would have known something.

And now the children had seen the mother. What would that do to them? Perhaps it was better that they knew everything. At least they would not be wondering what was going on, they would know that their mother was ill. But how would it have been for them seeing her, like she is now, in that little room. Margaret would have made an effort, surely, like she did when Maureen came. She would have made an effort for the children, but it may not have been enough. It took very little for that veneer to crack, for it to disappear entirely. And when she saw her beloved children walk into that room it would surely have been too much for her. She would not have been able to pretend. She would have cried, Maureen knew that she would have cried. And what would he have done? Did he hold her? Or did he stand back and watch? All four of them in that tiny room. It would have been too much, and his size would have dominated everything. Maureen could see it all. See them all crushed into that cell. Margaret would almost have been pushed up against the wall. She would have tried for the children but she would have been wary of him as well. Scared of him.

Maureen shook her head. She didn't want to think about it. She wanted to shake the thoughts out of her consciousness. She knew that the journey was moving to her part of the country now and she forced herself to think about Mama and Dada who would be waiting at Dungarvan, she knew they would be waiting there for her. And the thought of that made her smile.

At Waterford she had to rush to get on the local train home. It crossed the bridge going south and she felt comforted by the familiarity of it all, and by the peace and quiet of the country, peaceful even with the train steaming, puffing, through it. The mountains still there, solid on the right-hand side.

She was eighteen tomorrow, and she did feel more grown up

now. It had taken this bit of a journey, being away from the house in Bray, for her to know that she, herself, had changed over the last few months. She was not the girl who'd got on that train in September, not the girl who had waved goodbye to Mama and Dada as their figures became smaller in the distance. She had seen things that she didn't like, but she had met people that she did like, and met them in a way that would not have been possible if she'd stayed at home in Dungarvan. Met them as her own person, met them as Maureen herself, rather than as the Maureen Kelleher who everyone remembered running around like a little ragamuffin with scabs on her knees, or going to First Communion, or just being the sister of Theresa or Dympna or whoever it might be. No as Maureen herself. And she was very glad about that.

The train went the last few miles into Dungarvan. And she felt a pleasant familiarity with what she was seeing; a landscape and a view that she had known, one way or another, for the eighteen years that she had been alive, except, indeed, for these last few months in Bray.

As the train pulled into the station she lowered the window to look out and see who was there. And she saw Mama watching the carriages as they each slowly passed her, trying to catch a glimpse of Maureen and then, all of a sudden, seeing her, coming along with her head out of the window. She waved, they both waved.

Mama had looked older back on that platform in Dublin, with Dada, but she didn't now. Here on the platform in Dungarvan she looked her old self, alive, smiling, waiting for her daughter, she looked to Maureen like she always had, like her mother.

She got down from the train and gave her a hug.

'Where's Dada? There's nothing wrong is there?'

'No. He had to work today, that's all. He'll see you back at home.'

They walked off the platform, Maureen saying hello to Jimmy and Mick who were hanging about as usual.

It felt great to be back. There was something relaxing about being there. She knew which shop came next as they walked along the street and recognised the face, at least, of almost everyone she saw. They were stopped three times in the first couple of minutes while people asked her how it was all going, how she was enjoying Dublin, and Bray was it? Where your Mam said you were working now? A grand place Bray, so they say.

And they got the afternoon bus out to the house. Only a few minutes, but too far to walk, unless you had to.

And Dada was there. She had worried for a second when he had not been at the station, but he was fine. The level-crossing needed looking after and there was no-one else available. And he looked great as well, in his shirt sleeves, out in the garden now, doing a bit of tidying-up; like Mama, he looked more relaxed than he had in Dublin. They were happier here, almost younger here in some way.

And so the afternoon and the evening went. Tea and chat with Mama and Dada, and with the neighbours, Elizabeth and the other Maureen, and Joseph Kelly, all dropping in for a chat, curious to know how she'd been getting on working all that way from home. Would they be nice people you're working for? And you get your time off? And the children, what are they like? Do you get into the city much? It's a great place, Dublin, isn't it?

It was fun sitting there in the little kitchen just chatting away about nothing, and hearing the little bits of gossip, which were really no different to the bits of gossip that there had always been, and having a cup of tea and a scone that Mam had made specially because she knew that Maureen liked them. She felt like the little girl that she had always been in that house, but like a grown-up as well, a traveller who had returned with tales to tell.

The girls were working but dropped in at six. Ann and Annie and Greta, the three of them, whooping with delight when they saw her and all hugging each other in the tiny kitchen, with Mama and Dada, and Joseph who hadn't left yet, looking on, smiling at the four of them with their antics.

They arranged to go into town a little later. The four of them together. And they went to the dance and they danced, and sometimes they stood outside and chatted. And Maureen told them about everything, about how nice Margaret was and the children, and about Julia, who was as mad as a hatter, and about going in to Dublin, and going to Bewley's. But she didn't say anything about the troubles, about the breakdown, and Shaughnessy himself, or about the convent. For some reason she couldn't bring herself to say anything about those things, not here outside the dance hall anyway. Maybe at another time she would say something to them, but it would have felt like some kind of betrayal to just gossip to the girls about it, it was all too terrible for that. She would tell them, but at another time, in another place.

They danced and they laughed. And more boys asked her to dance than she could ever remember happening before. And she knew them all. And she accepted every offer with delight knowing it was a night to enjoy, a night where nothing would happen except this laughter and dancing, all taking place in the freedom of being home again for just these few happy hours. As she became eighteen.

She got home late. And slept. And was woken up for Mass. And went along to church with Mama and Dada, meeting the girls on the way. Chatting and saying hello in the warm spring morning sunshine. Almost everyone they saw waving and shouting out hello, and how's things, to her. And some, if they knew, shouting out their birthday greetings to her as well.

She had gone to communion in this church for many years. She walked and queued with all those that she had walked and queued with forever, or that's what it seemed like. And it was comforting in a friendly sort of way to be back here. The odd smile of recognition as people saw her, the odd smile of friendship or brief touch on the arm. She was at home here. Not like in Bray.

After Mass they stood outside for a while and even more people came up to her to see how she was, even the likes of the old Slattery brothers, and Phil Dwyer, the farmer, who wouldn't normally say much to her in the normal course of events.

Mama invited the girls to dinner as well. They had to eat early as Maureen had to get the train to Waterford and then up to Dublin; she wished now she'd agreed to go back Monday, but it was too late for that. And it was a great meal, lamb and potatoes and all the rest. Specially for the birthday girl. And a scarf from Ann and Annie and Greta, and another little brooch from Mama and Dada. She wore it straight away. And then she realised that she had to dash. The girls said they would go with her to the station. Michael, from down the lane, had said he would take her in the van when she was ready, Mama had organised this because there was no bus on the Sunday.

And so off they went, waving to Mama and Dada, and then a quick goodbye at the station because Michael would give the girls a lift back, but only if they went straight away. She waved and shouted goodbye to them as they left.

And Maureen walked out onto the platform. An empty platform, not one other person to be seen. It was a warm afternoon now, almost hot. She could smell the sea not far away, and the tang of tar and oil from the tracks and points and sleepers, a familiar smell to her. And she could taste that country smell as well, it was definitely there, hiding somewhere in the air, grass, silage and fertiliser, manure.

She wasn't exactly sure what being eighteen was all about. But, even so, she did feel different on that day, in this place. Seeing all those faces, those friends, those acquaintances in such a short time had sort of compressed her life for her. If she'd searched for particular memories she could have easily found them, but she didn't need to because every single memory was in those many different faces, those smells, that communion walk, the crowded kitchen, Mama's hug and Dada's shirtsleeves, the scones, and in the bed that she had fallen into last night, and had been gently woken from, that sunny, warm, spring morning.

So she stood on the platform breathing everything in. Happy. Content. Until she heard the chugging of the train and woke herself up. There were others on the platform now and Jimmy had appeared as well. Shouting her name and waving to her as he unrolled his flag, ready to get the train on its way when it was ready to go.

It was a quiet journey back. She felt used to it now, as if it was just any old journey. And, although she was sad to leave Mama and Dada again, she was looking forward to getting back to Bray, because it was a sort of home for her now. Well, for the moment at any rate.

CHAPTER TWENTY-FOUR

When Deidre had returned, after her couple of days away, she took over. Took over in the sense of being the lady of the house. But not in an unpleasant way, it has to be said. And neither did she try to make out she was taking Margaret's place. If asked, she always said she was the children's aunt and that she was helping out while their poor mother was recovering from her illness.

Mrs D had done further research. She would not leave things alone, as Maureen knew, she was like a dog with a bone. And to her, and Maureen's, surprise she discovered that Deidre was related, in some way, to Mrs S.

'She's a cousin of sorts, apparently, maybe fifth or sixth cousin if you can have such a thing. Seventh even.'

Maureen had come to like Deidre, but Mrs D was less convinced.

Nevertheless, she became a kind of housekeeper. Which was the best description really, because she had no real idea of how to be a housekeeper. It was Maureen who did everything, decided on the shopping lists, decided what they would eat, organised the laundry, got the children sorted for school. Deidre helped here and there, she went to the shops with Maureen at least a couple of times a week, she would sometimes help with the bedding, but she didn't do cleaning.

But Maureen liked her, and they had a bit of a laugh, and generally got on well. One day Maureen dared to ask her why she always locked her room, because she still did that, even after a month or so.

‘Why do you ask Maureen? Do you think I’ve got secrets that I want to keep locked away? Is that it? Things I don’t want you to find out?’

‘I’ve no idea Deidre, no idea at all.’

Maureen had called Deidre ma’am at the beginning but she wouldn’t have any of it and had insisted she be called Deidre. She didn’t seem to care if Shaughnessy approved or not.

‘Well, I’ll tell you. I do have secrets like anyone else, anyone who tells you they’ve no secrets is a liar. That’s the first thing you should know, every single person in the world has secrets. And you should remember it too. Everyone has their little secrets that they don’t want anyone else to know. I bet you do have secrets, Maureen. I bet you do. And you will have them in the future, Maureen, you will have them then, as well.’

She stopped talking after she said this and smiled at Maureen in a cheeky kind of way, leaving just a little a bit of space before she started again.

‘But, anyway, leaving that aside, the actual reason I lock the room is it’s just a habit, it’s as simple as that. I stayed in boarding houses and the like in London, and in New York, and in Boston as well, and you get in the habit of locking your room. Because if you don’t you’ll lose everything, there are thieves everywhere, I can tell you that for sure. So I just do it out of habit. That’s the absolute truth of it!’

Deidre smiled at her.

‘But it wouldn’t worry me if you went in there Maureen, because you wouldn’t steal anything and you certainly wouldn’t look at anything that you shouldn’t. I would trust you implicitly, Maureen, I would trust you entirely.’

And Maureen blushed inside, ashamed, hoping desperately

that it didn't show.

The bonus about having Deidre in the house was that Maureen now felt perfectly at ease going out in the evening and going to the dance at the weekends. She'd felt unsure about that when Margaret had gone away, but now she felt more relaxed about seeing Julia and having a bit of a good time. And, in fact, Deidre encouraged her to get out and enjoy herself, always making a point of asking for details the next day after breakfast. Maureen suspected that Deidre was a lot more like Julia than herself, suspected that she had been a bit of a wild thing when she was a younger woman. And, if it had been possible, acceptable, Deidre wouldn't have minded going dancing even now, would have loved it in fact.

Maureen was now prepared to have a good time on the summer Saturday evenings and Sunday afternoons. Rather surprisingly, though, Julia had become a little bit more sensible. Part of the reason being that she now had a boyfriend called Declan. And it was Declan that introduced Maureen to George.

CHAPTER TWENTY-FIVE

It was June when she met George. She had been going out again since Easter. Every week. She had met a few boys that she liked but there hadn't been one who had really grabbed her attention. Julia had started with Declan a few weeks before and this had sort of made things awkward for Maureen because there wasn't someone to go to the dance with, like two girls having a night out. She could still go with Julia, who might meet Declan on the way, or when she got there, but it wasn't quite the same as going out as two single girls.

One June Saturday evening when Maureen and Julia walked up to the dance hall they saw that Declan was talking to another boy. Maureen thought he might be just an acquaintance of Dec's who would disappear when the girls arrived. But he didn't.

'Hello there, girls, you have to say hello to my friend George. We went to school together. George, this is my lovely Julia and this is her friend Maureen.'

George looked ever so slightly embarrassed at Declan's introduction. There was no reason why he should have done, but he did nevertheless.

He was quite tall, a bit taller than Dec, dressed in his suit he looked smart, and clean as well. He had brown hair and a kind of roundish face, a very pleasant face, attractive, maybe not handsome, but attractive. And he had a smile. After his brief embarrassment, he smiled. And Maureen liked his smile.

Maureen looked quickly at Julia and realised immediately

that this was a kind of blind date that Dec and Julia had set up. But she didn't mind.

'Hello Maureen. It's a pleasure to meet you.'

He had a calm voice, a pleasant voice.

They went into the dance together but Maureen made sure that she danced with whoever asked. She had enjoyed her night out back in Dungarvan and she decided to do the same here. And, of course, George asked her to dance a couple of times and she did so, and then a third time as well. After their third dance he asked her if she'd like a mineral and after a second or two's hesitation she said yes. She drank her drink with him. And then she was approached and asked to dance by a boy she knew the name of, Dermot she thought, and she agreed. And after that she danced with other boys as well.

The two of them, Dec and George, went off somewhere, and Julia took Maureen outside for a break.

'He likes you Maureen. I could see that straight away.'

'Do you think so?'

'You know he does. It's plain obvious.'

'Oh well.'

Julia smoked a cigarette and told her about Declan, how nice he'd been to her, that she was thinking he might be the one for her. She thought he might even think about proposing. Maybe not at this exact point, but soon enough.

'And do you think you'd accept, Julia? If he did?'

She stopped for a second and thought, smoking her cigarette.

'Do you know, it's a funny thing, but now you ask I'm not exactly sure that I would. We'll have to see how things go. But anyway, that George is interested in you, that's definite. I'm one hundred percent sure of that.'

They went back inside and she danced with a couple of boys. But she found she was looking around, despite herself, to see if George was anywhere to be seen. He was still off somewhere with Declan it looked like. And then he appeared and when the dance finished he came straight over to her and they had the last couple of dances together. He asked if he could see her home. And she said yes, that would be fine.

They left the dance hall together and started their walk back, not saying anything at all for the first minute or so. And then he asked her about herself. She told him the usual things, the things she would tell anyone who asked, or most people who asked. The things she had told Margaret and Mrs Doyle, and Julia as well. Or some of it anyway. Where she came from, a bit about Mama and Dada and the family, her jobs and why she had come to Bray. She told him nothing at all about Margaret because she didn't want just anyone to know those things, she might tell him, but not yet. And she asked him about himself and he told her.

His family lived in Dún Laoghaire. His father worked at Guinness's, and he had three brothers and two sisters. The sisters were married and two of the brothers worked at Guinness's as well and the other brother was a priest. George was the youngest and the black sheep, or the disappointment at any rate. For some reason she wasn't surprised when he said this, she hadn't expected it but she wasn't surprised. And she said she was sure that could not be true, that he was a disappointment. He said he hadn't done as well at school as the others, and he'd got into a bit of trouble there as well, which the others had never done.

When she heard him speak she could, now, hear his disappointment in himself, he was annoyed at himself, as well, for letting people down. He had a job at the moment with the railway, he worked in a signal box near to Dublin but he was not going to stay there. He had decided that when he had saved a bit he would be going to England. To London probably.

She hadn't expected any of this. It was quite exhausting to listen to because in such a short time he had told her a lot about himself. He had listened to her speak about herself but he hadn't asked any questions and then he had immediately told her about his disappointment.

They reached her gate. Stopped. Silent first.

'Would you be free tomorrow afternoon? We could go for a walk along the prom, it promises to be another lovely day.'

Even at that hour of the night it was warm, comfortably warm, and the next day, in all likelihood would be a hot one.

Maureen thought she had two options. She could say she was busy, she could put him off, she could give him the message that she had considered him, and she had decided no. Or she could say yes. In those fractions of a second, and that's all they were, she decided that she wanted to see him again, even with his disappointments, and with his desire to go away and try and do better elsewhere.

'That would be nice. Like you say it'll be a hot day, and a walk by the sea would be nice. Could you call for me at half two, maybe?'

'I will. I'll be here at half-two on the dot.'

'Great. I'll see you then.'

He smiled, looking relieved at the same time, and after hesitating for a second, unsure, he turned to go, and she went directly up to the house without turning back.

As usual the house was quiet, no light in the kitchen, and she tiptoed up the stairs to her bedroom.

In bed she lay back and thought about George. She liked him.

He was nice looking and he had a nice voice. And she liked his disappointment, in an odd sort of way she liked his disappointment. She slept.

She was quite excited the next day, looking forward to seeing George. Deidre could see there was something going on and tried to get Maureen to tell her, and Maureen would only admit she was seeing someone later, although of course she couldn't help blushing. Which made Deidre roar with laughter.

She saw Julia at Mass, and Julia already knew that Maureen was seeing George that afternoon, Declan had found out and told her somehow. It had all been planned by Dec and Julia and, of course, they were very pleased that their little plan had come to fruition. Julia said she had met George a couple of times and he seemed a very nice boy. And his family had a bit of money, not rich of course, nothing like that, but they had a little bit of money, working in Guinness's. And there was a priest in the family as well, the older brother. Just right for a little country mouse like you Maureen. Julia loved all this, and Maureen was embarrassed. But at the same time she was glad, she discovered that she was glad she had met George, she didn't know exactly why she was glad, but she was, and she was glad she was seeing him later on that day. She was excited she was seeing him later on that day.

Maureen got the dinner sorted and cleaned up as quickly as she could. Deidre gave her a hand to put everything away and then shooed her upstairs to get ready for her 'date'.

She washed and tidied her hair and put on her summer frock and, it being almost time, she went downstairs to wait in the kitchen. Deidre came in as if to chat, stood herself by the kitchen door, and when the doorbell rang she made sure that it was her that opened it, edging Maureen away so she couldn't get there first.

'Oh hello. Is Maureen there?'

'She is, I think. Who shall I say?'

'It's George, she'll be expecting me.'

'Maureen, are you there? It's George.'

She knew that Deidre was doing all this for a laugh, when she turned as if to look for Maureen she gave a wink and then deliberately got in her way for a second before letting her past.

'You won't be late back now will you. Half-five at the latest!'

This was all a performance and Maureen knew it. She went through the front door and made sure she shut it behind her to stop Deidre from any more mischief.

'Is she the woman you work for?'

'She is, sort of. Mrs Shaughnessy is ill, she's away in hospital. And Miss Maguire, Deidre, she's a cousin of some kind, so she's a kind of temporary housekeeper.'

'She seemed pretty strict didn't she? Saying all that about getting back.'

'She was playing the fool, she's good fun really, but anyway I do have to get back to do the tea. She didn't mean anything by it though.'

George seemed to take it all seriously. She thought he was annoyed with Deidre for coming out with all that stuff about getting back.

They walked towards the town.

He asked her more about her family and about Dungarvan, so she told him about her little trip home for her birthday and how she had good fun when she was there. She also told him about her sisters in Watford and that Theresa was in London as well, but she didn't really know what she was doing there.

'Everyone has to leave, don't they? If you want to make a living you have to leave unless you're a priest or a lawyer or something.'

'Couldn't you have gone to work with your father? Didn't you say your brothers worked at the brewery, couldn't you have gone there as well?'

'I could have. I'm not sure, but probably. I didn't want to though. The truth is that I want to do something on my own. If I'm absolutely honest I want to show them I can do something on my own.'

'So when do you think you'll go?'

'I'm saving what I can. It's pointless going over there with no money so I'm saving everything I can and then I'm going to go. Next spring, March or April. At the very latest.'

She found that she was relieved he hadn't said he was going next week or next month.

'Shall we go along the promenade.'

And they walked all the way along. It was a very hot day and there were loads of people around, locals and trippers from Dublin, out for the day or the afternoon. He told her a bit about his job and the people he worked with, and how he had met Declan at school and they'd stayed friends.
He said that Declan liked Julia a lot and he tried to get Maureen to say whether she thought Julia liked Declan. Maybe he had been asked to find out, she thought. She said that Julia did like Dec but she wasn't sure how much.

They had an ice cream together and laughed when his dropped out of the cone onto the pavement and then they went for a cup of tea and he bought her the cake that she liked.

It was a very pleasant afternoon. She watched him as they walked and as they sat in the café. She watched his face as he talked and she listened to his calm voice. Even when he was talking about his disappointments his voice was calm.

She thought that she did like him. She thought that she liked him enough to keep seeing him, if he asked her of course. She decided that she liked him enough and that, in itself, was enough.

He took her back home and they arrived at twenty-five past five. He asked her if she would like to go to the pictures next week and she said she would. And then she went in.

Deidre had sorted most of the tea out, but the kitchen was, inevitably, in a bit of a mess, so after she'd got changed she dashed down to get everything back in order.

'So how was it with George?'

'It was very pleasant. We walked down to the promenade and walked all the way along and we had an ice cream and then we had a cup of tea, and a cake.'

'So where is he from?"

'Dún Laoghaire.'

'And what does his father do?'

'He works in Guinness's.'

'And what does he do, himself?'

'He works on the railway at the moment but he's going to England in the next few months. He says there's more opportunities there.'

'Right. That's probably true I'd say. Do you like him, then?'

'He's nice, yes.'

‘And are you seeing him again?’

‘We’re going to the cinema next week.’

‘So do you think you’ll be off to England as well? With him I mean?’

‘God, Deidre, it’s too early to think about anything like that. Could you pass me that tea towel, and then we’ll get them into tea, shall we?’

But the truth was that, despite herself, almost subconsciously, Maureen had already considered the idea of going to England with him. She had half thought that George was including her in his idea at the very moment he was talking about it. Of course, she had no real idea if this was true, but she felt that she existed in his plan somewhere, even if he didn’t really know it himself. Yet at the same time she knew that, even though she would like him very much, and possibly be with him, marry him, over there in England, she wasn’t sure that she would ever love him.

And, for some reason, she didn’t care about that because she had the idea that she had met someone with whom she could live, and even have children with, and that in itself would be enough.

CHAPTER TWENTY-SIX

They went out every week. On the Saturday, and on the Sunday afternoon if his work allowed it. They went to the dance or they went to the pictures or they went for a walk on the Sunday if the weather was fine. One Saturday they went into Dublin. For no real reason, just to enjoy themselves.

Sometimes he came round during the week. Deidre had said he was quite welcome to come to the house and he could eat with Maureen in the kitchen any time. She said she had spoken to Shaughnessy about it and he was fine with the idea, just in case she was worried that he might not like it.

George did come to the house, probably once a week. But he didn't like to. There was something about her being a sort of servant that he didn't like. He didn't like the idea of eating in the kitchen as if he was below stairs, so to speak. It annoyed him. Even though the children usually came in and sat down and chatted to him; Maria liked George, and Stephen was happy to have a chat with him. And Shaughnessy would pop in occasionally and say hello and Deidre, of course, was always in and out. Poking her nose in and doing her little flirting thing that she couldn't resist doing.

Maureen thought sometimes that her kitchen was like her little kingdom where people came to see her, where people asked if they could come in, asked if she would mind if they sat down, they all asked, even Shaughnessy. But George didn't like it. She could see that he thought it put him at a disadvantage, that it made him a kind of servant himself. Which he hated.

And, of course, he was never invited into the other rooms,

the sitting room, or the dining room. Why would he be? He'd come to see Maureen. And he knew this. But despite himself he felt excluded. He wanted to be invited in there by Shaughnessy for a chat about this or that, for a drink maybe, to have a laugh about something, to discuss the hurling or the football or politics.
But while he was the boyfriend of the maid he wouldn't be. Or that was how he saw it anyway.

Maureen was aware of this discomfort. She could see it in him. And he'd said to her a couple of times that he didn't really like coming to the house. She'd asked him why. And he'd told her he just felt uncomfortable. He'd said he didn't feel quite welcome. Maureen knew this was nonsense because everyone was always very nice to him, everyone was very friendly. It was his disappointment again, she understood this now. He was always feeling that he hadn't quite done as well as he should. And every time he came into the Shaughnessy's house he went from the front door straight to the kitchen, seeing the other rooms on his left as he passed, but never invited in.

She enjoyed his company and they had pleasant times together. She was satisfied with that. He was a good-looking man, which shouldn't have mattered but it did. She liked to walk along with her pleasant-looking man. And when he was relaxed he could be charming and friendly, to people he met and girls in the cafes and the like. When they ran into Mrs Doyle, one day along the promenade, he was very polite, and he had a little joke with her about something or other. Mrs Doyle had commented when she saw her the next day, saying what a charming young man he was. Which pleased Maureen, and pleased him as well when she told him.

They went out from June onwards and Maureen eventually began to wonder if he would take her to meet his parents one day. She didn't expect this straight away of course, but by October or November she did begin to wonder. If Mama and

Dada hadn't been such a distance away she would certainly have taken him to see them, introduced him to them. And Dún Laoghaire was just down the road, a few minutes away really.

For some reason she was wary of asking him if she would be meeting his mother and father, meeting his family, soon. Whenever he spoke about them it was obvious that he had respect for them, he obviously didn't dislike them or anything like that, but he was sensitive about them, and she wondered if he was scared of them in some way. And, as she thought about it more, she wondered if he was ashamed of her. She wondered if he was scared of meeting them with her, scared of bringing home a young woman who was nothing more than servant, a housemaid. Perhaps they had a maid themselves. It was possible. Perhaps he thought they would laugh at him, laugh at her, laugh at him for his lack of ambition, his lack of achievement, reflected again in his choice of this poor country girl for a girl-friend.

She thought of discussing this with Deidre or Julia. She realised immediately that Julia was an impossibility because she was unable, in any way, to keep any kind of secret, unable to keep her mouth shut, especially about something like this. She would certainly talk to Declan about it. They were still going out together, although Julia was expressing some dissatisfaction about him, Maureen did not expect it to last beyond Christmas. However, Deidre was a possibility. Deidre wouldn't talk to anyone else about it, except maybe to Shaughnessy.

Deidre's relationship with Shaughnessy was a bit of a puzzle to Maureen. They got on well, even better now after her being in the house for a few months. And Maureen did wonder, sometimes, whether there might be more to it than met the eye. She still heard the occasional movement at night, but that could be anything at all, could be someone going to the bathroom, or just the house creaking away as it did sometimes. Occasionally there was another late-night laugh, just occasionally though. But Deidre had made the house a bit of a happier place, for everyone, and Maureen was grateful for that.

She could talk to Deidre about it. But if she did Deidre might take against George a bit, especially if she felt he was making Maureen unhappy, and that might show, she might start talking to him differently, and that would only make things worse not better.

She decided that she would talk directly to him. Take the bull by the horns. She would say that she would like to meet his parents, and that she would like to go to Dungarvan with him to meet her Mama and Dada.

'I was thinking that we could go down to Dungarvan for a day, before Christmas I mean. I'd like you to meet Mama and Dada. I've written them about you and Mama says they'd like to meet you.'

They were walking along the promenade. It was chilly, a bit windy. And as Maureen heard what she was saying she understood the implications. She was saying to him, are we a permanent item now, are we going to go the whole way, are we going to think about getting engaged, getting married? Strange as it seemed they had not directly talked about these things before. He had talked about going to England and she, herself, had said that she would probably go there as well. And there had been that feeling inside her, that assumption that they were going to be a couple, but they had avoided talking about certainties, or time-scales, or commitment. And not meeting each other's parents was a way of not committing yourself to each other. If you didn't do that it was always easy to walk away because, then, you only had to explain yourself to friends, maybe Julia and Deidre, or, in his case, Declan. And in the main they would be sympathetic to you, saying there was plenty more fish in the sea etc. etc. But if you'd met the parents that would be a different thing altogether because, like it or not, it meant the wedding was already being planned.

'We could, although it's a bit of a trek in one day, isn't it?

He seemed perfectly happy with the idea. There had been no pause, no thinking about it, he had replied as if it was the most natural thing in the world. Maureen hadn't actually mentioned George in her letters to Mama but that was only a white lie and was very easily remedied.

'We could start early and it wouldn't be a great problem. Deidre would do the breakfast for me I'm sure. A Saturday would be best. Maybe in November some time.'

'Fine. OK.'

'What about your family? I'd love to meet them, and, sure, that's only down the road isn't it?'

This time the reply was not immediate.

'We could I suppose. Although I'd have to warn you that my family are not great for visitors. Da especially. You shouldn't expect too much. You shouldn't expect anything, really.'

His voice had changed. He must have known what was coming after she had mentioned going to Dungarvan, he had seemed quite relaxed about that, but even mentioning his own family had changed his voice into a slower, tenser tone. Whenever he talked about his family, which was not often, his voice seemed to reflect an inner unhappiness, almost a despair.

'Oh, don't worry about that! We can just go and have a cup of tea, say hello, and we can get away without any problem. It's not as if we have to travel for hours to get there and the same to get back. It's not much more half an hour away is it?'

'No. Although mother'll not let you get away with a cup of tea.'

'Well, anyway, you sort it out. There's no hurry, anyway, is there? Whenever it suits you and them is fine with me. And I'll write to Mama as well. We'll have to pick a Saturday when you're not working. Anyway, look it's too cold and windy here for walking, let's get a cup of tea shall we?

She linked with him, pulled him to her. She could feel the tension in his body as she swung him round to go back towards the town, but it eased a little as they walked. She didn't mention their proposed family visits again that afternoon or the next couple of times that they met. But she did write to Mama. She told her that she had met a young man called George, and they had been going out a little while. He worked on the railway and his family lived in Dún Laoghaire and his father and brothers worked in Guinness's, and he also had a brother who was a priest. Mama would like the fact that they had a priest in the family, it lent a bit of style to things, and Guinness's was a very respectable place to work as well. She didn't say that she had never met this family, never met the priest. And she said that she and George would like to come down and see them both, just for a day trip, and would that be alright? She added that George was just a boyfriend and there was definitely no talk of anything else at the moment!

She sent the letter on the Tuesday and had a reply by Thursday. Mama said it would be great to see them both, both she and Dada were looking forward to meeting George, and Ann and Annie and Greta were annoyed they were coming on a Saturday, when they all had to work, and Maureen and George were to go back to Dublin as late as possible so the girls could definitely meet him. Have a look at him, was what Mama actually wrote.

CHAPTER TWENTY-SEVEN

For whatever reason the visits to Margaret had almost become a scheduled event. He would go every week, not always on the same day but once a week nevertheless. He was sometimes accompanied by Deidre and every two or three weeks he would take the children on a Saturday morning. They desperately wanted to see their mother but, at the same time, they dreaded it. And Maureen knew exactly why. Every fortnight, usually on a Wednesday morning, Mrs Doyle would pull up outside in her car and she and Maureen would set off to go to the convent. When they got there Maureen would enter that small room on her own and spend ten or fifteen minutes with Margaret, and then Mrs Doyle might come in for just a few minutes before they left. In many ways there was not much point to the visit, Margaret certainly wasn't getting any better, on the contrary she seemed to be slowly retreating into some kind of shell, slowly but surely disappearing. But when she saw Maureen she would smile, and sometimes she would get up and hug her. Maureen told her about the children, and any other thing that came into her head, maybe a little joke about Julia, or something about the weather, or the garden. Margaret might listen and she might not, she never asked any questions. And when Mrs Doyle came in she just smiled weakly at her but often didn't show any real sign of recognition.

So when the children went to see her they were not seeing the mother they knew, not seeing the person that they wanted to hug, and talk to, and laugh with. And when they came home on Saturday lunchtime or early afternoon they were quiet and sad. Once in a while they might talk to Maureen about their visit, but they all knew there was nothing to say. Maureen never talked to Deidre about the visits she went on with Shaughnessy either. Mrs Doyle had told Maureen that the sisters had said that Deidre never left the car, she just waited outside for him to return. Except, occasionally, she got out of the car and walked around, on the drive, smoking, they'd said. Maureen wondered whether the nuns just sat behind the curtains spying on her for the whole time, or what. But she didn't ask Mrs Doyle.

The truth was that the visits to Margaret were a duty. It was not something that any of them resented, even though it was distressing, but, at the same time, it was little more than something that had to be done.

Maureen enjoyed the drive through the mountains. Every time. Even as the weather got colder and, usually, wetter, the scenery was impressive and beautiful to look at, never really the same from one journey to the other.

And Maureen enjoyed talking to Mrs Doyle as well. They had travelled together, now, quite a number of times and they had got used to each other. They talked about this and that, and had a laugh now and again as well. It was different in the car to when she might meet Mrs Doyle outside Mass or when she came to the Shaughnessy's house, those occasions were still sort of formal. Hello Maureen, how are you? I'm well Mrs Doyle, thank you very much.

In the car it was more relaxed. Mrs Doyle's tales and observations were scurrilous to say the least. She often talked about those little tea parties that the women hosted for each other, just as Margaret had done, and she was always keen to describe the pomposities and stupidities of some of the participants. The little snobberies and jealousies. She swore it was true that she had seen Mary Gallagher inch a tray full of tea and cakes slyly off the table, making it tip and crash to the floor, while no-one was looking, just so she could disrupt Bridget Murphy's event. Mary loathed Bridget, always calling her Bridie to her face because she knew she hated that name with a vengeance. And she said that Pattie Nevin had taken such a fancy to the curate, Father Pledger, that he never came to the teas any more, he was so embarrassed by her persistent attentions. Father O'Sullivan, she said, was hugely annoyed at this because the curate was now looking to be moved to another parish as well. Mrs Doyle said the parish priest was only annoyed because he was a lazy piece of work who relied on the curate to do everything.

'Mention any of that to anyone, Maureen, and I'll have your guts for garters.'

'Don't you worry Mrs Doyle, I'll not say a thing.'

It was bit like the confessional, because both of them said things that they wouldn't want heard by anyone else. Maureen talked about Deidre and how they had become sort of friends even though she wasn't sure about her at the beginning. Mrs D still thought there was something a bit suspect about Deidre but accepted that she was a nice enough person. Deidre didn't do the tea thing like Margaret had done because she wasn't quite the mistress of the house, so it didn't seem appropriate, and with Margaret 'away' it would have seemed in bad taste as well. Maureen was tempted to say that she wondered about the relationship between Shaughnessy and Deidre but decided that was not a wise thing to do. She had no proof, no proof at all, that there was anything going on.

Maureen spoke about George as well. She liked him and she wanted to talk about him. Mrs D said he seemed like a nice boy when she met him, and Maureen said he was, but he felt he was a bit of a disappointment to his family, and that got in the way a bit, she said, because it seemed to upset him. Mrs D said that men were like that, when you got to know a man you found out how weak he really was, how insecure they all were in fact, worried that they wouldn't be successful, worried about the opinions of others, worried they wouldn't have enough money. All those things. Which is why they spent so much time in the bars, spending the money they had, and worrying even more about their reputations.

'George isn't unusual Maureen, in fact he's probably the same as all the others. Even Mr D was a bit like that, believe it or not. His father was a terrible man, in my opinion anyway, treated everyone in the family in a very unpleasant way, a bully really. But once Francis was away from him, and with me of course, everything worked out fine. More or less, anyway.'

'Margaret and Mr Shaughnessy didn't really work though, did it? He bullied her, he hit her as well.'

'Do you know that for a fact Maureen? That he hit her?'

She thought she might have overstepped the mark. Could she say anything more?

'Well, once at least, I know he did. I'm pretty sure he did.'

'It wouldn't surprise me.'

Her voice said she was neither surprised not shocked.

'Maureen, the problem with the Shaughnessys was this. They were neither of them strong enough. Whatever demons he had, they made him into a difficult person, a drinker, a bully as well maybe. Only the Lord knows why. I don't know a lot about his family, but there was probably something there, that's usually where it starts. And she, a lovely woman as you know, didn't have enough for him. She didn't have the strength to make up for what was lacking in him. And she didn't really want to be with him in the first place, did she?'

'No, she didn't. She told me that.'

'Well, she said as much to me as well. Not in so many words, but reading between the lines. And if she didn't want to be with him, then it was impossible to give her strength to him, wasn't it? She didn't want him enough. Do you understand me?

'I think so.'

'I wanted to be with Francis, weaknesses included, almost from the moment I met him. I give him my strength, he gives me his. It works. Most of the time, anyway.'

Maureen was always impressed when Mrs D shared her thoughts with her. Mrs D was an open person, and she had ideas, and she was sensitive to people as well. At the beginning, Maureen had thought she was just a bit larger than life, someone who liked to take charge, someone who was, in fact, a bit insensitive to others. But that wasn't true. She could see through people, she understood how they worked. She understood Maureen as well, she knew she could trust her, and Maureen was flattered by that.

On that particular day, they hardly talked at all on the last twenty minutes of the journey. It was almost like Mrs D was giving her time to think over what she'd said. And Maureen did think about it because it was relevant. It was relevant to her and George. She knew that she liked him, knew that she could be with him and, as she had thought before, this would probably be enough. But was it? Mrs Doyle hadn't actually said you had to be desperately in love with someone had she? She'd just said you had to decide whether you wanted to be with someone enough, enough to give him your strength, to add your strength to his. And, just as important, you had to be sure he would do the same for you.

Mrs Doyle dropped her off at the house, saying she'd visit

Shaughnessy, and Deidre, later on in the week, or she would see her at Mass on Sunday. As Maureen got out of the car she became the maid again. It was the strangest feeling. Talking to Mrs D in the car it was like talking to a friend. Discussing serious things and frivolous things and laughing at some of them. Obviously Mrs D was older than her, in her forties Maureen thought, so she knew a lot more, she had more experience, but she didn't talk to Maureen as if she knew nothing. On the contrary she spoke to her as if she was an intelligent person. She listened to her, talked with her, appreciated her, laughed with her. So on that journey, there and back, inside that car it was almost like temporarily living a different life. Inside that car she, they, could talk about almost anything they wanted and they both knew it would stay there between them. It had taken Maureen a bit of time to get used to this idea, but now she understood it.

And when she stepped out of the car it was like stepping backwards into a different world. A world where she had to get on with getting the dinner or doing the shopping or tidying the bedrooms or sweeping the carpet. She didn't mind having to do all those jobs, in fact she enjoyed looking after the house and the people in it, but it was definitely a totally different existence.

She walked up the path and entered the house. As usual, on a weekday afternoon, it was quiet and empty. She went into the kitchen. No sign of Deidre, and no sound of Deidre either. She would usually have called out a greeting of some kind by now. Maureen was relieved. She wanted to get on with sorting out the dinner on her own in the kitchen. It was one of the best ways to give herself time to think, and she could consider her possible future with George, consider whether she had the strength for him, and, as well, whether he had the strength for her.

CHAPTER TWENTY-EIGHT

George surprised her. The following week, on the Tuesday, he had arranged to meet her for a few minutes when she was out shopping in town. They did occasionally meet like this, now and then, if George wasn't working on a particular day. They always had time for a cup of tea and a chat and maybe even a short stroll together down by the sea.

They went into a café and sat down, ordered some tea. Maureen could see that he had something to say. He leaned forward as if eager to speak.

'Well, I've spoken to my mother and father and arranged for us to go over there this Sunday afternoon. Maybe about four o' clock. How would that suit you?'

'That'd be good, George, that'd be great.'

She was pleased for him. And pleased for herself that he had done this.

They arranged to meet at the station at three o'clock. Most unusually Maureen was little bit late as there been some fuss from Maria, she'd got upset about this that and the other, and didn't want to talk to Deidre or her father. So Maureen had spent ten minutes with her in the kitchen, chatting to her and calming her down, aware all the time that she had to get going herself.

As she walked into town, hurrying now, she knew that she was anxious about going to Dún Laoghaire, anxious about meeting his parents and any of the others that might be there. He hadn't said if any of the brothers were expected. And the picture he'd painted of them all didn't make it any easier.

Luckily they hadn't missed the train.

She had passed through Dún Laoghaire before on the train, but she had never actually stopped there. The station was next to the harbour and there were ferry boats sitting there now. The two of them stopped briefly; they had a quick look at the activity going on around the ships, and then they turned away from the sea and started the walk to his parents' house.

It took ten minutes. They didn't really talk apart from Maureen making a comment about how it seemed very nice round here. They were both nervous. And then they came to the house. And it was just a house, an ordinary house, certainly not as big as the Shaughnessy's. So Maureen was relieved about that. Although it has to be said it was a lot grander than the little cottage back in Dungarvan.

'Right, here we go.'

He smiled at her and pushed the front door open.

'Mam, we're here.'

And the instant he said it she appeared. Maureen knew she'd probably been keeping an eye out for them, any mother would do that.

She was maybe in her fifties. About Maureen's height. A smile on her face, a friendly face as well. Greying hair and a reddish complexion.

'Well, Maureen, it's great to meet you.'

She shook hands with Maureen.

'Was your journey OK? Have you been to Dún Laoghaire before? Maybe you have?'

'It was easy, getting here I mean. Just a few minutes really. And no, I've never stopped here before, I've been through it of course, a number of times.'

'Of course you have. Anyway, look, come in and meet George's father.'

And she led them into a sitting room. Two armchairs and a small settee. There was also a desk squeezed in the corner and a man was sitting at it. He turned as they entered the room, and stood. He was quite a tall man, similar to George in fact, in height and stature. He had a short grey beard, and was wearing glasses. That's what she noticed. And his dark suit, with a waistcoat and a tie. And his face had some of George in it, she saw that immediately.

His face was not unfriendly but he wasn't smiling either.

'Da. This is Maureen.'

'Hello Maureen. It's a pleasure to meet you.'

He had a charming voice, like George's in a way, but older, more formal.

'It's a pleasure to meet you too, Mr Barry.'

'George has told us all about you. You're from Dungarvan I believe?'

'I am. Yes.'

She almost called him sir, but stopped herself.

'If I remember rightly it's a very nice town. And your parents, they work on the railway, is that right?'

'They do. They run one of the level crossings, not far from Cappagh.'

'Umm. A busy job I'd say, or could be anyway.'

Maureen was stuck for what to say now, and then she saw his eyes make contact with his wife, just for a second. George's mother responded.

'Maureen, come into the kitchen with me and we'll get you a cup of tea, you too George Junior. We'll eat at five, George, Michael'll be here by then.'

Mr Barry nodded, with a brief smile, and had already half-turned back towards the desk before they had left the room to go to the kitchen.

Maureen was relieved to be away from him. Not because he had been nasty in any way, not at all, but there had been a tension there, definitely. And when they got into the kitchen and sat down, the tension had disappeared. From them all.

She heard music start, in the room they had just left she supposed. Serious music, not Irish music, maybe like opera or something.

Mrs Barry fussed about with the kettle ready to make some tea. And there was also other food around which looked like it was being prepared for a bit later. There were some sandwiches in the making and some cake ready to be cut, all of it appetising. Maureen had done all that herself back in Bray loads of times and here she was being a guest, and having a nice tea prepared for her.

'So you're a housemaid in Bray, George tells me. Is that OK? Are they nice people to work for?'

'Well, they are yes. The children are lovely but Mrs Shaughnessy, the mistress, has been ill for a while, she's away in a rest home, so things are a bit sad at the moment.'

'So do you have to organise things yourself while she's gone?

That's some responsibility, I'd say, Maureen.'

'There's an aunt who's staying. She's very nice but, to be honest, she's hopeless with the house so it's me that does it all. Which I like. I like sorting everything out, it makes things more interesting really.'

'Oh yes, I could see that.'

'And Mr Shaughnessy pays me a bit more for that as well.'

'Well that's useful isn't it? Very useful. So his wife, she'll be home, soon enough, I expect?'

'We don't know, we just don't know.'

'That's a terrible thing isn't it, for the children, and for him as well I suppose. She can't be that old, I'd say?'

'In her forties, I think.'

Mrs Barry was fussing around, chatting away. Getting a little bit redder in the face as she got on with things. Maureen liked her, she wasn't that much different to Mama.

The door to the kitchen opened and, turning round to look, Maureen saw a priest coming in.

'Michael, you're here! That's great. Michael this is Maureen, George's girlfriend. Can I call you that Maureen, his girlfriend?'

'Yes, you can Mrs Barry, yes you can.'

She was standing up as she said this, pushing her chair back in the busy kitchen. Embarrassed now by the crowding, by the priest, by the girlfriend.

'It's a pleasure to meet you, Father.'

'It's a pleasure to meet you too, Maureen. George has told me a bit about you, haven't you George? And call me Michael, will ya?'

‘Michael, yes of course.’

She’d never called a priest by his Christian name before.

‘Da’s in the sitting-room, I suppose. I can hear the music from here. Verdi, I think it is. Nabucco if I’m not mistaken.’

‘Where else would he be, Michael, tell me that? Are you going in?’

‘I better do eh? He’ll be expecting me. I’ll see you all in a minute.’

And he left as quickly as he had appeared, and seconds later the music was turned down a bit, while they talked, presumably.

‘George’s father likes the opera, Maureen. Do you know anything about opera?’

‘God no, nothing at all I’m afraid. I’m not even really sure what it is, to be honest with you.’

‘Nor me! Although I do hear an awful lot of it through the walls!’

She winked at Maureen as she spoke, smiling.

‘Give me the Ink Spots, or Frank Sinatra any time!’

They sat at the kitchen table for the next twenty minutes or so. Mrs Barry making sure that the food was ready, chatting to George about his work and his friends, including Declan who she obviously liked, and asking Maureen bits and pieces about her family and her work. It was warm in there and comfortable and she was a nice person. George was also comfortable here. He was relaxed with his mother and they chatted in a friendly way.

Then she started to move the food into the dining-room and Maureen helped her sort out the table. She was glad to do that.

As a clock in the hall struck five Mrs Barry called them in for tea.

Mr Barry sat at the head of the table, George and Maureen sat on one side and Father Barry, Michael that is, sat on the other side. The kitchen had been warm, very warm, and quite bright as well. The small dining room felt cold in contrast, and it was a dark room as well, with slightly too much furniture in it, a mahogany chest of drawers and a dark brown glass-fronted cabinet with books in it. The fire was unlit.

When Mrs Barry had sorted things out she sat down at the opposite end to her husband.

'Would you say grace, Michael.'

They bowed their heads slightly.

'For what we are about to receive, may the Lord make us truly thankful. Amen.'

'Amen.'

The sandwiches were passed around and the tea was poured. They busied themselves with that for a moment or two.

'So tell me Maureen. You came to work in Bray after you left school, is that right?'

'Well not really no, I worked in Dungarvan before. I worked for an English family there.'

'Is that right? An English family you say. And what was that like?'

'They were very nice. I enjoyed it.'

'So why did you come to Bray. I mean if your job in Dungarvan was adequate, let's say.'

'My sister was working in Dublin and she encouraged me to

come up. More opportunities she thought.'

Maureen didn't say that the opportunities that Theresa had mentioned were mainly connected to dancing.

'And your sister? She's a housemaid, too is she?'

'Oh no. She worked in a solicitor's office in Dublin. A secretary she was for one of the bosses there.'

She wasn't a hundred percent sure Theresa had actually worked for one of the bosses, but that'd do for now, she thought.

His face changed slightly.

'She works for a solicitor? Well that's great isn't it. Wouldn't you say so Michael?'

Maureen looked towards the priest. He smiled at her.

'I would Da, I would. Still I'd bet Maureen's doing a great job where she is. Do you enjoy your work now?'

'Yes I do. That's not to say I wouldn't mind doing something a bit more important, but I enjoy it all the same.'

'Well that's the main thing, isn't it?

She sensed that Michael was prepared to help her out. And Mrs Barry too.

'Maureen's more or the less the housekeeper she was telling me, weren't you Maureen? The woman of the house has been very ill so Maureen's had to take over really, managing everything, checking on the children and the like. Which is an awful responsibility of someone of her age. She's only eighteen after all.'

'Is that right Maureen? You're running the house? More or less, you say?'

'Yes. I am. While Mrs Shaughnessy is away, I run everything.'

He looked at her slightly differently now that he was aware that she was a bit more than just a skivvy, or that was what Maureen was thinking anyway. But whenever he stopped eating to speak to her he tended to look over the top of his glasses, almost peering at her, narrowing his eyes. She found this irritating. But at the same time, his wife was very pleasant, the priest was friendly, and George was his son. So it wasn't all that bad, so far at any rate.

'Well, it's a good thing to be able to take on responsibility when it's offered, it's what we all should do, it's our duty in fact. Wouldn't you agree Michael?

'We all have different abilities and responsibilities Da, but yes, we must all do what we can when opportunities, and obligations, are offered to us, I agree with you there.'

The father laughed. He liked his son the priest.

'That sounds like a politician's answer to me, Michael, wouldn't you agree Maureen?'

She wasn't at all sure what she could say. She felt herself going red.

'Leave the girl alone George, she's not used to your nonsense.'

The mother said this with a laugh in her voice and things relaxed a bit.

'Anyway, young George, tell us all how it's going on the railway?'

There was a tone to the father's question which almost suggested a lack of real interest.

'It's fine Da.'

'Is that all? It's fine?'

'It's going OK. It's interesting.'

Last week George had told Maureen that he had been promoted to a bigger signal box, something like that, anyway.

'Why don't you tell your father about your promotion, George.'

'You've been promoted? Well, that's grand. It's a good job you came to tea, Maureen, or we'd never have been told a thing about it. So tell us, George, what's this big promotion?'

And so tea went on. For whatever reason the father treated George differently to Michael, the priest, and Maureen wasn't sure that her interruption had helped George really. From that point on he asked Maureen her view about the things they were discussing, almost as if he was really interested in her opinions, but he didn't ask George. Michael tried to bring him in, as did the mother, but none of it really worked. And it wasn't helped by the fact that George himself said nothing at all unless asked. Maureen couldn't help but be disappointed, in the situation, in the father, but in George himself as well.

When they had finished the mother started to clear the table and Maureen got up to help her. The father and the two sons stayed at the table while all this was going on, but he, George, was excluded still, just sitting there alone, an outsider.

And then they were leaving. George would take her home.

'It was a pleasure to meet you Maureen and I hope we'll see you again soon. Let's just pop in and say goodbye to George's father.'

The father had returned to the sitting-room with Michael, George sitting in the kitchen while Maureen and the mother sorted out the washing-up together. Maureen liked the mother and they had both chatted easily, about nothing at all, while they cleared everything up

The priest and the father both stood up when they all entered the sitting-room again, and both smiled at her and shook her hand and said they would be glad to see her again. And she thought, from their faces, that they were probably telling the truth.

Outside it was chilly, a breeze off the sea. They walked quickly back down to the station together. She linked with him and, of course, felt that tension which he so often carried with him.

'They seemed very pleasant, George, your Ma and Da, and Michael the priest as well, he was very friendly. I liked them all.'

And this was trueish anyway.

'And they liked you as well. I could see that. They liked you as well.'

There was nothing much more to be said.

CHAPTER TWENTY-NINE

When Deidre saw Maureen on the Sunday evening, after she got back, she said that Mrs Doyle had popped around the previous afternoon to say would Maureen go to her house on Tuesday morning, at around ten, because she needed to talk to her about something or other. Probably to do with going to the convent, said Deidre.

Deidre also asked her about the visit to Dún Laoghaire, of course, and Maureen said it had all gone well, and that George's mother was charming, and his brother, the priest, was a very friendly man. Deidre tried to get her to tell more but Maureen said that was all really, they'd had a bit of tea and it had been very nice to meet the family.

On Tuesday morning she arrived at Mrs Doyle's house exactly at ten o'clock. Mrs D herself answered the door and invited Maureen in.

'We'll go into the sitting-room, it's a bit warmer in there, and I've made a pot of tea for us, I knew you'd be on time.'

And so they went into the sitting-room and sat down next to the small table with the tea, and biscuits on it. Maureen liked the feeling of being in there, liked the comfortable armchairs they were sitting in, liked the fact that she had been invited to sit down in the sitting-room, not the kitchen, and have a cup of tea with Mrs Doyle. And, of course, she knew Mrs Doyle well enough not to feel too awkward about it all.

'How's things with the Shaughnessys?'

'Everything's fine. The same as usual really.'

'And George, is everything all right there?'

'We went to see his family on Sunday, they were very nice, one of his brothers is a priest. Michael, he was very pleasant himself.'

'It's Father Barry is it? I know a bit about him. He's well thought of I think.'

How on earth did she know these things?

Mrs D poured out the tea and offered the biscuits. Maureen took a chocolate one.

'Now look Maureen I was wondering what your plans are, for the future I mean. I can't see you staying at the Shaughnessy's for the rest of your life for a start. Are you going to marry this George, do you think?'

At that second Maureen had no plans at all that she could think of.

'Well, I don't know. I was thinking of going to England at some point, I suppose. That's where my sisters have gone. And George has said that he is going to go to England as well. And, yes, we might marry there. God, I don't really know to be honest with you, Mrs D. In a way I'm happy enough at the Shaughnessy's, but I'd like to do something else as well.'

'Well, Maureen, I've got to know you a little bit over the last few months, and I'd hate to think of you wasting your life away. I was thinking about you the other night, talking to Francis, in fact. And I said to Francis, she's got something about her that Maureen, she's only a youngster but she's got something about her. And he agreed with me.'

Embarrassing, she could feel herself blushing.

'But Mr Doyle, he hardly knows me at all!'

'No, you're right, that's true, he doesn't, but he always agrees with me. Almost always anyway!'

They both laughed.

'Now, look here Maureen, I've got a suggestion for you. You don't need to take it up, but I'd like you to think about it. It's a bit of an opportunity that you might like. Or you might not, of course. Which'll be fine as well, by the way.

'OK.'

'Now I have a niece, Janey, who's been living in the United States for the last few years. She's married to an American, and his company is transferring him to England in the New Year. They're going to be living in London. Now, Janey's been in touch with me saying she'll need some help in the house, she's got two children, and did I know anyone who might be interested?'

Maureen wasn't sure what to ask, or what to think. Mrs D looked at her for a few moments and continued.

'The thing is Maureen, it would be a bit of a step up for you, I think. You wouldn't be the maid, I mean. You'd almost be the housekeeper, with a bit of child-minding I'd say. And Janey'd be a good person to work for. And you'd be living in a very nice house in London as well. They're not short of a few bob I can tell you that.'

'And this Janey, is she Irish?'

'No. Her Mam, my sister, is Irish obviously, but her Da is English and she was brought up over there. But she's a clever girl, and she likes a good laugh as well. I think you'd get on with her fine.'

'Can I have another of those chocolate biscuits?'

'Of course you can, help yourself!'

She sat and thought for a few moments, having a sup of tea and eating the biscuit.

'What about George?'
'Well, he's already said he's going to England anyway, hasn't he? And he probably means London when he says England. It wouldn't matter if you went first, would it? Especially if you had a good job to go to.'

'I suppose not.'

Inside herself she knew now that she wanted to say yes to this immediately. She knew that Mrs D was thinking about her, knew she wouldn't suggest anything that she couldn't cope with, wouldn't suggest anything that might not be a good opportunity.

'And when would I have to start?'

'In the middle of January it'd be, and obviously they'd pay all your fares and everything.'

'I'd miss the Shaughnessys. And Margaret. God, I wouldn't see Margaret again would I?'

'The Shaughnessys will survive without you Maureen, they'll miss you but they'll get over it. And that Deidre's not such a bad old thing is she? She'll look after the children. And I don't think there's anything much more we can do for Margaret, but I promise you I'll visit her, the same as we always have together. I promise you that.'

They sat in silence for a minute, looking at each other. Half smiling.

'Mrs D I would love to do it. But I need a day or so to be certain. Is that OK?'

'Of course it is. That's the sensible thing to do. You might want to discuss it with George or with your Ma and Da?'

'No. I don't need to discuss it with anyone. I might think of a question or two for you about it, but I don't need to discuss it, I'll make up my own mind.'

'That's my girl. You make the decision yourself. Look, we're going to see Margaret next week aren't we? Why don't you tell me then what you've decided. I can let Janey know that you're interested and that we'll have a final decision by Wednesday next week, how would that suit ya?'

'That's great. And thanks for thinking of me Mrs D. It sounds like it could be a great idea, a great opportunity.'

'I suggested you, Maureen, because I like you, but also because I'm sure there's more to you than just being a housemaid, I'm absolutely sure of that. And London might be the place for you. I think it would be, I think it definitely would be.

Mrs D offered her another cup of tea but she refused, it was time to go.

When she left the house she couldn't help but feel really excited. She knew immediately that she was going to say yes, she was almost tempted to turn round and ring the door bell and just tell Mrs D that she wanted the job. If she didn't what would happen if this Janey found someone else during the next week? No, Mrs D would not let her take someone else, for sure she wouldn't do that.

No, she did need to think about it. She needed to think about what she was going to tell the Shaughnessys and what she was going to tell George as well. She wasn't sure how he would react to this news. They were going down to Dungarvan this Saturday, it had all been arranged now, and she would have made her mind up by then. If it felt right she would tell him on Saturday.

She would tell Mama and Dada at another time. They were

used to seeing their children set off for different places, it had happened so many times before.

She walked quickly back to the Shaughnessy's to get on with the rest of the day. Excited, excited, excited.

CHAPTER THIRTY

For the next few days Maureen thought about two things mainly. The first was the visit to Dungarvan on Saturday and the second was the job in London. And while she was thinking about those things, sometimes both intermingled in her mind, she was working in the house and talking to Deidre, and listening to the children, talking to them as well.

On the Thursday, after school, Maria came into the kitchen and sat down.

'Can I have some bread and jam, Maureen, please. I'm starving.'

'Well, you can get it yourself, can't you?'

'I'm starving and I'm too tired, Maureen.'

Maureen got the bread out of the bin and put it on the table, with the bread knife, and the butter dish and the jam jar, and a table knife.

'There you are. You can sort yourself out from there, can't ye? And don't get jam in the butter. Or butter in the jam come to that.'

'Yes I can, Maureen, and, no, I won't.'

And so she sat there cutting the bread, two thick slices, and putting butter on, and then quite a lot of jam, and then she held up one piece up to eat it, whole and uncut.

'Would you look at yourself with that huge slice of bread. Couldn't you cut it in half or something?'

'No. I like it like this. It reminds of me of when Ma was here, when I was small. She'd make it and I'd eat it. It was grand.'

Maureen looked at the girl sitting there, not sorry for herself or anything, just enjoying a memory of being with her mother, and eating a huge slice of bread and jam. She knew she'd miss her.

Maureen made a pot of tea for them both while the girl finished both slices of bread. Not talking, but comfortable there.

When she'd made the tea she sat down for a minute with Maria. The evening meal was all under control so she had a bit of time to spare. Maria looked at Maureen.

'How long do you think you'll be staying with us, Maureen?'

She couldn't believe that this question could have come at this exact time. As far as she could remember Maria had never asked her anything like that before.

'Why would you ask a thing like that, Maria?'

'I've no idea. But when I was walking home from school I was thinking about things, and the thought came to me. How long will Maureen stay with us? Because, I thought, she won't stay for ever will she?'

'No, I won't, that's true. I'll move on, I suppose, soon enough.'

'But you like it here, don't ya? And you get on with Deidre, don't ya? You two get on fine?'

She couldn't remember either of the children calling her Auntie Deidre, maybe they had at the beginning, but now it was plain Deidre. But it was said with an affection, an acceptance, even a friendship.

'Sure we do, yes. I mean Deidre's sort of part of your family isn't she, but, when all's said and done, I just work here. I mean your Da could give me notice any time, I suppose.'

'Well he's not going to do that, is he?'

Maureen laughed.

'I don't suppose he is, no. But look, Maria, I'm only young you know, I'm only eighteen, and I'll probably be moving on at some point, it could be sooner, or it could be later, who knows. Only God knows, I suppose. But, anyway, we'll always be friends won't we?'

Maria got up immediately and went round to Maureen's chair and gave her a hug as she sat there.

'Sure we will. We'll always be friends.'

Maureen almost cried, but didn't, and Maria, like she would, shot off immediately to go upstairs and do her homework.

Sitting there at the kitchen table, alone now, she realised that although the decision in itself might have been easy, there were other things which wouldn't be. She knew that she would be saying yes to Mrs D. She had already decided that. When she'd lain in bed over the last couple of nights the decision had become firmer and firmer. Even when Mrs D had asked she knew she would say yes, but now, if it were possible, she had become even more determined that she would go to London. And, the more she knew that, the more she realised how it might affect other people.

Maria would be upset. How strange it was that she would ask Maureen about leaving, in this week of all weeks. Was it possible that she could kind of feel that there was a change in the air? Maureen wondered whether she, herself, had become different in some way over the last couple of days. She didn't think so. But who knew?

Yes, Maria would be upset but she would manage. And Deidre was here. In some ways it was better if Deidre became more important, for the children's sake. Assuming Deidre was staying of course! Maureen knew that, in many ways, she, herself, was the main person in the house, at the moment, in the sense of running it and organising things. Even Shaughnessy, himself, left most things to her. And the children would, most times, come to her first before Deidre, or their father, if something had to be done, or if they wanted advice about something. Which, she thought, was ridiculous in a way, because she was only a couple of years older than them, wasn't she? If she left, then Deidre could properly take charge which would be better for everyone really.

And Stephen? She thought he would miss her as well. And she would miss him. He was a nice boy, a kind boy. But she remembered how both the children had been a bit off with her at the beginning, snooty almost; Maria more than Stephen, but him as well, a bit. But how things change.

If she told them next week that she was going it was going to be strange anyway over the following weeks. Even if it wasn't actually difficult, it would certainly be strange. And that wasn't even taking account of what George might say.

CHAPTER THIRTY-ONE

It was cold on the Saturday morning. Inside the house as well as out. Maureen made sure that everything was on, the fire going, the breakfast stuff on the table, before she got herself ready to leave. She had a quick cup of tea herself and then she was away. No-one else had got up yet.

Walking down the road towards the town she thought about the day ahead. She was looking forward to seeing Mama and Dada, that was for sure. And she was glad that they would meet George, and she hoped, before they set off back this evening, that they'd get to see the girls as well. But, at the same time, she wasn't sure about things. The very fact that she had decided to go to London would affect her and George, she knew that. She didn't think he would be very pleased, he would not be angry she didn't think, but he would be disappointed. Because she hadn't told him right away, because she had made her decision without discussing it with him.

She could pretend of course. She could say to him, on the train back to Dublin, she could say to him that she had been offered this job in London and she wanted to know what he thought, before she made any decision that is. And what would he say? He would say it was not a good idea. She was sure of that. He wouldn't like the idea of her going off to London on her own. She knew he trusted her but, at the same time, he would be scared, wouldn't he? He would be scared that she would leave him behind in some way. Which is what she would be doing, of course. He probably thought that going to England was his idea, his adventure, and he would go first, and she would join him later when he was settled. But now it would be different.

She would know all about London well before he arrived.

Or he could say he would come at the same time. They would go together. She would have her new job and he would find something pretty quick. He might say that. But Maureen knew that she would not like that solution to the problem. All of a sudden, on her winter morning walk into Bray, she realised that she wanted to go to London on her own. She was happy for him to come later, but she wanted this to be her own journey at the beginning, she wanted to get on that boat at Dún Laoghaire and set off on her own.

She decided that she wasn't going to pretend, she wasn't going to say that she hadn't made the decision, she would tell him that she had been offered the job and that she was going.

As she came towards the station she saw George waiting outside. Pointing at his watch. She hurried, not realising that she must have dawdled a bit while she was thinking.

The journey to Dungarvan was pleasant enough. The change in Dublin easy. George obviously knew the trains and had planned the times so that it would all be straightforward. Once they got on the train to Waterford he told her how much his Ma and Da had liked her, that they had enjoyed meeting her. And his father had said that she seemed like a very intelligent young woman. And Michael, the priest, had said that George was very lucky to have met a girl like Maureen, and that he should be careful not to lose her. And his mother had said she must come again soon. George was obviously very pleased by the reaction of his family to Maureen. She almost got the impression that he felt that he had done something right for a change and, obviously, that pleased him.

They changed at Waterford and got on the train to Dungarvan. George knew a bit about this section of railway, he said that it had been one of the most expensive ever built in Ireland because of the land it had to go through, and it had one of the longest level-crossings in Europe, he thought, as well, he said. Maureen told him he could talk to Dada about all of that when they arrived because he had worked on this railway most of his adult life and was more than happy to chat about it at great length. Very great length, she said, laughing.

Maureen had written Mama not to bother to meet them, that they would get the bus and go directly to the house. And so they did. And, as they walked up to the house itself, both Mama and Dada were leaning on the gate, wrapped up in their winter coats, waiting for them to arrive.

How strange people are she thought, after she'd introduced everyone and they'd gone inside. Her parents, Mama and Dada were almost like different people, almost, but not quite, like people she didn't know. They were both excited to meet him she could see that, but they were also a bit overawed by him. He was physically bigger than the rest of them and he seemed even bigger in the small cottage. As they shook hands with him they were both having to look up at him, they looked very small in comparison, almost like little old children. Of course, they probably didn't realise that he was as unsure as they were, Maureen could see the little signs of his nervousness, of his diffidence, perhaps not so obvious to them though.

There weren't sitting-rooms and dining-rooms here, that was for sure, so they were all in the same space as Mama put the kettle on for some tea. Maureen wondered, as they all sat down in a crowded kind of circle, whether she should be a little bit ashamed of this place, the place where she had been brought up. It was unlikely George was going to hear any of that Verdi stuff here, she thought, although Dada might possibly decide to give a little tune on his concertina!

She knew, as she was thinking all this, that she wasn't ashamed or embarrassed, she might have been in the past but she wasn't now, for whatever reason. This was where she came from, this was what she was, these were her parents, whom she loved, and respected as well. Take it or leave it, whoever you are.

And, of course, George would take it. Because he wasn't a man who looked down on people, not as far as she knew anyway.

She saw her Ma fussing around with the tea, and her Da, relaxing a bit now, as they'd sat down and George had asked him some question about his work on the railway. Da said they'd go out and have a look at the gates in a couple of minutes, the two of them, after they'd had a sup of tea. There was a bit of a chill in the air but a few minutes outside would do no harm.

They had tea, and then Da suggested that maybe, if they were going out anyway, that George and he could go for a pint together before they had their food. And so they did, leaving Maureen and Mama on their own in the kitchen.

'He seems a nice enough man now, this George. He's a good-looking man as well isn't he?'

'He is. And he's very pleasant, as well. Good company.'

'And he's got on well with your Da as well, I'd say.'

'He has.'

'So, do you think you'll be getting engaged or anything?'

'Well, I don't know about that. Not yet anyway. He hasn't asked me to marry him, if that's what you mean. But we've talked a bit about going to England, just in a general kind of way. So it'd be a possibility I suppose.'

'Would you like to go over to England? It'd be London you'd go to, I expect?'

'I suppose so, yes. Have you heard from the others at all?'

And they talked about Maureen's sisters who'd been in touch with their Ma quite recently. Even Theresa as well, who had said things were going fine.

And then, between them, they got the dinner together. Bacon and cabbage and potatoes. Maureen could smell the memories in the clouds of steam coming from the pots. And they had Mama's soda bread too. How many times had she eaten this meal in this house? It seemed like thousands.

About an hour after they'd left Da and George returned. They looked as if they'd had an enjoyable time, but not too much to drink. Just a couple of pints said Da and Maureen believed him. They all had a laugh about Jimmy Coughlan and his son Mickey that the two of them had met up at the bar; Jimmy was famous for his ridiculous stories, bargains he'd made, deals he'd done, bets on horses that had come in at 100 to 1. And then they ate.

It was a comfortable meal. The food was good. Maureen could see that Ma had made an effort to make sure there was more than enough for them all. Da asked George about his family and seemed suitably impressed with the employment at Guinness's and having a priest for a brother. And George asked about the rest of Maureen's family and Ma told him where everyone was and what they were doing, as far as she knew anyway. At the last count, she said, laughing.

After they had eaten and had another cup of tea Dada took George out to see his garden and to take him a few yards down the lane just to say hello to Michael. And so the afternoon passed. Maureen helping Mama do the washing-up and put things away, and then just sitting with her for a little while, chatting about this and that.

And then they had to go. Michael had said he'd give them a lift into town at four. And so they were ready to go when they heard the van pull up outside.

George shook hands with both her parents and Maureen

hugged them both and then they were away.

In town the three girls had all managed to get away a bit early and were waiting for them. There was only one café open and so they went in there for the half an hour or so they had before the train was due

It was a great laugh with George seemingly fluctuating between being totally embarrassed by the situation, and being flattered by all the attention he was getting. Because that's who the girls were concentrating on. George. Trying to find out as much as possible about him, trying to fluster him. And why wouldn't they? He was good-looking, friendly, not too full of himself or anything like that.

The girls walked down to the station with them and waved them off. Each of them individually having had a little private word with Maureen on the short walk, each saying that he seemed like a very nice boy, a very good-looking boy as well, and when were they getting engaged? When are ye getting engaged Maureen, will ye tell us that or not?

She just laughed.

On the train journey to Waterford they talked about the day. George said how much he liked her parents and that he had enjoyed the pub as well, all the men were interested to meet him, all of them saying how much they liked Maureen, and they'd told him how they used to see her cycling to the shop for her Ma, and about her brothers, who could be a bit wild at times, when they were just children mind, not now, at all, very respectable all of them, now. All got jobs, working hard.

As they stood on the platform at Waterford Maureen knew that, within a few minutes, she would be talking to George about going to London. She wondered, now, if she'd done the wrong thing, if she should have cancelled the trip to Dungarvan until she'd told him about London. Got it out of the way.

Seen what his reaction was. The day so far had been very pleasant, almost uneventful in a way, a natural progression where he met her parents, chatted, discussed, all got to know each other. Underneath it all a kind of understanding that this was part of the journey towards them getting engaged and then married.

And that was still possible, of course, still likely, in fact.

She didn't have to talk about it now. She could leave it. Leave it till next weekend. But by then she would have told Mrs D that she would take the job. If she left it till then she would not only have taken the decision without discussing it with him, she would actually have accepted the job as well.

If she talked with him now at least she would be able to say that she wanted to talk with him about it before she finally told Mrs Doyle that she would go London. In just six week's time.

The train pulled in and they got on. It wasn't too crowded. They found a seat with no-one opposite. No-one too close by. They settled into their seats.

'Oh, I forgot to tell you, I should have, I meant to, that Mrs Doyle asked me to pop in and see her earlier in the week.'

'What did she want?'

'Well, she wanted to talk to me about the future, I suppose. She knew that we'd been thinking about going to England. I'd told her that you were set on going, and me too as well, really.'

'So?'

'Well, actually, the truth is I was surprised by what she came up with.'

'And what was that then?'

'Well she said she thought there was a job going in London. Her niece needed someone to work in her house, and she thought I might be interested in doing it.'

'What kind of job would that be? A housemaid kind of thing, again?'

He didn't look too pleased with the idea of that.

'Well, not really, well sort of, but actually more like a housekeeper I think. She said the pay would be better. More opportunities and things. They're pretty well off, Mrs D said.'

'Would you be up to that, do you think? Being a housekeeper, are you maybe a bit too young for that?'

'Not at all, George! I'm more or less doing that now. Deidre's useless as you know. Very nice, but useless. I run the place really.'

'Well, there's a difference between doing that in a family house in Bray and doing it someplace in London where they've got a load of money. I'm not sure Maureen, it seems a lot of responsibility to me.'

'Well I think I could do it. And Mrs D thinks so as well.'

'Well maybe you could. I don't know. Maybe you could. But they'd be looking for someone now, wouldn't they? Is she going to hold the job open for you? I mean it could be another six months or a year before I go, and so it'd be even longer for you.'

'They want someone to start in the middle of January. They're moving over from America and setting up house in London then. The husband is American, he's moving with his company or something.'

'Well then, you can't do it, can you?'

'I'm thinking of taking it, George.'

'What do you mean?'

'I mean I'm thinking of telling Mrs D that I'll take the job.'

'How can you, they'll need someone straight away, I told you that.'

'Well. I'd have to go straight away. In January, I mean.'

'I can't go till later in the year, Maureen. It's impossible.'

'Well I can go first, can't I? I'd have a good job, and I'd have a place to stay. It wouldn't be a problem. And then you'd come when you could.'

'That's not what we agreed, Maureen, is it?'

'We only discussed it George, and we never agreed anything. Look, if someone offered you a good job in London, you'd go wouldn't you?'

'Probably, but that's not the same thing at all.'

'I don't see why it's not the same. My sisters have all gone on their own.'

He was quiet. The train rattled on. It was dark outside. There was chatter and laughter elsewhere in the carriage.

'So have you already said you'd go? Have you already accepted the job? It sounds to me like you have.'

'No, I haven't. I wanted to talk to you first about it. I wanted to get your opinion before I finally decided. I told Mrs Doyle that I'd tell her my decision on Wednesday, when we go to see Margaret.'

'And what have you decided?'

'I'm going.'

'I thought so.'

He was disappointed.

CHAPTER THIRTY-TWO

It was Mrs Doyle who took her to Dún Laoghaire, to the port, on that Saturday evening. In the end it had seemed the most convenient, least upsetting, way to go about it. Shaughnessy had offered to take her, which probably would have involved Stephen and Maria coming along, and Deidre as well. That would have been too fussy for Maureen, she just wanted to get on with things with as few tears as possible. At the port, anyway. George had said he could come to Bray and take her on the train, carry her suitcase. He said he would like to do that. And then Mrs Doyle had said she would be quite happy just to pick her up at the Shaughnessy's and drop her off at the port. A bit like a taxi almost. So she told George she would see him there. George's mother had even suggested she could stay at their house and just go down to the boat from their house, but she definitely didn't want to do that.

Early Saturday evening Mrs D turned up in the car and came up to the house. The family and Maureen had eaten an early tea together, one that Deidre had made. It was a tad awkward because there was nothing to talk about any more, all the questions had been answered by then, but, nevertheless, it was pleasant to sit with them for the last time, in the sitting-room. When the doorbell rang they all got up and went into the hall. Maureen answered the door and Mrs D said she was ready to go.

Maureen put on her coat. She hugged Maria and Stephen, he towered over her now and Maria as well was taller. She hugged Deidre as well, and she shook hands with Shaughnessy. He held her hand in both of his and he gave her a smile.

And she left. Finally she was going, and she was relieved. Once in the car she turned and waved, seeing the four different-shaped figures silhouetted by the lights in the hall. All waving, themselves.

Mrs D was only driving slowly at first.

'Right. You've got everything now? Your money and your Travel Card, and your tickets? Double-check now, Maureen, we don't want to be coming back now, do we?'

She checked in her bag, even though she knew everything was there, having checked herself half a dozen times in the last two hours or so.

She confirmed she had everything and Mrs D speeded up. They were on their way.

They didn't talk much at all on the journey, but it was not awkward, they were used to travelling together like this. Only that previous Wednesday they had done the last trip out to see Margaret. Maureen hadn't really known what to say to her, so she just said that she wouldn't be coming for a while, but hoped to see her soon, one way or another. Margaret hadn't really understood as far as Maureen could see. She was glad, though, that Mrs D had said she would continue to visit.

Mrs D made sure that Maureen knew what she was to do when she got to London. Made sure that Maureen had the letter from Janey with the instructions on it.

'It'll seem a bit confusing at first Maureen, but it'll be easy enough, don't you worry yourself about it.'

And so they arrived at the port. Maureen saw George waiting. Mrs D stopped the car a little away from him at first.

'I hope you have a good journey Maureen. Just think, this time tomorrow night you'll be safely at Janey's house. Starting a new adventure! I envy you Maureen, I really do. Now, you'll write me a line now and then, won't you? You make sure you do.'

'I will Mrs D, I will. And thanks.'

'You're a good girl, Maureen. Make sure you come and see me when you come home for a visit won't you?'

'I will. I will.'

And Mrs D leaned over and gave her a hug. Maureen felt her warmth and smelt her perfume, felt her friendship too.

She started the car and drove the few yards to where George was standing, Maureen could see that he hadn't recognised the car. And then he saw her. He helped Maureen out and took her case. Mrs D waved to them both and set off, beeping as she pulled away. She'd said all she wanted to say already.

It was cold outside of the car, and it was windy as well. A rough winter night.

They had about twenty minutes before Maureen had to board. Probably longer if she wanted it, but Maureen didn't want to spend a long time saying goodbye to George. They went across to the station to get out of the wind, and away from the milling about that was going on near the boats. George carried the suitcase.

'So, you're all ready to go? Have you got your money and everything?'

'I have. Mrs D made me check. Everything's there.'

'Well, I hope your journey goes well, although it looks as if it might be a bit rough out there.'

'It'll be fine.'

'Ma sends her best wishes and Da as well.'

'Thank them for me, would you?'

'I will, yeah......Look, Maureen, I'll miss you, you know. I wish you weren't going, but you know that already don't you?'

'I do. Everything'll be fine George, don't you worry. And you'll be over yourself soon enough, won't you?'

'Yes, that's true.'

There was nothing more to say. They stood looking out towards the sea for a minute or two and then Maureen said she had better get going, so she could try and get a seat for the crossing.

When they reached the gate they stopped and Maureen hugged George. She hugged him tightly. She liked him very much, he was a good man.

'I'll miss you Maureen.'

“I know you will, George, I know.'

She smiled, and gave him another brief hug before picking up her case to go through towards the boat.

CHAPTER THIRTY-THREE

It was a bit of a rough and tumble getting on board. Loads of people around with their cases and their bags, individuals and groups, laughing and shouting, and sailors as well doing this and that all over the place. Maureen had never been on a boat before, any kind of boat. And this one seemed like a very big one to her.

Once she'd got through, and showed everything she needed to show, she found herself inside. At first it was difficult to work out where she should go, and then she realised that the best thing was just to follow everyone else. Mrs D, and Shaughnessy also, separately, had told her to take care of her money and look after her luggage. Most people were fine, they had both said, but there's always someone who'll take advantage of you if they can. Shaughnessy had said that she should find herself a seat if she could and stick to it. The journey wasn't that long once the boat got going.

And, luckily, she did find a seat. Next to a small number of older men, who had settled down together and didn't look as if they intended moving. A couple of them smiled at her, but they didn't say anything, and she was happy with that.

She sat down and unbuttoned her coat. It wasn't that warm in the lounge, that's what they called it. She watched the boat filling up. She realised now, or it seemed anyway, that very few people were travelling alone, a lot of the travellers were men in small groups, a few women as well together. If she had to guess she would say that most of the men had had a drink or two. It was a Saturday night after all, and why wouldn't they? It became noisier and noisier in the lounge, more and more crowded so that chairs were pushed together and bags and cases piled up. The smoke from the cigarettes, and pipes as well, became thicker and thicker, she could even see a real cloud of it hovering above everyone, blue and grey smoke. It was a lot warmer now, too.

She wasn't sure how long she had been sitting there before things started to happen, an hour possibly longer. She sensed that the noise of the engines had changed in some way, and she could see sailors walking through, looking as if they were on their way to do something, not dawdling, and waiters and barmen became more evident moving about the lounge. It was as if the whole place had started up suddenly.

And then the boat moved, she could feel the actual movement now, hear the engines taking charge and pushing the boat along. She was on her way.

She was nervous about her journey. She would not have admitted that to anyone, but she was very nervous. It was like a step into the unknown, even stepping onto this boat was like that, she had no idea what you had to do, where you had to go. So she'd just followed the others. And, luckily, no-one seemed to be taking a blind bit of notice of her, apart from those initial little smiles from the men next to her.

She could feel the boat rocking slightly as it moved, perhaps it was turning; she definitely knew that Holyhead would be the next stop, now.

After speaking to George on that Sunday she had felt sorry for him really. He hadn't expected it at all, and he was unhappy about her going. She should have felt flattered, but she didn't. And she had gone ahead with her plan. On the Wednesday, only five and a bit weeks ago now, she had got into the car and she had said, almost immediately after saying hello, that she would go to London, that she would work for Janey. She didn't actually say Janey, of course, she'd said 'your niece'. Mrs D was delighted. She said she'd made the right decision, in her opinion anyway. And they had talked about making arrangements and sorting out the tickets. Mrs D had said she would write to Janey, in America, that afternoon, telling her about Maureen's decision and she thought that Janey, who didn't worry about money too much, would telephone her before the weekend, she expected she would anyway. And she did. She arranged for Mrs D to buy the tickets and help Maureen sort out any documents that might be needed.

It all became exciting, and Mrs D was excited about the whole thing as well, which added to it all of course. She arranged for Maureen to come round and talk to her about the money she needed and the ferry times, and the Irish Mail, and how she would travel overnight to London. Janey was flexible about when she arrived so Maureen and Mrs D talked about it and they decided on that particular Saturday night. The Saturday night on which now found herself on the crowded ferry moving out onto the Irish Sea.

She wondered, too late, if George had waited on the dock till the ship had sailed, wondered if he had waited for her to come out and wave goodbye to him. She thought he probably had, and she hadn't given it a second thought. Admittedly she had been desperate not to lose her seat, but one of the men next to her would probably have looked after it for her, and her case, as well, for a minute or two, but she hadn't given George a thought.

All of a sudden the boat started to creak and roll and turn, and she could hear people saying it was going to be a rough one tonight. And it was.

The initial small movements changed into very big movements, up and down and around it seemed, again and again. At the beginning passengers in the lounge ooohed as the ship moved, and men walking from the bar with trays of pints had to move sideways, then backwards, then stop, then lean and try again. Laughing at first. But, as it got worse, less was said, less was laughed at; looking around she could see that many of the passengers were very uncomfortable with all this, were scared. A lot of crossing was going on. Men and women both. And as the journey progressed people just sat, waiting, praying some of them, for it all to be over, or ran to the toilets, or even outside into the weather, to be sick, she realised. The men next to her seemed unaffected though, half asleep the lot of them, and she, herself, although surprised by what was happening, and a bit scared initially, got used to it, and rode with it all. And she saw the waiters, and the occasional sailor passing through from outside, looking unconcerned, so she thought they weren't about to sink or anything, not yet anyway.

She sat back in her seat, closing her eyes. Feeling the movement, ignoring what was going on about her.

She had gone to see Shaughnessy that same day. The same day she had told Mrs D. She didn't want to wait, she wanted to get it over with. After they had eaten in the evening, and she had cleared away, she went back to the sitting-room where Shaughnessy was sitting smoking and reading the paper. Deidre was upstairs somewhere.

'Could I have word, sir?'

'Of course you can, Maureen, come in, sit down if you like.'

He folded the paper and dropped it onto the floor beside him.

'Are you OK, Maureen?

'Oh, I'm fine sir, I'm fine.'

'OK then, what's the problem?'

'Well, sir I wanted to tell you that I've been offered a job in

London and I'll be wanting to leave in January, sir.'

'Well, that's a surprise Maureen, I can tell you straight away I wasn't expecting that.'

Then he didn't say anything for a second or two. He looked at her, and she felt uncomfortable.

'So this job in London? What kind of thing is it?'

'It's a sort of housekeeper's job sir. I was going anyway, at some stage, to England I mean, but this came up, and it's too good to miss, I'd say.'

'So was it one of your sisters or someone that found it for you?'

She paused, unsure.

'No, it was Mrs Doyle, it's working for her niece.'

'Oh, right. She looks after you doesn't she, Mrs D? She likes you a lot. And so do we, by the way, so do we.'

'Thank you, sir.'

Unexpectedly he smiled.

'Well, I wish you the best of luck Maureen. We'll miss you, the children'll miss you, and Margaret too, I would say, she'll miss you as well. But you have to do what you have to do, and if it's a good opportunity you should take it. I'm sure you'll do a grand job.'

'Thank you.'

'So, when will you be off?'

'It's not exactly decided yet, the second or third week in January probably. If that would that be OK?'

'Just let me know when you've decided.'

He smiled again and she didn't know what to do. She was unsure what to do next.

She said 'thanks' again and turned to leave.

'Maureen. A second.'

He was standing now.

'I have appreciated everything you've done for the children, Maureen, and for Mrs Shaughnessy, for Margaret. I want you to know that.'

He stopped for a moment.

'Look, Maureen, there have been times when I've wanted to explain to you that things can sometimes be more complicated than they might seem, here in this house I mean. A lot more complicated, in fact. But the right opportunity never seemed to come. I would have liked you to know a bit more, helped you to understand what was going on.'

He seemed confused, almost upset. In a way that she'd never seen before. But his face then changed, he reconsidered, she could see that.

'Anyway, forget it, Maureen, it doesn't matter. Look, forget it. Ignore me. Forget I said a word. Shall I tell the children you're leaving, or would you like to do that yourself. That might be better, mightn't it?'

He had been going to tell her, but he'd changed his mind.

'I would like to tell them myself, if that's alright with you, tomorrow afternoon maybe?'

'That's fine, that's fine. Thanks for letting me know, anyway.'

She left the sitting room and went back to the kitchen, relieved that she'd told him and a little puzzled by him as well. What could he have told her that she didn't already know?

She felt a tap on her shoulder and she opened her eyes. It was one of the men.

'I'm going to the bar, would you like a cup of tea?'

'I would, that'd be great.'

She watched as he walked across, moving with the ship as he did so. It didn't seem to bother him, and it was easy to get served because it looked like most people were still feeling too sick or too scared to move around. He came back with a tray and handed her a cup of tea.

She offered to pay but he shook his head, and she drank the tea. It was relief to taste it. She was pleased with herself. If she'd been sick, like many of the others, the journey would have been unbearable. A nightmare in fact.

The children had been upset, of course. They'd been mystified. Maria especially. She couldn't understand why Maureen had to go. She had cried. Maureen had explained that she would have gone to England at some point anyway, it just happened to be bit sooner than she expected. She didn't mention Mrs D, she just said that someone had offered her a good job. Deidre asked her about George, what was he going to do? Maureen said he would follow later on in the year probably.

Shaughnessy said to her a few days later that he and the children, and Deidre, would be very pleased if she would join them for Christmas dinner. He laughed, saying if she was cooking it anyway, it'd be better if she ate it with them, wouldn't it? She accepted his offer, although the very thought of it made her nervous.

She dozed for the second half of the journey until she felt a light tap again on her shoulder.

'It won't be too long now Miss. We're coming into the harbour.'

It was the same man. She woke up properly. She wondered if

she should try and wash her face in the toilets, she needed a pee anyway. She asked the man if he would keep an eye on her bag, and he nodded.

The toilets were disgusting. The floors swimming in water, with vomit in the washbasins and the toilet bowls as well, and it also looked like some people didn't know how to use the toilet at all. For the first time on the journey Maureen did feel like being sick. She wouldn't wash herself in there, and she thought she could manage without the toilet till they got on the train. She would have to, because she was not going to use any of these toilets, for definite.

She went back. The boat was not moving about at all now, and people were starting to get themselves together, putting their coats on, sorting out their bags. And talking had started again and laughter as well. Relief that this part of the journey was over.

She felt more confident now. She had survived the first bit, and better than a load of the others by the look of it.

It took longer than expected for them to finally dock. The boat seemed to go back and forward quite a bit before it finally stopped. She followed the crowd, not wanting to get left behind. Mrs D had warned her it might be difficult to get a seat on the train if she wasn't quick about it.

There was a rush from the boat to the train, just a short walk, but everyone was compressed together and anxious, with their luggage and their friends, and even a few children as well, Maureen noticed. She pushed along with the rest and managed, just about, to get the last seat in a compartment. She would really have liked to go to the toilet but she decided to wait for the train to get going, you weren't meant to use the toilet when it wasn't moving anyway. There were three men in the compartment, not together she didn't think, and a couple of girls as well, about her age, maybe a touch older.

They all looked tired. Two of the men were smoking already. And there were people standing directly outside in the corridor as well, including two young lads trying to catch the eye of the two girls. They all sat tight against each other in their winter coats, the girls chatting to each other, mainly about being sick on the boat, laughing about it now, sort of. One of the men was asleep, and snoring. And it was cold. She hoped it would heat up as the train got going.

It didn't. The ticket collector, when he came round later said the heating was broken and there was nothing he could do about it, and they would be late in to Euston because of delays at Crewe. He said it an accent that Maureen hadn't heard before, it certainly wasn't like the Graham's accent. They had spoken a very nice English, Maureen remembered.

She pushed her way to the toilet when the train got going. She queued for at least ten minutes, and it wasn't really much better than on the ship, although there was a small amount of toilet paper left so she could clean the seat before she sat down. She would not go again on the train either, that was for definite as well.

Back in the compartment everyone was trying to sleep, or doze anyway, although one of the men was reading a paper and almost chain-smoking it seemed. Which made the atmosphere very unpleasant, cold and very unpleasant.

She thought about that Christmas dinner. Yes, she had been nervous about it, but as it got closer the nervousness gave way to excitement. She planned it all with Deidre, they had a great laugh together, working out what they would eat and when they would buy the goose and the bacon, and all the rest, and who would do what. In the end Maureen, on the day, was in charge because Deidre had no real idea, but she was willing to learn and was happy enough to do preparation of various types.

And they had a great Christmas dinner. She needn't have worried. There was no awkwardness at all. They ate and they laughed and they even pulled some crackers that Mr S had found in Dublin. Of course, Maureen had to do the tidying up, and most of the washing-up, and putting things away. But she didn't mind. George came round later and she told him all about it, in the kitchen.

Shaughnessy had told her not to worry about presents but she had bought a little thing for each of them, just a token, some sweets for the children and a cigar for Mr S and a nice little scarf for Deidre. Stephen and Maria bought her a bracelet, a nice one, to remember them by, and Deidre had bought her a scarf as well, a better one it has to be said, and Mr S gave her an envelope with five pounds in it.

She felt the rhythm of the train and, despite the smoke and the cold, she managed to fall asleep for a couple of hours as they sped towards London.

CHAPTER THIRTY-FOUR

The slowing down of the train woke her up. The windows were half steamed-up, and dirty as well, but she could see that it was getting light outside. They were still in the countryside, she thought, but they could not have been that far from London now. And, as if to tell her the information that she needed, right there and then, the train went slowly through a station. Watford Junction. Where Nan and Julia were living. She didn't really know where Watford was, but she did know that it wasn't that far from London.

The others in the compartment were awake, apart from one of the girls, and one of the men was standing, fiddling about with his case in the rack, and putting on a coat that had been sitting on top of the case. She asked him how long it would be, did he think? He smiled at her, he had a nice face, she hadn't really noticed before, in the night, but he looked tired as well. Twenty minutes maybe. The atmosphere in the compartment was unpleasant, what with the smoke and the cold and the smell of people as well, she'd be glad to get out of there.

She sat and waited. The train was not going particularly fast and, although she wasn't next to the window, she could just about see what was going past. Houses, thousands of them, street after street, and chimneys and smoke everywhere. She'd just sit and wait. Everything, up to now, had been fairly straightforward, get on the boat, find a seat, walk across to the train, get on the train, find a seat, just follow the person in front, because you were all going the same way. But when she got to Euston she'd be on her own. All the people on the train would be going off in different directions. Some of them would be met by friends or family. And if she'd waited until George had come over, and followed him to England, then she would have been met as well. She didn't care about that. She looked in her handbag to check the instructions for getting to Janey's house. It was safely there, and it didn't seem too complicated.

And then Euston arrived. As slowly as anything the train came into the platform. The men in the compartment had stood up and had their coats on and their bags ready to go. It wasn't really possible to go out in the corridor yet, though, because everyone else was ready to go as well. The two girls were sitting down waiting, they looked nervous themselves, Maureen caught the eye of one of them and they smiled at each other.

The train lurched to a stop and everyone started to get off, she could see people outside on the platform already, rushing on to wherever they were going. When the men had left, gone into the corridor, Maureen pulled her own case down, as did the two girls with their bags.

'Can you tell us where the Underground is? Neither of us have been before.'

Maureen was surprised to be asked, almost flattered that they would have thought she knew the way.

'It's just there in the station, it's easy enough.'

She knew this because Mrs D had told her, and it was on her instructions as well.

'Can we follow you then?'

'Sure. Where are you going off to, then?'

'Tooting Bec, they call it. That's a funny name isn't it? Tooting, I mean. Do you know it? And you, where are you going?'

'East Finchley. No, I don't know where Tooting is I'm, afraid.'

And the three girls traipsed together down the platform together, with Maureen in the lead, now, idiotically, feeling confident because she had been asked the way, almost as if she lived there.

She was glad they were together, glad she was with someone else, because she didn't think she had ever heard such noise and seen so many people in her life, it would have been really frightening on her own, with porters rushing their barrows, and steam shooting out from the engines, and people pushing past in a hurry to get wherever they were going, and shouting as well, shouting and calling everywhere. The building was big, and old, with a tall ceiling, and it was dirty and smoky, and grimy too, not a nice place at all.

Maureen looked for signs and saw one that pointed towards the Underground. She led them along and down to where she would get the train to East Finchley. They couldn't really talk but they had introduced themselves, Mary and Joan were their names. They were from Tipperary and were going to stay with an aunt who had found them jobs in a hotel somewhere.

In the Underground station they looked quickly at the ticket machines, but then they decided it would be easier to go to the ticket office, which they did, and bought their tickets and were told where to get their separate trains. The man behind the glass was very helpful to them. And then they parted to go on their different journeys.

Maureen went to her platform, Platform 1, and waited for the train to High Barnet or Mill Hill East. And the first one roared into the station with High Barnet on the front and on the indicator thing as well. She got on and sat down. It was not packed, but most of the seats were taken, a lot of the people reading a newspaper, if they weren't talking to the person next to them. No one took a blind bit of notice of Maureen.

The noise of the train was tremendous to Maureen's ears, and it was a bit odd knowing you were travelling underground, she wondered what on earth was over the top of them as they flew along. Mrs D had said that she would know when she was close to her station because the train would come out into the open air again, just before they arrived. It took about twenty minutes and then she was there. She jumped up and made sure she had everything, and the train stopped, and she got out onto a cold platform that seemed to be above the street in some way. Higher than the road.

Outside she checked her directions and walked, with her case, toward Janey's.

She found the house easily, less than ten minute's walk. A big house, bigger even than Mrs Doyle's. She breathed deeply and rang the bell.

A woman in her thirties or so answered. She was wearing some kind of slacks and a blouse and a headscarf. She was pretty.

'Maureen! You've got here! Come in, come in, come in.'

'Hello Mrs.....'

She'd forgotten her second name.

'Janey, call me Janey.'

She had an English accent which also sounded a little bit American as well.

'Now, I'll show you your room, and you can have a wash, and a bit of breakfast, and then a rest. You have the day to yourself, and I'll talk to you a bit later about what I'd like you to do. And you can start properly tomorrow. OK? It's only me here today. Jed's away on business and the children are with their grand-parents, so we can have a nice talk later. OK.'

Whenever she said OK, she sounded very American.

CHAPTER THIRTY-FIVE

Janey had made her eggs and bacon, and tea, and bread and butter, and had asked her about her journey, and had been very kind. Maureen's room was on the same floor as all the other bedrooms, the smallest one she discovered later, but it was the nicest room she had ever seen, even with a window looking out over the long garden. It was obvious, immediately, that the family had only just moved in, there were packing cases still around and things looked a bit disorganised.

Janey told Maureen that for the first couple of days, starting tomorrow they would work together getting the house in order. The children would be back Tuesday evening, and Jed would be here by Friday at the latest.

On that first day, she slept for most of the day, she was exhausted, and when Janey had explained how everything worked, she had a bath as well. She had never had a bath like that in her whole life. She thought she liked Janey. It was only right at the end of the day that she realised that she had missed Mass.

She got up early on the Monday and waited for Janey to arrive downstairs, which she did at half-seven. After some tea and toast they worked together, unpacking stuff, and moving furniture around, and cleaning as well. The two of them together, except when Janey was on the phone, which she was quite a lot. But it was fun working with her.

At lunchtime Maureen made some sandwiches from what was in the fridge, and they sat down in the kitchen.

'Right Maureen. Listen to me. I want you to be my right-hand woman. I know that you'll have to learn quickly but my Aunt, the formidable Mrs D, tells me you have a lot of potential. It won't be easy, but I can see already that you've got what it takes.'

And she explained that Maureen would do most of the everyday cooking, if that was OK, especially for the children, but she herself liked cooking so it wouldn't all be down to Maureen. And she would guide her through what the family liked to eat and help her when she needed it. And that Maureen would be a part of the family, that she would eat with them, and when they went on holiday she would come with them too. They had dinner parties, which were often part of Jed's work, and Maureen probably wouldn't want to get involved in those, not at the beginning anyway, and she didn't have to worry about the cooking for that because they would get caterers in. And she should expect to baby sit a couple of times a week. And she could have a day off a week and they could arrange that on a weekly basis if that was alright. And once she got used to everything she would take responsibility for arranging things like the caterers, and getting people in for cleaning etc. etc.

It was difficult to take everything in and it was scary as well, because, really, she didn't even know what caterers were, and she'd have to use the phone, and Janey said it would be better if she could learn to drive, because that would be very useful.

And after lunch they got back to sorting things out. Moving furniture around, this time, because Janey didn't like where the movers had put the stuff, and between the two of them they moved beds, and chests of drawers, and wardrobes, and started to unpack clothes to go in the drawers and cupboards. And they made the beds, properly as well, so that everything even after one day started to look more ordered, and sensible and clean. And Maureen felt she had contributed to that, which felt good.

Janey insisted that she would cook that evening, and made spaghetti with some kind of tomato sauce. Maureen hadn't eaten anything like that ever before. It reminded her of once on a train, when she was six or seven, or maybe even younger, with Mama, being offered a tomato by a nice lady sitting opposite. Maureen had never seen a tomato before and she had bitten right into it, expecting it to be sweet, and she'd been totally shocked by the taste, and had screwed her face up and spat it out, into her hand, and everyone had laughed. The spaghetti and the tomato sauce tasted different too, from what she was used to, but she found that she liked it, apart from the difficulty of keeping the spaghetti on the fork. Janey demonstrated how to do it, and they had a good laugh as Maureen got it wrong again and again, and then finally got it right.

CHAPTER THIRTY-SIX

Maureen enjoyed those first two days with Janey. They got on well. But, at the same time, she understood that, underneath it all, Janey liked to get her own way. She heard her on the phone a few times talking to a plumber and to a man who was going to do something big to the kitchen, she told them exactly what she wanted, there was no argument. And when she asked Maureen to do things, it was always said nicely, but it was always Janey's way or no way. Maureen didn't mind.

Even in those couple of days she was learning things, there was an electric food mixer in the kitchen, brand new, that Janey'd brought from the US, and they both learnt how to use it, they did a cake mixture in it. Maureen didn't even know that something like that existed. And the Hoover that Janey'd brought as well, it was so easy to clean the floors and the carpets with. In the Shaughnessy's Maureen just had one of those floor sweepers that you pushed back and forth, this was a totally different thing altogether.

And Janey made her do things. Insisted. On that first Tuesday she said they needed to ring the grocers in Muswell Hill to get some stuff delivered, and Maureen should do it. Maureen froze. She had answered the phone in Bray, but that was different. Janey told her exactly what to say, who she was, what she wanted, and when she wanted it. And she stood by her, encouraging her with nods and gestures as she made the call. And she told her to say 'This is Maureen Kelleher, the housekeeper at Mrs Solomon's, in Woodside Avenue'. She told her to be confident.

'If you don't, they'll walk all over you, Maureen. Show them who's boss!'

She laughed when she said this. But she meant it.

Late on Tuesday afternoon the children arrived. Ruth and Michael. She was seven and he was five. Their grandmother brought them. She was about the same age as Mrs D, had the same look about her and, of course, she had an Irish accent, not quite as strong as Mrs D's though.

'It's great to meet you Maureen, Mary says you're a real gem. And I hope you enjoy working here with Janey. She's a bit of a whirlwind, difficult to keep up with, I know that myself, but you'll be fine I'm sure.'

The children were very polite to Maureen, and Ruth asked her where she came from and did she know their great-aunt, Mary? Maureen said she did. She liked them both.

They sat at the kitchen table, all five of them, and they ate a small piece of the cake that Janey and Maureen had made with the food mixer. Then Janey said that, after they'd said good-bye to their Nana, Maureen would take the children upstairs to sort out their clothes and their rooms, and make sure that they had everything ready, because they had to go to school the next day. And everyone did what they were told.

The week got into a routine. Maureen got herself up and made sure the children were up, made sure they washed and put their uniform on, and then they had some breakfast, usually cereal and some toast. She then had to make sure they went back to the bathroom and brushed their teeth. And then she walked them to school. It was a fifteen-minute relaxed walk up to Highgate, although Michael always said he wanted to get the bus, but they never did.

Maureen walked back to the house and quickly sorted the

bedrooms out, and any washing-up that may have been left over in the kitchen. Janey always left a list on the hall table saying what was to be done that day, initially, for the first week or two, it would have everything on it, but after that just the things that were extra or different. Maureen learnt what she had to do and got on with it. And Janey, who went out most days for at least a couple of hours, left Maureen with more and more responsibility, ringing up the kitchen man, ordering, even booking tickets for a concert.

The husband Jed, turned up on the Saturday, although he had been expected on the Friday. His flight had been delayed. He must have forgotten his key because Maureen had to open the door to him, when the doorbell rang.

'Hi! You must be Maureen. Good to meet you! Is Janey around? Where is she, where are the kids?'

A real American accent.

He came in, dumped his case in the hall and went looking for the family, who all appeared almost instantly. The children jumping up on him, and Janey giving him a kiss.

He was tall, with dark hair and a darkish complexion. And he was very handsome, and he was friendly. Call me Jed, Maureen. Yes, sir, I will. No, Maureen! Jed, I tell you, Jed!

Janey was different around him. Which was nice to see.

So, with him back, and the house becoming more settled and organised, it was easier to settle into a rhythm. Maureen enjoyed her job, and enjoyed the responsibility that Janey gave her, knowing, at the same time, that Janey had high expectations and would not be happy with things going wrong, or things being done badly.

'Maureen, we'll go up to Finchley tomorrow I'd like us to get a few things and I'd like to get you a couple of dresses as well.

Something that you can wear for work, practical but nice looking if you know what I mean. No offence but what you've got at the moment is......is a bit kinda Bray, if you know what I mean. Is that OK?'

'Of course it is. And I'm happy to pay for them, I know the stuff I've got is a bit old-fashioned, if you like'

'No need. Think of it as a requirement for work, so I pay for that!'

Days off were a bit strange. In the main everyone found it convenient if Maureen took the Sunday off. She would go to Mass and then she had the rest of the day to herself. Janey would cook the lunch, and Maureen was welcome to stay if she wanted. But she felt that it was their family day and it would be better, really, if she was out, and if she did stay she felt obliged to at least help with the lunch. So usually she would go into London, at least for a couple of hours.

She could get the underground in or the bus. The bus was the more interesting because of the simple fact that you saw more of London that way.

Although she knew that lots of Irishmen had fought in the war, and there was a bit of bombing at home, and terrible shortages as well, she realised on these Sundays how different it must have been in London. There were still huge areas of bombed land, bomb sites, and rationing still, of course. When she walked round she also got to understand that Janey and Jed were well-off, that she was working for people who, although they were relaxed and friendly, were rich in comparison to most people in London. That she, herself, was privileged in a way as well, working for them. With her own lovely little room, and eating with the family, almost like being treated as one of them. Not quite, but as near as you'd hardly notice the difference.

After about a month, she arranged to go and see Julia and Nan in Watford. Julia said that she should come to her house and they'd all have Sunday dinner together.

After nine o' clock Mass she went on the tube to get the train from Euston to Watford Junction. It wasn't as quick as the Irish Mail, that was for sure, stopping at all the stations on the way. Julia had given her instructions and it took her about twenty minutes to find their house. It was on a long road with small terraced houses all the way down, not far from the hospital it seemed, which would be convenient for both Nan and Julia.

Julia had got married to Jim, he worked on the buildings, and they lived in part of the house, the downstairs flat. Maureen was surprised how small it was, certainly in comparison to where she was living. Her 'small' bedroom was the same size as Julia's living room. Nan turned up with her husband, Danny, at about half twelve. They obviously all got on pretty well, Maureen could imagine that they saw a lot of each other, because the girls worked in the same hospital for a start. After a couple of minutes the two boys said they'd would go for a pint and would be back just after two.

It was great to sit down with them, because, although she'd sent them a letter now and then, she hadn't actually seen either of them for three years or more. She told them a bit about home, and about Bray, and they told her about Watford and the jobs they had, and who they'd seen. Two or three people from the Dungarvan area were living in or around as well. None of them had seen Theresa, although they'd all had a letter or two. Julia and Nan had always been close, but they'd never been great pals with Theresa. They'd laugh that Theresa was a bit above herself, gave herself airs, and, although they laughed, that was what they thought.

As they chatted Maureen looked at both the women. Married

now. Nan said she lived in a similar kind of place not too far away, they hoped to get something bigger off the council eventually. And she said also, as if it was half a secret, that she was pregnant as well. Julia obviously knew already. And as Maureen looked at them she could see that they looked older than they were, older than the mid-twenties that they were, already they looked downtrodden, a bit poor almost. Friendly, and obviously close to each other, but worn out as well.

At about twenty-past two Jim and Danny turned up. Jim seemed OK, but Danny had obviously overdone it. Maureen could see that Nan looked nervous, or was she just embarrassed? Maureen wasn't sure.

They all squeezed into the kitchen, around the small table, where Julia served up a bit of bacon with potatoes and cabbage. The men each had a pint bottle of Guinness to see them through the meal. The women didn't say a great deal now, they looked happy enough but said little, and the men asked Maureen about where she was working, telling her they knew that area well, working for Murphy's like they did. The food was fine, it reminded her of home, but there was something that she didn't like about being squeezed into this rather grubby little kitchen, close up to, listening to, the two men who went on about this and that, a bit of football, a bit of hurling, a bit about work. It wasn't interesting, she didn't feel part of it. And she realised also that she didn't know these two sisters that well either, in fact she hardly knew them at all.

She was glad to get out of there, felt liberated, almost, walking back up towards the town and on towards the station. And she liked the journey back to Euston, and felt happy getting on the tube, and even happier walking back from the station to the house in Woodside Avenue.

CHAPTER THIRTY-SEVEN

She wrote home to George after the first week and then every one or two weeks depending on his reply, and she wrote to Julia soon after arriving, and then occasionally, and she wrote to Mama and Dada once in a while, as she did to Mrs D. Mrs D deserved that, at the very least. And, of course, she wrote to Maria and Stephen.

Her letters were not long, to any of them. She told them she was having a great time and everything was going well, and she got on with the family, and she was glad she had come. And she asked after other people as well; Margaret, or Declan, or the Barry family, or Mr S and Deidre.

She wrote her letters on the Sunday night usually, and posted them on Monday morning after she had dropped the children off at school, maybe just one or two letters a week. She knew as she sat down to write her letters, and as she wrote them, that she was not telling them exactly how it was.

This was because she thought it was almost impossible to explain this different kind of life to them. Mama and Dada had never been inside a house like this, she was pretty sure of that, and the existence of all the others, even Mrs D really, was not like it was in this house, with this family, in London.

She knew that Janey had sort of taken her under her wing, that she was training her in some way. And when she thought about it she realised that she wasn't training her to be a housekeeper, although that was obviously part of it, no, she was sort of training her to be like herself.

When they went to buy the dresses, she wanted Maureen to start thinking about how she looked to other people. The dresses themselves were not expensive, but they did have a bit of a different look about them, different to what Maureen owned, or might have thought of buying herself. And, when they were there, she suggested a pair of slacks might be useful. When Maureen herself decided to buy a new coat she asked Janey to help her choose, and she did, pointing her towards things which had a little bit of style.

Of course, it wasn't all easy, Janey didn't believe that things should be easy, for herself or anyone else, she knew that if you wanted something you had to try, you had to put in the effort. She said as much to Maureen, and to her children as well.

At the beginning, the social events were the most difficult for Maureen. The Solomon's had a house-warming party after about a month. Janey planned it all, with Maureen's help, or assistance anyway, they talked to caterers, looked at menus, and decided what drinks there would be. And, on the night, there were a couple of waitresses with the drinks, and the caterers serving the food. Janey told Maureen that she wanted her to keep an eye on things, make sure everything was done right, make sure that people were getting drink and food, and she was to talk to people as well, try and chat to people.

Maureen made herself as smart as she could for the evening, and of course Janey looked fantastic. Once the evening started it was as if Janey had become a different person, a performer really. And the guests arrived all smart and, obviously, well off. Maureen made sure that coats were taken and drinks were offered and everyone knew where they were going, and Janey kept performing. But, for all that, Maureen knew that Janey was keeping an eye on things, and at least three times during the evening she came past Maureen to give her an order about drinks for a particular person, checking where the desserts were, and telling her to stop one of the waitresses spending too much time with a particular group of men. And Maureen did all this, and made sure that she was keeping an eye on things herself. It taught her to see, to take notice. She spoke to people as well, mainly because they spoke to her, asking her who she was, how come she was here, did she work for Jed, was she a friend of Janey's? And she said she was the housekeeper. It sounded strange saying it out loud, a number of times, to different people, to people she didn't know. And seeing their reactions, as well, of course. To one or two people it meant the conversation stopped right there, they smiled, politely enough, and moved on. To others it was interesting, and they asked her where she came from, you're Irish obviously, and how she liked working for the Solomon's, and where had she worked before. And she chatted to them. Luckily she didn't have to keep going for too long, she learnt that she could say, oh, excuse me, I'd better go and sort out those drinks over there, or I must go and check something with the caterers.

It was difficult, but even on that first big evening it got easier as the evening went on. She didn't drink anything but a bit of lemonade, now and then, all evening. She probably wouldn't have drunk any alcohol anyway, but Janey had said to her it's better to keep a clear head for these things, so she'd not touched a drop.

And, of course, she had to keep half an eye on the children. They'd got a baby sitter in for the evening, and the children had been allowed to see everything start, but then they'd gone upstairs. Every half hour or so Maureen dashed up to see all was well, using it as an opportunity to get her breath back, and check herself in the mirror as well.

Everything finished, finally, at about half-one, Maureen making sure the waitresses and caterers did all the cleaning up, and washing-up, that they had been contracted to do before they left. Then she went to bed.

She had most of the Sunday off although she had spent an hour or two in the morning, after Mass, making sure that any remaining signs of the party were cleaned up or put away. On the Monday morning, when she arrived back from taking the children to school, Janey asked her to sit down with her in the kitchen for a post-mortem.

And she went through the whole evening. And made notes. Had they got the right amount of drink, and the right type? Was the food good enough, did people eat it? Were the caterers any good, and the waitresses? And she told Maureen that she had done very well, but she would be expected to be a bit more evident in future, she wanted to work towards the point where Maureen could run things, where she could really leave things to her. But she said, also, that she had seen her talking to guests, and one or two had actually told Jane how much they'd liked Maureen. So well done!

CHAPTER THIRTY-EIGHT

Maureen had not heard from Theresa, even though she had written her a short letter to say that she was working in London. Mama had said a couple of times, in letters, that Maureen should visit Theresa. Mama's letters were just little notes really.

'Hope you are well, Dada's fine. Could you go and see Theresa one day? The girls send their love.'

She decided that she would go and see her. It was the beginning of April. Lent still. Maureen was not observing Lent with maybe the same rigour that she might have done at home, but she'd given up sweets and was sticking to that. Janey didn't observe Lent, although she had been brought up a Catholic. And, of course, Jed was Jewish.

Maureen went to Mass at ten, not too early, no communion that day, she hadn't been to confession, and then she took the tube down to Camden where Theresa was living. As far as she knew anyway.

She'd been through Camden before on the train, on the way to Euston, or into London, but she'd never stopped there, there was also a station called Mornington Crescent nearby, which, she thought, sounded quite nice. She got off at Camden Town and looked at the map in the station, and then asked for help from the ticket collector. He pointed her in the right direction.

'Five minutes, straight up Camden Road, darlin', you can't miss it.'

And so she walked away from the station, toward Theresa's street.

It looked dismal around here, dirty. She walked past the big ABC bakery, she hadn't realised they made their bread in Camden, and then, a minute or two later, she turned into Theresa's street. Small houses. She was nervous, she was almost tempted to turn back, to run away. She wasn't quite sure why. If Theresa had wanted her to visit she would have asked her, wouldn't she?

She kept going and rang the doorbell.

It was answered almost immediately. Not Theresa, but a young woman. Not unfriendly, but brief nevertheless.

'Yeah?'

'Does Theresa Kelleher live her?'

'Yeah. Upstairs. Theresa! Someone for you! Hang on, love, she'll be down in a minute.'

And the girl disappeared.

Maureen waited. At least a minute. And then she heard footsteps coming down the stairs. The door opened. It was Theresa.

Initially, she'd only looked round the door, so Maureen really only saw her face. It was definitely Theresa, but she looked a bit tired, not as smart as she always had been, her hair a bit higgledy-piggledy.

'Oh... God save us...... Hello Maureen. What on earth are you doing here?'

She looked shocked, taken aback, surprised definitely.

'I thought I'd come and see you. You didn't reply when I wrote you, so I thought I'd come and see how you were. I'm kind of doing the rounds, I went to Watford to see Nan and Julia the other week. And Mama said as well, would I try and call on you, see how you were?'

'OK. Well, you'd better come in I suppose.'

She opened the door to let Maureen come into the hall, and then shut it behind her.

'I'm upstairs. Follow me.'

And she did.

Theresa was wearing a kind of housedress and a pair of slippers, she looked like a housewife who'd been caught unawares, which, of course, she had been. Nothing at all wrong with those clothes on a Sunday morning at home, but they weren't the kind of thing that she would have expected on Theresa, not back in Dublin anyway.

'You're in Finchley or somewhere, aren't you?'

She spoke as she walked upstairs. So she'd read the letter anyway.

'It's kind of between East Finchley and Highgate. Highgate really I suppose.'

Janey always said it was Highgate they lived in, but Jed teased her and said weren't they actually nearer to East Finchley? And she'd get annoyed about that.

It was only a short flight of stairs. The house was two storeys high, Maureen had seen that from outside, so presumably Theresa had the upstairs, just like Julia had the downstairs of that house in Watford. The girl who answered the door must have the rooms or the flat downstairs. She could hear the radio on down there and someone laughing, not the girl, it was a man.

'Right, here we are.'

There was a very small landing, hardly enough space to turn round in, and three doors.

Theresa opened one of the doors and went into the room, Maureen followed.

It was the room at the front of the house. In a small play pen near the window there was a child, a baby really. Maureen was both surprised and not surprised at the same time.

'This is James. Say hello, James, this is your Auntie Maureen come to see you.'

The baby was too young to say hello, that was obvious, but he did look towards them, holding out his arms to Theresa and smiling as well.

Theresa looked at the baby, and looked at Maureen. She had a wry smile on her face.

'So, Maureen. There you are. That's the reason I've been a bit difficult to get hold of.'

Maureen went over to the child and smiled, and leant over and put out her arms to him, and he put out his arms to her, and she picked him up and held him close to her.

'Hello, James, you're a lovely boy, aren't you? I'm your Auntie Maureen and I'm very pleased to meet you, very pleased indeed.'

She could smell him, and feel his warmth next to her, hear the noises he was making. She held him out to look at him and he smiled at her as she did so. He was lovely.

'He has the look of Dada about him, don't you think?'

'Don't be ridiculous, Theresa, why would you say a thing like that!'

And they both laughed.

'I'll make some tea.'

She left the room, leaving Maureen with James. He looked anxious for a second, his eyes following his mother's departure through the door, seeing her disappearance, but then he was OK. He looked back at Maureen and giggled and gurgled. She walked around the small room with the baby in her arms, looking at everything.

There was an armchair, and a small sofa, and a table with two chairs, and the play pen. Which just left a small square of carpet in the middle, in front of the fireplace. The fire was lit and there was a fireguard in front of it. On the mantel there were some photos. One of Mama and Dada, one of Maureen and Julia and Nan and Theresa, together outside the front gate at home, when they were years younger. Theresa looked as if she was sixteen or so, and Maureen just a child. And there were three photos of James. There was a little clock in the centre and a mirror above. On the table, there was an ashtray with the remains of a couple of cigarettes, lipstick on one, and some letters, bills they looked like. A standard lamp in the corner, behind the armchair. Not much else. Toys in the play pen. Curtains and nets at the window. She looked out quickly at the road she had walked down just a few minutes ago. Rocking the baby, cooing in his ear.

She heard the noise of the tea being made, and then Theresa reappeared, with a small tray which she put on the table.

'Give him here.'

She took James and laid him gently down in the play pen, for a second he thought about crying and then he just got on with playing and standing, and sitting and playing.

They sat at the table.

When Maureen had seen Theresa last, that afternoon in Bray, she had seemed so much more grown up than Maureen, so much more adult. What was it, eighteen months or so? Now things were a bit different.

'So I suppose you want to know all about it, do you?'

'Only if you want to tell me.'

'You'll have guessed most of it in the last five minutes I would say. Didn't you have any idea? Any of you?'

'No. Not really. You always did what you wanted to anyway, didn't you? I suppose we just thought you'd moved on a bit, away a bit, from us I mean.'

'Well, I've moved on alright, that's true enough.'

'What happened then?'

'I got involved with one of the partners at work. Not the one I was working for, one of the others. A bit younger he was, still is, of course. I started to see him, just for a drink at first, but then it got more complicated, and he's married anyway. There was no way it was going to be anything more than a bit on the side for him, it couldn't be anything else could it? But I suppose I had some kind of ridiculous hopes. And then I got pregnant.'

She looked sad as she spoke.

'Did you tell him?'

'Oh, yes, I told him alright.. I thought he ought to know. I mean I didn't threaten him or anything, I didn't say I'd tell his wife, or tell the other partners. I just told him I was pregnant, and it was his child.'

'So what did he say to that?'

'Well, first he said, was I sure it was his? So I said it was definitely his, there was not a shadow of a doubt about that. And he was quite calm about the whole thing, I was surprised. Maybe it was because he's a lawyer, I don't know.'

'What happened then.'

'He said he would help me all he could, with money he meant, but he wouldn't admit to being the father. In fact, if asked, he would deny being the father, if I said anything he would deny it, and there'd be no more money either. He said it might be better if I considered going elsewhere with the child. He even said maybe I should go to Australia or New Zealand. He said I could be a widow or something, someone who'd lost their husband and had to bring up the child on their own. No-one would know the difference, he said. And he would help with expenses, and, possibly, a bit of an allowance.'

'You didn't want to do that?'

'Not really. It seems a bit silly, considering I haven't been in contact with anyone for ages, but I didn't want to go so far away that it would be difficult to see anyone any more. I'd miss you all, I suppose.'

'So you decided London?'

'Yes. He would have preferred a greater distance but, to be fair, he said he would give me some money and would try and give some support for the child if he could. But he also asked me if I'd thought of getting rid of the child. In London it would be possible to do that, even if it wasn't legal. He said he would pay for that, said he knew people who might be able to organise that for me. I said no to that, straight away, that was never going to happen. I would have the child, with or without his money. I told him that straight.'

'So, when I saw you, it was all decided?'

'It was. I thought about talking to you about it. But, to be honest, you seemed such a child, on that first day and when I saw you again, such a child. So I didn't, it didn't seem fair.'

'I remember thinking that you looked different, you looked worried, not like the usual confident Theresa.'

'I let you down a bit, didn't I? Leaving you like that?'

'No, not at all. Forget it, I was fine. So you came to London?'

'I had some savings and some money from him, so I came over and got this place, and I got a job in an office for a few months. Luckily I never got that big so I worked without any questions till almost the seventh month. And then, two months later, I had the baby.'

'All on your own, though, that's terrible.'

'Not totally, Sheila, downstairs, she's great. She worked out pretty quick what was going on and helped me, and looked after me a bit as well. It wasn't terrible at all. And I work part of the week again now, Sheila looks after James, I pay her. It's OK, I've got enough money to get by, and to look after him as well. And I get that bit of money from Dublin as well, which helps.'

'Are you going to tell everyone? But look, if you want me to keep it secret, I will. If you want.'

'What do you think, Maureen, what do you think I should do?'

'I think you should tell everyone, the family I mean, absolutely. Mama and Dada won't mind, they might be surprised, maybe a bit shocked, but they won't mind Theresa, they really won't. They'd want to know, now that's the truth of it, they'd want to know.'

'And Nan and Julia and all the rest?'

'Well, I'd say that Nan and Julia would have a bit of a laugh about it all. Theresa with all her big ways and there she is with a child and no father! And Nan'll be annoyed you beat her to it as well! But they'd want to know and they'd like to help, I'm sure of that, sure of it. And all the others as well.'

'Well, maybe I should write a few letters and tell them all about their nephew and their grandson.'

'I think you should, definitely.'

They looked over at James. He was asleep.

Maureen stayed for another couple of hours with Theresa.

Theresa showed her the flat. It was just three rooms, the front room where they had talked, a tiny kitchen, and a small bedroom. There was a single bed and the cot squeezed in there. The shared toilet was out the back. She had a tin bath which she filled a couple of times a week, or, occasionally, she said, she used the public baths which were not too far away.

Maureen told Theresa about Bray, and Margaret, and Julia and George. And told her about her new job in Highgate. But she didn't give too much detail about that. She would have liked to tell Theresa about the luxury she was living in, and the type of people the Solomon's were, about Janey, and the housewarming party. She would have liked to, but it didn't seem quite right to do that at the moment, when Theresa was living like this. It wasn't a slum or anything, it was comfortable enough in its own way, but it was nowhere near the comfort that Maureen had. Without the problem, as well, of having to bring up a child on her own, a child with no father. She wondered about that lawyer in Dublin as well, wondered whether he ever thought about his child living like this in the backstreets of dirty old Camden.

Theresa made them both some bacon and eggs, and she'd made a bit of soda bread as well, so it was almost like having breakfast back home. And they had another pot of tea as well, while Theresa smoked a cigarette while they chatted and played with James.

Theresa said she would write to everyone in the next day or so, and she would say that Maureen had visited and that she already knew. And they would see what would happen then.

Maureen promised that she would come and see Theresa in two weeks' time, and she gave her the address in Highgate in case she wanted to get in touch in the meantime. She gave a big hug to James before she left, and a hug to Theresa as well. Both of them waved her away from the front door as she set off back to the station.

Theresa seemed happy enough, she thought. She didn't seem upset or resentful or anything like that. But if anyone had told her, two years ago, that Theresa would be living in a place like that, with her own little baby boy, and no father, she would not have believed them. It would have been impossible to predict. Smart, efficient, ambitious Theresa. Absolutely impossible to predict.

Maureen wasn't in any way glad that things had turned out like that for Theresa, except for the fact she now had a lovely baby, of course. James was a lovely, happy, baby. But, as she got on the train for High Barnet, she couldn't help but feel relieved with the way that things had turned out for herself.

CHAPTER THIRTY-NINE

Janey had got into the habit, after the house-warming party post-mortem, of having a kind of business meeting with Maureen every Monday morning, after she'd arrived back from taking the children to school. Maureen probably would not have been around on the Sunday, so it was a time they could catch up with things and plan the week as well. Usually it was friendly and they had a bit of a laugh together. On the Monday after her visit to Theresa's Maureen had thought of telling Janey about her sister, and the baby, but decided not to, not just yet. But, anyway, on that particular Monday something else came up that Janey wanted to discuss.

'Maureen I wanted to talk to you about something this morning, and I don't want you to be upset about what I'm going to say, do you understand?'

Janey was being unusually serious and Maureen was worried that she might have done something terribly wrong without realising it, or worse, that Janey was going to let her go, sack her. Which would teach her to be so smug about her situation in comparison to Theresa's. Pride comes before a fall, Mama had always said that.

'Yes, of course.'

'Right. The thing is Maureen I think you have to do something about your writing and how you put things down on paper. To be honest, my love, your handwriting is appalling and your written vocabulary and the way you express things in writing is almost as bad. Even on the little notes you do for telephone messages.'

Maureen could feel herself going red with shame and embarrassment. She had not expected this at all.

'I'm sorry Janey, I don't know what to say.'

And then, to her further shame, she cried. She couldn't help herself. Sitting there at the kitchen table in that lovely house, with the garden through the window, and a cup of tea in front of her, she cried.

Janey got up and came round to her side and gave her a hug.

'Maureen, Maureen, it's not worth crying about, that doesn't help at all. We've just got to find a way to improve it, that's all. You're an intelligent young woman and you need to make use of your intelligence, and expressing yourself in writing is part of it. Even writing letters, they need to be done properly.'

'I don't know what to do about it, Janey. I could practice I suppose, could I do that?'

'You could, but you'd have to know what to practice, wouldn't you? Look, I've decided that, just for a short period of time, just until the summer holidays I'm going to get someone to come every week to help you, to give you exercises for your handwriting and help you with putting stuff down on paper. Is that OK?'

'But I'd have to pay for it, I'm not sure I could afford it, Janey.'

'I'll pay, that's not a problem, for this first bit anyway. He's coming tomorrow at seven for your first lesson. Better to get on with things, that's what I say. Finished crying? Good. We'd better get on with it this week hadn't we? Oh, by the way, I need you to get a provisional driving licence because I want you to learn to drive as well, if possible before the summer holidays. Anyway, let's get on.'

Mr Gordon arrived at seven the following evening. An older

man, Maureen wasn't sure what age he might be. He asked her to copy out a piece of writing from a book and then he dictated a short piece to her. And he looked at what she produced for a minute or two.

'You went to school in Ireland I suppose? How old were you when you left?'

'Thirteen.'

'Blimey, that's a bit young. And did you enjoy school?

'I did, but I don't suppose I did that well.'

'Do you read books?'

'Not really no.'

'Do you read the newspaper?'

'Sometimes. Occasionally.'

'And are the papers delivered here?'

'Yes. We get the Times, I think, and the Manchester Guardian, and the Daily Herald.'

'That's quite a lot.'

'Mr Solomon says he likes to keep up with the news, but I'm not sure he always has time, he's very busy. He works in advertising.'

'Well, Miss Kelleher, I'd like you to make sure you read a newspaper every day, not from cover to cover but read the main parts. You don't have any problem reading do you?'

'No, I don't, although I don't always know some of the more complicated words.'

'There's a dictionary in the house?'

'Yes, there is.'

'Well, use it then. Start with the Daily Herald probably. Every day.'

'Sure.'

'And I have these cards with writing exercises on. One every day. Very careful, no need to rush. Look I'll show you.'

And he took a card and he copied the writing on it very slowly, making sure it looked exactly the same.

'There. Just like that. And I think it won't take you long, Miss Kelleher, to improve.'

'Maureen. Call me Maureen.'

'Maureen then.'

'And last of all I want you to write a little piece about home. Just fifty words, no more, describing your house or your school, or even someone you know. In that kind of handwriting. Can you do that?'

'I can.'

He was a nice man, she liked him. And she did exactly what he said. Mostly in the evening when the children had gone to bed, but if she had a moment during the day she might take a look at the newspaper. And if she had to write a note or a shopping list she made sure she wrote it carefully and clearly.

Each week he came and he helped her improve and he talked to her about what she had read and he even brought her books to read, a variety of them. A simple one called 'The Little House on the Prairie' which she loved and read a bit of to the children, who wanted to hear more, and he brought a book of short stories by James Joyce, whom she'd heard of all right but had never read. But she did know he'd lived in Bray, in Martello Terrace, not far from the station. She enjoyed the books he brought, and she found that she like reading more than she'd thought.

The driving was something different altogether. She was scared stiff at the beginning. Janey had found someone to teach her, a local man who did driving instruction as a kind of hobby. The one thing that did keep her going was the memory of being driven by Mrs D, who'd have been proud of her if she could see her now. In fact, once she got used to it, the driving was not that difficult, and she began to enjoy it as well. Her instructor, Mr Slade, was actually quite amused by the idea of this nineteen-year-old learning to drive in Mr Solomon's quite big Austin. The traffic could sometimes be very busy but she got used to it and she passed her test first time, which was pretty good according to Mr Slade, because, he said, only about half of people passed first time.

It was a strange summer in a way because she started every weekday taking the children to school and then, at some time during that day, she would do some kind of learning herself. She might do some writing practice or some reading, or she might be having a driving lesson. It was busy because everything else had to be packed in as well. Janey's expectations never changed, she was friendly and amusing, and a very demanding woman. And Maureen liked her a lot.

At the beginning of July the lessons with Mr Gordon finished. Janey had spoken to him about continuing and he said he could but that Maureen had picked up things quickly and tried hard and was perfectly competent really, she'd just needed a bit of advice, a bit of help. So they left it at that. And she could drive now as well.

CHAPTER FORTY

Maureen visited Theresa a fortnight later. She knew that Theresa had told them at home, about the baby, because Mama had already written. She wanted to know about Theresa and about James, mainly she wanted to know that they were alright. And she said that she and Dada might try and come over and see her, but they weren't sure when they could manage that, or if it was possible at all.

Theresa looked better than before. And, on the Sunday that Maureen went over, it was bright and warm so, after a quick cup of tea, Theresa smartened herself up and got James dressed and the three of them went out for a walk. They walked down to Regent's Park. It was very pleasant to sit out on the grass and let James crawl around and enjoy himself. He could have a bit of space and a bit of sun, and he could see all the other people, the other children and the babies out on a Sunday afternoon.

Theresa said that she felt relieved, happier, now that she had told Mama and Dada, and had written to the others as well. She said that she had got a letter back from Nan, a letter from Julia and Nan together really. And they had said that she must bring James out to see them as soon as possible. And they said that Nan was due very soon so James would have a cousin as well, which would be great, wouldn't it? Nan and Julia were very close and you were never quite sure about them, Theresa and Maureen agreed on that. Sometimes Maureen thought that, despite the age gap, she and Theresa had more in common with each other than either of them did with the other sisters.

'Shall we go to Watford then? Go and see them?'

'We should I suppose. It'd be the right thing to do and James here needs to meet his family, doesn't he?'

They decided they would go in two weeks' time, as long as it was OK with the other two.

Maureen met Theresa at Euston at eleven o'clock. Theresa had really made an effort. She looked much closer to the Theresa of before. She'd got out some of her smart clothes, she looked quite elegant really. And James was dressed in new baby clothes. So they would both make a good impression.

They got on the train and chatted about this and that. Maureen had just started her writing and her driving lessons.

'God, Maureen, that Janey sounds great to me. Sorting out all that. She must think a great deal of you to do that, if nothing else it's costing her a few bob isn't it?'

'Well, I suppose it is. I was a bit upset at first, with the writing and everything, but she thinks everything can be solved if you put a bit of effort into it. She always says that.'

'She's probably right, for the most part anyway. I'll look forward to seeing you drive. You can drive us all back home if you like, that'd impress 'em wouldn't it? You turning up at the wheel of a big old car, and me sitting in the back with little Jamie here.'

And they roared with laughter at the very idea.

They got off at Watford Junction and walked through the town pushing James in the pram. They didn't say much, but Maureen thought they were probably both thinking much the same thing. What would the response be to James and Theresa, by the sisters and by their husbands?

They arrived. Julia opened the door and immediately went to look at James and lifted him out of his pram; she held him up and marvelled at him. James seemed a bit disconcerted by this and wasn't sure whether he should cry or not, looking anxiously towards his mother, and towards Maureen as well.

They went in to the kitchen where Nan was sitting. Very large now. She looked tired and hot.

'Will you look at this one now, Nan, isn't he a dote? Isn't he a little beauty. You are, aren't you James, you're a little beauty alright. He's lovely Theresa, he's lovely. Now say hello to your Auntie Nan, will you?'

And she passed him to Nan, who held him, and looked at him, and cooed at him. And then he started to cry, and Theresa took him back.

'The boys have gone for a pint, we'll have a bit of dinner when they get back. It'll give us time for a chat.'

So she made tea and they chatted. They asked Theresa how she was getting on. They probably wanted to ask about the father, but they didn't, apart from saying was she getting a bit of money from him. Theresa was non-committal on that. Theresa asked Nan about her pregnancy and how was it going, they had that in common to talk about, which the other two, of course, didn't. And Julia got on with making the dinner. And they talked about Mama and Dada, how they felt about the baby. And everyone seemed to think they were fine about it. After all it's not the first time it's happened is it? Philomena Duggan appeared with a baby not that long ago, at home, and no-one was too bothered. Oh, they didn't approve or anything and there was a bit of nasty gossip, but it's all died down now, Julia said. And anyway, Theresa, you're in London, so what does it matter? It happens all the time.

Maureen watched Theresa while all this chat was going on. It was well meant, sort of, but she thought Theresa found it all a bit irritating, it was a relief for her to feed James and change him.

Like in the last visit the two boys turned up at about half two. Jim and Danny. Had Theresa thought about that coincidence, of the name? Why had she called him James? Certainly not after Julia's husband. She hadn't met him before, for a start. But, of course, he was rather pleased that the baby had the same name as him, rather taken with the idea. Jim was the friendlier of the two men, a pleasanter man altogether.

It was even more crowded than last time now. Theresa and the baby and the increase in Nan's size as well. They'd stuck the pram out the back, so James was on Theresa's lap.

Danny had drunk more. While Jim had seemed amiable enough last time and this as well, Danny was not so pleasant.

'It'll be difficult bringing a child up on your own, I'd say?'

'It's tough sometimes alright, but I manage OK.'

'Do you have enough money, for your rent and that, and food?'

'I've got some savings and I work a couple of days a week.'

'Theresa used to work in a solicitors' office in Dublin, Danny, I told you that. She had a great job, didn't you Theresa?'

'Oh, you work now, as well, do you? Not in a solicitor's I wouldn't say, some other kind of work I expect?'

He smiled around the table, and then pointed his fork towards Nan.

'Nan'll not be working, she'll look after the child. Won't you? You'll look after the child?'

'Yes, at the beginning, anyway, I suppose, but we can't do without the money for ever, can we?'

'Well, at the beginning you'll look after the child, I've told you that!'

He opened a bottle of Guinness and poured some in his glass and in Jim's as well. He took a drink, almost downing half the glass in one go.

Maureen felt a tension around the table. It had been there last time as well, but it was greater now, being so crowded together didn't help, of course.

'So, Theresa, do you know who the father is? Of young James here, I mean? Because you'll want money off of him, won't you? He'll have been someone you worked with I'd say? Or was it someone you picked up somewhere, on a night out in Dublin eh?

There was a silence. He was looking at Theresa with a smile on his face, pleased with himself for asking his questions. He was still eating as well, had been chewing while he spoke.

Maureen looked quickly at the others. They weren't going to say anything to Danny. They looked uncomfortable, but they weren't going to object to him talking like that. Perhaps he'd asked the questions they'd all wanted to know the answer to, themselves.

She looked at Theresa who looked stunned, unhappy, holding James tight in her lap. Protecting him.

Maureen stood up.

'I'm sorry Julia, Nan. We're going. Theresa, shall we go now? I'll get the pram, shall I?'

She wasn't going to stay there. If she'd had a glass of Guinness herself she would have thrown it into his face.

She got the pram and pushed it through the kitchen forcing them to move their chairs. Theresa had gathered up James and his stuff and followed Maureen out to the hall. Julia came as well but the others stayed in the kitchen.

'I'm sorry Theresa, he's had too much to drink. He's alright really, except when he's got drink taken. Jimmy should have slowed him down.'

It was Maureen who spoke, while Theresa sorted James out in his pram

'We'll see you again sometime, I expect, but when that would be I have no idea, not soon I wouldn't say. And I tell you now Julia, I feel really sorry for Nan, I can tell you that now. Anyway, Julia, goodbye.'

She could hear some low talking in the kitchen behind them, and a laugh, and she was sure she heard the word bastard.

'Are we ready?'

Theresa nodded. They went out and walked away from the house, not looking back.

CHAPTER FORTY-ONE

George wrote every couple of weeks. It was the same letter each time really. Saying how he missed her, and telling her anything of interest that might have happened at work, and in his family, and asking her how it was going. It was pleasant to hear from him. Her letters back to him, she had to admit, were probably not any more captivating than his, although she did try, now, to write them well, and make them a bit more than just a note or two. However, she didn't tell him everything. She didn't, in fact, tell him the more interesting things at all. She didn't tell him about Mr Gordon, about his lessons in writing, or about the books he had given her; and she didn't tell him about Mr Slade and his driving lessons, or the fact that she had passed her test. And she mentioned Theresa but gave no detail about what had happened to her, and she didn't tell him about the dreadful visit to the sisters in Watford.

She didn't know why she didn't tell him, except for the fact that she didn't want to, she just didn't want to tell him the most important things. She didn't want to share those things with him. Not because she didn't like him, she did like him as a person, he was a very nice man. But he wasn't important enough for her to tell him the most important things, and she knew that he wouldn't understand those things, anyway, in the same way that she did. She knew that.

In late June his letters didn't arrive when they should have done. She didn't notice at first. She didn't notice that he hadn't written, and then she realised that a letter hadn't arrived when it probably should have done. She didn't think it had anyway. Maureen didn't keep George's letters, so she couldn't go back and check when he had last written. And because he hadn't written to her she didn't write back.

In the second week of July a letter arrived.

'Dear Maureen,

I am sorry that I haven't written to you as normal. The truth is that I have been thinking about things, and thinking about us. You seem to be enjoying being in London, and I am very glad about that. I have been thinking as well about when I will go to England. Three weeks ago, however, I was offered a promotion. I was not expecting it but it is a very good opportunity and I have decided to take it. I hope this will not be too much of a shock for you, because it will mean that I will not come to England as planned.

In the circumstances I think it would be better if we stopped writing to each other.

I hope that all goes well for you in London. I am sure that it will.

Yours sincerely

George

She read the letter a couple of times. Not because she was shocked by it. Or upset really. She read it a couple of times just to make sure she hadn't misunderstood it.

The truth be told, she was slightly annoyed with herself for giving George the opportunity to reject her, rather than the other way round, but on the whole she read the letter with a great deal of relief.

And she was pleased for George as well. George was not an adventurer, he would not really have liked to live and work in London, she didn't think. He would be very pleased with his better job on the railway, she knew that for a fact, he might even tell his father about it.

She read it once more for luck, and then tore it up and put it into the waste basket.

A week later she got one of her irregular letters from Julia. Julia liked to write when there was a bit of scandal or a bit of hot news, she couldn't be bothered with the normal day to day. And Maureen noticed now, of course, how bad her handwriting was, and that she didn't always use proper sentences.

Dear Maureen

Hope everything's great in London. I envy you, Bray is a real old bore I can tell you.

Dec told me that George told you he wasn't coming over. Bet that was a relief!

Anyway, just letting you know he's started with some girl from his work. I met her, a plain old thing, nice enough I suppose, but plain as you like.

Look, I want to get a job in London. What do think?

Love

Julia

It was no surprise that George had found someone else. In his own way, he was a bit of a catch, she supposed, he'd got a good job on the railway, he was reliable enough, and he was presentable, good looking enough. The best of luck to him. She couldn't help wondering whether he'd already started with the new girl, the plain old thing, before he'd written his letter. It didn't matter if he had, really, did it?

And Julia wanted to come over. In a way that was no surprise either, that's what so many people did, including herself, of course. She wasn't sure if Julia was suggesting she help her in some way. She didn't really know what she could do. She certainly wouldn't encourage her to turn up here, that was for definite. Julia and Janey wouldn't really hit it off, she was pretty sure of that.

CHAPTER FORTY-TWO

Janey made Maureen drive to the shops a couple of times a week, usually going with her, but not always. Maureen still felt nervous driving the car but, at the same time, it was fun. As well as that she noticed people looking at her, a bit surprised to see a young girl out driving. And the lorry drivers and bus drivers usually had something to say if she pulled up next to them at a traffic light. Always friendly though.

At the beginning of July, Janey told her, on a Monday, what they would be doing for the summer.

'We're going to Devon for a whole month. Near Ilfracombe. We've rented a house just outside the town, it should be great.'

'Everyone?'

'Everyone. You included, of course. Jed will come for the third week and then possibly for a couple of days right at the end. He has to work, I'm afraid. My mother's coming as well, dad said he might come with Jed for the last bit, but I doubt if he will. He doesn't like holidays, doesn't like the seaside. Misery guts that he is.'

Maureen had met Janey's dad. He was, in fact, a very pleasant man.

'And when will we go, then?'

'The third week in July.'

'Right.'

'There is something else though.'

'What's that?'

'Well, Maureen, the truth is, I need you to drive us there. We could go by train but then we'll be stuck for getting around, and for going to the beaches, and going out for the day, and that could be difficult for a whole month. So we need the car.'

Maureen wasn't sure why she hadn't asked before.

'Can't you drive us? I'm not even sure where Devon is, but it'll be some distance won't it?'

'Well, look, I haven't told you this before. It didn't matter really. But in the past, not for a long time though, in the past, I've had fits, epileptic fits, small ones really. I haven't had one for a long time now, but I'm nervous about driving and more especially with the children. I did pass my test, but I haven't really driven since.'

'Right.'

'Look, Maureen, it's no big secret, about the fits I mean, but, all the same, I'd prefer it if you didn't tell anyone. People get the wrong idea. Normally, if anyone asks I just say I don't like driving, and leave it at that. Anyway, what do you think about driving to Devon? It'll take most of a day, it'd be hard work.'

'I won't tell anyone Janey. It's no-one's business but your own. And that'll be fine, the driving I mean, you'll have to tell me where to go though, I won't have a clue. Not a clue.'

'Great.'

Janey looked relieved, and Maureen thought how odd it was that you immediately saw a person differently when they told you something private, when they shared a secret. All that time, six months or so anyway, that she had known Janey, and she hadn't realised that she carried that little secret around with her, not the driving, the fits; that it worried her, and she didn't really want people to know. And she probably worried as well that the children would have it too. And now she had told Maureen. Maureen felt flattered that she had been told, felt they were closer because of it. But, when she thought about it, she also realised that she admired Janey even more; always bustling, always trying to do things better, always helping her children, and Maureen as well, to do things better, while she carried that little secret around with her.

But before the holiday there was the garden party. Janey said it was important for Jed's work that they did some entertaining at home, clients and colleagues she called the people from work, but friends were always invited as well. And the summer event was going to be the garden party.

They spent almost a month, one way or another, organising that Sunday afternoon party. They had to organise a marquee, better safe than sorry, in case it rained. And summer foods had to be decided upon, and drinks, and invites sent out. Once the overall plan was done Janey gave Maureen the responsibility for ensuring that everything was running to schedule, checking with the caterers and the marquee people, as well as checking on who had replied, checking on who was coming. Jed, of course, did nothing, except occasionally ask if everything was running to schedule. He had every faith in Janey to get these things done efficiently with no fuss.

They did all the final checks on the Thursday before.

'You've been brilliant Maureen. Well done.'

'Thanks, it wasn't that difficult. Let's hope it all works on Sunday though.'

'I'm sure it will. Anyway, I was wondering if you wanted to invite anyone? I should have asked you before. I know it's not that easy if you're organising things and everything, but maybe a friend, or someone from your family, might like to come. Only if they'd enjoy that type of thing I mean, not everyone does.'

She didn't really want to invite anyone, she couldn't think of anyone she knew who would fit in to that type of thing. Except maybe Theresa?

'Well, there's my sister Theresa. She'd have to bring her baby though.'

'Other people will bring children, that wouldn't be a problem. Invite her if you think she'd like to come, if you think she'd enjoy it.'

Maureen knew what Janey meant. She meant if she'd fit in OK.

'There's one thing though. Between you and me and the gate-post, there's no father, if you know what I mean.'

'She's bringing up the child on her own? Well maybe she'd enjoy an afternoon out. She can tell people anything she wants, as far as I'm concerned, I won't say anything. As long as she'd enjoy it all, and not be uncomfortable with the other guests, she's very welcome to come.'

'Oh, she'd be fine. I'm sure of that.'

'Ask her then, ask her.'

Maureen went quickly down to Camden that evening and spoke to Theresa about going to the garden party. Theresa was unsure, but Maureen said she'd be fine, she could just pop in if she wanted, she could stay for as long as, or as little as, she wanted. And she said that Janey understood about James, and wouldn't say anything. And Theresa said yes, she'd come, and she'd go out and spend some money on a new dress. Why not!

It was a beautiful hot afternoon. Maureen had prayed that morning, at early Mass, that the garden party would go well, and that Theresa would enjoy herself, and that Janey was pleased with things, and that everything else went perfectly. And so it did. The caterers arrived on time, the waitresses were conscientious, the important guests that Jed wanted to come all arrived, Janey greeted everyone with a kiss, including Theresa, and everyone enjoyed themselves. Theresa, looking like she used to look, in her new dress, talked and laughed with people, and let James play on the grass, and had a little drink, and some bites to eat. And Maureen was so pleased that Theresa could see her as she was now, the young woman who was managing this rather important garden party, with all these rather important people. Theresa stayed for about an hour and a half, only leaving when James started to get a little bit grizzly, and after making sure she said goodbye, and thank you, to Janey and Jed before she left. Maureen was proud of her sister that afternoon, and she hoped Theresa was equally proud of her as well.

Janey and Jed were very pleased with how things had gone, and both of them said how much they had enjoyed meeting Theresa. She should be invited to their parties in future, they both said that.

And then it was holiday time. Janey's mother stayed for the couple of days before they left and she and Maureen made sure that everything was packed. They had decided that, as space would be limited in the car, they would send two trunks by rail to arrive two days later, so the pair of them got that organised. Maureen also got a local mechanic to come and look at the car and make sure it was up to the journey, He said it was fine, but to make sure to carry some water and a petrol can, with petrol in it, and a fan belt. He left a new fan belt with them. Maureen had no idea what it was, but she packed it away in the boot anyway.

They decided they would leave on the Saturday morning, as early as possible. They had packed the car the night before, leaving it ready to go on the driveway. Everyone was excited before going to sleep, the children especially of course. Maureen got up at five and went into Ruth and Michael's bedrooms and woke them up. She then gave a little knock at Janey and Jed's door, and at the spare room for Janey's mother.

It was a warm sunny morning, so quiet at that time on a Saturday. Except for the distant clink of a milkman up the road. They all had cereal and a cup of tea together in the kitchen, Jed as well. And then they got themselves into the car. Janey's mother, Ann, in the back with the two children, and Janey in the front passenger seat with the maps. It was quite crowded because there were a couple of picnic bags in the car as well, and books and drinks, and macs as well, just in case. Maureen checked that everyone was comfortable and that they'd been to the toilet, and the doors were shut, and then she got in the driver's seat herself. Jed was standing by the side ready to wave them off. Maureen started the engine, everything sounded fine, and she edged out to the road. Jed waving and the children shouting goodbye, and Janey waving to him out of the window as well.

She slowly turned right and moved away, everyone still waving and shouting in that warm, quiet, summer morning. The car felt heavier than it had ever felt before, slower as well, but Maureen decided she would just take it easy. It was six o'clock in the morning and they had the whole day to get to Ilfracombe, she would just drive carefully all the way.

Janey directed them towards the North Circular Road and, when they got on to it, she just left Maureen to drive. It was busier than the other roads but not too bad. Maureen realised that within about fifteen minutes she had already driven further than she ever had done before. But she was enjoying it, and the children were laughing with their Nana in the back, and Janey was carefully looking at the map, with the window half open next to her, letting in the warm air. It took them a while but eventually they reached a roundabout and Janey said that they must go onto the Great West Road, on the A4, now. It was busier here and Maureen wasn't really used to roundabouts. Janey was saying take the left to the A4, Maureen, the left to the Great West Road and Maureen not quite sure which one it was, the left to the A4 Maureen, and then she was sure and they were onto the Great West Road. And everyone cheered.

This was easier, a wider road. Janey said that in about eight or ten miles they had to go on the A30, and then they just followed that for ages and ages, which would be a piece of cake, they'd go all the way to Yeovil in Somerset on the same road.

They arrived at the house at a quarter to nine that night.

CHAPTER FORTY-THREE

Their house was a little outside the town, but near enough so that they could walk in within ten minutes or so. It was like a large cottage, with ivy growing on it and a small garden at both the back and the front. Mrs Cooper owned thc house, she lived just a couple of hundred yards away, and she had been there when they arrived to show them how everything worked.

'I heard the car coming up the hill, dears, it has to be you this time of night.'

Mrs Cooper had an accent Maureen hadn't heard before, the children tried to mimic it when she'd left, but Janey shushed them, laughing. They all got used to it, of course, because everyone spoke like that round there. Mrs Cooper left them some milk and a little hand-drawn map of the town and the beaches close by.

That first evening they were exhausted, but excited as well, so they all had a cup of tea and some toast and jam together in the kitchen. Ann and Janey doing all the work, insisting that Maureen should do absolutely nothing at all, after having driven all that way. When they'd eaten they all had a little wander round the gardens, front and back, and a look out into the lane as well. It was warm, and quiet, and there was a smell of flowers lingering in the air. The quietness and the warmth, and the fragrance as well, reminded Maureen of how it could be sometimes back home in Dungarvan, late on in a summer evening when the trains had stopped running.

The children shared a room, somewhat unwillingly, although

they had already been told this before they'd set off from London, and the adults had a room each to themselves. They slept.

The next morning was relaxed, everyone got up by about half eight and they had breakfast together, there was a small table in the back garden and they decided to eat out there, the children eating quickly and then exploring the garden, and the little garden shed at the back. That first day, Janey said, they would go to the town together and they could explore a little and get their bearings. Luckily, they had enough food and drink with them for a day or so because there wouldn't be much, if anything, to buy on a Sunday.

Maureen thought about Mass. Next week would be fine she decided.

It was a slight walk downhill to the town, along a quiet lane for the most part. The three women trooped along together, the children running ahead and running back, all looking into the gardens of the other houses and cottages, saying hello, as well, to three people they met on the way, and hearing that accent again in reply. And then they got into the town and saw where the shops were for the next day, the butcher's and the grocer's and the greengrocer's, and Ann bought a paper as well. There wasn't a refrigerator in the cottage like there was at home, so they hoped the milk that Mrs Cooper had given them would be alright overnight in the pantry, she'd probably give them more if they asked.

It was a day of getting used to where they were. They had sandwiches at lunchtime and then they strolled around the town again and saw where the two beaches were, excited about going through the Tunnels, although Janey said they couldn't go there all the time because of the cost.

And so they got into a rhythm of getting up not too early, and having breakfast together, and going down the town, one of the women staying behind to give the place a bit of a clean and tidy the beds, and wash the breakfast things. Then they would have a small lunch and go to the beach, everyone together. Once, in that first week, they went to the Tunnels and on the other days to Wilder beach, and to Woolacombe and Combe Martin in the car. It was fun. Everyone enjoyed everyone else's company.

As the days went on Maureen realised that the holiday was like nothing she had ever experienced before, never in her life. She had been to the beach before near Dungarvan, and been to Youghal, been to the seaside, she was no stranger to that. But there was something altogether different about this. It felt like an odd kind of freedom. She forgot she was actually an employee of Janey's, she didn't really feel much like that back in London, but here the whole idea had disappeared. The three women and the children were enjoying life together in the sun, eating together, going to the beach, everyone looking after each other, taking turns with whatever had to be done, cooking or cleaning or washing a few clothes. And in the evening when things had quietened down the three of them would sit in the back garden just chatting about anything that came up.

Ann asked Maureen about Dungarvan and her family, and she described growing up there, in that big family. It seemed a bit distant now, even though it was only a few years ago that she had left. And, of course in some ways, Ann had more in common with Maureen than with her own daughter, Janey. Ann and Maureen had both been brought up in Ireland, in the country as well, not at the same time obviously, but, when they talked, their descriptions didn't seem that different. Going to Mass and confession, the dances, and the little gossips and goings-on that took place in every little Irish town, nothing seemed to have changed that much. And Janey talked, herself, about growing up in London, going to school, and the war, and getting a job and meeting Jed, who'd been working for the

US government in London. Maureen was surprised that they'd met and got married almost straight away. It didn't take a lot of intelligence to work out that Janey was probably pregnant when they got married, or might have been anyway. Perhaps that's why she was sympathetic to Theresa, she knew that things like that could happen, although Janey was luckier in her choice of men. And they'd gone to live in the States. She described living in New York, which she said she liked a lot, but, at the same time, she was glad to get back to London. Once the war was over she wanted the children to grow up in London. Like she had.

All these discussions wandered around through the air as they sat out together. They might have a little drink of wine, although Ann preferred a whisky which surprised Maureen. Janey liked wine and had brought half a dozen bottles with her. Maureen sipped at her glass of wine, she didn't like to refuse, but she didn't like it that much, she'd be just as happy, happier in fact, with a cup of tea.

As they talked, each night, they opened up with each other more and more, the mother and daughter especially; not in an explosive kind of way, but in a gradual, almost invisible, way. Janey talked about how difficult things had been for her at school, she hadn't got on with some of the teachers, the nuns, in the convent she went to, she'd hated it. And Ann was surprised, she knew things hadn't been great but hadn't realised how badly things had gone. And Janey hadn't realised the extent of her mother's upset when she'd gone off to the States. With hardly even a goodbye, or so it had seemed to her. And Ann said she hadn't liked Jed at the beginning, hadn't liked him at all, and him being Jewish hadn't helped, of course. But everything was calm, they talked and they seemed to understand each other.

Maureen felt as if she had nothing terrible to talk about. Her life, in many ways, had been smooth and uneventful in its own way. But she did talk about Margaret Shaughnessy, and about Theresa as well, about what happens to people sometimes, how things could get beyond them before they've even realised what was happening; until it's too late for them to do anything about it, until it's totally beyond their control, anyway. Ann knew about Margaret, from Mrs D, and wasn't surprised about Theresa, she'd met her at the garden party. She said that things happen, she seemed philosophical, you have to make the best of things. And, of course, Janey disagreed. Yes, she said, you had to make the best of things, but you could change things yourself, couldn't you? Everything was possible. Margaret could have walked out, couldn't she? And Maureen thought about that woman crying in the kitchen that night, and she wondered whether Margaret could have walked out. Janey didn't know Margaret, of course, it was easy to say those things without really knowing the person or the situation. Isn't that what Shaughnessy himself had said, or implied anyway, before she'd left?

But it wasn't all serious. Ann told some terrible tales of what went on in the factory she worked in when she first came over, the goings on were absolutely hilarious. Mainly things of a sexual nature which rather embarrassed Maureen, although she couldn't help herself laughing as hard as the others. And Ann described meeting Janey's father for the first time at a dance, and how awkward he was, and how she'd decided there and then that he was the man for her, and how she'd made sure she'd get him, especially when she saw that Eleanor Murphy had her eyes on him as well. He didn't have a clue, she said, he didn't have a clue! Oh mum, shut up, I don't need to know all that!

Every day in those first two weeks was fun, or funny, or interesting, or relaxing. Or all of them together. And it was different. Different from living that day to day, working existence in London, where things had to be done at a particular time, or by a particular date, or for a particular purpose. Maureen was glad to see that, here, even Janey could let things go a little and just enjoy companionship, and the children, and relaxing on the beach, and chatting away till midnight or beyond.

Jed arrived on the Saturday, two weeks after them. They all went down to the station to meet him. He was a friendly man, Maureen liked him although she didn't feel that she knew him that well. At home he left quite early, and he worked late most days as well. But he was usually around at the weekend, when he was polite, friendly, and helpful.

The children and Janey were really looking forward to his arrival. Once he was there he tried to make the best of the time, he drove everyone to the big beaches every day, insisting everyone went. Maureen had to admit, to herself, that this annoyed her. Not the going to the beaches, but the driving. She had got used to driving, she liked to be the driver now, and anyway the car was too crowded now with all of them in it. It was uncomfortable, and they could only go when he wanted to go, either to the beach, or back home again. She was annoyed with herself for getting annoyed, but she was, and that was it.

In the week that Jed was there, Ann and Maureen spent more time in each other's company than before, they would go and get the shopping, leaving Jed and Janey and the kids to enjoy their time together, and they would sit together when they all went to the beach, and one evening they babysat the children so that Jed and Janey could go and have a meal by themselves in the town. Maureen liked Ann, so, although it was different to the first two weeks, it was very pleasant all the same.

On the Sunday after Jed had left, he wasn't able to stay any longer than that, Maureen and Ann went to Mass. Neither had been on the first two Sundays. Ann said she was not a regular Mass-goer these days, and Maureen realised that, as time went on, she was becoming more forgetful about it herself. Nevertheless, it had a pleasant reminder of home about it when she went. The children asked if they could go as well, Janey certainly never took them, and they probably only wanted to go out of curiosity. So the four of them went together, tidied up and a bit smarter than they'd been for the last three weeks. Janey was happy to stay at home and clean up.

It was a pleasant walk to the church and the Mass itself was quite crowded, locals and holidaymakers together. Maureen watched the children during the service, she saw them fascinated and, also, a bit bewildered by the standing up and down, and the kneeling, and the smell of the incense. And they looked at her, questioning, when the queues for the communion formed. Should they go as well? Maureen shook her head, mouthing 'just sit down, just sit down'. Neither Maureen or Ann were taking communion, they hadn't been to confession for a start. Looking at the children, she wondered whether she had ever felt like them, going to church and wondering what on earth was going on. She thought she hadn't really, because when she was a child at home, it was where everyone went, it was what everyone did, on a Sunday.

After Mass they each had an ice cream before walking back to the house.

The last week was, in many ways, like the first two. They reverted back to what they did before Jed had arrived and they did enjoy it. However, in Maureen's mind, and in everyone else's as well, it seemed, the week did have a different feel about it because they knew that the holiday was coming to an end, and, even in their conversations with each other, and with the children, the focus started to be on what would be happening in the future more than anything else. Going back to school, getting back to work, getting back into a routine. They even started to pack from the Tuesday onwards, putting away things that would not be needed again.

Janey, in particular, seemed to be moving back quite definitely into her efficient self, talking about school uniforms, and school books, and how they would organise work that had to be done on the house, and thinking about decorating the bedrooms.

On their last evening they walked into the town, all together, and had fish and chips and, when they got back to the house, and the children had gone to bed, the three women sat out for the last time. It was still as warm as it had been, but there was a sad feeling in the air as well. Or Maureen thought there was, she felt sad anyway. When they got home they wouldn't have these moments together, these talks, these laughs. Janey had the very last of her wine, and Ann had her whisky, and Maureen sipped at the half glass of wine that Janey had poured for her, and they agreed that it had been a great holiday. But they didn't stay there very long that night, they went to bed early, in order to be up and away on the Saturday morning.

The journey home was uneventful. Maureen found that she was looking forward to the drive that Saturday morning, early again, like on the first day. Mrs Cooper came out to wave them off and away they went. Another pleasant summer's day. On the trip down it had felt like they were leaving something behind as they moved further and further away from London. The journey back was the opposite, from quiet country roads they joined the bigger roads and saw more traffic and even found themselves in small traffic jams as London became closer. Everything was noisier, and busier, and more complicated, and Ruth felt sick, twice, so they had to stop and let her recover. And they had lunch at a busy café on the A30. And the journey took even longer than on the way down. When they eventually got on the North Circular Road it was almost ten o' clock. Janey turned to the children and Ann, in the back, to tell them they were almost there, but everyone was asleep.

Jed was waiting for them, he said he'd been worried they'd got lost or something. Maureen and he unpacked the main suitcases, she helped to put the children to bed, and then she slept herself.

CHAPTER FORTY-FOUR

Sometime in the second week in September Maureen got back from taking the children to school as usual. Janey was obviously waiting for her arrival.

'Maureen. Thank goodness! Jed's been on the phone. He left these documents behind and he needs them at the office urgently. Could you take them down to him? He doesn't want to risk putting them in a cab for some reason.'

'Of course I will.'

'You know where it is don't you? It's easiest on the tube, go to Tottenham Court Road, it's only a couple of minutes from there. The address is on one of the envelopes anyway. Thanks Maureen, you're a lifesaver!'

Maureen had been there once when Janey and she had gone into town, Janey had wanted to see Jed for a few minutes about something or other.

Maureen walked up to East Finchley Station and got the tube to Tottenham Court Road. She found, when she got there, that she did remember the way, and when she reached his office she took the lift up to Jed's floor. It only took a few seconds. Jed was in a meeting but the receptionist, Sheila, was expecting Maureen and the documents, she took them and disappeared, saying Maureen should wait in case Mr Solomon's needed her for anything else. Maureen wasn't quite sure what that could be, but sat down in the reception anyway. She wasn't in any particular hurry.

'Hello.'

A young man had come from the offices out into reception.

'Hello.'

'Are you alright? Is someone dealing with you?'

'Yes. I'm fine. Just waiting.'

'OK. Are you here for an interview or something?'

She looked at him again. He was quite tall, with dark hair, he was smiling at her. Suit and tie. In his twenties she supposed.

'No, just waiting for the receptionist to come back.'

'You're Irish.'

'I am, yes.'

She knew he expected her to say more than this. Ask where he came from, things like that, it was always the same. She didn't say any more.

He stood waiting, still smiling

'So what are you waiting for then? If it's not an interview, I mean?'

She smiled at him.

'Why would you want to know?'

'I'm just being nosey, I suppose.'

'Well, you tell me who you are, and maybe I'll tell you what I'm doing here. Maybe.'

'I work here. My name's Stuart.'

'And, so, Stuart, what is it you do here? Apart from checking up on people in Reception I mean?'

'I'm an accountant. So that's me. What about you?'

‘I work for Mr Solomons and his wife. I’m their housekeeper.’

He looked at her for a second.

‘I hope you don’t mind me saying but you look a bit young to be a housekeeper. Mr Solomon’s got a big house hasn’t he, in Highgate?’

‘Are you saying that you don’t believe me? Because I could say you don’t look much like an accountant yourself.’

‘No, I’m not saying I don’t believe you......What was your name again?’

‘I didn’t tell you.’

‘So what is it? I told you mine after all, didn’t I?’

‘It’s Maureen Kelleher.’

‘So, Maureen, I was just thinking that you must be a very good housekeeper to be working for the Solomons when you’re so young. Relatively young, I mean.’

‘Actually, you’re right. I am a very good housekeeper. And it’s got nothing to do with whether I’m relatively young, as you put it. So, anyway, what does an accountant do? Here I mean. With all the advertising and things?

‘Deals with the money basically, deals with the money.’
‘Right.’

The receptionist appeared through the door. She looked at them both talking.

‘Maureen, he’s not bothering you, is he? Stuart, please don’t bother the visitors will you!’

The girls looked at each other and laughed, and Stuart laughed as well, although he went slightly red at the same time.

‘Maureen, Jed says there’s nothing else, but thank you so much for getting down here so quickly.'

'OK, thanks, Sheila, I'll be off. See you again sometime.'

She went over to the lift.

'I'll come down with you if that's OK? I'm going out to get some cigarettes.'

They waited until it arrived. Not speaking. And they got in.

'Ground floor?'

'Obviously.'

'So you're getting the tube back to Highgate then?'

'I am. I have work to do when I get back. It's a busy life being a housekeeper, you know. Believe it or not.'

'I'm sure it is Maureen, I'm sure it is.'

They got to the bottom and went out into the street together.

'It was nice to meet you Maureen.'

'And you Stuart.'

And they went their different ways.

CHAPTER FORTY-FIVE

Jed came home relatively early a couple of days later. The children had finished their supper, Janey and Maureen had tidied up and were having a cup of tea before Maureen checked the children's homework and started to get them ready for bed.

He came into the kitchen.

'Ahhaa! It's the famous Maureen!'

He stood there looking tall and dark, and very amused.

The two women looked back at him, wondering what on earth he was going on about. Jed could be funny at times, and odd and jokey, it could be something, or it could be nothing at all.

'Well, Janey, my darling, I can tell you that it's a very risky business sending our Maureen out on errands and the like. Because you never know what is going to happen. You just never know!'

'Jed, for god's sake, what are you going on about?'

'Well, you'll remember that just two days ago you asked our Maureen to deliver some very important packages to the office for me?'

'I do remember. So what?'

'Well, Maureen delivered them to Sheila on Reception as asked. Thank you, Maureen for doing that, so promptly as well.'

'It was no problem Jed, no problem at all.'

'But, tell me, who did you meet there?'

'Where?'

"In Reception!!!'

'Sheila, of course.'

'Not Sheila. I know you met Sheila. Who else?'

'Stuart.'

'Who's Stuart, Maureen? You didn't say anything about meeting anyone called Stuart.'

'He was just a boy who came through while I was there.'

'And Maureen did you like our Stuart?'

'He was nice enough, I suppose.'

'Nice enough eh? Only nice enough? Well, I have to tell you that he thought you were a bit more than nice enough.'

As he said this he took an envelope from his jacket pocket, and waved it in the air, still with a little grin on his face.

'Jed. Will you tell us what is going on!'

'OK. OK. Well young Stuart is a trainee accountant at the office. To be honest I hardly know him. I've seen him around but I don't have much to do with trainee accountants. Not that there's anything wrong with them, trainee accountants, I just don't meet them very much on a day to day basis. Anyway, he came upstairs to my office today, I admire his nerve really, he asked me if I would give this note to Maureen.'

He waved the envelope again in his hand again.

'So, Maureen, there you are!'

He handed it over to Maureen.

She was embarrassed but rather pleased at the same time.

'Aren't you going to open it?'

'Shut up Jed! Give her a minute.'

She looked at them both, smiling, opened the envelope and slid the single sheet out, unfolded it.

'Dear Maureen

I hope you don't mind me telling you this, but you made a big impression on me the other day.

So, because of that, I decided to write you this letter and ask you if you would like to go on a date with me.

I don't know when you have time off so let me know an evening or a time on a Saturday or Sunday when we can meet (if you would like to that is).

You've got nothing to lose from one date have you? Especially as Mr Solomons would know who you were with.

We can meet in town or I can come and pick you up.

I look forward to your reply.

Stuart'

'What does he say?'

"He's asked me out on a date.'

'Are you going to go?'

Maureen thought for a second or two.

'Yes. Why not?'

PART TWO

CHAPTER FORTY-SIX

She had decided that she needed a few minutes break. It would not make a mite of difference whether she was there or not, but she knew she had to be, it was the right thing to do. Nevertheless, every so often, she did need twenty minutes or so to herself. Sometimes she just bought herself a cup of tea in the café nearby, but this time she bought herself an ice cream and strolled down the road towards Tufnell Park. It was relief to be out in the fresh air. A sunny July day. Flags out in some places too.

Theresa had been great. She picked the children up from school every day almost, walked them home and gave them a bit of tea. The children could see to themselves really, but they seemed to like it that Theresa looked after them so. And she brought them over as well. The children wanted to come, of course they did. And others came as well. Stuart's mother every day, which is what you'd expect, and his Da too.

She'd got herself a cone. Just vanilla. It reminded her of the ice cream back home, those creamy blocks you could buy. An ice cream was always a lovely thing to have, whether it be an English cone or an Irish wafer. She sat on the wall, resting for a moment, licking quickly the ice-cream that was starting to drip down the side of the cone. When she'd taken them to Ireland, the children, they'd bought ice cream at the little shop near the creamery, still the same place as when she was a child. It would have been a bit of a luxury then, not something that Mama and Dad could easily afford, just a bit of a treat now and then. Stuart had come over once but she knew he regarded it as all a bit primitive, the toilet facilities and the tin bath. After that first time he always found an excuse not to come, but he thought he made up for it by insisting she and the kids went by plane, that time, to Dublin, which the children absolutely loved. And Maureen had to admit it was a lot better than the train journey and the ferry.

He'd have told the mother about her parents' place, that was for sure, and Lynda would have loved that, definite proof that Maureen was unworthy. To be fair Stuart probably wouldn't have been saying it to be nasty, she didn't think so anyway, but nevertheless.

The children actually loved it back home. The countryside and the people, everyone friendly and interested, and the toilet and everything was just a bit of a laugh to them. They got on well with Mama and Dada, and their uncles as well. And the girls took them out to the town and spoilt them rotten. Once they'd managed a trip to Bray and called in to see Deirdre and Shaughnessy, and Mrs Doyle as well.

She'd finished the ice cream and knew she had to get back. Harder to go back, much, much, harder.

Back at the hospital she went up to the ward. Stuart was lying there, still not awake.

Sister Murphy had seen her come in and came over to her. Cathy Murphy was from Cahir, not that far from where Maureen had been brought up. They got on pretty well.

'How are you, Maureen?'

'Ok, not so bad. I've just treated myself to an ice cream.'

'Lovely.....Look, it'll be today or tomorrow. You know that, don't you?'

'Yes, I do. Dr Williams said as much.'

'He's pretty comfortable, all things considered, with the morphine and that. It'll be peaceful I would say.'

'Well, we can only hope so. God willing, anyway.'

'Will you get the priest?'

'Stuart's family is Jewish if it's anything at all, way back I mean, but no priest or rabbi I don't think.'

'OK. Like I say, it won't be long now.'

Cathy touched her on the arm and smiled before she set off back to the Sister's Office.

He had been ill for more than a year, eighteen months almost, at first just a cough that wouldn't go away, but it had got worse than that, or even more persistent anyway. He'd gone to the doctor, but only because Maureen had insisted. The first couple of times the doctor had said it was bronchitis that would clear up in a week or two, especially if he cut down a bit on his smoking. Stuart didn't take any notice of that, he smoked twenty Player's a day, which he said was not a great deal, and anyway he needed the cigarettes for his concentration. Eventually the doctor said he'd better go for an X-Ray, and that's when they discovered the real reason. He had a shadow on his lung and they did more tests. Maureen thought it might be TB. She'd known people at home who'd had TB, she knew Kitty who'd died from it, but these days she thought it could be cured.

Stuart had an appointment with the consultant and Maureen went too, she thought he might object to her coming along, but he didn't. And that was when they found out. Stuart had lung cancer. The consultant was a very nice man, Mr Davis was his name. He said they could try treatment, yes, they would definitely try to treat it, but he was afraid the prognosis was not good. Stuart and Maureen both looked at him, she didn't know what to say, didn't know what questions to ask. Would he die? She wanted to know, but didn't want to ask it directly. Mr Davis said they would start the treatment the next week, and they'd see how things went. There was a silence. She remembered that silence. She glanced sideways at Stuart, he was pale, she could see he was worried, scared. And Mr Davis stood up and leaned across the desk to shake their hands, he said his secretary would write to them that afternoon with an appointment.

They drove home; most unusually Stuart asked Maureen if she would drive.

The treatment started the following week. Maureen had spoken to Janey about it and Janey contacted some medical friends of hers, they said that Davis was well known in that field and Stuart was in good hands. But Janey wondered as well about private treatment and got Stuart an appointment with someone in Harley Street. He looked at the X-Rays and examined Stuart. He said that he thought Davis was offering the best options but, unfortunately, the prognosis was not good. Maureen was with Stuart and this time she did ask. What did that mean? The doctor paused a moment and then said that he thought Stuart had a year at the most, although you could never be definite about these things and the treatment might help, might delay, but it wouldn't get rid of the disease, it definitely wouldn't do that.

The treatment didn't really help and Stuart deteriorated rapidly. And it became clear he was going to die. They faced it together or as much as you can face a thing like that together. He was scared and he became physically weaker and thinner until eventually he was admitted to hospital and everyone knew that he would never come out alive.

And so she sat next to his bed knowing he would be gone within the next twenty-four hours.

CHAPTER FORTY-SEVEN

She didn't really know why she'd married him. She thought back to that day of meeting him in the office, laughing with Sheila the receptionist. Laughing at him really. He was eager, a little bit pushy, in a nice enough way she supposed. And then the letter. To be honest it was a good letter, putting his cards on the table, saying he liked her, that she'd made a big impression on him. She was flattered and she almost felt that Jed and Janey were quite keen on the whole idea as well. And he was presentable, good-looking almost, and he had a good job, didn't he? An accountant. It was possible that all those little things had flown rapidly through her head after she'd read the letter and Jed and Janey had asked her if she was going to see him.

She didn't know if the boys back at home were really any different to Stuart, probably not, but this felt different. An Englishman with a good job, and she herself had a good job with a well-off family that liked her and supported her. This little Irish girl from Dungarvan. She decided she would see him, which in itself was nothing, was it? Nothing more than a date.

But it became more than that. That first time they walked on the Heath, and had tea in a café, and he walked her home. And then they went to the pictures, and then they ate in Lyons' Corner House, and then they met every week, twice, usually on a Wednesday and Sunday. And then Saturday as well. She liked him of course. He was amusing, and he tried hard, and he bought her little presents. He took her home to meet his mother and father. Lynda was pleasant enough initially, asking about her home, and Ireland, and her family. But Maureen felt it became a bit of an interrogation really, she wanted to know about Dada's job and what her brothers did, she even managed to find out that Maureen had left school at thirteen, and had been just a housemaid until fairly recently. Lynda made sure she knew that Stuart had an accountancy qualification and could have gone to university if he'd really wanted to. His dad, Jim, was actually very nice to Maureen, right from the beginning, giving her a little wink behind Lynda's back, but Maureen realised pretty quickly that he was very definitely under Lynda's thumb.

In a funny kind of way it was all Lynda's fault. Maureen became almost bloody-minded about the whole thing, she refused to be intimidated by Lynda. She would go to the house and hold her own, in the nicest possible way. She'd even insist on helping Lynda in the kitchen with the tea or whatever, almost as if she was already part of the family. A couple of times Lynda mentioned one of Stuart's previous girlfriends, Gillian, how it was a pity that it never worked out, she'd thought they would be married, perhaps even have children by now. And Maureen would smile, and Stuart would look embarrassed. 'Muum, Maureen doesn't want to know about Gillian, that's all in the past anyway.' And he would hug Maureen or give her a quick kiss.

No, she didn't really know why she married him. But she had.

They hadn't been going out long at all before Stuart started to talk about the future. They had been round to see Theresa. She remembered that afternoon, they'd all gone out to the park like before and Stuart had really enjoyed playing with James. On the way home he'd said how much he'd like children, and put his arm round her as he said it, giving her a little hug. She knew. She could feel the inevitability of it. Part of her could almost see the logic of it; people got married and had children, that's what they did. They did it at home, and they did it here, they did it everywhere, as far as she knew anyway. And she didn't mind Stuart at all. At the same time she was nervous about it, she couldn't help but think of Margaret Shaughnessy in that kitchen back in Bray. Had she wanted to get married to him? Why had she done it, why had she married? She didn't think that Margaret would ever have been in love with Shaughnessy, but at the same time Deidre seemed to like him fine, she appeared to have no complaints at all, although she herself was a totally different person to Margaret, that was definite.

The trouble was, Maureen thought, trying desperately to work it out, the trouble was this, she liked to spend time with Stuart, but she didn't love him or anything like that, although she didn't really know what that meant anyway. If she never saw him again, would that matter to her? She wasn't sure it would.

Although he didn't directly mention the word marriage he did keep talking about the future, the children thing, and getting a house like Jed's, and starting his own company now he was fully qualified. And it all took place very quickly.

One Sunday afternoon he suggested they go to the Heath again. It was a pleasant, warmish, autumn day. They walked from Kenwood across the Heath; he led them away from the path and found a bench for them to sit on. She wondered afterwards if he'd planned it, if he'd checked before if there was somewhere they could sit.

She could feel his tension although she wasn't sure what it was about. Perhaps Lynda had said something to him, saying she didn't want Maureen to visit or something, and he was scared to tell her. Which was ridiculous, Lynda wouldn't say that, even though she definitely thought it.

'Maureen, I've got a question to ask you. An important one.'

'OK.'

She really wasn't expecting it.

'I want to ask you to marry me.'

And then he got down on his knee and took something from his pocket, a little box.

And Maureen couldn't stop herself thinking, 'Shouldn't he get on his knee first?'

'Maureen, will you marry me?'

She could see him looking up at her.

And after a few seconds hesitation she said yes, and immediately regretted it.

She sensed a movement in the hospital bed and looked across. He was awake, drowsy, he smiled and edged his hand towards her, she smiled, and took hold of his hand and squeezed it, lightly.

CHAPTER FORTY-EIGHT

Once he had got his yes, everything seemed to get a momentum of its own. And there were good bits and bad bits. The worst, of course, was connected to Lynda. She was clear that it was obvious that Maureen and her family would not be able to put on a wedding that was in any way appropriate for the marriage of her son. There were lots of questions about where it would be and who would be invited. Lynda saw that she could take over the whole affair, or that's how it seemed to Maureen. Her initial regret was now compounded.

But Janey, of course, came to the rescue.

When she had told Jed and Janey, who were the first people she told after Theresa, they were both very pleased for her. But Janey wasn't stupid and, later on that day, talked to Maureen on her own.

'You're OK with this Maureen? Stuart's a nice man I know, but you don't seem actually overjoyed to be honest.'

'No, it's fine, I'm just a bit overwhelmed I suppose, with the pace of it an'all. And Lynda as well of course, she'll want to take over. But I'm OK, Stuart's a good man.'

'Is that enough for you Maureen? That he's a good man?'

'He'll be fine, he'll be a good husband. Which is more than a lot get isn't it?'

'Well, as long as you're sure.....

They looked at each other. They both knew.

'......anyway don't worry about Lynda. I'll deal with her. We'll have the reception here and it'll be on us, she'll hardly get a look in.'

'You can't do that Janey, that's not fair on you.'

'We'd love to do it. And your mother and father can stay here for a few days as well can't they? It'll be fine.'

And Janey took charge.

They had decided to get married in the Spring. Stuart had said they could find a flat or a house by then, he had a deposit and knew he could get a mortgage. Maureen didn't really understand all of that but they started to look at places, around Highgate and Muswell Hill and bits of Finchley as well. It was exciting. She realised that she would have her own place, it looked like they might even be able to afford a three-bedroomed house. Maybe in East Finchley somewhere.

Maureen remembered the meetings at Janey's house, planning things. Janey and her, and Theresa, and, of course, Lynda. Lynda seemed to be in a permanent state of fury about the fact that everything had been more or less taken out of her hands. Maureen knew she had been convinced that it would be her show. And it seemed that almost everything involved over-ruling Lynda. For a start, she didn't want the wedding to take place in a Catholic church; she had already talked to the Anglican vicar and made a provisional booking. Maureen said that she could only get married in a Catholic Church, and Theresa backed her of course, and Janey as well. Maureen knew that Lynda never ever went to church and had that Jewish background, anyway, way back. When she discussed it with Stuart he didn't seem to mind one way or another, although he was definitely worried about his mother being upset. Maureen didn't mention anything about children at that point, he'd have to agree to them being raised as Catholics. That might not go down too well either.

Maureen also had a thought about asking Father Michael to officiate at the wedding for her, she didn't know if it was possible or if the local parish priest would be upset but she thought she could try. Michael had been to London a few times over the last year. A church thing and a rugby match. When he was here he always invited her to tea at a nice hotel in the Strand. He had a way with him that might even impress Lynda. Maureen liked him very much. And he was a handsome man as well.

All these ups and downs were complicated by dresses and bridesmaids and menu and guest lists and honeymoon and house-buying. And contacting Mama and Dada to make sure they could come, and brothers and sisters too. So much so that Maureen forgot whether she wanted to or not, totally forgot.

She went to see Theresa one Sunday afternoon.

'You know you're lucky really. All the others did it in the local church and had a few friends to a little thing after, in a pub or at the Irish Club. Yours is becoming more like a society wedding, what with Janey and Lynda competing and trying to outdo each other.'

'I suppose so. I'll have to try and calm them down, even Stuart's getting worried that the whole thing's getting out of hand

'Anyway, what did your priest say, have you been in touch with him?'

'He said he'd be honoured but he said he'd contact Father O'Connor to check if there'd be any problems with it.'

'Good.'

'Don't you want to get married, Theresa?'

She had met a musician, Paul, who worked in a dance band. Maureen and Stuart had seen him playing at Hammersmith Palais one evening a few weeks ago, a saxophonist. Theresa and Paul seemed to have a good time together. He got on with Stuart as well which was a good thing. Maureen also knew that he stayed over two or three times a week.

'I don't know. I don't think so. I like Paul but I'm not sure a marriage would work.'

'What about James though.....couldn't it bc a bit awkward for him, at school and everything, him not having a father?'

'Being illegitimate you mean?'

For a second she looked annoyed, and then sad.

'It might be I suppose. But he's not the only one. And we can just say his father still lives in Ireland, in Dublin. Which is true. It's what I say to him when he asks now and then.'

They didn't say anything more about it.

CHAPTER FORTY-NINE

Sitting there by the bed she could hear the World Cup fuss all around the place. Everyone was excited and Maureen could hear the match being played on radios, and could hear people gasping and exclaiming and shouting as the match went on. It didn't seem so long ago that Stuart had said that they must get some tickets for the Final if they could because, he thought, England had a pretty good chance of reaching it. Stuart really liked football, he supported Spurs, and he would have loved to have been there that afternoon, he would absolutely have loved it. But instead he was going through the last moments of his life, barely conscious, not knowing what was going on in the big wide world outside. And Maureen sat with him, holding his hand.

He'd relapsed again into that semi-conscious state after his smile, virtually unconscious. It was upsetting for the children of course. The mere fact that they knew he was going to die was upsetting in itself, but seeing him unconscious and sometimes in pain only added to that. They usually came in the late afternoon. Elizabeth was older than Michael, fourteen now, and she seemed to be managing. She sat with her dad and talked to him, even if he couldn't hear, telling him about school and what she'd done and who she'd seen. It almost made Maureen cry just to watch her being so brave. Elizabeth'd discovered an interest in medicine over the last year, she'd found out all about her dad's illness and, although it made her unhappy when she realised the finality of it all, in some ways the knowledge seemed to help her. She asked the consultant questions about the disease and he was obviously impressed with her grasp of things.

A week or two ago they had been sitting in the kitchen at home and Elizabeth had said that she had decided she would become a doctor. She went to a very good girls' grammar school, she was ambitious, which Maureen wanted her to be, and she was encouraged by Janey and by Theresa as well. Maureen wasn't one hundred percent sure how you became a doctor, or whether the whole idea would pass when Stuart had died, but she was pleased, she couldn't help but feel pleased by her daughter's confidence about doing something like that. She mentioned it to Theresa the next day.

'Jeez, a bloody doctor! And she'll do it as well won't she? That one aims for what she wants and gets it as well.'

Michael was more withdrawn than Elizabeth, he was a great deal quieter about his father's illness. In the ward he would just hold his dad's hand for a second or two and say hello to him, and then retreat, sitting in a chair behind the others, kind of looking on. He didn't know what to make of it at all. Last week he had disappeared out of the ward without Maureen noticing and, when she did notice, she had gone to look for him. She found him in the stairwell, just crying. A year and a bit younger than his sister, perhaps he understood less. Although he had passed his 11+, Maureen thought he had probably only just scraped through. He wasn't as bright as her, not as inquisitive, but maybe more sensitive in a way. Margaret was very protective of him but their father's illness put immense pressure on the both of them, Maureen knew that.

There was a roar down the corridor which Maureen assumed meant that someone had scored, and at that moment the children arrived with Theresa.

'England have equalised, mum.....Is it alright if I go and watch, Sister said it would be OK.'

Michael liked football, a Spurs fan like his dad.

'Just say hello to dad, and tell him where you're going. He'll understand.'

Michael went over to the bed. Stuart wasn't really there. Michael leant over close to him.

'Dad, I'm going to watch the World Cup down the corridor. It's one-all at the moment, first half. England are doing pretty well. I'll come back and tell you how it's going.'

He looked back towards his mum, his face asking if that was alright, and could he go?

Maureen nodded. She looked towards Theresa.

'Elizabeth and I are OK here for the moment, why don't you go and get a cup of tea?'

Maureen checked with her daughter, who nodded.

'I'll just be downstairs.'

She went down and got herself a cup of tea, lit a cigarette. She used to have the odd cigarette with Janey, she hadn't liked them particularly at the beginning but it was a thing to do, Janey looked sophisticated with hers. Then she bought packets of ten which'd last a couple of days, and when Stuart became ill she just started smoking more, maybe ten a day, maybe just eight. Theresa smoked so they'd often light up when they were chatting together. Stuart didn't know she smoked. She wasn't sure what he would have thought.

They hadn't really agreed about the house. Once they'd started looking Maureen thought it would be fairly easy. It was exciting, looking at different places, she enjoyed it. Until Lynda started to take a more prominent part. They saw a place in East Finchley which Maureen liked, it was a pretty street and there were three bedrooms, and it just looked nice.

She didn't really know how you made decisions about houses but she liked this one. And Stuart seemed to be OK with it, pleased, actually, that they'd found somewhere she was happy with. But Lynda said no. She said she had found a real bargain not far from Ally Pally, no more than five minutes' walk from her own house. Maureen didn't want to be that close to her. But they went and saw it. There was nothing wrong with it, if anything it was slightly bigger than the house she liked, and it was a little bit cheaper. Stuart and Lynda decided that this would be the house, and so it was.

The tea in the hospital café was as weak as washing-up water. The English say it's their national drink and as often as not it's undrinkable, it always was in this place, although she forgot every time and ordered it again and again.

Looking back she couldn't really understand why she hadn't said more. It wasn't as if she didn't have allies. Theresa and Janey were always prepared to give their opinion about anything and they would have backed her. They had both asked her separately if she was happy with the house, would she be happy living so close to Lynda? And what had she said? She'd said she thought it would be OK, that the house was very nice, that she liked it. And, of course she didn't dislike it at all, it was the proximity that was the problem.

But of course there was something else as well, she knew that now, and she knew it at the time as well, she was acutely aware of it. In effect Stuart and his family were paying for the house. When he'd said he had the deposit he actually meant that he could get the deposit. And where would he get the deposit from? From Lynda and Jim. That wasn't totally fair. She knew he did have some savings, but not enough. And she had a little bit saved in a savings account, but the bulk of the deposit would be borrowed from his mum and dad. Which meant Lynda's opinion had to be taken into account, no, more than that, Lynda's opinion almost became the only opinion.

Yet she kept going. And that was the mystery. Why had she kept going? Liking Stuart hadn't been enough even then. She'd become a kind of pawn in it all, moved around here and there. Was she just taken with the idea of having a nice house in London, having a pleasant husband, having children? Maybe she just saw it as the next step, an inevitable one. The job with Janey was interesting but it didn't pay a huge amount, but she got board and lodging, of course, which made up for some of that. But although it was an interesting job, a very interesting job, and fun sometimes as well, although it was all those things, she didn't know where she could go next. That was the truth of it.

She was an Irish girl with no qualifications, she'd been lucky up to that point but she really wasn't sure what type of future she had. And London then was really only just starting up after the war. As she sat in the hospital café she thought how different it was now, in the sixties. The Beatles and all that, it was like a different world now, full of opportunities.

She'd taken a pragmatic decision, that was the truth of it. Stuart had offered her the chance to become something different from her past, to step up in a way. Lynda didn't like that idea, that he should marry someone from a kind of lower class, an Irish lower class, she didn't think it was right, she probably thought it was risky as well. What would this Irish girl turn out like? And, of course, they didn't even much like each other, did they? That didn't help.

Anyway, she'd decided to accept the offer. She would become an English housewife, with a three-bedroomed house, and children, probably, as well. He'd said he'd like a boy and a girl. Well. She'd like that as well, obviously. Who wouldn't?

'Mum. Auntie Theresa says could you come back up. Dad's woken up a bit.'

It was Elizabeth. She seemed quite calm. It wasn't an emergency, it wasn't the end. He had just woken up. She edged through the café tables and chairs, following her daughter towards the foyer. They walked slowly up the stairs together, not saying anything, Elizabeth linking arms with her mum as they started to climb. It was such a pleasure to walk with her, saying nothing, but joined together. Maureen realised Elizabeth was on the very verge of becoming a young woman. Just slightly older than Maureen had been when she left school and went to work in the railway dormitory.

CHAPTER FIFTY

When they reached the ward she could see that he was quite awake. He saw her come through the door, smiled, even waved slightly. There was only Theresa there. Michael was still watching the football.

'Lizzy, go and find Michael will you, tell him to come and give his dad an update on the football. Quickly now.'

Elizabeth ran out.

'So, it's good to see you awake. How do you feel? Do you have any pain?'

'I'm OK. Woozy, of course, with the morphine, but not too bad. Are the children OK? Are they coping?'

His voice was croaky and weak.

'They're fine. Well, you know what I mean, they're managing OK. Theresa's doing a grand job, picking them up from school and everything, giving them their tea, checking their homework.'

Theresa laughed at that.

'Checking they've done it. I wouldn't have a clue about helping them with it. God, you should see some of the science stuff that Lizzy's doing. Jeez, it's all Greek to me. I tell you. But, anyway, they're coping fine, Stuart.'

The children came in.

Stuart tried to sit himself up a bit.

'How's the football going, then?'

'Well there's fifteen minutes to go, dad. It's still one-all.'

'Who scored our goal then?'

'Geoff Hurst, and Haller got theirs, scored first.'

'OK. Go and see how it's going, keep me up to date, OK?'

'OK, dad.'

And Michael shot off.

'Have mum and dad been in?'

'No. they'll be along soon.'

'OK.'

And the effort was all too much. His face lost its interest and its smile, blanked over almost instantly, he slept.

Theresa and Maureen moved him into a more comfortable position. He didn't wake.

CHAPTER FIFTY-ONE

Michael dashed back in to tell them, to tell his dad, that it had gone into extra time. He looked desperately disappointed when he saw that Stuart was not conscious. Maureen told him to go and watch the rest of the match. Theresa said they would go home straight after. Elizabeth said she would go with him and watch some of the football. The two sisters were surprised to be left alone.

'I was thinking just now about when we bought the first house in Ally Pally. What did you think about me getting married and everything?'

After Elizabeth left they had both moved to the window, looking out, just a few feet away from Stuart. They spoke quietly as if he might hear.

Theresa didn't say anything for a little while.

'I suppose I was surprised and not surprised at all. It's a while ago now, isn't it? Stuart seemed nice enough, probably a good person to marry if that's what you wanted. But at the same time you'd seemed quite independent for a while, working for Janey and everything, and then you seemed to kind of change direction overnight. I wasn't sure why. And I don't know how you dealt with her, God, she was a right pain in the arse, wasn't she?'

She looked, glanced quickly, towards Stuart as she said this. As if to check whether he could hear her or not.

'I suppose she was, yeah.'

'Why do y'ask anyway?'

'Just thinking about things, I suppose. With all this waiting and sitting and wondering you get a lot of time to think.'

'Yeah, I guess...'

They heard someone behind them, near the bed, they turned. Lynda.

Almost seventy now, not as sprightly as she was when Maureen had first met her. She had a lot of energy for her busybodiness back then. But, to be fair, she kept herself well, always looked smart, always seemed to have her hair just done. These days a tightish perm, grey-blue sort of.

She'd gone straight to Stuart. Leaning over to give him a kiss, touching his hair, looking sad. Well, she was his mum even now, thought Maureen. She was entitled.

'Hello there, Lynda.'

It was Theresa who spoke first. Maureen smiled to herself, whether deliberately or not Theresa's accent seemed to get just that bit more Irish when she spoke to Lynda. A little reminder, like.

'Lynda, how are you?'

'Not bad. Jim'll be along soon, he's parking the car. How's things going?'

'Well, you probably know, the doctor says that we're almost at the end. Today or tomorrow.'

Lynda nodded. Maureen could see that the words upset her, even though she knew already. She'd been in earlier and would have spoken to the doctor herself.

Maureen walked around the bed and stood next to her. She held her hand, and Lynda gripped her back, just for a moment, before releasing herself and starting to tidy the bed, tidy the bedside cabinet, put things in order. None of which really needed doing at all. And then she sat down. At that moment Jim appeared.

'Had to park down the street.'

Lynda just nodded, still looking at her son.

Maureen went to him and gave him a hug, and Theresa did the same. They both liked him. He was a good man.

And all this time there had been shouting going on and cheering. Then they heard a scampering down the corridor. The two children arrived, Michael, and then Margaret with slightly more decorum.

'We won! Right at the end, we won! It was great wasn't it, Lizzy?'

'It was good, yeah.'

'Don't say yeah, Elizabeth!"

'OK, Nan.'

They both looked at their father, an instant sadness taking over.

'I'm going to tell Dad.'

And Michael went up to the bed and leant over and spoke quietly in his father's ear.

'It was a great match, dad, and England won, right at the very end, after extra time. Geoff Hurst was brilliant. You would have loved it.'

Michael stood up.

'Do you think he heard me?'

'I'm sure he did, I'm sure he did, Michael.'

There was silence for the moment and then Sister arrived.

'Well, there's an awful lot of you here, aren't there? God, six of you, if matron saw this I'd be in real trouble, I can tell you that now.'

'It's OK Cathy, I'm taking the children home now, and Theresa's leaving as well I think, so it'll just be Stuart's mum and dad, for a while.'

'Right, OK, and I'll call you right away if there's anything you need to know.'

After their goodbyes they set off for home, Theresa leaving them just outside the hospital to get the bus to Camden.

CHAPTER FIFTY-TWO

She made the children some scrambled eggs on toast, some for herself as well. And they ate in the kitchen. All three subdued. The children knew what was going to happen. Maureen had made sure she had prepared them. It had been a gradual but inevitable thing. Once the real diagnosis was made everyone became aware of how things would turn out. And of course Elizabeth's research had made it clear to her what the reality would be. Maureen knew that the children talked to each other about their father's illness and the fact that he was going to die. He had even tried to talk to them about it himself but it had been difficult for him, and for them. Now they were almost there, almost at the end point

'Will it be tonight, mum?'

'I don't know love, but you know the doctor says it'll be soon. We'll see what happens, just like every day. You're both being so brave, you know. And Dad was pleased to see you, and to talk to you, wasn't he? Anyway, you both look tired. Why don't you get your stuff ready for tomorrow and then think about bed? You can read for a while and I'll come and tuck you in.'

Not that long ago they would have moaned or said they wanted to watch the TV for a while, but they both nodded and, after putting their plates in the sink, they went upstairs.

She heard them in the bathroom and talking to each other and moving about and, after about twenty minutes, there was quiet, she waited five more and then went upstairs.

To Michael first. He was asleep already, he must have just lain down and fallen asleep instantly. Maureen was disappointed because she had wanted to chat to him and give him a cuddle and a kiss before he slept. She almost felt cheated. Elizabeth was reading. Maureen sat on the bed and looked at the book. The Secret Garden. Elizabeth had read it at least three times. Comfort in some way.

'Are you OK, love?'

Lizzy closed the book and pulled her mother to her, hugged her.

'I'm going to miss daddy so much.'

How long was it since she had called him 'daddy'? Years. It was always dad now wasn't it?

'I know, darling, I know.'

There wasn't really anything more to say. They hugged each other and then her daughter settled down, Maureen kissed her goodnight and left the room, turning the light off as she did so, but not quite closing the door.

Maureen went back down to the kitchen. The house was dark and quiet. She sat at the kitchen table. On her own. It reminded her of that night back in Bray, when she had come in and discovered Margaret sitting in the almost dark. That little housemaid had returned from her night out and come in and sat down and they had talked. Except this time it was herself, that

little girl of years ago, sitting alone in the kitchen. And there'd be nobody coming in from their night out to talk to her.

She lit a cigarette and inhaled deeply.

PART THREE

CHAPTER FIFTY-THREE

Mama and Dada had arrived one day before the wedding. Dada couldn't get a load of time off, they had to get back again on the day after. It was tiring for them but they seemed happy enough. On the way home they would stay in Dublin for just one night.

And they liked their room in Jed and Janey's, they liked the house. It would be the first time they had ever stayed in a place like that, real luxury in their eyes. And Da in particular got on famously with everyone. He liked a chat and, it seemed to Maureen, always had seemed, that he treated everyone in exactly the same way. Interested, friendly, not overawed by anyone, he got on well with them all, and they liked him too. Jed and him discussed a bit of football, and Jim joined in when he turned up with Lynda to meet the other in-laws. Even Lynda seemed somewhat charmed by his gentle, unperturbed, open chattiness. She liked him, and oddly enough that seemed to make her seem like a nicer person, for a while anyway. Mama was less outgoing, maybe a little shy, but, when she had relaxed a bit, she was open and friendly too.

The men even went out for a pint together, Stuart as well. Maureen doubted if Jed had ever been in the local pub, and Jim and Stuart were not regular pub goers. But they went off happily, walking up the road to the place near the station. The saloon bar Maureen hoped.

The wedding itself was pleasant enough. And it was terrible that she should think about it in that way. Yes, it had been exciting, sorting out all the arrangements, buying the house, even sorting out the honeymoon, but the day itself did not excite Maureen. Not in the way she might have liked or hoped. She hadn't really thought about it before, but now she was actually getting married she knew that she would have wanted a marriage that she was looking forward to, that she was dying for, that she couldn't wait for. And this wasn't it.

But, yes, paradoxically, it was a happy enough day. The weather was good, things went to timetable, Father Michael officiated, Dada led her up the aisle, and of her brothers and sisters, only Conny couldn't make it, even Tommy made sure he was home from sea to be there. And Tommy behaved himself at the reception as well, he could sometimes be troublesome after a few drinks.

The food was good and speeches were made and after a bit of initial hesitation the two families got together and got on pretty well, Janey and Jed using their skills to introduce everyone to everyone.

And in the late afternoon Maureen changed into her going away stuff, and they were seen off by everyone as they took a taxi down to the Strand where they were staying in a nice hotel that Lynda and Jim had paid for, and then getting the train the next day to Bournemouth. Maureen had suggested Devon but Stuart thought it would be too difficult to get to by train and, anyway, there would be more to do in somewhere like Bournemouth.

Maureen hadn't stayed in a proper hotel before. She hadn't said that to Stuart. She didn't want to admit it, and he hadn't asked. She was nervous about it, in a way, but she knew she could cope, there wouldn't be a problem. She was nervous about something else as well. Stuart and she had kissed and he had touched her a bit, on her breasts, nowhere else, if you didn't count sometimes letting his hand drift down to her bottom when they danced, or kissed. She was quite strict about it all, not letting anything go any further than that. They hadn't talked about sex at all, although he talked about children, he'd done more and more of that as the wedding approached, and, of course, there's no children without sex.

Maureen knew what happened, she wasn't stupid, and she'd been brought up in the country so what animals did was nothing strange to her. And Theresa had talked to her about it as well. Which had led to some hilarity for the pair of them, of course. But she was nervous. She thought it might have been another matter if she felt about him in a different way, she thought she might even have been looking forward to it, but she just liked him, and not in that way.

He was probably nervous as well. She had no idea if he'd done it with other girlfriends, with whatsername, Gillian, for example. They hadn't talked about it at all. Why would they?

The hotel was rather grand, with a big entrance hall and lots of staff; they didn't have to carry any of their luggage, and after Stuart registered them they followed the porter up to the room. When they got there the porter showed them the bathroom and how things worked, as if they couldn't work that out for themselves, and then left after Stuart had tipped him.

It was a lovely room, there was even a small separate sitting-room. On the table was a bottle of champagne and a card from Lynda and Jim. Wishing them all the best.

During the day Maureen and Stuart had been together and apart, apart longer than together in fact. They'd been together at the altar and the photos and at the reception for a while but then they'd separated because they had to talk to everyone and anyone. Making sure their own families were OK, making sure they had said hello to the other family, had a little joke with them, moved on and started again. Maureen was surprised by the fact that a number of his family had commented on her Irishness, asked where she came from exactly, called her a colleen, and said how lovely her Da was. And commented as well on Father Michael, they liked him. All of it said in the nicest way. As the afternoon went on she sat down with Mama and Dada, chatted with them, and let people come to her, she was starting to get a bit tired and she was also thinking about getting changed and moving on. Stuart was still circulating, he appeared to be enjoying himself. He'd made a nice speech and her Da had said a few words, as well, and proposed a toast. It had been a good day.

And then they moved together again, pushed a bit by Janey and Lynda saying they had better start thinking about changing and leaving.

Stuart had to do very little, he was wearing a dark suit, and he'd keep that on, taking the buttonhole out was all he really had to do. Their cases had been packed the day before, so all that was left was for Maureen to change. Theresa offered to go up with her but she said no, she'd manage OK on her own.

It was a relief to go up her room. Small though it was and packed with all kinds of wedding stuff. She sat on the bed. She was pleased that it had been a good day. But she knew also that her life was going to change, she wouldn't be staying in this room anymore and, although she had insisted on keeping her job with Janey, she knew that Stuart would pressurise her, with his mother's help, to concentrate on being a housewife, and a mother as well, as soon as possible.

She wasn't sure she was ready for that. She was only twenty after all. She wondered again how she'd got herself into this situation. She knew that most people thought she'd done well, fallen on her feet, stepped up a bit in life, met a good man, an accountant begod! They'd even bought a house in London. What more could a young Irish girl want? She wasn't altogether sure, but she did know that she had regrets. Already.

She took the wedding dress off, slowly and carefully, feeling, oddly, that she wanted to preserve it even though the wedding itself was not all she desired.

With Theresa's help, she'd decided on a smart dress for the trip to the hotel. She put it on, thinking about the hotel, and what would happen, as she did so.

They both looked around the hotel suite, for that's what it was. Looking in the drawers, and in the bathroom. Stuart popped the champagne and poured it into the two glasses on the tray.

'Cheers, Mrs Johnson!'

He lifted his glass, waiting for her to lift hers. She did so, and they clinked together.

'Cheers, Stuart.'

And then, all of a sudden, they didn't know what to do. Or Maureen certainly didn't anyway, and, looking at Stuart, she thought he didn't either.

'It's been a long day, hasn't it? And it's a bit of a journey tomorrow. Should we get ready for bed, do you think?'

'OK. You use the bathroom first.'

He sat down on the small sofa with his glass of champagne and watched her get a few things from her case, her nightdress and her washing stuff and make-up bag.

She went into the bathroom, washed and removed her make-up but put a little bit back on, put on her nightdress, and sat for a minute or so on the side of the bath. She knew what to expect next but, at the same time she had no idea at all. None whatsoever.

She returned to the bedroom, quickly hung her dress up,

and hid her underwear in the case along with the washing and make-up stuff. He was sitting watching her. Smiling, she smiled back, they said nothing.

She went and climbed into the bed.

'Right!'

He went to his suitcase took out a smaller bag and went into the bathroom himself.

Five minutes or so later he came out, hung up his clothes put some other bits in his bag, and came over to the bed. In his pyjamas. She thought he looked ridiculous.

CHAPTER FIFTY-FOUR

They went down to breakfast together at eight-thirty.

They had managed adequately. He had kissed her and undone her nightdress and touched her on her breasts and down below as well. And she could feel that he was hard, and she could feel him entering her. It hurt a bit but not unduly. It was not particularly pleasurable but not wholly unpleasant either. However, as he reached his climax, he became very energetic and noisy, and she almost wanted to laugh.

And he said:

'Was that OK?'

And he fell asleep before she had a chance to respond.

She had turned the lights off, by the bed, and lain in the dark for a while before drifting off herself. She wouldn't have minded a cigarette.

She woke before him and wondered what would happen when he woke up. Eventually he did wake, he pecked her on the cheek and said they should get dressed and go down to breakfast.

After breakfast they got their bags and took a taxi to Waterloo where they got a train to Bournemouth, where they got another taxi to take them to a nice hotel up on the cliff.

They spent a week in Bournemouth. It was sunny, they ate in the hotel and in an Italian restaurant, they walked, and they sat on the beach. They went to the Winter gardens for a concert which Maureen quite liked but then got bored by.

They made love four times. Maureen did not initiate any of this, she waited for Stuart. He did it all in a very similar way to the first time.

And then they returned home. To their new house.

In a way things returned to normal for a while. Maureen continued to go to Janey's every day, it was slightly strange turning up at the front door rather than just coming down the stairs, but she had a key and she arrived at the same time as she would have done previously. Stuart moaned about this because it meant that he had to get his own breakfast. He laughed about it, saying what was the use of having a wife if you had to get your breakfast yourself. He laughed about it, but he meant it. She said the money was useful and she had to leave early because of getting the children to school.

And the money really was useful to Maureen because it meant she had her own cash, she didn't really have to ask Stuart for pocket money or money for clothes or anything.

Their life was OK. Generally friendly enough. Maureen cooked dinner every night, they ate together, sometimes they went to the pictures, sometimes they walked on the Heath. Maureen was relieved that it all seemed fairly easy, but was disappointed, occasionally, when she looked at Stuart across the dinner table, or listened to him go on about work. He wasn't as interesting, or indeed amusing, as the keen Stuart she had met in the office had seemed to be.

Two things happened which changed everything, no, three things really.

Six months after the wedding Janey told Maureen that she and Jed and the children were returning to the States. He had been offered a really good promotion and, she said, he was getting a bit bored with the London job, it just wasn't big enough. Maureen was shocked. She had not been expecting this at all. She hadn't even considered it, she thought that she would work with the family for as long as she wanted really, she almost thought of it as a job for life, though it obviously wasn't. Sitting there listening to Janey she could feel the tears welling up. She didn't see how she would be able to get a similar job, she had got this one through Mrs Doyle really, she didn't even know how you would go about looking. She didn't even know if she wanted to work for someone else, it would never be the same as working with Janey. And she knew that Stuart would be glad. He liked Janey and Jed, he liked the fact that he knew these people who were quite well off and high up, but he didn't like the fact that Maureen worked for them. Looked after their children and the house. She knew he thought she was little more than a glorified housemaid; he had never actually said it, but she knew that was what he thought. And Lynda thought so too, of course.

And he would say that she didn't need to work, that he earned enough for both of them. Maureen wasn't exactly sure if this was true, he had never told her what he earned. But one thing she knew for definite was that she would then be reliant on him for money, she would have to ask him for money.

Janey said they would be leaving at the end of the month, so it would be almost a full four weeks before they left. Maureen asked her if it was possible to keep it a kind of secret between them for a week or so, she felt she needed a bit of time to get used to the idea. Janey told her not to worry, Jed wasn't letting people know for at least ten days, so it could just be between them for a while. Although the packing would have to start straight away and she was relying on Maureen for help in doing that.

Janey also said that she'd pay her an extra month's wages to make up for the short notice and to show how much she had appreciated having Maureen as her assistant.

Ten days later Maureen realised her period was late. It had happened occasionally before but this time Maureen had the feeling that this was the real thing.

She now had to tell Stuart about Jed's move, Janey had told her it would be public knowledge at the beginning of the next week, but she wasn't going to tell him about anything else for the moment. The pregnancy, if that's what it was, was not definite yet. She wanted to keep that to herself for now, if it turned out to be true she wanted to be the only person who knew.

It was Thursday evening. Janey had told her earlier that day that it would all be public soon, next Monday.

'I had some bad news today.'

They were eating liver and bacon and potatoes and peas.

He looked up, stopped eating.

'Oh yeah, what was that then?'

'Jed and Janey are moving back to the States.'

'No, really!'

'They're going in a couple of weeks, he's been promoted or something.'

'No-one's said anything at work.'

'I think it'll be announced on Monday. Don't tell anyone tomorrow, will you? It's a bit of a secret at the moment.'

'Ok. Well, that's a real surprise. So, obviously, they're letting you go.'

'Yes.'

'Well, actually, I'm glad. I know you've enjoyed working for Janey but it'd be better if you stayed at home really, wouldn't it? You don't have to work, you can be a woman of leisure. I earn enough for both of us. Mum's always saying that she doesn't understand why you want to work. She never has.'

'I know that, Stuart. She's always been very clear about that.'

They continued eating in silence.

CHAPTER FIFTY-FIVE

Maureen went to the airport to say goodbye. Flying off to New York, it seemed so glamorous. She was sad to see them all go, the children in particular. They weren't sure, either of them, that they wanted to return to America, not because they didn't like it but because of the friends they'd made over here. They hugged her as well, hugged her tightly, and she wanted to cry.

She watched them all go through to the other side. Waving, and then they were gone. Maureen felt a big part of her life had disappeared with them, even a big part of what her life might have become had probably gone with them. She was scared that their departure symbolised a change in her life too, and not necessarily a positive one. Even going to the bus stop outside the terminal was a bit odd, she was free now of course, but she had no purpose, nowhere she had to be, except back at home. She went to Hounslow and got the underground back home.

She had made an appointment with the doctor for that afternoon.

She couldn't think of the last time she had been there although she did vaguely remember him, their doctor. A nice old man who smoked a pipe almost continuously.

He talked to her about her period, examined her briefly, talked again about the timing of the periods, and told her, yes, she was pregnant. About eight weeks he thought. He congratulated her. He said a bit about the ante-natal procedures, saying they could sort all that out in the next couple of weeks. He was a nice chap, he meant well.

'Have you told your husband?'

'No, not yet, I didn't want to until I was sure.'

'Quite right too. Well, he'll have a lovely surprise when you tell him won't he, my dear?'

'He will, doctor, he will.'

She walked home from the doctor, taking the longer route through the local park. The truth was that she felt good about the child. Over the last week she had grown more convinced that she was pregnant, the missing period hadn't turned up for a start, but it was more than that, she could feel that there was a child inside her. And she felt good about that.

She didn't think that Stuart would be a bad father, but, at the same time, she was sad that he was the father of her child. So there was happiness and a regret.

She thought about keeping the baby a secret for a while longer, maybe even another month, keeping it as something that only she knew. She wasn't being sick or anything, and nothing showed as yet. No-one would know.

She looked at her watch. Julia was coming around for a quick cup of tea. She had arranged it last week, Julia had arranged it, in fact. Julia'd come over from Bray not that long after Maureen, and Maureen had helped her find a job in a pub and then in a small hotel. Actually it had been Theresa who had helped most, she knew more people than Maureen, or more people in that kind of business.

And, after a wild eighteen months or so, Julia had met Bobby, a postman who worked in Camden, and settled down. They were saving to get married and hoped to get a council flat off the Prince of Wales Road somewhere.

She came round for a cup of tea and a chat every week or two.

And she was waiting outside the house as Maureen appeared.

'Jeez, Maureen, you're late, leaving me hanging around in the street like this, what'll people think!'

They went in and sat down in the kitchen, Maureen putting on the kettle first.

'So? How's yer luck. You're looking a bit peaky if the truth be told Mo.'

'Don't call me Mo, for god's sake, I hate it'

Stuart occasionally called her Mo when he was being affectionate, she loathed it. Julia just did it to wind her up.

'OK, OK. Maureeeen, then. You're still looking a bit peaky. Everything OK?'

'Yes, I'm fine.'

'You're not OK. I can tell that just by looking at you. Pale and peaky. What's up? Not pregnant are ya?'

Julia laughed as she said this, but Maureen's face must have given her away.

'Oh Jeez, you are, aren't ya! Have you told his highness yet? And the queen mother as well?'

Maureen got up to make the tea.

'I only just found out for definite. I've just come from the doctor.'

'Well, anyway that's great. He'll be pleased, I'd say, he's always going on about kids, isn't he?'

Julia was not awfully keen on Stuart. She didn't actually dislike him, but she did think he was a drip, thought he was a bit wet.

They had their tea and Julia talked about this and that, and Bobby, and the pregnancy, and she was especially pleased when she realised that she was the first to know, even before Theresa.

They heard the key in the front door. Stuart was home. Earlier than usual. Maureen looked fiercely at Julia, giving her the message that nothing must be said, nothing at all. Julia nodded. Don't worry, don't worry.

Stuart came in looking happy. He saw Julia and didn't look quite so happy.

'Hi Julia. You alright?'

'I'm fine Stuart, I'm fine. How's yourself. You're looking well.'

'Thanks. Maureen, everything OK?'

Maureen nodded.

'Well, I'll be off anyway. Look after yourself now.'

She gave Maureen a quick hug and smiled at Stuart.

'I'll see myself out.'

And she was away. The door shutting with just a bit of a slam.

'Julia gets on my nerves, Maureen. And she's so common. Mum was shocked by her at the wedding, her language and everything. I don't know why you're friends with her. Still friends with her, anyway. And Bobby as well. God!'

'She's alright, she means well. And she was a good friend back home, even if she has got a bit of a wild streak. And Bobby's nice, he's good for her.'

'What did she want?'

'She didn't want anything she just came round for a sup o'tea and a chat.'

She knew he hated her saying that. Sup o'tea. Too Irish. So she said it. Get him back for Mo.

'So anything new in the land of postmen and barmaids?'

'She works in a hotel now.'

'Same thing.'

'Anyway, you're home early, you wouldn't have seen her if you'd come home at the normal time.'

'I've got some news.'

'And what would that be?'

'Well, in a way it's similar to Jed's.'

He looked at her smiling.

'What, we're moving to New York? Jeez that'll be great. I've always wanted to go there, and to live there as well! What about your mother, is she coming as well?'

Now he looked annoyed.

'No, don't be stupid. Of course we're not going to New York.'

'Well, what then?'

'I've handed in my notice.'

'When. Today?'

'Yes.'

'And why would that be?'

'Because I'm starting my own business, my own accountancy firm. Obviously it'll be small at the beginning, just me, but I think it could grow.'

Well, this meant she could safely leave the pregnancy news for a few days at least.

'And do you not think it might have been a good thing to discuss this with me first?'

'Why?'

'I'm your wife for a start. It's a big move. How are we going to manage with money and that? You're not going to make your fortune straight away are you?'

'Don't worry yourself. It's all sorted out. I've made sure I've got the promise of a few clients to start with. I've saved a bit, and mum and dad have said they will back me, they've already lent me a little bit and said there's some in reserve there if I need it.'

'So, when do you start?'

'I leave in four weeks, but I've already got some work to get going on. I can do it in the evening and I've got a few days holiday to use up, so I can get on with it then as well.'

'OK. Well let's hope it all works, but I wish you'd told me first, Stuart, I really do.'

'Don't worry, everything will be fine.'

CHAPTER FIFTY-SIX

The pregnancy was easy. She wasn't sick and she enjoyed the feeling of having her first child inside her. She told Stuart a week later. He was overjoyed. She didn't tell him that she'd kept the news secret for a week, from him anyway. She had seen Theresa and told her. But she hadn't told anyone else. Stuart had insisted that they drive immediately round the corner to his mum's to tell her and Jim the news. They were both very pleased, and Maureen thought that Lynda seemed quite genuine in her pleasure.

The accountancy business started well enough. Stuart worked very hard. A lot harder really than when he was working for the firm in Soho. He left at about eight in the morning and often was not home till eight at night. But he said that they could make a good living out of it.

The bonus for Maureen of course was that she had lots of time to herself. And she got used to that.

Elizabeth was born with no problems at all. To Maureen it had all seemed so easy, she almost wondered what all the fuss was about. She saw lots of Julia and Theresa during her pregnancy, in fact she spent loads more time with them than with Stuart, and when Elizabeth was born this continued. The only other person she saw regularly was Lynda who insisted on coming around a couple of times a week, and also insisted that Maureen take an hour or two off to go shopping or whatever so that she, Lynda, could spend time with the baby. Maureen didn't mind.

Maureen had chosen the name. It was Mrs Doyle's name. Obviously she could have chosen her mother's name, or Lynda's name, or Theresa's, or any other. A saint's name it would have to be of course. But she had decided on Elizabeth. It was a name she liked and she felt that Mrs Doyle had been good to her, had looked out for her. She had changed Maureen's life. Mostly for the better, and if the marriage wasn't exactly what Maureen would have wished for, that wasn't Mrs Doyle's fault. She knew that.

Lynda didn't really like the name Elizabeth, and Maureen wasn't sure that Stuart did either, but Maureen insisted.

And they all went to the Catholic church and she was baptised Elizabeth. The mother of John the Baptist. She remembered that.

Stuart and Maureen didn't start having sex again for quite a while, months. Maureen discouraged him saying that it would be painful for her. He was disappointed but, to give him some credit, he was understanding. When they did start Maureen became pregnant again almost immediately. Stuart was happy with this. Maureen had some sickness with this pregnancy and, because she had Elizabeth to look after at the same time, she found things more difficult, more tiring, more stressful. But Michael arrived without too much trouble, and although he was a little more demanding than Elizabeth had been, she managed them fine, and enjoyed them too.

Stuart's business had become quite successful even in that short space of time. He had employed another junior accountant, Gerry, and a secretary as well, Kathy, whom he always called Kat. This irritated Maureen, she wasn't jealous, just irritated.

And he was never home. He had taken up golf because that was the thing to do, absolutely essential for business he said, and he had joined the chamber of commerce and the masons as well. It was so important to meet people. Occasionally he brought business acquaintances or clients home, Maureen was nice to them, but she didn't really like them. She didn't feel the same about all that as she had when she worked for Janey and Jed.

CHAPTER FIFTY-SEVEN

But, oddly, despite all this, she found that her life became her own again. Obviously the two children took up most of it, in a particular way, but she found that she was free to think again. Because he was rarely there. They did sleep together of course. She didn't like that, it didn't disgust her or anything like that, but she didn't like it. They had sex occasionally, in a perfunctory kind of way, and she insisted he wear something, a johnny he called it. She didn't like saying it, but she insisted he wear something. She didn't want another child. Definitely not straight away, anyway. And, inside herself, she knew she didn't really want another child with him.

She sometimes wondered whether he had a girlfriend, what was it they called it, 'a bit on the side'? She thought he probably did, but as long as he was discreet, it didn't bother her a great deal.

But he was not a bad man. They had arguments now and then, about money, or about holidays, or about his mother, or because he thought she should have ensured there was a meal ready when he got home late. But the arguments were short and not violent, not even particularly unpleasant. They came and they went.

When Elizabeth was three and Michael about eighteen months Maureen decided she would take the children home for a holiday. To see their Irish grandparents, it was only right, seeing that Lynda and Jim saw the children two or three times a week at least.

Maureen first of all said to Stuart that it would be nice if they all went to Ireland in the summer, to see Mama and Dada. Maybe for a month. She knew he wouldn't go for a month, a week possibly, she thought, would be his limit. He thought about it, and said he would love to go, it would be great, and a rest for him as well. And then a couple of days later he said it might be more difficult than he thought, with the pressure of work, but he'd give it some thought, he would find some time. When exactly was she thinking of going? And then a day later he said it would be impossible, there was too much going on at the office, even in August. Why don't you take the children on your own? Or maybe Theresa, or even Julia, could go with you?

It couldn't have worked out better.

And so in late July he took them down to Euston in the car and settled them into their first-class compartment and waved them off. It had worked out fine. Maureen's cousin Bernie, who lived in Streatham, had a daughter of fourteen, Bernadette as well, and Maureen had asked if she would like to come along. She could help with the children and have a little holiday at home. Bernadette's grandparents lived less than ten miles from Mama and Dada so she could see them as well. It was great fun for Maureen and Bernadette, neither of them having been in a first-class carriage before. Luckily there was only one other person in the compartment, an older women, Irish, who didn't seem bothered by the children. She smiled occasionally but left them alone.

Rather than rush down to Dungarvan Maureen had booked a hotel in Bray for two nights. She had told Mrs Doyle, and Deirdre, Deidre Shaughnessy as she was now, that she was coming and Mrs D had said she would pick them up from Dun Laoghaire and take them straight to the hotel.

As the boat docked they looked over the side and Maureen spotted Mrs D, and Deidre was with her as well. Maureen was taken aback by how she felt. When she saw the two women down there waiting for her, waving when they spotted her, she felt all kinds of memories rushing back into her, as if they had been stored elsewhere, somewhere outside her, while she was away, and they weren't real memories of events but rather memories of feelings, memories of sensations, memories of colours and moods. It was the strangest feeling, a happy feeling that almost made her cry, would have made her cry if she hadn't been holding Michael's hand, and lifting up Elizabeth at the same time to look down as the ship docked.

They disembarked and, as soon as they'd got everything together, they went to meet the two women. She hugged them both. And she felt, now, that she was hugging them as a woman, a woman who was different from that girl who had left, the young girl who had left from this very place just those few years ago.

Mrs D did look a bit older maybe, tiredness in her eyes, and Deidre now looked like a cheerful woman in her forties, a bit chubbier but definitely still the same Deidre, dressed in a slightly chaotic but colourful way, a bright summer dress and a cardigan that only just matched. Mrs D, as always, dressed in respectable, darker, clothes with a neat hat poised on her head.

It was great to see them. Maureen introduced the children. Michael. 'Oh, isn't he a dote!' And Elizabeth saying hello, shyly, in an English accent that Maureen had never properly noticed before. And Bernadette as well, hanging back slightly, waiting to be ushered forward by Maureen.

And they squeezed into the car. Mrs D had borrowed Mr D's bigger machine as they'd never have managed the six of them and the luggage in Mrs D's little car, but even then it was still really tight, and they laughed as they contorted themselves inside and laughed again as Mrs D started off, initially with a few lurches as she failed to get the right gear, and then they were away on the road to Bray.

CHAPTER FIFTY-EIGHT

Even though it was a bit of a way Maureen decided that they would walk down to the Shaughnessy's the next morning. They could have got a taxi of course but Maureen preferred to walk. Bernadette was happy to do whatever, her first trip to Ireland, her first holiday without her family, Michael in the pram, and Elizabeth walking a bit and sitting in her little chair on the pram a bit, chatting and asking questions now and then.

It was a beautiful day and they'd had a nice breakfast in the hotel, an Irish breakfast including white pudding and black pudding and soda bread. It was different from London without being totally strange. And from the hotel they could see the strand and the sea as well, stretching back toward Wales.

As they walked along Maureen told Bernadette about the first time that she had walked from the centre of town out to the Shaughnessy's, that evening after the trip up from Dungarvan. With Theresa, not on her own, but it became her first real night away from home.

She told her a bit about Margaret Shaughnessy and how much she had liked her, but she didn't mention anything else about her, apart from saying that Margaret had got ill and had died quite young. And she made sure that she said that Deidre was a nice woman who she'd got on with. She couldn't think of anything to say about Shaughnessy himself.

Deidre had invited them over, saying they should visit and Mrs D would come as well and they could all have a chat together, better in the morning after they'd had a chance to rest after their journey.

It was a strange experience walking towards the house. It wasn't that long ago that she had arrived here but it seemed like an eternity and once again she had that feeling of being a woman now rather than a girl, but still possessing, somewhere, all the feelings and emotions that she had on the day she arrived here for the first time.

She wondered whether Maureen, the girl, would have approved of what she had done, what she had become.

The door was opened by the maid. Inside Maureen almost cried. It could have been herself standing there. A girl of fifteen maybe, in not-very-well-fitting housemaid's black, rather awkwardly telling them that the mistress was expecting them. They entered the hall and Deidre appeared from the kitchen, looking cheerful and slightly flustered at the same time.

She welcomed them all, giving a little hug and a kiss to everyone, including Bernadette, and ushering them into the living room, sitting them down and telling Mary, the maid, to look out for the kettle and see that everything was ready.

They sat and relaxed a bit, Deidre as well.

'So, was the hotel OK? It's got a pretty good reputation I'd say, so it should have been alright.'

'It was fine. A great breakfast and everything. Wasn't it Bernadette?'

'Yes, it was great. I loved the sausages.'

'Good.'

'John sends his regards, he may get to see you a bit later on. And Stephen and Maria too. They're both at University, Trinity College. Who'd have thought it? Two children at Trinity. Margaret would have been so proud of them, so proud.'

John was Shaughnessy of course. She'd never even thought of him having a Christian name, always just Shaughnessy.

And then the poor little maid came in, struggling a bit with the tray of tea and scones and bread and jam. Maureen could see she'd put too much on it. Everyone leapt up to help and, at that moment, the doorbell rang and the maid was sent to open the door, and Mrs D arrived, and they all sorted out the tea together.

And they chatted and laughed and played with the children. Maureen told them about her job with Janey, Mrs D would know all about that anyway, and about her marriage and her house and the children. And as she talked she could hear that what she was saying sounded so positive and successful. With Stuart a business man, and a house in London, and two lovely children.

And, of course, it was exactly that, she wasn't lying in any way at all, about any of it. But it wasn't the whole story either.

Maureen felt relaxed there, in that company, though. It was like being at home, being with people she liked and people who liked her. With some shared history too, and memories of Margaret. Glancing around the room Maureen saw the photos of Margaret and the children, much younger, in pride of place on the sideboard.

And John Shaughnessy did turn up as well. Maureen heard the front door opening and knew it was him, somewhere in her memory was the sound of how he opened the door, all the different members of the family did it in a slightly different way and, at that moment, she knew it was him.

And she was surprised. He came into the room. And he smiled at her. He was an older man, older than she was expecting, smaller as well. He came toward her with his hand outstretched.

'Maureen, it's great to see you. How are you? And these here are your lovely children?'

He clasped her hand, not letting go. And she was surprised, there was a warmth about him that she had not expected, he sounded genuinely pleased to see her.

'We've all missed you, you know, even after however many years it is. We've missed you. Isn't that right Deidre? We've missed her, haven't we?'

'Of course we have, all of us. And I'm sorry we didn't get to the wedding as well. It would have been great to see ya getting hitched!'

'God, Deird, what kind of word is that to use! Hitched, she says!'

Maureen had invited both the Doyles and the Shaughnessys to the wedding but only Maria had been able to make it, the Doyles being away in America and Deidre and Shaughnessy himself having some kind of family obligation that weekend, Stephen had just sent his apologies. Presents from all of them, of course.

It would have been lovely to see them all there, but at the same time, Maureen thought, it was a pleasure for her to keep these friends to herself, these friends who were her own, even if she only saw them once in a blue moon.

Shaughnessy sat down with them for twenty minutes or so and then excused himself saying he had to return to the office and, as he left, Maria turned up. And there was more hugging and going over the little bits of news and gossip and memories that would make them laugh, and, maybe, make them sad for a moment. And make them think.

Maureen said they must go. Mrs D offered to get the car and drive them back into town but Maureen said they'd walk, and

Maria said she go along with them.

As they walked, Bernadette pushing the pram slightly in front, Maureen knew that Maria wanted to talk to her. She could feel it.

'Maureen, look, I've a favour to ask of you.'

It didn't sound too serious from her tone.

'And what would that be?'

'Well, you know I finish university this year and, really, I want to go to London. I want to be a journalist. I know it'd be difficult to get a job anywhere but I'd like to try London, and even if I didn't get a newspaper job I could still work somewhere, see somewhere different. Elizabeth Doyle knows a few people who might help as well. With the journalism bit, I mean.'

Bernadette smiled back at the pair of them as she walked along with the children.

'OK. I don't know any newspapermen I'm afraid, at least I don't think I do, so I couldn't really help with that.'

'No, look, I was wondering if I could stay with you for a while, at the beginning anyway. I'd pay rent and everything. What would you think?'

Maureen's first thought was happiness, if happiness is a thought. The idea of having Maria stay with them pleased her. What would Stuart think? She didn't know. He might not care. He'd met Maria at the wedding, but only briefly, to say hello to, to shake her hand, Maureen didn't know if he'd even noticed her. They hadn't discussed the guests afterwards. They had a spare room. In the long term it would be a room for one of the children, at the moment they shared, but it was used as a guest room and a bit of a spare room at the moment.

Maureen was also ashamed to admit to herself that she

couldn't help thinking about Maria's rent as well, she might have a little bit of cash for herself. Stuart wouldn't be interested in Maria's rent she didn't think. And she felt guilty at even thinking that.

'I'll tell you what, when I write to Stuart in a day or so I'll mention it to him. I'm sure it would be fine. It'd be nice to have you there. If Stuart's OK with it you can stay for a month rent-free while you get your bearings, so to speak, and then if you want to stay on with us we'll agree some kind of rent. How does that sound?'

'That'd be great, Maureen, absolutely great!'

'OK, I'll let you know in a week or so, I'd say, and if there's no problems you can come anytime from September onwards.'

When they got into town they walked along by the sea and had an ice-cream together before Maria headed back into Dublin and Maureen, Bernadette and the children went back to the hotel.

CHAPTER FIFTY-NINE

They spent almost four weeks in Dungarvan with Mama and Dada. The weather was outstandingly good, hot most of the time, and no rain apart from a few summer thunderstorms.

It was a different life. No luxury at all really, but relaxed. Maureen and the children and Bernadette had to sleep in one room, with two small beds and a cot. Elizabeth sometimes in with Maureen and sometimes in with Bernadette, her choice. Going up the hill to the shop together, stopping to talk about this and that with whomsoever they met on the way. And Bernadette made friends with two girls and a boy from down the road, disappearing for hours, returning eager, full of stories, and suntanned, her brown hair bleached a little as well by the sun. She looked like a different girl. Maureen wondered if she, herself, had looked like that at her age. What was it? Less than ten years ago.

The difference being of course that Maureen was already working then, not a lot of time for gallivanting, running wild through the fields and down to the streams, swimming and diving and screaming and laughing.

She wrote a short letter to Stuart every week just to say how things were going, and to keep him in touch with the children, she even managed to put a couple of photos in as well. She'd got a Kodak Brownie with her. He only responded to the letter that mentioned the idea of Maria staying. He said that would be fine, although he didn't want Maria to think it would be permanent as Elizabeth would want that room eventually, a month's notice either side, and how much would the rent be?

She didn't say anything about the idea in her next letter, although she did write a brief note to Maria saying it would be fine and to let her know when she would be arriving.

It was another existence for those four weeks, one that she had forgotten about, one that she had thought she was glad to leave behind. Admittedly her only real obligation was to look after the children and make sure that Bernadette was not getting into too much trouble, or too many bad ways. Smiling she wondered how easy it would be for Bernadette to fit in back at school after a summer like this, easily probably, she was only a child, a child enjoying an unexpected, temporary, and very different, kind of freedom.

And when she met the girls, her friends from the past, she realised that dissatisfactions exist everywhere. The three of them were jealous of her life in London. Maureen knew that they thought she was loaded, that Stuart was rich, which in a comparative kind of way he was. But also they were jealous of the idea of London life, of all the things you could do, all the places you could go. In this little village and around about there were dances and the like, and the pub for the men, but not much else. And everyone knew your business of course, everyone knew, and the priest knew as well. In London there was the chance to be anonymous wasn't there? Or to know the people you wanted to know and ignore the rest. And the opportunity to meet a boy as well, one of the three was getting married soon but the other two had no-one in particular, laughing that one of them would probably have to marry Martin Flynn pretty soon, the choice being so limited. Martin, poor thing, was a simple soul, with no sense or malice, who wandered around all day long saying hello, how-are-ye, to every single person he met before looking embarrassed and tongue-tied if they actually replied.

Late in the evenings, when even Bernadette had vanished to

the bedroom, Maureen often sat with Mama, and Dada as well, if he was not working that night. She realised that they too thought she had stumbled on some kind of paradise back in London. They had seen Janey and Jed's house, and had a peek at her house as well when they came over for the wedding, it was a different world to them. And she knew that she was a woman to them now, an independent person with children of her own, one of whom talked in rather a nice English accent, which was slightly strange to them. Sitting there in the light of the paraffin lamp, smoking a cigarette with Mam, or both of them, she saw that they were slightly in awe of her, she had accomplished something which was, in a way, beyond them. Most of her brothers or sisters, except Theresa really, even if they lived abroad, were still the Irish people they once were, still lived in that kind of milieu, still went to the Irish club and knew the priest, were part of it all. But Maureen wasn't. Not in the same way anyway. She was divorced from it. She went to Mass with the children, but not necessarily every week, and, if the truth were known, it didn't really bother her. The priest had dropped in a couple of times and had even made his point about the importance of the faith and regular attendance and its importance for the children. And she had nodded and gotten him another cup of tea, a small scotch on one occasion. But it wasn't important to her.

But, at the same time, it was. Sitting in this tiny country kitchen with her ageing parents, door open, twilight lit, hearing the nearby summer night sounds that you would never, ever, hear in London, was important to her, although she knew that she would never be fully part of it anymore. Once you have known something else you could never fully return to what was, a dire impossibility because of what you have come to understand. But these people, and the people in Bray in a slightly different way, were what she had come from, they had made her; she had a fleeting, minute, thought, that her mother and father had actually physically made her, just as they had made Theresa and Tommy and all the rest. It almost made her laugh to think of such a thing. Almost, affectionately, looking at the two of them sitting opposite her now, smoking, taking just a small drink, talking about the children, interested, friendly, wondering about her life and her future. They had made her and they were her past.

And the last week came. As they knew it must. They did go to Mass on the Sunday and Maureen knew that they would be back in London by the time the next Sunday arrived. They started to think about packing, there wasn't much but they didn't want to forget anything. The children and Bernadette were brown as berries, they looked so healthy. Relaxed as well, in a sort of way they would never be at home. Home. In London the word home always signified Ireland, but here it meant London, to Maureen and Bernadette and to Elizabeth, too, who had started asking when they would go home, and when they would see daddy again, not moaning, not crying, just asking. Bernadette also said she was looking forward to being back in Streatham, as much as anything to tell her friends about her great holiday in Ireland. She had only seen her grandparents twice, Maureen had insisted they drive over there, borrowing a car to do so. It would have been a crime not to have made that visit, Bernie, her mum, would not have been pleased if they had not made the journey once at least.

And without overdoing it they dressed themselves up a bit for the journey back to England, feeling slightly uncomfortable after weeks of loose dresses, no stockings, little make-up, and sandals on their feet. They drove down to the station, the girls were there to see them off as well, and away they went, waving as before to the diminishing figures of Mama and Dada and those three girls, no, those three women, who had been Maureen's friends for so long.

CHAPTER SIXTY

Things changed. The month away from the house, the month in Ireland, the month without Stuart, that month changed things. Changed everything in fact.

Although Maureen did become aware of this it didn't necessarily enter her consciousness immediately.

Stuart was pleased to see the children when they got back. He picked them all up from the station and it was very jolly, he gave her a peck on the cheek and picked up each of the children and whirred them around. Elizabeth laughed and Michael looked worried, bemused.

But as Maureen looked at him, at the station, and as he drove, and as they re-entered the house, something seemed to be different. Physically he looked different. He looked not exactly fatter but more substantial in a way, glossier, and his suit looked expensive, and he was louder as well. She thought he could well have looked like this before she left, but she had only noticed it now. And, in a way, he was not the Stuart that she used to know. Still friendly, still the children's father, still caring too, she thought, but not the Stuart of before. And, of course, she had only liked Stuart before, she had never loved him. And this Stuart seemed more distant, further away from her somehow.

When they got back to the house he helped unpack the car but then said he had to be off, he had a meeting.

'At the weekend, Stuart?'

'Never stops Mo, never stops. It's great to see you back.'

He kissed the children and her. Michael cried and Elizabeth looked a bit puzzled. They were tired after their journey. So was she. She could have done with a hand, or at least another adult in the house.

And then she looked around. The house was quiet, not just quiet in terms of noise, but quiet in another way too. It lacked being, it felt colder than she expected, almost unused, it felt as if no-one had been in there since she and the children had left a month ago. He'd probably slept there and that was it, he'd probably eaten out, breakfast as well, since she left, and gone to his golf club and the other places he frequented. She wondered if he'd slept elsewhere as well. Possibly.

But she had been away as well, spent time away from him, and she had enjoyed it, she hadn't missed him. She hadn't missed him at all.

And life entered this new phase with hardly a jolt.

Maria came to stay, and then stayed for two years. Maureen enjoyed her company. Both women now.

Maureen had never spoken to Maria about her mother, or about Deidre either. Maureen would have liked to know how much Maria knew about everything that had happened, but it was not something that was easily raised. Even when they were sitting around having a little drink after the children were well asleep. Whenever Maria mentioned Margaret, or Deidre, or Shaughnessy as well, it was always with affection, with sadness also about her mum. Maureen was somehow surprised that Maria should feel so positive about her father. The person that she said little about was Stephen. He had started to train as a solicitor and it seemed that they saw not much of each other now.

Elizabeth started school. And so Catholicism raised its head again. Paradoxically, despite Maureen's ambivalence towards the church, she did want Elizabeth to go the Catholic school. It seemed a way to keep some kind of contact with her own history although she didn't explain it to herself in that way, but many of the other parents were Irish and it was not unpleasant to have those Irish kind of conversations at the school gate.

And of course Elizabeth had to learn her Catechism and eventually make her first confession and take her first holy communion.

'Who made you?' - 'God made me'

'Why did God make you?' – 'God made me to know him, love him and serve him in this world, and to be happy with him forever in the next.'

Maureen had known early on that Elizabeth was bright and outgoing, much more sociable than Michael seemed to be, but she was somewhat intense as well.

Elizabeth took the Catechism seriously, learning it every day and even discussing religious matters with Maureen and Maria.

'Mum, how did God make me, do you think? Or do *you* know, Maria? How God made me, I mean?'

'Maria, how long would forever be, do you think, would it be longer than a year?'

They answered as best they could. And Maureen went to Mass every Sunday, with Michael as well, Elizabeth getting very annoyed if there was any suggestion at all that they should miss Mass for any reason. Maria often came as well, although she did sometimes say to the children that she had decided to go to an early evening mass instead, with her friends, at another church not so far away.

Stuart was bemused by all this. The truth was that he didn't like it. And Lynda didn't like it either. Maureen knew that she didn't like the Irishness of it all, she didn't care particularly about the religion itself, it was the connection with another culture that annoyed her, a culture that she regarded as lacking in some way, a lower-class culture as she saw it. But Maureen didn't care and Stuart's total involvement in his work, and whatever else he was up to, meant that Maureen could do whatever she liked as well.

Maria went home after about two years. She had done a bit of work for a local paper but most of the time she had jobs in offices doing fairly menial work, and even had as stint working in a local grocery shop. Maureen thought she was wasting her education and when an offer of a job came from home she encouraged Maria to take it.

And at more or less the same time Michael started school. And the change multiplied.

CHAPTER SIXTY-ONE

There was the loneliness.

When Michael went to school, on his first day, after she had taken both of them to school, she returned to the house. There was a feeling similar to that day when they had returned from Ireland, all of a sudden the house had become colder and somehow impersonal, even judgmental in a peculiar way. When the children were there, as they had been an hour ago, talking, eating their breakfast, getting ready, Michael feeling nervous on that particular day, the coldness was not evident. In fact Maureen did not even think about the house in those circumstances, it was a place where their lives took place, but it was not an entity to itself. But when it was empty, when she returned from the school on that day and turned the key in the lock, and went inside it felt different. The atmosphere told her something about her life, something that she avoided thinking about mostly.

She felt the loneliness and the emptiness of her existence. When the children were there they gave meaning to her life and, in a practical sense, also gave her loads of things to do, loads of things to get done, things that she mainly enjoyed, because they were for her children.

But when the children were gone there was a vacuum, a void. They would be back later, at half past three, or four o'clock, but this daily absence would confront her continually with the truth. Stuart was not there, he was away on business this week. She'd forgotten where, and she didn't really care. He was happy with what he was doing. He was pleasant to her and the children, he provided money. In that sense she could not complain. They slept in separate beds now, in the same room, but separate beds. He said it would be easier, not disturbing her with his erratic hours. There was no sex, had not been for a while now, and she was grateful for that, she didn't want to have sex with him, and, to be honest, she didn't want more children either. She loved them both, Michael and Elizabeth, didn't know what she would do without them, but she did not want more.

In the kitchen she sat down after making some tea, and had a cigarette, seeing out onto the garden behind the house, with the two apple trees looking full with almost ready fruit.

When Maria had been staying she had been a close friend, almost a sister for a lot of the time. They got on really well, laughing about how they had been back in the house in Bray, Maureen the maid and Maria the jumped-up little schoolgirl. Talking about almost everything. Almost everything. Just as Maureen avoided talking to Maria about Shaughnessy and Margaret, the relationship between them, so the subject of Stuart and Maureen was avoided as well. Maureen was not even sure if Maria had any views on how Stuart and Maureen lived. But why would she not? She was not a stupid girl, not a stupid woman. Living there in the house for two years or so she must have noticed all kinds of things, must have wanted to ask. She didn't really get on with Stuart for a start, they always said hello and were civil to each other but Maureen couldn't remember them actually having a conversation or a joke together in all that time. And Maria could still sound a little sharp, like she had been as a girl. Stuart didn't like that, he had commented to Maureen about it a couple of times. And Lynda, as well, had said a few times that she didn't know why that girl was staying for so long, it wasn't as if Maureen and Stuart needed the money was it?

In fact, Maureen charged Maria very little, but she enjoyed

that tiny bit of extra cash, it wasn't something that she had to ask Stuart for.

When Maria went home Maureen envied her. Envied her freedom to do just that, to go home again, even though Maria would probably have preferred to stay in London, if she could have got the right kind of job.

What was the use of it all? Things had seemed exciting, in a way, working in other people's houses, being involved, learning things. And moving on to places which seemed better, more adventurous. Coming to London. It had all seemed so hopeful.

Theresa, of course, was not as reticent as Maria when it came to talking about Stuart. She didn't dislike him but she did ask questions. And she made Maureen answer as well. About what he might or might not be up to, and whether they were still having sex. Theresa knew about the beds, of course. But at the same time Theresa also thought that Maureen had fallen on her feet, with the house and the money. She assumed that Stuart was earning loads of cash, and Maureen had to admit that she had no real idea about the money at all, apart from the fact that there always seemed to be enough.

But none of that made up for the fact that she felt so desperately lonely. At that table, the cigarette in the ashtray, smoke rising across the garden view, clouding it slightly.

She almost wanted to cry but there was no point in that was there? Crying didn't solve anything at all. But there was still the solitude. Why had that only come now, was she a different person before? Before now? Was she different then?

And she thought she was. Different that is. There was no comparison with who she was then. She could think back to when she was a child, playing outside, doing whatever chores and shopping that Mama asked her to do, going to school, leaving school. It had seemed straightforward, it was what happened, just like going to Mass every Sunday, going to confession, going to communion. It all just happened.

There were changes of course. Her body changed, and her periods started. And Mama told her what to do. Yes, that had been a big change but still it was just accepted as what happened. And those exact same things were happening to the other girls as well, and they whispered a bit about them, and sniggered and giggled together.

Had she ever felt lonely as a child? Had there been even one time that she had felt lonely? She couldn't think of a time. She had been upset of course. She had got into trouble at school with the teacher once or twice and he had complained to Dada. She had been worried about going back the next day, but the teacher seemed to have forgotten about whatever it was she had done. And when she had fallen in the dyke and broken her wrist she had been upset. And when Jimmy the dog died. Silly nothings. She might have cried a bit but they were of little consequence. And they were not the same as being lonely.

She thought about when she had taken Bernadette over to Ireland with the children; watching her play with those other kids from down the road, spending the day out in the countryside, coming home, laughing and exhausted. That was how it had been for her. She just lived then, just lived.

Even when she had gone to Bray. That first night in her little room, seeing the stars through the window, that was probably the first time she had been really alone, but she still felt the connection. Hadn't she thought then that she was looking at the same night sky that Dada and she had looked at together? She still felt the connection with home, still felt the connection with others.

She lit herself another cigarette. Looking at the ash-tray she saw, to her surprise, that she had already smoked two. Lipstick-ended filters crushed into the grey ash.

She stood and walked out into the garden. It was warm, comfortable. They had a little man who came round every couple of weeks. He kept the garden looking nice. The grass cut and the roses dead-headed. He was the same man that Lynda used, he came on her recommendation, or, if the truth were known, on her insistence. Maureen thought that Dada would laugh at all that. He liked flowers, she knew he did. But he would have seen that garden as an opportunity to grow things they could use. Some vegetables and fruit. Not waste it all on flowers, and definitely not pay a man to keep it tidy. Sidney was a nice man, though, he did a good job. She'd make him a cup of tea and have a little chat with him when he came round. Elizabeth often followed Sidney around if she wasn't at school and he didn't seem to mind, even explained what he was doing to her.

Where had it all gone wrong? When she looked around the garden and turned to look back at the house she knew that many people would have envied her. It wasn't a huge house by any means, three bedrooms and a decent-sized garden. Stuart had started saying that they must move soon, get something better. She knew he had the desire to own a house like Jed and Janey's, he really wanted somewhere like that. It was important for business, he said, to look as if you were successful, success builds on success, he was always saying that, or something very like it.

She didn't care. The house they lived in was fine. It was big enough. The children were happy here. She wasn't going to have any more children, although Stuart had said recently that they should think about having another child, or two even. They could afford it. She would do her best to make sure that there was no chance of that, and in purely practical terms the necessary acts for producing children were non-existent at the moment. To her relief.

The garden smelt fresh and green. The grass still a bit wet from dew, or maybe there had been some rain during the night. She wasn't sure. The dampness seeped through the gaps in her sandals making her feet wet. Mama had been furious that time when they'd just returned from town with new shoes, shoes for school and Mass really, and she and Paddy had gone out together and had paddled, shoes on, in the stream looking for the tiny fish you sometimes saw there, black ones and silver ones. And she had got home with the shoes soaked. Mama had left them to dry out overnight and made Maureen polish them the next morning, and then every day for a week.

Stuart and his ambition. In a way she would have preferred it if she hated him. It would be so much easier. But she didn't. She still liked him, in a way. He always provided for them, and when he got home he always talked to the children, and they looked forward to seeing him, jumping up on him, and clinging on to him as he walked through to the kitchen or the dining-room, or the sitting-room. Of course, this was partly to do with the fact that they knew he would probably have a chocolate bar or a Mars bar or something like that for them.

When she thought of herself, those not so many years ago, she thought of herself as a little waif of a thing. Not like Julia, but almost, in a way. If you looked at Julia now you could still see the shadow of her past, still thin, almost gaunt sometimes, especially when she was tired, smoking away, always puffing on a cigarette. Julia brought her past with her, she thought, it was always there lingering in the background.

Maureen threw her cigarette into the bushes at the thought, and went back to the kitchen.

CHAPTER SIXTY-TWO

Stuart had been rather full of himself over the last few weeks, maybe over the last couple of months. That glossiness had become even more glossy. He seemed to have got a little fatter as well, more pleased with himself. Business must have been doing well. He was keen on saying what that Macmillan had said, 'We've never had it so good', and he'd give her a little peck on the cheek as he said it. He even said he might buy her a little car for herself. She did use his sometimes, but he didn't really like her doing that and, anyway, it wasn't often there, outside, for her to use.

He'd met a man called Jonathan Gray at the golf club, or somewhere, and they'd become quite good friends, in a very short time. Stuart had even invited him home for dinner, telling Maureen to try and make it something special.

They had a nice steak and chips with some ice cream afterwards. He, Jonathan, had bought two bottles of wine. And, between the three of them they drank both bottles, the men having slightly more than Maureen. They ate in the dining-room.

Maureen found herself watching both of them. Jonathan was an 'Englishman', quite handsome in a way, tall. Charming, without overdoing it. Friendly. Good company. Stuart obviously liked him and was a bit in awe of him, Maureen thought, almost a bit subservient, which Maureen didn't really like. But Jonathan didn't lord it in any way, and he made sure that he spoke to Maureen, included her. This wasn't always the case with Stuart's pals from the golf club, they often more or less ignored her, just about saying thank you if she filled their glass or served them some food, and often, like Mr Graham, at the house in Dungarvan, if they did talk to her they'd do it in a funny kind of Irish accent. This annoyed her intensely now, which it hadn't really when Mr Graham had done the same thing such a long time ago.

When Gray had left, Stuart came into the kitchen. Maureen was still finishing off the washing-up and putting things away.

'He's alright isn't he? Jonathan, I mean.'

'He seems very nice, very charming. Nicer than some of those other eejits from the golf club, at least he spoke to me.'

'Yes, I like him. We might even do a bit of business together. Nothing definite yet.'

And Stuart disappeared back to the lounge without saying anything more.

Stuart never discussed the details of business with Maureen, after all what was there to know? He ran an accountancy business, they did the books for people, did audits and things like that. Stuart had made lots of contacts and the firm had grown, there were now, she thought, five or six accountants working for Stuart. Gerry was a junior partner in the firm and Kat was the office manager, running two offices in fact. The original one, in Finchley, and another in Archway. Kat came over occasionally, if they were having drinks, or supper with friends. Maureen didn't really mind her, she'd got used to her although it did niggle slightly that Kat knew much more about Stuart's business than she did. Not that it mattered, it didn't.

It was only a couple of days later that Stuart got home from work slightly earlier than usual, coming straight into the kitchen where she was preparing tea for the children.

'Mo, I was talking to Jonathan again today,' he said with no preamble, smiling, pleased with himself, 'He asked me if I want to get involved with a new building project up in Barnet.'

'Oh yes?'

'Looks like a good opportunity. Put our cash into something different, diversify a bit.'

'So, not just doing the books?'

'No, no, no, no. Investing. I think it's time to start moving into something a bit bigger, accountancy's OK but we need to diversify, like I said. If we want the bigger house, if you want your car.'

'Right.'

And Stuart threw himself fully into this new venture. Gerry and Kat ran the offices but Stuart was looking for bigger things now. Jonathan popped in a few times and he seemed very upbeat about what they were doing and seemed happy to be working with Stuart.

Maureen had known Stuart for a long time now. She knew his moods, she could tell instantly if things were going well, if he'd had a good day or a bad day, even if he tried to cover up things sometimes.

It was obvious he was excited by this new project, they were going to build houses somewhere up in Barnet, he was really positive about everything. And, although Maureen was happy enough in their house, she started to get affected by his enthusiasms and even found herself looking in estate agents' windows, checking the prices of bigger houses in better areas. And thinking about what little car she would like.

She chatted to the children about what car they thought would be best if Daddy had the money to buy Mummy a car. Elizabeth did not really respond at first, but looked at her in that quizzical way she had, as if she was thinking, 'I don't really care what kind of car you have, why on earth should

I?' But Michael entered into the spirit of it. He wondered first whether it would be possible to get some kind of sports car like an MG or a Sunbeam Alpine but then said that would be stupid because people like Mum didn't have sports cars did they? Maybe a Ford Anglia or an Austin A35. Something small? She would have quite liked the sports car, but maybe he was right. Michael said he would look every day as he walked to school and he would tell her the best car to have, tell her by the end of the week. And then Elizabeth said, 'Is it possible to get a red one, Mummy? I think I'd quite like a red one.'

CHAPTER SIXTY-THREE

What Maureen didn't find out until later was that there was no pot of cash from the accountancy firm, no big money waiting to be invested in other projects. The firm paid its way, certainly, provided a good living for Stuart and paid the wages of Kat and the others, but there were no huge excess profits. Starting up the second office had taken quite a bit of money in itself.

Without knowing all this, Maureen watched as Stuart got more involved in the building project, leaving the day-to-day office stuff to Kat and Gerry. She could see he was really taken with the idea of moving up a league, of working with people who dealt in big sums of money. She watched and watched as he came home every day, chatting about who he had met, and what Jonathan had said, and what the next step was. He was excited, and, in a way, so was she.

But over a period of time things changed. In simple terms Stuart started to become stressed rather than excited. She didn't really think much of this at first. After all, sometimes, one could almost be mistaken for the other and she realised that no project was going to be plain sailing anyway. But, very quickly, he became stressed all the time. She could see it in his face. He was never unpleasant to her, a bit short with her occasionally but never unpleasant. She could see the change though.

'How are things at work, Stuart? You look as if it's tough going. You should slow down a bit, you know.'

'No, no. Everything's fine, everything's fine.'

He smiled for a moment, and then didn't.

He went to work early and came home late. She noticed over a period of two weeks or so that he was gone for much longer each day. She could smell the drink on him when he got home. He often, over the years, had a drink with friends after work and she would smell those drinks on his breath, but now, in an odd sort of way, it had a different flavour to it. And it came from his pores as well as his breath. There was an odour of panic about him, intermingled with the gin and tonics, and the slices of lemon.

And then came the last day. He arrived home at seven. She heard the news start on the radio. He looked different. Did he look smaller? Afterwards she thought he did. The children were finishing their homework. He sat in the lounge on his own. She could see him in there, he'd hardly said a word.

She brought him a drink. She didn't know why she did that. She never got Stuart a drink, he always got his own, if he wanted one.

Although it was early she shooed the children upstairs to have a bath and go to bed. She said they could read. They knew something was wrong, she knew they could feel it, they went upstairs not moaning, but looking slightly anxious, looking back as they climbed the stairs.

She came and stood in the door of the lounge. He was sitting in his chair, the drink on the table. He looked at her. She could see that his face was different, something of himself was not there anymore.

'We have to talk.'

She started to move into the lounge but he got up.

'No, let's go in the kitchen.'

He took his drink and they went and sat at the kitchen table. She had no real idea at all what was going on. She felt almost calm because she couldn't think what could be so bad. She didn't think he was going to leave her, she didn't think there was another woman, he didn't seem ill or anything like that. Something to do with work?

He sat opposite her in his dark blue suit, waistcoat undone, and his tie now pulled loose. His face was flushed, sweaty, swollen in some way, distended almost, his hair greasy.

'I've got some bad news.'

She waited.

'I invested in Gray's project and the whole thing's gone belly-up. It looks like I've lost everything.'

It took her a little while to make sense of this, and even then she couldn't.

'I thought you said you were investing money, profits, from Johnson Accountants? That's what you said wasn't it? Money that you'd made from there, it needed investing, that's what you said. You can't have lost everything, I don't understand what you mean.'

'I know that's what I said but there weren't any profits to invest, not big profits anyway, not enough.'

'I still don't understand.'

'There wasn't any extra money there, it paid everyone's salaries and we could expand, yes, the business was doing OK, but there wasn't any excess, if you like.'

'Why did you say there was, then?'

'It was an opportunity. I saw an opportunity to make some real money. So we could move up a bit, get that house you wanted.'

'I wanted? I didn't say I wanted a bigger house, Stuart.'

'No. Maybe you didn't.'

'So there was no money. So what happened?'

He didn't say anything for a number of seconds, he looked down at the table and then up, he directly looked at her.

'I borrowed money.'

'Where from.'

'Some from the bank, and other places. And some from Mum'

'You borrowed from Lynda as well. Jesus!'

'It looked like a dead cert, Mo, Jonathan showed me how we couldn't possibly lose.'

'But you're an accountant, Stuart, you must have known there was some kind of risk?'

'It seemed like we couldn't lose. I believed him.'

There was a long silence in the kitchen. Maureen could hear the children talking and laughing upstairs, something which seemed so normal and usual, happening just a few feet away from this conversation.

'So what happened?'

'There were planning problems with the council, and some kind of supply problems as well, a supplier went bust after taking a load of money. The project's off now, finished.'

'And you'll get the money back?'

'No. It's gone. Jonathan's lost some as well, of course.'

'You have to pay back the loans?'

‘I can’t. There’s no money to pay it back.’

‘How much was it then?’

‘In total it’s about £5000.’

‘You borrowed £5000! Jesus Christ, Stuart, are you fucking mad!’

‘Shhh, the children.’

Maureen had never sworn like that in her life. She was shocked at herself, it had come out of god knows where inside her.

‘How are you going to pay it back Stuart? Will you have to sell the business?’

‘I’m bankrupt Maureen. They’ve called in the loans and I’m bankrupt.’

CHAPTER SIXTY-FOUR

Maureen didn't really understand what being bankrupt meant, or, when he told her, didn't fully understand the implications anyway.

But they very soon became clear. The family had to move out of the house almost immediately and lose most of their possessions, everything apart from essential furniture and clothes. All the rest was claimed to go towards paying off the creditors. Life had changed totally within a space of no time at all. One minute she was the wife of an accountant with a nice house and money to spend and the next she was the wife of a ruined man with no possessions. None of any consequence. No house, no car, just what they stood up in almost.

It was totally bewildering for Maureen and, of course, the children could make no sense of it at all. Maureen tried to explain that there had been problems with Daddy's business and they were going to live elsewhere for a while, but everything would be alright, everything would return to normal very soon, everything would be fine. And as she said this she understood that she was lying to them. Nothing would return to what it was, nothing.

Stuart had spoken to his parents. She discovered, in fact, that he had told them first, told them before he had told her. This made her angry, but there was no time to deal with that anger at the moment. Lynda and Jim had said they must move in with them, there was space in their house. And Maureen was grateful to them for that.

Maureen spoke to Theresa immediately, and then to Lynda

as well. It was like talking about a death in the family, except it was worse in a way because there was shame attached. If someone died there was no shame, only grief, but Maureen learnt almost immediately about the shame, and disgust as well, that went with bankruptcy. And the pity allied with contempt.

Julia and Billy came to help with removing the bits that they were allowed to take from the house. There was something comic about all this because, god knows how, Billy had got one of the vans from the post office to use. They did it on the second evening after Stuart had told her, Billy said they'd have to do it the dark, and be quick about it too. But he was so nice and gentle, friendly, and careful with those little bits of furniture they were allowed to take. And funny as well.

'Come on, darlin', it's not the end of the world, happens to the best of us. 'Ere I bet you didn't know this did ya? Abraham Lincoln, he went bankrupt twice. Course he got shot in the end, perhaps that's not such a great example.'

How did he know that, she thought.

Lynda wasn't keen on Billy.

Maureen would remember that evening forever. Leaving her own house behind for the last time. The short ride around to Lynda and Jim's with their stuff, crowded into the van. They'd laughed a bit with Billy but they were all silent now. Realising what had happened, realising that everything had changed.

They pulled up in front of the house. Lynda came out and she gave Maureen a hug, and it was genuine, Maureen knew that, and she was grateful.

'Put everything in the garage for now. Your rooms are ready for you. And there's a meal. We'll eat together and then you can put the children to bed. OK?'

It only took them half an hour to unload the van and put the beds and little bits of furniture in the garage. Billy shot off, eager to get the van back. They took their few suitcased belongings inside and upstairs to their rooms. Two rooms with two single beds in each. The children were quiet and Stuart was almost invisible, there all the time, but invisible nevertheless.

Maureen helped the children put their clothes into the chest of drawers in their room. They hadn't shared since they were toddlers and now, although they didn't want to share, they were much too old for that, they were reluctant, but they were relieved at the same time. It wasn't said, but Maureen could see that they were glad they were together on that night.

All four of them went down and sat with Jim while Lynda served up a stew she had made. They were quiet, Jim trying to cheer people up a bit, and failing. No-one wanted pudding, even though Lynda had made a nice apple tart. They decided to go to bed. Maureen gave Lynda a hug before she went upstairs. Maureen thanked her. And she meant it.

The room was small. The children were in Stuart's old room which was slightly bigger. This was the spare room, the room that was used for nothing. The two of them had hardly spoken over the last few days. Stuart had been called for two interviews with the Official Receivers. He returned from each meeting looking worse than before, smaller than before. Ill. The two of them hadn't really spoken because there seemed to be nothing to say. He had ruined them, and he hadn't discussed it with her, and he hadn't even told her first when it all started to unravel.

She undressed in the cold, small room. Was it cold? It felt cold to Maureen. She stripped down to her slip, she didn't want to take any more off in front of him. He lay on his bed in his clothes. They said nothing. She sat on the side of the bed at first and then got inside, it felt damp and cold and unused. She turned away from him. She heard him stand and go to turn the light off, heard him undress, and put himself inside his small, creaking bed. And they lay there. They knew each other's breathing, and they knew that neither of them was asleep.

Maureen lay and thought. About everything and nothing. How had it come to this, what would they do now, where would they get money from, how long could they stay here, how long did she want to stay here, how would the children cope, where would they get money from, should she just leave him, what could she tell Mama and Dada, should she just take the children home, they'd be happy there, wouldn't that be better, where would they get money from, where would they get money from, where would they get money from?

'I'm sorry Maureen, I'm so sorry.'

She didn't respond.

CHAPTER SIXTY-FIVE

Maureen got up early. Too early for the children.

She went down to the kitchen and made a pot of tea. She wasn't a real guest in the house, she felt like an interloper of some kind, almost worried that Lynda would catch her making tea and demand to know what she was doing, making tea without asking.

But Lynda didn't appear for twenty minutes or more. Maureen smoked two cigarettes and had just the one cup of tea in that time. She had slept, in the end she had slept. But she felt tired and useless.

Lynda came into the kitchen, housecoat over nightdress, her face unmade-up, looking wrinkled, and old. Lynda always looked well turned out, made up, hair done; but not this morning. Maureen felt sorry for her. She wasn't a stupid woman, she would know that Stuart was to blame for all this. In truth Maureen was surprised that Lynda had even lent Stuart money without checking that it was fairly secure. Maureen didn't know yet exactly how much Jim and Lynda had lent him, she didn't dare ask. She didn't really want to know, but she would have to know eventually, soon. It was bad enough having to rely on their charity without knowing that they also owed them loads of money.

'Is that tea drinkable?'

'Probably not, it's been in the pot for a while, it'll be stewed and cold probably. I'll make some more, sit down and I'll make some more'

'I'll do it, stay where you are.'

And she made tea. A woman in her own kitchen, Maureen envied her.

Lynda said nothing while the kettle boiled, while she heated the pot, while she spooned the tea, while she poured the boiling water, while she got another cup and saucer. And then she sat down. She pointed at Maureen's packet of cigarettes and Maureen pushed it towards her. Lynda rarely smoked. She lit up.

'How did you sleep?'

'Well enough, considering.'

'And the children?'

'I peeked in, they seemed alright. Glad to be in the same room, I think.'

Lynda said nothing, smoked, had a sip of tea.

'I'm sorry Maureen. For all this.'

'It's not your fault. If anything it's me, I should have, I don't know, done something, made Stuart be more careful, I don't know.'

'Did he tell you about the project?'

'A bit. I met that man Gray. But business was Stuart's thing, I didn't really understand any of it.'

'Stuart was always like that, always very keen on the ideas of other people, ambitious, but easily taken in, a bit insecure. I knew that, I should have made him be more careful. Should have made him think twice. But I didn't.'

'You lent him some money, you and Jim, I mean.'

'Of course. He's our son. Our only son. You always believe the best, despite yourself. You always do.'

She had a sad smile on her face, and she reached across to touch Maureen's hand with her own.

Maureen had never seen this person before, although her hug last night might have been a clue.

'Try and keep everything normal for the children, Maureen. It's going to be very difficult for you all, possibly for years. They're going to rely on you, they're going to need you to be strong, because I don't expect Stuart will be, I really don't. And you can stay here for as long as you like. It's your home for as long as you like. Don't forget that......God, is that the time, I must get dressed, and you'd better get the children ready for school hadn't you? Keep everything normal, it's the best way, believe me.'

She put her cigarette out, smiled and got up quickly to leave and get back upstairs.

Maureen sat for a minute or two, letting Lynda get back to her bedroom, then she went upstairs herself. She went into the children's bedroom and woke them up gently. Each in their own bed. They woke with uncertainty already on their faces, they were in a strange room and they still knew that something was wrong, knew it even before they had fully woken up.

'School, then, you two. We're a bit late already. My fault. Let's go.'

She forced them, cajoled them, to get on, as if it was any old normal day.

'Do we have to, mum? Can't we stay at home today. Please can we?'

They were at the kitchen table, eating cereal. Elizabeth was doing the talking and Michael's face was agreeing with her.

'Of course not, what's the matter with ye both?'

Both of the children laughed despite themselves.

'Mum, you sound so Irish, no-one says ye any more.'

'Well I do, get on wit' ye.'

She was glad they'd laughed together.

Staying at Lynda and Jim's, the children could continue at their school, which was something to be grateful for. At last, a reason for appreciating the fact that Lynda lived around the corner! When she dropped the children off Maureen told the school they had changed addresses but didn't say why, didn't want to say why. But things got around. Because Stuart was involved in a local building project the bankruptcy was reported in the local paper. Maureen was not aware of this until one of the other mothers approached her at the school gate. Said how sorry she was to hear the news, and Maureen could see the pity and contempt, and became aware of the other mothers watching, all of them knowing what was being discussed.

Back at home, it looked like Lynda and Jim were out.

Maureen went upstairs. He was sitting on the side of the bed. It looked like he could have been there for hours. Sitting, staring into space. A shrunken man, in his trousers and his vest. Unshaven. His dark hair greasy, unclean.

Stuart had always been tidy, smart, clean, proud of himself, too much so sometimes. But now it was if he had lost himself, lost his pride, lost his self-respect, become nothing.

She tidied up her bed, and the clothes around it. She didn't say anything. He didn't move, although his head had moved slightly to check who had entered the room.

'Your ma says we can stay as long as we like. She's being very nice.'

He didn't reply.

'Right Stuart, look, what's done is done. I don't know what happened but it's done now. You deal with the bankruptcy, do whatever that has to be done. That's your responsibility. But we have to find some money as well, and we can't stay here forever. We have to look after the children.'

'So it's just as simple as that, is it?'

He spoke quietly.

She paused before replying.

'In the end, Stuart, yes, it damn well is. What's done is done. I'm going to look for a job today and you better as well, otherwise we'll have nothing.'

She looked at him, still sitting there. And then she dug out some smarter clothes and went to the bathroom to wash and dress.

CHAPTER SIXTY-SIX

By the time she went to pick up the children that afternoon she had interviews for three cleaning jobs. One in a solicitor's office in the early morning and two in houses nearby, bigger houses, richer people, but not too far away. It had been easy, she had looked in the local paper and at the postcards in two newsagent's windows. Cleaning seemed easiest straight away, she was no stranger to it, after all. She hoped that Lynda would be able to get the children up and give them their breakfast, although it was possible she'd be back in time to take them to school.

When she arrived at the school that afternoon, the school secretary came out and said that the Headmaster, Mr Jones, wanted to see her.

She went in. He was a Welshman, a bit unusual for a Catholic school, in his fifties or sixties maybe, sometimes a bit abrupt but friendly nevertheless. The children complained that every Friday morning he played the violin for the hymns in Assembly, and he was awful.

'It just screeches, mum, and he doesn't care!'

Maureen went into the school.

'Come in Mrs Johnson. Sit down, sit down, sit down. Thanks, Mrs Perkins.'

The secretary left them to it, closing the door quietly.

'I'm sorry to hear about your troubles, Mrs Johnson.'

'Thank you.'

'The gossip gets around and, I have to admit, I did look in the paper when I heard.'

'Like everyone else, I suppose.'

'Yes, I would say so. Look here, the reason I wanted to see you, there's been a few things happen today, in the classroom and in the playground. The other children know as well, of course, their parents will have told them, or discussed it any rate within their hearing.'

'So what's happened?

'A bit of name-calling, a bit of nastiness, if I'm being truthful. Teasing, bullying, if you like. But I've dealt with it, there'll be no more of that tomorrow, or there better not be anyway. The children will tell you all about it I'm sure.'

'Perhaps I should move them to another school.'

'No, no, no, no, no! That won't be necessary. Elizabeth and Michael are good children, I won't have them bullied out of my school. Look, Mrs Johnson, when I started teaching in Port Talbot, I saw children bullied, in fact I saw the children of a local grocer who'd fallen on hard times, a bit like yourselves, bullied until they could take no more, and I swore that would never happen in any school where I was the headmaster. And it won't Mrs Johnson, it won't, I promise you that.'

She believed him.

The children looked unhappy when they came out. As they walked they said about Bobby saying this, and June saying that, and Jimmy Conway, an Irish boy, calling them tinkers for some reason. But they said that Mr Jones had spoken to their class, and Maureen said she had spoken to Mr Jones as well. And they didn't say they didn't want to go back.

'Have we really lost all our money, mum?'

'Yes, I'm afraid we have. Just a bit of bad luck really, happens to everyone once in a while. But we'll be OK, we'll be OK, don't you worry, we'll be OK.'

When they got home, to Maureen's surprise, Lynda had made some tea for them and there was toast and jam as well. Maureen mentioned quietly to Lynda that she might have got an early morning job and could she get the children up and ready for school, for a little while anyway. She said it would be no problem, no problem at all.

CHAPTER SIXTY-SEVEN

Everyone was unhappy. The turmoil that it created had affected them all in different ways, but it did affect them all. The children had been moved from everything they knew, had been moved from their own place, from where they were comfortable. Lynda had her own method of doing things which was different from Maureen's, more organised in a way, more obviously organised, let's say. Meals at an exact particular time, staying at the table till everyone had finished, taking shoes off at the front door, just little things really, but different. And these tiny things upset the children not only because they were different, but because, they seemed to signify that, like it or not, their mother was not in charge any more, not as long as they were living in that house. Elizabeth, or Michael, would look pleadingly at Maureen but all she could do was shrug her shoulders, hug them, and whisper it would be alright soon. When she wasn't at all sure it would be.

But Lynda was unhappy as well, disappointed for her son, but disappointed with her son as well. Maureen could see that she had expected more of Stuart, especially after he had taken that loan from her and Jim. And now he wasn't showing himself to have strength. He was letting them all down, and his parents were more obviously affected than anyone else. Maureen was concentrating on working and supporting the children, and the children weren't properly aware of how Stuart was dealing with the whole business.

Maureen knew that Lynda had spoken to Stuart both in a caring way but also angrily, because she was frustrated by his apparent inertia. He was doing what he had to do for the Receiver but, apparently, little more. He hadn't found a job, and had hardly looked for one it seemed. Jim, who was always quiet, seemed, himself, to reflect his son's decline, he now looked depressed and anxious, said little, smiled little, and had a shrunken look about him. The only thing that did cheer him was the children, but they made him sad as well, disappointed that his son, his family, had let them down.

Stuart had fallen further into his state of despondency. He must have known about the impending bankruptcy before it happened, knew it was on the cards, maybe for weeks or even a month before it occurred. Maureen had worked all this out, because it was obvious, everything wasn't perfect one day and a disaster the next, was it? But once it did happen he lost not only his money, but himself as well.

Maureen started her jobs within two days. She had given Janey as a reference, and all three seemed happy enough to start her on trial, subject to a satisfactory reference, even though it had to come from the States. She left at six-fifteen to do the solicitors, they had said she could do it in the evening if she wanted but she decided to stick with the morning. It was easy enough, tidying, hoovering, polishing, cleaning the fireplace and setting a fire, windows twice a week, wash the towels, and clean the little kitchenette they had, and the toilet. A piece o'cake, she thought.

The two houses were different to the office, but not too arduous. She went to the first one after leaving the children off at school and did the other from just after twelve. The woman at the later one would have preferred her to start earlier, but was happy enough. It wasn't hard at all. For a start they all had pretty good hoovers these days which made a real difference to doing the floors and the carpets, the old carpet beaters and sweepers were murder by comparison.

And she enjoyed the work. The money was not great but it was a start and she felt at least she was doing something. She got satisfaction from doing something, from being active.

She watched Stuart every day over that first week or so. She encouraged him to get out and find a job, it didn't matter what it was. She hadn't looked into it properly but she thought that getting an accountant's job as a bankrupt, undischarged they called it, would be impossible, it might even be illegal, she didn't know. Maybe he could be a book-keeper? Do people's books for them, she wasn't sure.

His inertia, however, got to her, as it had done to Lynda. It made her angry. And she was angry with him anyway, very angry, for putting themselves in this position. But the anger was mainly kept inside her, living in that house made it difficult for her express any real feelings about what was going on,

'I've got an afternoon off today, Stuart, she's having some people to lunch. When I get home I want you ready to go out and get a job. Suit, shaved, tidy. No excuses, d'ya hear?

She'd lied about the lunch, she'd taken the afternoon off, 'on urgent family business', the woman had been OK about it, more or less anyway.

He just looked at her, sitting at the kitchen table with a cup of tea in front of him.

Lynda heard her and said he'd be ready.

She arrived home at twelve. Lynda had worked on him. He looked respectable, not the same as he could be, but respectable enough. She took him up to Muswell Hill and then on to Archway. It was like dragging a child around the shops; it annoyed her and it made her want to cry as well, which she hated beyond belief. They looked in every shop and in every newsagent's window. And they saw two cards for bookkeepers. There were loads of other jobs as well, building work, kitchen work, shop work. She wasn't sure he could manage those types of things the state he was in, simple though they were. She said they'd focus on the bookkeepers. The first one was in a rather run-down insurance office just off the Archway Road. Not far from where his old business was, where it actually still was in fact, but not his anymore.

She said to him he'd have to go in and get the job himself.

'Do you understand Stuart? You have to get this, we need the money. Think of the children for god's sake!'

He looked at her for a moment.

'You're not going to stand outside, are you?'

She didn't reply immediately, angry and frustrated as she was. All of a sudden full up with those feelings, almost unable to respond.

'No, I'll wait around the corner.'

He waited, standing there in his suit, almost, but not quite, like Stuart.

She went and stood around the corner in the Archway Road. But she could still see him in the reflection of the shop window on the other corner. She watched. He stood there, he lit a cigarette and looked in the window of a small newsagents next to the insurance office. She could see him standing there, doing nothing. Then he walked away down the side road, further away, disappearing out of the reflection as he did so.

She waited there for at least ten minutes. She had decided she would just wait, she would do nothing but wait. Watching the traffic going down towards Highbury Corner or across towards Tufnell Park. And the buses. The 27 bus near the station going towards Camden and to Teddington. They had once got that bus all the way to Richmond, Stuart and her, and the children. A long way. They got the train back. It had been fun, during the school holidays, and they'd rowed on the river which had been so funny, they had all laughed so much. She remembered it, that hot day on the river. The children had wanted Tizer and they'd bought a big bottle for them to have with their sandwiches.

She wasn't really thinking about Stuart now. Just waiting. Lynda said she would get the children if they weren't back, so she didn't have to worry about that.

She turned again to the reflection. He had come back into view.

Still smoking. He must have lit up again, he'd been longer than one cigarette's worth. He stood around, looking in the newsagent's again. Then he straightened himself up, he was getting ready to come back. She could see him prepare himself, prepare his face. A small part of her was sorry for him.

He came round the corner. She smiled at him.

'Well?'

He was already shaking his head in that sad, regretful kind of way.

'No. Already gone. They interviewed someone this morning, and offered it to him. Said if I'd got there it would have been mine, better qualified.'

She still smiled at him. For a moment or two.

'I saw you Stuart. You didn't go in there at all. You're lying to me. Well that's no good to me or the children, Stuart. No good at all. Now get back down there and get that bloody job. Stop feeling so sorry for yourself and get that bloody job. D'ye hear me Stuart, do ye damn well hear me?'

She was almost raising her voice, raising her voice within her whisper to him on the busy street corner.

He looked at her, and then went back around the corner. She

watched in the reflection until he had opened the door and gone inside.

CHAPTER SIXTY-EIGHT

About two months after she'd started the cleaning jobs the woman in the twelve o'clock house sat her down with a cup of tea. They did that occasionally. Friendly enough, but not pally or anything. Christian names though, Maureen and Stella

'Maureen, look, I thought we'd be staying here for a least a year but my husband has been moved, we're going to Hong Kong, for three years it'll be. And we're going to let the house out. I was wondering if you could do a big house clean for me. Give the whole place a kind of deep clean. Some of the walls have got a bit grubby as well, they'll need washing. And I'll recommend you to the tenants, it's a family, English, he's in the army. Maybe three day's work to do the big clean, what do you think?'

She offered Maureen a cigarette and lit it for her. Time to think.

'I could do it, of course. But I'd need a bit of help to do it properly, you'd get a better job that way. With the walls and everything.'

Stella nodded.

'You know someone?'

'Oh yes, I could get someone to help me.'

'Well, if you sort it and let me know how much it'll cost, that would be wonderful.'

Maureen got Julia to help her with that first job.

And almost immediately she was in demand, other people contacted her, they had heard she could organise house cleaning, and end of let cleaning, things like that. Maureen was surprised that there was that amount of work available, surprised that the word got round so quickly. Obviously, she couldn't do all the work herself but with Julia's help, and Theresa's as well, she got the names of women, Irish usually, but West Indian sometimes as well, who might be interested.

At first she did it from Lynda's. Lynda was happy to help at the beginning, taking messages on her telephone. She had taken quite a shine to Maureen since the disaster happened, impressed, in some way, with how Maureen had approached things. But after a while she said, in a nice way, that maybe Maureen should think about renting a little office. And so she did. Not doing cleaning herself anymore, but organising it, with Julia's help. The office, once again, was in Archway, a convenient central point to manage work in Highgate and Kentish Town and Hornsey, and Hampstead as well.

And her agency started. 'Maureen's Cleaning Company'? 'Johnson's Cleaning Service'? No, that wouldn't do at all. 'Kelleher's Kleening Services.' Yes, that would do for a start, she liked that.

Stuart had got that job. He didn't appear for half an hour but she knew he was in there, had seen his reflection enter the brokers. When he came out he walked straight around to see her.

'OK. I got the job. It's only part-time though, two or three days a week but he said his brother has the same type of business and could probably use me for the other days in the week. They're Jewish. He seemed OK.'

Stuart looked different. Even if it was only a slight change there was an air of having achieved something about him. He was pleased that he had got the job. She was relieved because there'd be a bit more money and he might even become more like his old self, the children needed that, and she would find life easier if he was functioning more or less normally. He got the other job as well, so he was fully employed. Of course the money was not great but it was an income, and, added to Maureen's cleaner money, they could manage at a very limited level.

The transition to running the agency, Kelleher's Kleening Services happened over a number of months, of course. Initially she was just finding people to do jobs in a kind of informal way and was still doing her cleaning jobs as well. It was tiring but sort of fun and, even as it started, she had an inkling that something more might come of it. Obviously Stuart was aware of what was happening, how could he not be, and she had a concern that he might not be keen on her making more money than him, or starting a small business. They didn't discuss it initially.

Their relationship, once he had started his book-keeping, once he was earning, had become a friendly enough thing. They looked after the children, they worked, they shared a room, but not a bed. There was no passion, but had there ever been? No, was the answer. Not on Maureen's side anyway. The disaster, the bankruptcy, had changed their relationship totally, and made clearer what it was and what it wasn't. Maureen, before, had acted as wife, as a housekeeper, as a mother. And the truth was that Stuart had made all the decisions about money. But now they had become equals, almost overnight. If anything Maureen had become more powerful than Stuart, she was the one who had taken the initiative about her own work, and about his work as well. And he had shown himself to be lacking, lacking in courage. Maureen wasn't exactly sure if he realised that, but she definitely did. And she suspected that the children had felt it was well. She still liked him well enough, in her own way, but there was little more than that

As Maureen changed what she was doing her status within the house changed as well, especially as Lynda was helping her, almost giving Maureen her imprimatur, giving a recognition that Maureen was someone to be reckoned with. The children liked this, they felt that their mother was becoming more important and they liked it.

Maureen had told Lynda that she needed to talk to Stuart about moving. Lynda said they didn't have to move, they could stay as long as they liked. The disaster had changed Lynda as well, she had become a nicer woman, maybe she had always been nicer but Maureen had seen a different, more positive, side to her since they had moved into the house. One that cared about her son, obviously, but cared very much about her grandchildren and Maureen too. Not that she couldn't still be picky and irritating and pompous, she definitely could. But.

'We need to move Lynda. Find a place of our own. Get started again, it's got to happen. And sooner rather than later really.'

Lynda said that Jim and her were going out the following Sunday afternoon, going to friends up in Southgate, and the kids were going to a birthday party round the corner, so Maureen decided to talk to Stuart then.

They'd had an early lunch and the others had all left. They sat in the kitchen having another cup of tea and a cigarette.

'Stuart, I was thinking the other day that we need to move. We can't stay here forever. And it'd be better for the kids. Wouldn't it? What do you think?'

He looked as if he didn't want to discuss it. Stubbing out his cigarette as if he was about to get up and go.

'No, no. We haven't got the money, Mo. It's rent-free here, I'm still paying back, and will be for ages, years probably. We're better off here.'

He sounded certain.

'Well, you may think that but the truth is this, we can't stay here, it's bad for the children, they don't like being in someone else's place all the time. And we have to stand on our own feet, have to make a go of things, despite whatever's happened in the past. Look, Stuart, I'm going to start my own business, properly I mean, the cleaning thing, I can make a business out of it. It already is really. And your mum said I should rent a small office, start to get a bit more professional she said.'

'And buy a house as well, I suppose. Now you're a professional.'

'Don't be stupid, Stuart, we won't be buying a house for a while yet. The business will pay for the office, I've worked all that out, and we can rent a flat. If you're working, and I am as well, we can rent a flat. I'm not saying it'll be easy but we can do it.'

'I think we should stay here, for another year maybe, and then when I'm back on my feet we could look into buying a small place maybe. I've still got contacts. I'll sort something out. It's better if we stay here, Mo. Let's wait until I'm on my feet and then I'll sort it.

They moved three weeks later, the flat in Maureen's name.

CHAPTER SIXTY-NINE

The new place was a little way away, near Ally Pally, but the children were able to go to the same school. It was more difficult certainly, a greater distance, but between them, and with Jim's help mainly, the children got to school and home every day. Jim either walked them there and back or took them in his car if time was short or the weather was bad.

It was Elizabeth's final year at the primary school, she had passed her eleven-plus, which was a relief but no real surprise, and they had been looking at girls' grammar schools for her. She was very excited about all of that, which, possibly, took her mind off the problems she could see or feel at home. Michael still had a year to go and was a lot less positive, he had been more moody recently, recalcitrant. The school expected that he too would pass the eleven-plus, but the result wasn't quite as certain as with Elizabeth.

The flat was different to Lynda and Jim's house. It was the upper floor of a two-storey house, bigger than the flat that Theresa had in Camden, years ago, but not much more salubrious. Living in a place like this told the family how tight things actually were, the other house had disguised this in a way. Two bedrooms, a small living room, a small kitchenette, and a bathroom. Not well-decorated, shabby really. And there was a smell to it. An indefinable smell of food that was always there, day and night. It didn't come from the flat downstairs, it was almost like it was baked into the wallpaper, baked into the walls, to be there forever.

There was a Greek family downstairs who they said hello to,

but didn't really talk to, the husband was never there, the wife's English was limited, and the two children went to the school round the corner so Michael and Elizabeth didn't really make friends with them, or play with them outside either.

Maureen and Stuart had disagreed about the flat. They had disagreed about moving and they had disagreed about the choice of flat. Maureen had been pragmatic, she thought. They didn't have a lot of money, beggars can't be choosers, but having their own place would be a step forward. Stuart just wanted to stay at home, that was the truth of it. While Lynda and Jim were definitely not rich they were comfortable, and their house was comfortable as well, and Stuart had never known anything different. She remembered how unimpressed he'd been with Mama and Dada's house back home. Because he was so intransigent Maureen had gone ahead on her own, finding four places to look at and then dragging him along. They had brief arguments on the pavement outside two of the flats they had seen together. But Maureen had persisted, and Lynda and Jim had supported her, at least in the way of trying to persuade Stuart that this was the right thing to do. He probably felt betrayed by them all.

The turning point came at the dinner table one evening. They were all there, Lynda and Jim, Maureen and Stuart, Elizabeth and Michael. The children knew a move was being considered and Elizabeth, out of nowhere, had asked how long it would be before they actually went.

'I think it'll be nice to have our own place again, even if it's not as good as our old house. Don't you think so, daddy?'

And nothing more had to be said.

The bedrooms in the flat were small. A furnished flat. There were two small single beds in the children's room, and a double bed in the other room. She had known from the first visit that they probably wouldn't be able to change the double bed, they'd be stuck with it. She had thought of asking the landlord if it was possible to have two single beds, make up some story about back problems or something, but decided against it, she didn't want that kind of fuss. And it wasn't a huge double bed either. But everything else was acceptable, including the price. So they slept together again. She hoped they would only be here for a few months, and hoped Stuart wouldn't be interested in sex anyway.

He didn't like the fact that she had signed the lease, and dealt with the money. It annoyed him, she could see that, she could feel it. She could feel it every day. He wasn't unpleasant. Stuart had rarely ever been unpleasant, but it all added to his disappointment with life, and it always showed in him, in one way or another, this disappointment, and a current of anger always there beneath.

Their relationship became a functional one, quite efficient in a way, but not close any more, friendly enough, but in a distant way. The bed was the most uncomfortable part of the whole affair, their bodies close together, the shared warmth, shared and unwanted, the audible breathing, the impossibility of moving without touching, the waiting for sleep.

Maureen hated it, and she suspected that Stuart did too.

But they had their own flat, she was busy with her agency, the children were going to school, and Stuart didn't seem to mind working for the Abraham brothers in their two different insurance brokers. He'd said that he could do her books as well if she wanted, but she said she was alright for the moment, maybe when the business really took off. She was surprised to discover how much she didn't want him involved in her business, and didn't want him knowing about the money either, definitely not that.

Every day that she set off for her little office, one room with a desk and a telephone and a filing cabinet, she had a feeling of elation, every day; it was impossible for her not to, that feeling just arrived every day. She had set up her own business and, in her business, it felt like she was absolutely in charge of what she was doing, for the first time in her life.

CHAPTER SEVENTY

Initially, at the very start, Maureen had been surprised by the amount of work she'd got just through word of mouth. In the first six weeks, when she was doing the actual cleaning work herself, with Julia usually, and with a little bit of help from Theresa, they had done four big houses and the owners had seemed grateful and happy to pay up quickly, in cash, for what had been done. Complimenting them, in fact, on how efficient they had been, and being surprised that Maureen was organising everything. One of the owners hadn't quite believed that there was not a man behind the whole venture, hadn't quite believed that the two of them were not just cleaners. Maureen could see that he was almost reluctant to hand over the money directly to a woman, even though all the arrangements had been done entirely with her.

Once she'd got the office, once she'd started Kelleher's Kleening properly she started to realise that running a business was not necessarily that straightforward. She had to make money to pay anyone who worked for her, and she had to pay for the office and the telephone, and she had to make some money for herself. She advertised in the local paper, and she rang estate agents and letting agents to say what services she was offering. Some of them were interested, most were not, saying they already had firms that they used for that kind of work. And some asked who the boss was, assuming, she thought, that she was the secretary or something like that.

During the next week she also had a couple of visits from those other firms. The estate agents must have told them about her. Two men came from one lot and one man from another. They just turned up, walked in, sat down. Both lots looked the same, suits but not smart, spivvish almost, cocky. Not obviously unpleasant, or threatening, not directly anyway. They said they just wanted to introduce themselves, said it was a difficult business to set up, this cleaning lark, especially for a woman, the one on his own one said especially for 'a bird'. They hoped she wasn't expecting to take work away from them because they were already well established in the trade, they had contacts, and contracts, with a number of agents and expected to keep them. They didn't want her to even try to take them away. Yes, she was going to find it all very difficult. If she found other business, small stuff, like, that was fine, and they might even put a little bit of work her way now and then. Maybe she should stick to charring, that kind of stuff, because they weren't particularly bothered about that, and it was more of a woman's thing wasn't it? You're Irish aren't you love? Kelleher, that's Irish isn't it? Used to be a Kelleher up North Finchley way, he related to you, is he?

Julia wasn't there on either occasion, to Maureen's relief. She could imagine what she might have said to them. And that would not have been particularly helpful. She wasn't going to be intimidated by them and she wasn't going to 'stick to charring' either, but there was no sense in deliberately rocking the boat straight away.

So she continued with her newspaper adverts and cards in newsagents and work did come in. Of course, she wasn't able to actually offer real jobs to the women who worked for her, full-time official jobs. At the beginning she was relying on women wanting part-time work, cash in hand. She knew it was risky but that was the only way she could start. Some of the women told her about the other firms, because they did work for them as well. Those companies were obviously more organised, they'd been at it longer for a start, run by men who probably had never cleaned anything in their lives. The women preferred to work for her, the money wasn't better, the work was much the same, but they preferred it, if the work was available.

Lynda had asked her about the legality of it all. Paying tax and stamps and that kind of thing. Lynda said they'd catch up with her eventually, sooner rather than later, in fact, as she now had an office and a name. If she didn't watch it she'd get into trouble, and it could happen pretty quickly. Look what had happened to Stuart. That was because of what he owed, which was different, but it had all happened so quickly. There was a kind of blurred line between when she had been doing the cleaning all herself with Julia's help, and the occasional help of a few other women, and with what the firm was now becoming. For a short period of time she thought she would get away with it, her optimism and the excitement of managing everything on her own had blinded her to some of the practicalities. When Lynda spoke to her she realised she was skating on thin ice. And she almost panicked, right there and then. When she went into the office the next day she was scared there would be someone from the tax or the national insurance waiting for her.

She knew that lots of people tried to avoid paying taxes of any kind, she'd heard tales of people who'd worked on the buildings and done everything they could to avoid stamps and tax and the like. And she knew loads of Irish men got picked up in vans and lorries for building work at Archway every day with no intention of paying anything they could get away with.

But she had an office and an address and she wanted to run her own business and she wanted to be successful, she didn't actually want to be illegal, she knew that now.

She could have asked Stuart for his advice about tax and the like but she didn't, didn't even mention anything to him, and asked Lynda not to as well. She found an accountant in North Finchley and went to him instead. Used the name Kelleher rather than Johnson just in case he thought of Stuart for some reason. It cost money. But within a short space of time she had set up a limited company and had organised how she was going to manage the tax and all that other stuff. She only hoped she hadn't now priced herself out of the market, because she'd bet any money that those other lots, those other men, were as dodgy as you like.

When she'd just started those two cleaning jobs the people she worked for had always seemed grateful, thanked her for doing such a good job. But she discovered that this wasn't always the case. Now they were often working for landlords or estate agents and they could be very demanding, unreasonably so in some cases. Wanting walls cleaned when they actually need redecorating or doing a kitchen that was so old and decrepit that no amount of cleaning would make it look good. And then trying to not pay, or withhold the money or even, in a couple of cases, just disappearing. Maureen preferred to work for the landlords and agents who were reliable, and there were a few of them, but if she was doing an end-of-let clean for a leaving tenant she would get some of it up front, explaining that she was sure they were as honest as the day was long but she'd had bad experiences in the past. 'I'm sure you understand.'

She also found in some cases that Julia's straightforward belligerence was a useful weapon in the agency's armoury. Julia had an aggression that Maureen had never convincingly mastered. When people were very slow in paying, the private customers not the agents in the main, she got Julia to go and have a word with them and it usually paid off, not always, but usually.

About six months after she had 'regularised' everything she went to see her accountant with the latest bank statements, invoices and the like and he told her that there had been a bit of a purge by the revenue and national insurance people during the last few weeks. He said she was lucky things were in order now, because that would have been a big problem. The next day Jack Green turned up again. He was the man who had come on his own when she had started. Warning her off in his friendly enough way. He said he was just popping in because he had decided that he was going to move into another area of work. Going back to second-hand cars which, he said, was what he preferred.

‘I started off in the car trade, Maureen. My dad had a small plot after the war. A few old jalopies and some old army surplus stuff, lorries and vans. Yep, I started there after I left school. Cleaning them, washing them, really, at the beginning, but pretty soon I was doing a bit of selling. Loved it.’

He had sat down and lit up. She hadn’t asked him to do either, but she didn’t particularly mind. Not yet anyway. He smiled when he talked about the car sales as if he had really enjoyed it. Then he looked more sombre.

‘But the old man retired and then he died. Just like that. Cor, what a shock. Only fifty-eight. I didn’t have the money for the motors so mum and I sold up and I moved into the cleaning lark.’

‘Not as much fun, eh?’

‘Oh, it’s alright, it’s a living innit? You know that Maureen, yourself. But anyway that’s not why I’ve popped in.’

‘Why is it then?’

“I’m going back to the motor trade. That’s what I love doing, the cars, and a really good opportunity’s come up, down in Bromley. But, anyway, look, I’ve got something that might be of interest to you.’

'What would that be....Jack.'

'My list.'

'Your list?'

'Yep. My client list. Names, addresses, telephone numbers. Not just the agents, private stuff as well.'

'What good is that to me?'

'Come on Maureen, don't be dense. I give you the list. I tell them that I'm recommending you. And your business is increased by maybe 100% overnight.'

'Well, that's very kind of you Jack. Unexpected, I have to say.'

He smiled at her.

'Five hundred quid.'

'Five hundred quid?'

'Yeah. Five hundred quid for the list. Worth every penny. I know the others'll be interested if you're not, but I liked you Maureen, when we met, you got that Irish thing haven't you? A bit of charm but hard underneath.'

She knew it would be useful to have, if he hadn't already sold it to five other people.

'How many on the list?'

'About fifty. That's why I've priced it at five hundred. Only a tenner each and you'll easily make that back. Dead easy.'

'I don't have that kind of money Jack, certainly not five hundred. And, by the way I'm not an eejit, and I know it's not worth anything like that. Nothing like that at all. Sorry. Look Jack I've got to go out now. Let me know if you can come up with a better deal, I might be interested then.'

She stood up ready to go. He said nothing but stood as well. Still smiling, still smoking.

She was fairly certain he'd been hit by the tax people. He needed money, and she doubted if the car sales in Bromley was anything more than a figment of his imagination. And if he was out of the business, locally, she could safely contact the local agents anyway.

Maureen heard Julia clumping up the stairs, heard the door opening. She came in breathless after the climb, cigarette in hand. She stopped when she saw Jack, looked towards Maureen.

'Oh, great, Julia, you're here, we'd better get going otherwise we'll be late.'

And they hurried him out as they left the office, Julia immediately understanding what to do.

He came back the next day and they agreed a very small initial price, with a bonus for him after six months if the work came through as he said it would.

Her business did double in size, not overnight, but within three months. And later she heard that Jack spent a short time inside for tax evasion.

CHAPTER SEVENTY-ONE

The increase in business meant that Julia took a greater part in organising and managing things. To Maureen's surprise she took to it well, enjoyed the responsibility and, also, she modified herself a bit; she looked smarter and she was not quite so abrupt as before. Maureen had thought of offering a kind of partnership, after all she had been there from the beginning, and Maureen was not sure what she would have done without her. But when the idea was mentioned, just floated, by Maureen, Julia said no, she said she was happy to be a manager and all that, but she didn't want to have the responsibility that Maureen had, didn't want to take that risk.

And the cash flow increased and Maureen decided that it was time for the family to move. She wanted them to have their own place again. The kids had moaned about the flat for a long time now, and Elizabeth, with friends at school who had very nice houses, did complain occasionally about bringing people back to 'this place'. It was very unlike her to complain so it must have been important to her. Michael didn't seem so bothered. He was happier now, he'd got in to grammar school but seemed mainly interested in football. Playing for the school team and going to matches with Stuart. Spurs.

Stuart was still working as a bookkeeper. Still with the Abrahams' but he'd modified his times so he could do some other work as well, and he was doing little bits of extra stuff in the evening, at home. He seemed happy enough although they didn't really talk about anything now, just day to day living. Maureen was pleased that he spent time with Michael, it made them both happy.

She had worked out what they could afford and where it might be possible to buy a house. And she had decided that it would be her to buy it. Stuart had not been discharged as a bankrupt yet so it was easy for her to take the lead, his room for financial movement was still very restricted.

Although the children didn't need to be right next to their schools, now they were older, they still had to be in the same general area they were now. Maureen looked in Ally Pally and Finchley, from the end of Highgate up to North Finchley. When she had identified three or four houses she spoke to Stuart.

'I was thinking we ought to move, you know. We can do better than this now. You're earning a bit and the agency's going fine. Three years in a place like this is more than enough. Don't you think?'

'I can't do anything about it yet. There's still a lot owing. It's OK here anyway, for the moment.'

'You know it isn't OK. It smells and Elizabeth, for one, is ashamed of it. She doesn't want to bring her friends back here, does she? None of us really like bringing people back here, not you either, don't pretend you do. And it'd be nice to live somewhere nice, somewhere a bit like the old place. Wouldn't it, Stuart?'

'We can't afford to move.'

'We can. The agency's doing well and I've got the money for a deposit.'

He looked downwards at the carpet for ten, maybe fifteen seconds then he looked up again, directly at her. His expression had changed from being friendly enough, mildly interested in what she was saying, to one of pain, resentment and hurt. And dismay as well. Portrayed all too obviously in his mouth, and his eyes, and the lines and features which surrounded them. Just those few seconds had collapsed the friendly, smiling, pretence of hope which he carried round as his defence these days. It didn't take much to do that. Not much at all.

'You've already decided, haven't you? It's you that makes the decisions now, whether I like it or not. Do you know something, Maureen? You make all the decisions about everything, whether you think you do or not. Who we see, where we go, what we eat. And where we live, where we damn well live as well. You make the damn decisions about everything. The children ask you first about anything because they know it's you that says yes or no. Everything damn thing depends on you now. What I say is irrelevant, not that anyone ever asks. Just because of that one mistake.'

He was angry, and humiliated, and she thought he might cry as well. And he was right. She had taken over everything since the bankruptcy. Because she had to, that was the only way they were going to survive. She felt sorry for him, sort of, but she knew she had to go on. She couldn't stop now.

'That's not true Stuart. The children love you, Michael thinks it's great to go to football with you, and he loves it when you go to see him play. And you do that maths homework with Elizabeth, I haven't got a clue about that, not a clue……Look I've spoken to two estate agents and we can go and see three houses on Saturday. Just you and me, together, we'll go in your car. OK?.....OK Stuart?'

He nodded and then got up silently to leave the room. She heard him go downstairs and heard the front door close behind him.

They saw three houses that Saturday morning and two more the week after, and another two the week after. Maureen knew which one she wanted. And in the end the decision was hers. A four-bedroomed house in East Finchley, not that far from the one she had wanted right at the beginning.

CHAPTER SEVENTY-TWO

It was only four weeks after they'd moved in that Mama died.

The move had gone better than expected. Stuart had, at first, been resigned to it all but had then become enthusiastic, taken up by the excitement that the children were showing. And Maureen, and Lynda, and Jim as well. In a way it was like going back to what they were before, almost as if they could regard those intervening years as something that could be forgotten. Stuart was happy to do the bit of decorating that was required, something he had never been that keen on before. Maureen was surprised at his positive attitude, it was almost like he had deliberately turned a corner, deliberately tried to look on the bright side. And the discharge from the bankruptcy was about to come through as well. In some ways he could return to normal.

The children loved their new rooms, their first experience of this as teenagers, a place that was all their own so they could close the door on everyone else. And Elizabeth even brought two friends home from school in the first week just to show them.

The main bedroom was big, bigger, in fact, than the one they had years ago. They got two nice single beds, on the large side, so that each of them had what was almost a small double bed to themselves. The fourth room they made into a study cum spare room with a small bed that could be used as a sort of sofa, and a bed 'for anyone that needed it.'

Once the deposit payments had been made, and the solicitor's and the estate agent's money had been dealt with, and the mortgage organised, it was everybody's house. The fact that it was all Maureen's money was irrelevant, and the children didn't know anyway. Why would they?

On that Monday morning Theresa rang Maureen. She was in the office, she'd started work early that day.

'I tried you at home but Stuart said you'd already left. It's bad news, Maureen, really bad news, it's Mama. She passed away during the night.'

Maureen didn't quite understand for an instant. Passed away? What did that mean? And then she did know. She understood.

'How? What happened? Who told you?'

'Paddy rang me this morning. First thing. Poor Mama had a cold or something, nothing serious, and then all of a sudden it got worse. And then she was gone. The doctor said it was probably heart failure.'

'Is Dada OK?'

'Paddy says he's sort of alright, very quiet though. They've got someone else to take over the crossing so at least doesn't he have to worry about that.'

It was difficult to take in. Mama wasn't really old, only sixty-five. And she's always been healthy. As far as Maureen knew anyway.

'OK. God, I don't believe it. What about the funeral and everything?'

'It'll be in a few days. Thursday or Friday they think. Look I'm going to go today. I'll get the train this afternoon. Paul says that'll be fine, he can look after the pub. I want to see Dada, it must be such a shock for him.'

Theresa and Paul had bought a pub in Camden Town. They were trying to make it into a music pub. What with the

Beatles and the Stones and the like there was an opening there, they thought. Paul, being a musician, had a few contacts in the business which helped. James, her son, was involved as well, but he wasn't a great deal of help apparently. There was a family rumour he was into drugs and that kind of stuff.

'Right. Look, Theresa, I'll need today to sort things but I'll come over tomorrow. I'll book this morning. You didn't speak to Dada?'

'No, Paddy says he's staying at home. No phone there, so it's not possible...'

'Do you think I should bring the children?'

'I don't know, love, James is not coming. Do what you think is right. And I'll try and phone about the funeral and everything. Paddy says he's contacted the others.'

'OK. Poor Mama. Poor Mama. I'll see you Wednesday Theresa, God willing.'

'OK. God bless.'

And Maureen was left alone in her office. Thinking about Mama. It had never entered her mind that Mama would die. Obviously she knew it would happen eventually, but not really, not actually, not like this. She didn't cry, but she felt terribly sad. She could see Mam's face on the railway platform, see it at the wedding, laughing, but a bit shy as well. Dada always needed Mama, he relied on her throughout all his adult life, and she relied on him as well. At the little cottage next to the railway.

She sat and thought for twenty minutes or more, not about anything particular, but of her life back there with them both, little images and little events. Walking along the lanes to the creamery or the shop. The outing to Youghal, the trip to Dublin. Picking blackberries together and making bread. All crushed together into a huge all-encompassing sensation of life. Mostly laughing and enjoying, not all, but mostly.

And then she heard Julia. Whom she told and who hugged her tight, just for a moment.

'I'm off tomorrow, I'll book a ticket today and, I suppose, I'll be back for next Monday, all being well. Is that OK? You'll manage?'

'I'll manage fine. Don't you worry yourself one little bit, everything here'll be fine.'

CHAPTER SEVENTY-THREE

She rang Stuart. He already knew of course, Theresa had told him. He was sympathetic, he liked Mama and Dada, often laughing, in a fond way, about that trip to the pub with Dada. He said she should fly, it would be quicker. She knew he was right, and had considered it. To be honest she had thought that money was a bit too tight after the move and everything, and a flight would be an extravagance, but he was right. It was easier. If she could get a ticket she could fly from London Airport to Dublin tomorrow morning, and be in Dungarvan by the evening. It would save a load of time and avoid the journey on the Irish Mail as well, which was never great.

She'd mentioned taking the children and Stuart had said it was probably not a great idea, Michael had a football trial on Saturday and Elizabeth was going on some theatre thing wasn't she, with the school? Maureen wanted to take them both, she did want them to be there, but at the same time she wanted to get it done with the smallest fuss possible, and in a selfish kind of way she also wanted to concentrate on herself and Mama, to not be distracted from Mama.

She went out to the travel agent's round the corner, they did loads of Irish stuff there because of the amount of Irish living round there. And she'd booked a ticket, just for herself, by eleven o' clock.

When she saw the children that evening they were both upset about Mama, Stuart had talked to them when they got in from school, and they were both annoyed with their mother for not taking them, Michael a little less than Elizabeth maybe. Elizabeth said they would write a letter to Grandad from them both, which she was to take with her, and she had to tell Grandad that they had both wanted to come to the funeral but Maureen hadn't let them. She had to tell him that. Elizabeth was annoyed with Maureen, very annoyed, and Maureen knew she had done the wrong thing.

And that upset her. She went up to the spare room, the 'study', saying she had a bit of sorting out to do and she cried. For the first time that day she actually cried. And Elizabeth knew, of course. Maureen didn't know how she knew, but she did know. And she came upstairs and held her mother and cried herself as well.

The journey was easy. Almost fun, despite the circumstances. On a Vickers Viscount, that's what they called the plane. And at Dublin she got the bus into town and managed to get a train to Waterford and then to Dungarvan. All easier than she thought.

And a taxi. Mickey's taxi from the station out to Mama and Dada's. He chatted to her about Mama and said how sorry he was, she was a great woman altogether. Mickey had driven the taxi forever, but Maureen couldn't remember ever being in it, except maybe once with Dada, she wasn't sure. And here she was getting in and being driven off as if it was the most natural thing in the world. Except for the fact that when she was in Dungarvan she was still that girl, even though she was a grown woman, in Dungarvan she felt like that little girl, always.

Theresa and Dada came out when they heard the car and she hugged them both. Dada looked glad to see her, tired, a bit older. But not too bad considering. Paddy was inside waiting as well. And they sat and talked. About everything. About Mama, and Mickey's taxi, and the aeroplane, and what a pity the children couldn't come, and what a lovely letter they'd written. Which they had. And the funeral itself, of course.

On the Thursday, they all went to the chapel of rest. And there was Mama laid out in the open coffin. Rosaried hands clasped over the front of her best dress. A dress that Maureen remembered, a dress that Mama had been proud of. They sat next to her there, Dada closest. And the people came. The long line of them, shaking hands and saying a few words to Dada and Paddy and Theresa and Maureen and Tommy, to all of them. And everyone stood and talked, quietly in the main, for two hours or so. And then the rosary was said and the coffin removed to the house. Where Mama lay again for all to see while sandwiches and tea, and cake as well, were served and drunk and eaten.

Maureen had been to wakes before. This time was different of course, but it was both strange and comforting to see Mama still there amongst them. As natural as anything, yet, at the same time, disconcerting. She wondered what Michael and Elizabeth would have made of it, and she regretted, deeply regretted, not bringing them with her. They would have been a comfort to her, their presence would have been a comfort to her, but that wasn't it, that wasn't it at all. They had a right to be there. And she regretted what she had done.

There was laughter here, and chat, and children too. Maureen talked to everyone about Mama, but also answered each enquiry about herself and her family, and how she was now a businesswoman back in London, is that true now, that you run your own business? Who would have believed it, eh? Maureen Kelleher running a business now in London. Who would have believed it? And you call it Kelleher's? Jeez that's great! Your Mama would be proud of you now, that's for sure, Maureen.

And the house was quiet when they were all gone. Dada and the brothers and sisters sitting around chatting and having just a small drink before sleeping. Four of them down the road with neighbours just for the night, and the others, Maureen included, squeezed inside this tiny house.

For those few hours Maureen was back in a place that she thought she had long forgotten. A place that was more than just the cottage and the houses and the farms and the local fields and lanes. For those few hours she was part of what she had come from; people, custom, tradition, religion, belonging, and superstition too. All those things. And she'd not really forgotten them at all, she'd just put them aside for a while, and now, despite the circumstances, she was thankful to be part of them all again.

They were quiet in the morning again, joined by the others from down the road.

And the coffin was sealed and neighbours and friends turned up outside, waiting, talking, smoking, smiling, the occasional laugh. All as it should be.

But more solemn today, more solemn than last night when Mama had lain amongst them. More solemn now.

They followed the hearse down to the church, walking, not so far away. And then the Requiem Mass, responses and hymns that everyone knew, and the burial. Just behind the church. All so near. Everyone crowded in, waiting for it all to end, praying and singing and then slowly walking away. Maureen and Theresa and Paddy closest to Dada.
Refreshment at the house and slowly it emptied until there was just the family. And, when it was just them, it was clear that Mama had finally gone.

CHAPTER SEVENTY-FOUR

Maureen had decided to stay until Saturday and then go to Dublin. She had arranged to see Maria there, stay in a hotel, and then get the plane back to London on Sunday so she was home and ready for Monday.

The rest of Friday was spent with Dada and the others. Once again just talking, mainly about Mama and the past, although the difference in ages of the brothers and sisters meant that their histories often didn't really coincide at all. However Dada's little stories about each of them did give them feelings in common for a while, and made them smile and laugh. And late in the evening he played three small tunes on the accordion, and they all knew these, and they listened, and clapped quietly when he had finished. And all of them had tears for those few moments there.

On Saturday morning she met the girls in town. To have tea and a chat in the café that they used to go to. They'd all been at the funeral of course, but there had been little time to talk.

They had stories to tell, each of them, about their marriages and their children. All of them married now, all of them with at least two children, even Annie who had always said she'd never find anyone she wanted in this damn town.

It was great to talk. And while they talked Maureen looked at the three of them. Ann, Annie, and Greta. They seemed to be the same people as long ago, from their laughs and their gossip, but they all looked different now. Ann was fat now, there was no other way to put it. And Greta had grown out a bit as well but was still curvy as she had always been, still an attractive woman, while Annie, for some reason, looked skinny, haggard, worn away somehow, and when she laughed there was some sadness there. And she chain-smoked too, never once without a cigarette in her hand.

And while they talked Maureen also wondered what they made of her. What did they see when they looked at her across the table? They saw what she saw. Women now, not girls, carrying their worries around with them in one way or another, loving their children, and mentioning their husbands, just mentioning them. The difference being of course that Maureen knew exactly who their husbands were, and they might have met Stuart for a few short minutes, years ago when he visited once, when he was a successful London accountant of all things. Not now though, not now.

And she had a business of course, which none of them did. All housewives and mothers. And sort of happy with their lot. As far as she could see anyway.

She kissed them all and told them to visit her in London anytime, and then she rushed back to Dada to say goodbye. He said he was coming to the station with her in the taxi, he wanted to see her off.

As the car set off towards town she asked him.

'Have we been in Mickey's taxi before, you and me, I mean, Dada?'

'I'd say that was very unlikely, Maureen. Why would we, anyway? I don't recall that at all. Do ye think we did?'

'No, Dada, I just wondered that's all. Just wondered.'

'I wouldn't pay your extortionate fares now, would I Mickey?'

'No, Pat, you wouldn't, that's for sure, not in a million years.'

And both the men roared with laughter.

As the train left the platform, it was just Dada standing there. He didn't walk away this time, but waved until the train was out of sight.

CHAPTER SEVENTY-FIVE

Maria was waiting for her at the station in Dublin. They went to Bewley's. She asked after the funeral, how things had gone, was her father OK?

Sitting in Bewley's brought back the memory of Mama sitting there opposite her, Dada as well. How nervous she had felt taking them in there, and how proud she was that she'd done it. How grown up it had felt to treat them both to tea. She felt as if she might cry, but didn't.

'It was all as fine as a thing like that can be, it was fine, and everyone was there. She would have loved it. Anyway, it's smashing to see you Maria, you're looking great as well. How's things? And everyone else, how are they?

'Everyone's fine, more or less anyway. Deirdre's the same as ever, of course. God, that woman, she's as mad as a hatter, you never know what she's going to do next, or what she's going to wear either, but she's lovely all the same. And she looks after Dad, and that's the main thing. And to be honest with you I don't go home that often these days, which is ridiculous considering it's half an hour or so on the train.'

'But you see them, anyway?'

'Maybe once a month, I suppose. I'm busy with work.'

'And how's that going?'

'It's great. I love it. I get little bits of work from the big papers, the Irish Times and the others, no real job unfortunately, but I meet people, which is important. And I get to go to all kinds of things. Anyway, you'll never guess who I met in November?'

'I have no idea. The Pope?'

'No, better than that.'

'Ok. Who did you meet?'

'The Beatles.'

'You met The Beatles?'

'I did. When they came to the Adelphi. I was at the press conference. And I said hello to Paul and Ringo and they both said hello to me.'

'Was that it? You said hello to each other?'

'Have you said hello to Paul McCartney and Ringo Starr, Maureen Kelleher? Have you?'

'No, you're right I haven't. Wait till I tell Elizabeth and Michael, though. They'll be jealous as hell.'

'And then just a couple of weeks after that there was John Kennedy, dead in the car. Jeez that was terrible, wasn't it? I tell you the papers were doing ninety after that, it was mad, I tell you, it was mad.'

'What kind of shock was that, eh? We were watching the TV that evening and then the news came on. I couldn't believe it, I felt sick to my stomach. I cried. And Elizabeth too. And then you still couldn't believe it, could you? Even though you knew it had happened, even though you'd seen it. I just didn't want it to be true. And Jackie as well, she was so... so dignified wasn't she ?

'Yes, she was. You're right.'

For a second they stopped talking. Shocked again.

'Well, anyway, are you seeing anybody? If you have any time

what with your Beatles and everything?'

'Not really. Well, yes, I'm seeing someone called David, he's a journalist too, but he's going to England, he's got a job in Liverpool. I don't think it's going anywhere. Him and me, I mean. I thought I might go back to London, but jobs are so difficult to find, anywhere really.'

'Well you can always stay with us, you know that.'

'Thanks. And anyway, tell me how Kelleher enterprises is going? The big businesswoman! How's all that going?'

'It's brilliant. It really is. And I'm thinking of starting something new. Property management. There's an opening there, so I'm looking into it. Anyway. So, Stephen, the solicitor how's he?'

'He's OK, I suppose.'

'You don't seem so sure'

At that moment the waitress came and took away their empty plates, and Maureen ordered some more tea. She watched Maria's face, watched Maria thinking what she was going to say next.

'Look, if I tell you must promise not to say anything to anyone else. Definitely not to Dad and Deirdre. Do you promise?'

'Of course.'

'Well Stephen has had problems. You haven't really seen him over the years have you? No, well he did his degree, did a lot of drinking and that, which is not that unusual obviously, but he did a helluva lot of it. And there was a bit of gossip about him as well, now and then. And then he got his job and he married Tess, she's a really nice girl. But things have happened since. Tess had an accident at home a month or two ago, where she got quite badly bruised, fell over she said, but a couple of years before, I remember, there was something else, a bruise on her face. Said it was a door, got in the way.'

'You don't think Stephen did it, do you? He's such a quiet boy isn't he? And accidents happen, don't they, to all of us?'

'Maybe they do. But that's not all. I hear things in my job, about people. And Dub is such a tiny place, you hear all kinds of things. Things that never get published. Look, the truth is, there's been a number of complaints about Stephen at work. Complaints from women, about him touching them, and then there was something that sounded like it was a lot worse. You know, real sexual assault. A woman from his work that he met in a bar. Apparently by chance, but he might have followed her there.

'You don't mean he raped her?'

'I don't know, I really don't. But she made a complaint at work, and threatened to go to the police, and then it was all hushed up. He knows people does Stephen, in the law, and the police as well obviously... They say she was paid off and sent back to Limerick. Virtually the next train home.'

'Jesus!'

'And the rumours about him at college were about girls, touching them and the like.'

'God. Have you asked him about all this?'

'You're joking, aren't you? Stephen, I hear you're assaulting women and beating up your wife. Pack it up now, will ya! There's a good lad.'

'OK. Maybe not. And your Dad and Deidre know nothing?'

'Not as far as I know. But they will, soon enough. Like I said, it's a very small place. They can't hush it up forever, especially if he keeps doing it. Anyway, I've told you now, and I feel better for it, to be honest. Thanks. Now, for God's sake, tell me about something more cheerful. Elizabeth and Michael for a start.'

They chatted for another half hour or so. Laughing for a lot of it. And then they parted outside Bewley's, Maureen to return to her hotel, Maria to meet David and some friends for a drink. Maureen was invited along but decided she could do with some sleep before her earlyish start back to London the next day.

Walking through the streets of Dublin back to the hotel she thought about Stephen. How shocking it was that he was acting in that way, how shocking that it could all be hushed up so easily. She felt sorry for Maria, having to carry the burden of knowing all that.

When she got back to her room she made a very expensive phone call to Elizabeth and Michael, warmed by their voices, their enthusiasm, and even their worried enquiries about their Grandad. But when they heard about Maria and The Beatles they were ecstatic, she knew it would be all around their school the next day.

After she had put the phone down she sat on her bed, alone in the very quiet hotel room, the door locked and bolted. Despite herself, she thought back all those years to Margaret in the darkened kitchen that night, and to those threatening steps creaking on the stairs outside her room, and then waiting there, silent. Maybe it hadn't been Shaughnessy at all. She shuddered at the thought.

CHAPTER SEVENTY-SIX

On the flight back they went over the Bristol Channel. It was a bright morning and she could see right across, see the coasts slowly moving towards each other. She didn't know it was the Bristol Channel but she heard the man sitting in front of her telling his wife, saying it was a damn long way round to London, the wife didn't seem that interested. Maureen thought it was a beautiful sight, the sun shining on the waters and the sand on either side.

She was glad to be going home, looking forward to seeing the children, even looking forward to seeing Stuart. He'd been good, quite happy for her to go on her own, happy to look after the children. Of course, part of that was that he was keen to see Michael do well in the football trials, but that was fair enough.

She thought briefly about Stephen. He'd always been a strange one, quiet anyway, worried and anxious too. But she'd never thought there was anything horrible about him, never thought there was anything that she should be worried about. Had she? God, it was so long ago now. He'd been a boy of her sort of age. Would he have done that, stood outside her room like that? Maybe he would have. She'd never know, would she? And he couldn't have hit his mother, could he? Why on earth would he have wanted to do that? Had Margaret actually said it was Shaughnessy? Or had Maureen just assumed it? Which would be fairly logical wouldn't it? It was all a bit of a mystery.

Stuart and the children had come to meet her and they drove home together, it reminded her of when she had driven back from Devon, that last bit on the Great West Road and the North Circular. Different children then, though. She told them it had gone well, all things considered, and told them a bit about her meeting with Maria, and said Maria might even come and stay with them if she came to work in London. Michael told her about the football which he thought had been great, and Stuart thought he had every chance of getting into a local youth team which had connections with Spurs and other clubs too. So the two of them were pleased. Elizabeth was still annoyed that she hadn't been taken to the funeral, although obviously she was interested in how her Mum had got on, and how things had been. And she had enjoyed the Romeo and Juliet trip with the school. She said that the film West Side Story was based on it, she bet them they didn't know that. Maureen certainly didn't, and Elizabeth was pleased.

Maureen hadn't been lying when she'd said to Maria about Kelleher's Property Management although possibly she was jumping the gun a bit. But it was her project now. Julia had become a different person as she'd got older and had settled down with Billy. She'd become more mature, more considerate, friendlier, but also more focused as well. She took her work with Maureen very seriously, and she acted as a very loyal second in command. Admittedly there were times when you saw the old Julia come through, occasionally drawing deeply on a cigarette and then saying something incredibly rude about one of their clients or one of their girls, but those lapses were rare. And Julia now ran the cleaning part of their work, she was already doing it. Maureen had told Julia that she was the day to day manager and she would leave everything to her. Especially as now she, herself, was looking into that property management stuff.

This had come about in the same way as the cleaning. She had dabbled in bits of management for one or two people, letting a flat for someone who was going abroad, and finding a rentable house for a friend of a friend from Ireland. Just favours really. But she realised there was an opportunity and the cleaning was going well with Julia. So she started to advertise services that complemented the cleaning, looking after rented property while people were away, or for people who owned one or two places and didn't want to be faffed with managing it all themselves. Obviously it impinged a bit on local estate agents and letting agents but she thought she could manage that alright. It was her contacts that really got her going, some Irish owners or landlords, or people from Irish families, a load of them around Archway and Camden and the like, and with the other businesses and owners that she'd met over the years. She had a good reputation so work came in, and she enjoyed the new challenge of it all. It was different.

They still stuck with the same offices, although they'd also taken over the other office on the same floor for a bit more room, so Julia and Maureen saw each other every day, and kept up with each other. They also employed a lady who did the typing and general office stuff and answered the phone, Gloria, and Harry as well, an older man who did the handyman stuff on the properties and small building works where necessary.

Maureen enjoyed every minute and bought herself one of those little Minis to take herself around in. Stuart said she should have got something bigger but she just wanted that beautiful little red Mini, and she got one. She loved the day she parked it outside the house and went in to drag the kids, and Stuart, out to look at it. She hadn't told them she was buying it. The children were amazed and made her take them round the block three times. Stuart wasn't so sure, he liked his big old Zodiac which Maureen was never really fond of, she thought it looked like a monster next to her lovely little Mini.

Stuart and Maureen got on well these days. He still did his book-keeping, the bankruptcy was behind him now and he had started his own 'self-employed' little business, and he even did a bit of work for Maureen now and then; he still did the Abrahams' books as well but had taken on a load of other work as well.

They slept in separate beds and sometimes, if she was working late, she slept in the spare room.

Oddly enough it was when she was sleeping in the other room that she first really noticed his coughing. One night it was so bad that she went in to see if he was alright.

'Yes, I'm OK Mo, just a bit of bronchitis or something. It's nothing. I'll read a bit while it settles down.'

And he plumped up the pillow behind him, lit a cigarette, and started to read a book, a book about the war, that he'd picked up from the bedside table, giving her a little wink first, as if to reassure her.

She went back to the study.

CHAPTER SEVENTY-SEVEN

The cough continued, sporadically at first. He took cough medicine. The cough would calm down and then it would return. The doctor said it would clear up, especially if he stopped smoking. He didn't and it didn't. There came a point with the cough that Maureen realised it was probably, or possibly, something more serious than just a bit of bronchitis. Stuart waved away any concern, saying it was nothing, but she could tell from the way he was acting that he was starting to get worried himself. And they all noticed the cough. At breakfast one morning, they were sitting around together, unusual, really, for them all to be there, and Stuart started a coughing fit, eventually leaving the table and going out to the garden till he recovered. The children and Maureen looked at each other, they couldn't help it, and Maureen could see that the children were worried too.

Maureen went with him to the various doctors and pretty soon the truth was told, Stuart was very ill. The illness was probably, almost definitely, terminal.

She drove him home that day, in his Zodiac. She'd only driven it a couple of times before and it certainly wasn't as much fun as the Mini.

They didn't talk for a minute or two. The place near Harley Street.

'Will we tell the children? Do you want to tell them straight away?'

'Let's leave it for a while, love. To be honest I need a bit of time, Mo. I really didn't expect that. Oh, maybe I did expect it, but I didn't want to, I really didn't want to.'

'I know, love, I know.'

She reached across and held his hand for a second.

'We'll do it whenever you're ready Stuart. And what about your mum and dad? Shall we leave that as well.'

'Yes, I think so.'

'OK, my love, ok.'

It was in that short journey that she realised, that she understood, her affection for Stuart.

She made a conscious decision that, from that moment, she would do everything she could for him. He had been a friend, he was the father of their lovely children, he cared about her and he deserved to be looked after, to be comforted, to be supported. For the children's sake as well. It was true that she didn't love him, true that, in some ways, she had made a mistake marrying him. But that was all done, that was in the past.

From that moment on she always slept in their bedroom, she talked to him every night before they went to sleep, heard his discomfort and his coughing, heard his worry and sometimes his panic, and tears as well, sometimes, quiet tears as well. She went to every hospital appointment and every consultation. And she sat with him when, three weeks later, he decided to tell the children.

'Do you mean you're going to die, Daddy?'

Elizabeth needed exact clarification.

'Yes, darling, the cancer means I will die. Not yet. But the doctor thinks within eighteen months or so.'

'And they can't do anything about it?'

'No, darling, they can't. They can give me drugs and things but they can't cure it.'

Both the children had gone pale, with fear, anxiety, shock at being told their father was going to die.

After a silence, Maureen stood, she gathered them up and cuddled them both, enfolded them with Stuart as well, so they could hear and feel each other breathing, feel the shared warmth of each other together, tightly held; and then the sobbing of the children, the sobbing of them all, in fact, bound them even closer, bound them together for however long it would take.

PART FOUR

CHAPTER SEVENTY-EIGHT

'Mum, mum! Wake up, mum!'

She heard Elizabeth's voice, first at a distance, a muzzy distance, and then directly inside her head. She started, gulping for breath as she did so.

'What is it? What's up?'

She sat up, now realizing that she had fallen asleep at the kitchen table. The ashtray was full. She could see that it was daylight outside, but not fully day, still early.

'It's Nan. She rang from the hospital. We must go in now, she says. Right now!'

There was no need to know why. No need to say why.

'Right. OK. Give me one minute and get Michael out in the car. Hurry.'

She ran to the bathroom, went to the loo, threw some water on her face and gave her teeth a brush, all quickly. And then she ran downstairs, picking up her bag and the keys from the hall table, and going outside to the car. She started it, and sat waiting for the children. After a minute or so they came out of the front door, Elizabeth closing it and, at the same time, dragging Michael behind her. In other circumstances it might even have been funny to see them both like that. But today it wasn't.

They got in the car and she zoomed off down the road towards Archway.

They were quiet. They all knew what was going to happen. They were going to see and be at an inevitability, something the children had never seen before and would never see again, the death of their father. Going to an event that they never wanted to be at, but had to be at. There was no alternative, none whatsoever.

Michael was in the back, Elizabeth in the front, next to her mother.

'Did your Nan say anything else?'

'No. She just said we should get there as soon as possible.'

'How did she sound?'

'She was calm, I suppose. Just like herself really.'

'OK.'

The Sunday morning roads were not busy and it only took a few minutes or so to get to the hospital. She parked and they walked into the building. She linked with them both, one on either side. She could feel the tension rise as they went through the main entrance, in herself as well as the children. The hospital was starting up, cleaners around, staff going home after the night shift, saying bye as they went their different ways. An ordinary day.

They went up in the lift and straight to the ward. Maureen had brisked up her walk, moving them along with courage, she hoped, making it clear they were there to be with their dad, and they all had to be strong for him, and for each other.

Of course, nothing was actually different from the evening before. Lynda and Jim were beside the bed. Stuart was lying there, eyes closed, the tubes going in and out of him as before. It was quiet.

The Ward Sister came in after a couple of minutes. Maureen knew her by sight but had not spoken to her before. She took Maureen outside for a second.

'It's great that you got here, Mrs Johnson, with the children as well. Look, like I told Stuart's mum, it could be any time, any time now. It will be any time now, in fact. But you knew that, of course. I'll be in and out, but definitely call me if you need me. God bless.'

She was Irish too, of course.

And the five of them sat around the bed. Maureen held Stuart's hand. And they sat and waited. His breathing was laboured even though it was assisted with oxygen. He was asleep but not comfortable, that was obvious. Now they had been told that his death was just around the corner they couldn't leave, not to go the toilet, or to get a tea, or even to go for a little walk. They talked sporadically about nothing. They waited for maybe an hour and then, as if she knew, the Sister returned. She checked him over and said it was probably only a matter of minutes now. And Maureen was sure, at that very moment, that she felt Stuart squeeze her hand, just lightly, twice in succession, she was sure of it. And then there was a noise from Stuart's throat or his lungs. From his throat, she thought. And then a kind of almost invisible collapse. As if he was no longer inside there, no longer inside that container that had failed him so prematurely.

He had gone.

The Sister said that he had passed away.

'I'll leave you there just for a minute or two.'

And when the nurse had gone there was a silence amongst

them. Maureen stood and gave Stuart a kiss on the forehead, she encouraged the children to do the same. While he was still warm. And Jim did the same. And Lynda also, but she held him tightly as well, put her arms around him, just for a second.

They stood around the bed. He looked relaxed now, the pain gone, himself gone as well though. Maureen was relieved it was all over. She looked at the children, both with tears in their eyes, and she put her arms around them both. Jim and Lynda holding each other as well. Maureen found that she felt more sorry for all the others than for herself, the loss was certainly greater for them.

After a few minutes the Sister returned with a young doctor and one of her nurses. The doctor examined Stuart and confirmed, rather apologetically, that Stuart had passed away. The Sister said they would have to prepare Stuart now, but it wouldn't take long, and they could see him again soon, if they wished to.

CHAPTER SEVENTY-NINE

Stuart had said that he wanted to be cremated, he'd been very definite about that.

Everything was organised for a week later. At Golders Green.

Maureen was surprised by how many people had inquired about Stuart and said they wished to come to the service. She knew he had been liked but nevertheless she was taken aback by the number of people who got in touch by phone, or called round, or stopped her in the street. Some of those in the street she didn't know herself. How had he known these people, how had they known him? It was like discovering a whole new side to a person that she had lived with for fifteen years or more.

Dada said he would come over. And Maria as well from Dublin, she said that Shaughnessy and Deidre would like to come as well, not that they knew Stuart particularly but they wanted to be there for her in some way. Would that be alright? Of course it would. As with Mam's death Maureen discovered again that funerals and the like highlight friendships and attachments that may have lapsed or faded slightly, but are oddly reinvigorated by death.

The children helped her. They were still shocked by the loss of their father but they seemed to be helped, themselves, by being involved, by talking to people, and Maureen wondered also if the fact that they had known, for a long time, that he would leave had helped them, some way, to deal with the whole thing.

Julia took over all the business for the week, she had in fact been doing a lot of that for the last month or so. Maureen knew she could rely on her. And Lynda and Jim were involved in the funeral matters as well, Lynda particularly. She seemed to be dealing with the loss of her son in a pragmatic way and was focusing on supporting her grandchildren and helping Maureen.

During that week they viewed the body at the funeral director's. They had all seen Stuart again in the hospital, before he was removed, but they went to see him again. This was different from seeing him immediately after death. That had seemed natural, he had only just gone, the body was still Stuart. Going to the funeral director's was like going to see a corpse, a prepared corpse. And it had a finality about it.

They stood in the small room and viewed him, lying there in that suit that they knew was his best one, with his tie and white shirt, looking waxed and artificial, looking similar to Stuart, but only similar. The children both kissed him, not before the slightest hesitation, and Maureen did so too, feeling the not-human temperature of his skin on her lips.

Another step towards the end, thought Maureen.

On the day before the cremation, the evening before, family and close friends dropped in, Dada was staying with them, and Maria was in a bed and breakfast nearby. It wasn't like Ireland, Maureen thought. It was more formal, and Stuart was lying elsewhere. On his own that night.

CHAPTER EIGHTY

The day of the cremation dawned and there was a tense feeling in the house. Relief that the day had finally arrived, but worry as well. In truth Maureen wasn't worried about her own reaction to the cremation, it would be sad, certainly it would be sad, but that would not be the problem, no, she was worried more about the children. Seeing their dad disappear. Into the flames. Michael more than Elizabeth. He had been quiet while Elizabeth had been sad but curiously efficient as well. Reiterating, at times, her definite wish to be a doctor, her desire to make something positive out of her father's death. Maureen had no doubt at all that she would achieve her ambition, but also wondered if, at some time in the future, a more concrete grief might hit her. A later realisation. Michael was quiet and sad, and had cried. Perhaps that was, in fact, better.

They gathered in the kitchen and the hall. Maureen, the children, Dada, Lynda, Jim; and in the background, Julia and Maria and Theresa, definitely there, definitely present, but taking subsidiary parts today, supportive parts, let's say.

Waiting for the hearse, waiting for the cars.

Standing, waiting. Talking quietly. Holding hands. Some still smoking before they left. Everyone dressed smartly. Michael's hair combed and straight, much more than it ever was. She smiled, inside, to look at him there. Smart and trying hard. Stuart would have been proud of him.

'They're here.'

And so they went. Driving through the streets. Aware of being noticed by everyone they passed, looking out, themselves, at other people's ordinary days.

It was short. Short enough. Lynda had found a minister to say the words, someone who had known Stuart when he was younger. There were three hymns. Stuart had chosen them with the children, and Maureen. Two were light enough, 'Morning Has Broken' and 'Amazing Grace' and Lynda had wanted 'Ave Maria,' as well, so they agreed on that. And Stuart had suggested 'The Sound of Silence', for at the end. Maureen wondered if that just wasn't too sad. Beautiful, certainly. But too sad.

They watched the coffin disappear behind the curtains. She held the children's hands tightly as it went slowly, creaking, away, and then put her arms around their shoulders and hugged them to her, she felt them hug her back, each putting an arm around her waist.

And then they walked out. The PA system played 'I am a rock.' She had changed it at the last minute, the other song was just too sad. At least it was still Simon and Garfunkel, she thought.

CHAPTER EIGHTY-ONE

Because so many people had wanted to come Maureen had hired the hall attached to a local pub, and got some caterers that she'd done some work for to provide the food.

There was relief in the air, in the family anyway, now that the cremation was over.

Maureen walked around and said hello to anyone and everyone and said nice things about Stuart, which was not a difficult thing to do at all.

It was only here, at the pub, that she really noticed who had come.

Theresa and Paul. Theresa's son James was there. Her own children's cousin. Looking not very well. It was more than just rumours about the drugs and everything she thought, but he was pleasant enough when they had a few words. And her sisters from Watford had come, with their children running wild now, round the hall and everywhere. No harm there really. Gloria and Harry chatting in the corner with a drink each, a small sherry it looked like and a beer, just a half. And Dada was having a good chat with Billy, who was now very respectable, he ran the sorting office apparently, a big wheel in the local GPO. Julia was very proud of him. And Deirdre and Shaughnessy said hello. It was so nice to see them both. A bit older, to be sure, but still the same. She a bit scatty, he polite and friendly now. Maureen had the thought that she would have loved to see Mrs Doyle there too. Oh well.

A tall man approached, familiar, very smart.

'Hello Maureen, I was so sorry to hear about your husband, about Stuart. I was in London on business and Maria told me, I was so glad I was able to come. It's not an intrusion?'

Irish, well-off. She knew him. Stephen.

'Stephen, how are you? I'm so glad you could come. Maria too of course.'

She hadn't immediately realised but he had held her hand when he had come close to her, an automatic thing, a shaking of hands. He was still holding it lightly. Not letting go.

'Believe it or not, I think of you a great deal, Maureen. Back in those days. The young girl from Dungarvan. You were very important to us, you know. Very important. Up in that little room of yours. Do you remember? I certainly do. Yes I often thought of you, alone, up there, at the end of those creaking stairs'

She felt a chill and she knew he was still holding her hand, just so lightly. Looking at her, smiling in a knowing kind of way.

'Anyway, look, it's grand to see you, even in such sad circumstances, but I know you have many people waiting to talk to you, so I'll leave you now. Get in touch if you're in Dublin at all. We could have dinner together, maybe?'

He smiled down at her. She felt immediately that she didn't like him. He looked directly into her eyes for longer than was necessary, and then he was gone.

CHAPTER EIGHTY-TWO

It was not an Irish wake, that was for sure, but it did what was necessary. The children talked to a load of people, all of whom said something positive, something lovely about their father. And they laughed about things he had done and things he had said. And it was a celebration of sorts. Maureen felt they had done him justice.

Eventually they went back to the house. Maureen, the children, Dada, Lynda, and Jim. They had tea and then just one more drink. Lynda and Jim walked home after hugging or shaking hands with everyone. And Lynda said thank you to Maureen.

And it was quieter now in the kitchen. Dada had decided to go up to bed, it was still early but he was tired after the day, and he'd drunk a little bit as well. Dada was never troublesome with the drink, but he did get tired these days.

The three of them sat in silence for a while. And then the children said they would go to bed. Perhaps they wanted to be on their own for a while.

She kissed them and pulled them to her, yet again, warmth and closeness.

She heard them talking together for a little while and then their separate doors could be heard shutting. All was silent.

She sat in that silence. Relieved to be on her own, herself. She lit a cigarette and opened the back door to go out into the garden.

The sky was clear. A million stars above her. Warmish, comfortable. Alone in the garden. She looked back at the house and saw the light on in the children's rooms and in Dada's room, the study. No faces though, looking out. Just the lights. Perhaps they were all lying on their beds, thinking.

And the strangest words came into her head. Unbidden.

'Free at last. Free at last.'

CHAPTER EIGHTY-THREE

She sat on the garden bench for a long time. And over that time the bedroom lights went out. One, two, three. The garden became totally dark as the illumination from the house disappeared from the reflecting grass, from the gardened lawn. There was only the starred night above now.

She went back inside, quietly, and took the phone from the hall table into the sitting-room, manoeuvring the awkward cord, and then closing the door.

She dialled a number, and waited while it rang.

'Hello, it's me.'

Acknowledgement

Although this definitely isn't the story of my mother's life it was inspired by her tales of a childhood in Dungarvan, and of her time as a housemaid, both in Ireland and in England. Her sisters, my aunts, also contributed, over the years, with anecdotes and stories about their lives 'at home' in Ireland and over here in England. Thanks to all them.

Thanks also to the friends who have read drafts of the book and given me their very valuable feedback.

About The Author

Peter was brought up in an Irish family, living in London for most of his life. He worked as a merchant seaman, factory worker, labourer and milkman before becoming a teacher.

Peter eventually became a headteacher, and educational consultant, working with children and young people with very challenging behavioural and psychological difficulties.

He now writes thrillers, novels and poetry.

www.peter-f-doyle.com

BOOKS BY THIS AUTHOR

Closed City

Earth

The Accident Of Touch

Lightning

Card

Printed in Poland
by Amazon Fulfillment
Poland Sp. z o.o., Wrocław

63020714R00284